He had only been out of prison a few days, and this was the last thing he needed…

Sam coughed from smoke as his horse slid to a stop. He could see only two bodies that seemed intact in any conceivably survivable manner. He chose one near a red post at the water's edge and leapt from his saddle. Mark grabbed the reins to keep Sam's horse from running off.

Sam pulled the knife at his waist and jumped down next to the man whose fishing waders were filling with water because his chest belt had come off. Sam cut the waders' suspenders, freeing the man of the water weight that was slowly pulling him under. The waders sank out of sight. He noticed that the muddy bank and water were tinted red. Only then did he see that the man's left forearm was not tucked under him as he had thought, but had been brutally severed just below the elbow. He knew from experience that the wound was bad but survivable with proper emergency aid. He rolled the injured man onto his back and checked for signs of life. Though he seemed dead, blood spurted from the grotesque stump. "This guy's alive!" he yelled as he whipped off his own belt and wrapped it around what was left of the arm in an attempt to staunch the pulsing flow of vital arterial blood.

After securing the horses' reins, Mark rushed over to help.

"The embankment protected this guy from most of the mortar and tree shrapnel," Sam said. "Let's get him out of the water."

Mark slid his hands under the injured man's armpits and pulled him to dry ground. He dipped his Stetson into the bloody water and poured it over the man's mud-caked face, then checked that his airway was clear. Sam climbed out of the water and began tightening his makeshift tourniquet. He heard his brother gasp.

Sam Calder knows prison changed him, and not for the better. Still, when he's suddenly freed, he goes home, wanting to make things right. Unfortunately, that hope fades when he stumbles into the midst of an assault on none other than the President of the United States and the one-time Navy SEAL leaps to the man's aid. In the aftermath, the nation comes to believe its leader is dead and the ex-convict is somehow involved. With no other option, Sam flees with the badly injured chief executive in tow and the real assassins and every cop in the land in hot pursuit. Their only chance at survival now lies in Sam's willingness to unleash that part of himself he wanted left in prison, and this time he can't hold back.

KUDOS for *Forced Succession*

In *Forced Succession* by Dave Bullock, Sam Calder has just gotten out of prison after being falsely accused of murdering his wife. Finally exonerated when new evidence comes to light, all Sam wants now is peace and quiet, but, alas, that is not to be. On a peaceful fishing trip with his brother, Sam runs head long into a VIP assassination attempt with some powerful people behind it. Now he's on the run with only his wits and his special forces training to help him survive. Bullock tells a gripping tale, filled with realistic, well-developed characters, fast-paced action, and numerous twists and turns. An enthralling read. ~ *Taylor Jones, The Review Team of Taylor Jones and Regan Murphy*

Forced Succession by Dave Bullock is the story of a man who happens to be in the wrong place at the wrong time. Coming out of a restaurant with his wife, Sam Calder runs into some drunken cops, resulting in the shooting death of Sam's wife. Falsely accused of her murder, Sam goes to prison until new evidence finally clears him. Once released, he returns home to Montana, hoping to repair his relationship with his father and brother. But a few days later, while on a fishing trip with his brother, Sam is in the wrong place again, witnessing a political assassination and even rescuing one of the intended targets. Now Sam is running for his life, trying to keep an important political figure alive as well, and the only thing Sam has on his side is his Special Forces training—and his smarts—against the forces of a corrupt shadow government. Will it be enough? *Forced Succession* is definitely a page turner, hooking you from the very first one. I couldn't put it down. ~ *Taylor Jones, The Review Team of Taylor Jones and Regan Murphy*

FORCED SUCCESSION

DAVE BULLOCK

A Black Opal Books Publication

FORCED SUCCESSION
Copyright © 2013 by Dave Bullock
Cover Design by Peter Greene
All cover art copyright © 2017
All Rights Reserved
Print ISBN: 978-1-626947-15-3

First Publication: AUGUST 2017

Published by Black Opal Books **http://www.blackopalbooks.com**

DEDICATION

This book is dedicated to my wife's unwavering willingness to ensure I had the undisturbed time needed to write it. That meant she mowed the lawn and took out the trash while I sat on my keister, typing comfortably in the air conditioning. Of course, I know payback's coming now.

CHAPTER 1

Sam Calder stared down at the jam-packed New York City street five floors below. *Rush hour, damn it*, he thought. *We're not gonna make it if she doesn't get her ass in gear.*

"You'd better hustle up, babe," he said. "The concierge got us a cab for seven."

"What time is it now?"

"You've got four and a half minutes. He'll probably start the meter if he has to wait."

Judith Calder paused with her eyeliner brush and leaned around the edge of the bathroom door. "He can't start the meter without a fare, and you know it. Now stop rushing me, or I'll end up looking like a kabuki dancer." Her head disappeared, but she continued speaking. "We're just going to dinner and a show, not on one of your precisely timed SEAL missions. This is a celebration, remember?"

She's right, he thought as he walked over and sat on the edge of the bed. *I need to chill out, get used to the idea of being a civilian again, and becoming a father.* Both scared the hell out of him.

When they climbed into the cab twelve minutes later, Sam was sure they would have to forget the show, but the

Pakistani-born cabbie assured them he knew of a nearby restaurant that didn't require a reservation and served excellent seafood, Judith's favorite.

Maybe we'll make it after all, Sam hoped as they inched their way into the heavy traffic.

But when they pulled to the curb in front of a dingy downtown bistro twenty minutes later, Sam's concern returned. As he climbed out and held the door for Judith, his nose was assaulted by the aroma of something spoiled.

He looked around for the source and saw a dozen overloaded garbage cans lining the alley alongside the restaurant. The overwhelming stench countered his hunger but didn't seem to deter the rats scurrying about.

"Oh my, that stinks," Judith said as she joined him on the sidewalk, pinching her nose.

"This place looks kinda sketchy, babe."

"No, no. It is a fine restaurant," the driver called out from the cab. "My good friend from Islamabad is owner."

"I'm too hungry to look for another, Sam. Besides, the show starts in less than two hours, and the theater's back uptown."

Sam relented, paid the cabbie, and led her to the door. He reconsidered that concession the moment they entered and saw only empty tables. "That's not a good sign, either," he whispered in Judith's ear as an elderly woman in a blue burqa moved toward them.

"Shhh," Judith answered, elbowing him gently in his ribs.

"Good evening to you. Welcome," the woman said in thickly accented English. "Please to follow."

She seated them in the center of the dimly lit dining room, handing each a menu.

"Thank you," Sam said. "Just give us a minute, please."

As the woman turned away, Judith squealed and erupted from her chair, knocking it over.

Sam looked up from his menu and saw the cause skittering across their tabletop. He smashed the scampering roach with his plastic-coated menu and dropped it there. As he stood to join his creeped-out wife, she shrieked again and began stamping her feet like a Mexican hat dancer. He glanced down to see another roach riding atop her sandaled foot.

"Let's go, let's go," she insisted when the creature fell off.

Sam stepped on it and pushed Judith's elbow toward the door of the foul eatery, ignoring the old woman's offer of free desserts.

Outside, they found no cabs in sight.

Sam turned back to the door. "I'll get us one."

"I'm not going back in there," Judith declared.

"Okay, stay here," Sam told her. "I'll be right back."

He was forced to give the now angry old woman five dollars to summon a ride. He watched to make sure she did so before he stepped outside again.

Judith was several yards down the sidewalk, surrounded by three men she seemed to be trying to dodge. They countered each move she made, keeping her in the center of their triangle. All three wore open sport coats with holstered pistols and gold badges visible at their waists. Their slurred voices and stumbling stances told Sam all three were intoxicated. *Oh well, drunk cops are better than gangbangers*, he thought as he started toward them.

Though his wife was ten weeks pregnant, her twenty-one-year-old figure gave no hint of her condition, so Sam assumed the inebriated men were simply trying to cajole a strikingly beautiful woman standing alone on a New York City sidewalk to join them.

He expected they would apologize and move on once

they realized she was not a hooker, nor alone. Before he could make his presence known, though, one reached out and groped her breast, braless under her thin-strapped summer dress. His pals ignored her terrified shriek and quickly fumbled to cop a feel in kind.

Enraged, Sam fell upon them like a vengeful wraith, five years of SEAL training and combat providing more than enough skill to match his fury. Grunts and howls of pain accompanied the discernible splintering of bone during those few seconds it took him to end the drunks' bawdy revelry with his wife. In moments, the three lay sprawled on the pavement, blood gushing from mouths and noses and two arms bent at unnatural angles.

The first fondler yanked his revolver from its holster and shakily pointed it up at Sam.

Drooling a mixture of blood and spittle, he slurred, "Don't fucking move, you—"

BANG!

As the gunshot echoed off the surrounding buildings, Sam kicked the detective in the head, removing several teeth, fracturing his jaw, and rendering him unconscious. The pistol fell away. He quickly spun to the others and found them down for the count, too. Then he turned to Judith.

Instead of rushing to him as he expected, she was on her back, motionless, her blood-soaked blonde hair matted over what was no longer a face.

*****

Sam woke as he always did at that exact moment in the nightmare, startled, sweat-drenched, and panting. His eyes snapped open in the semi-dark and strained to focus on the gray cement ceiling, trying unsuccessfully to blot out the image seared into his mind's eye five years before. His jaw ached. *I was grinding my teeth again*, he thought as he flexed it and unclenched his white-knuckled fists.

Mercifully, warning whistles distracted him from his ghastly mental picture. A few heartbeats later, his ears picked up the stomp of heavy boots climbing the steel stairway beyond his door. *Who're they coming for?* If he were the target, there would be at least three approaching. There were never fewer, though sometimes there would be more if they were training new people. He lay still, listening. *Yep, three*, he wagered himself. *It's me they want, but it's early.*

He heaved his muscled, 210-pound frame from the thin mattress atop the steel platform of his upper bunk, and faced the door with both hands clasped behind his head, elbows pointing at opposite walls only six feet apart. *The position is assumed.*

In response to his movement, the forty-something obese man sprawled on the bottom bunk produced a loud fart and turned his scraggly, bearded face to the wall.

The stench sickened Sam almost as much as the vile tattoos covering the fleshy man's jelly-like flab and shaved skull. Sam knew each marking to be a tribute to some racial or ethnic prejudice the fat hater too frequently barked about. He also knew the faded ink evidenced decades of incarceration that would deservedly continue. Sam dreaded that thought. He loathed every waking minute he and Clyde Bucher had shared the cramped space.

Sam stifled a gag as he stared straight ahead and thought back on their first meeting, when Bucher had tried to establish some inane form of dominance over their two-man world as soon as the door closed him in it.

"Get your crap off my bed, asshole," he'd said in greeting as he grabbed a handful of Sam's hospital-cornered bedding and yanked everything onto the floor.

Sam conceded without argument, assuming the rotund newcomer would never be able to lift his bulk to the upper bunk anyway and not wanting to be underneath it should he miraculously manage to do so.

At lights-out that night, having foolishly misinterpreted Sam's compliance as weakness, Bucher had stepped close behind and demanded a more personal act of submission.

A slight smile creased Sam's lips as he recalled dropping to his knees and spinning to face the flabby man's exposed genitals. Instead of giving Bucher what he expected, though, Sam's fist slammed upward, and Bucher released a brief, girlish squeal.

Unable to determine where the cry had originated, searching guards found both inmates prone on their bunks, though only Sam, doing his best at pretend snoring, was conscious.

He quietly chuckled, remembering how Bucher had been unable to stand for the next morning's head count. It had taken six guards to move the whimpering hulk to the infirmary. He returned days later, still pissing more blood than urine and carping each time.

Five years without a civil conversation, Sam thought. *Five years of pretending the other doesn't exist. Seems kinda pointless, with our toilet only four feet from where we sleep.* That thought brought him to glance around the seven-by-nine-foot cage he considered his quarters. *It certainly isn't a home*, he told himself. *That's where you live willingly.*

Still, despite Bucher's loathsome presence, he preferred the highly restrictive maximum-security abode to the general population zoo where the prison staff had initially placed him.

His thoughts drifted again, this time to the day his confinement in Attica State Prison had begun. During his three days in the orientation cell block, another inmate—a repeat offender—explained how things worked.

"How old are you, kid?" asked the balding, middle-aged man.

"Twenty-three," Sam replied.

"How long you in for?"

"I got five to life."

"Damn. Well, at least you'll get a shot at parole at some point, if you can keep your nose clean."

"I will."

"You're big, and you look strong. That'll help you some, but you're also young and good-looking. That'll go against you. Once they move you into general pop, you'll only have two options to keep the predators at bay. You can ask for protective custody, and they'll move you into segregation with the stool pigeons, child molesters, and cross-dressing freaks, or you can join a gang for the safety of numbers."

Sam knew residing amongst the perverted would never be an option for him, but his mentor made it clear that joining a racially oriented gang came with costly risks.

"They'll demand unquestioned loyalty, demonstrated by your willingness to participate in their activities. In prison, those are generally limited to smuggling drugs up your ass and violence against other gangs, either of which can extend your sentence if you're caught. But refusal to do as you're ordered means death at your own gang's hands. Believe me, I know. I hung out with the Aryan Brotherhood last time I was inside, and they ordered me to shiv some black dude a week before I was scheduled to be paroled. I said no and talked the guards into putting me into segregation until my release. If they hadn't, those bastards would've killed me for sure."

"So how're you going to avoid them now?"

"I ain't worried. That was eight years ago down in Ossining. None of the Brotherhood here will know me."

Sam gloomily recalled the man being found on the shower floor the next day, a hand-honed toothbrush handle imbedded in his throat. As guards wheeled the sheet-covered corpse past, he overheard one say, "The camera caught that lifer who transferred up from Ossining following him in there."

Sam judged gang membership a losing gambit, primarily because he found the majority of white inmates incapable of forming any sort of coherent band for security, and the white supremacists' mentality held no appeal for him.

He was escorted to a general population cell the next afternoon. Standing just inside its barred door with his pillow, blanket, and sheet resting on his forearms, he sized up the three men staring at him from their bunks. *No problem*, he thought, but said, "I'm Sam."

The biggest of the trio—all with swastikas tattooed on their necks—slid off his lower bunk and approached. "You queer?"

"Nope," Sam replied as he stepped past the man and set his armload on the only empty mattress. He leapt up to sit on it with his legs hanging over the side.

The other two fell in behind the big one as he slapped at Sam's dangling feet. "That's too bad. You're still gonna suck my dick."

"Then mine," another said from behind.

"Mine, too," the third one added, laughing.

Sam was one second away from showing the three how wrong they were when a whistle sounded and a passing guard announced, "Fall out, yard time."

His cellmates turned to the door, which automatically slid open.

Sam followed, keeping the three in sight as the entire cell block marched in single file. As the long line emerged into a bright summer afternoon, he watched inmates fanning out across the huge open space as if they all knew where they were supposed to go.

He did not.

He saw his cellmates meet up with a dozen other similarly tattooed brethren. The big cellmate pointed, and the entire group began moving Sam's way. Thankfully, a couple of guards followed close behind.

At a whistle from someone, the gang made an abrupt left, with the big one calling out, "Later, bitch!"

Sam remembered how relieved he had been at not having had to kill anyone on his first day. The largest gathering of inmates, the blacks, took over all four hoops of side-by-side basketball courts. About half as many Hispanics crowded an area filled with weight-lifting equipment, and the white supremacists were lined up with their backs against the cell block wall, staring his way.

There were a few others scattered about in ones and twos. The closest were two old, white inmates playing checkers on a concrete picnic table, and a lone white man who looked to be in his mid-thirties lying on the grass near them. He was smoking a cigarette and appeared relaxed, as if he were spending his lunch break in the park.

That was when Sam noticed a roofed enclosure in a more distant section of the yard. It reminded him of the handball courts he had enjoyed at the Navy base, so he walked over to the checker players and asked about it.

And that changed everything, he thought as he recalled the incident.

"Yeah, it's supposed to be a handball court," one old man said, "but guys kept getting shived in there, so nobody goes there anymore."

The other added, "Stay outta there, kid. There's only the one door, and those Nazis over there are watching you like buzzards."

Sam glanced at his cellmates, then at the figure sitting on the grass.

"Who's the loner?"

"That's Tony Deluca, Salvatore Deluca's kid."

"Who's that?"

"He's just the head of the New York mafia, that's all."

"Oh, okay," Sam said, unimpressed. "Thanks for the info." He turned and headed toward the enclosure.

"You're asking for trouble, kid," one of the old men warned from behind.

Sam offered a half-wave of thanks as he walked to the concrete structure and stepped inside. He stood looking around at the huge, empty space. *Yeah, this'll do*, he thought as he closed the squeaky steel door. After a few stretching exercises, he started jogging slowly along the wall, loosening up. His speed increased after only one lap. By the third, he was sprinting on the straight-aways and slowing in the turns to just below the point at which centrifugal force would slam him against the wall. With his mouth closed and his breathing deep and controlled, he began to relax.

The door opened with a loud clang. Sam stopped, expecting to see tattooed necks filing in. Instead, Tony Deluca entered after a shove from a guard.

"Got a handball?" Sam asked.

The mobster's Bronx accent was thick as he answered, "F'get about it, kid. The bulls threw me in here. I think maybe they got a little surprise coming for me."

Sam glanced at the still-open door and saw the camera above it swivel to face the wall. *Uh-oh*, he thought just before four black inmates sauntered in and a guard behind them closed the door.

"You voodoo-pray'n sons-o'-bitches are asking for trouble," Deluca barked. He backed up and motioned for Sam to stay out of the way, as if he would handle the menacing-looking foursome by himself. "Anyone moves on me, and my old man'll whack your whole family, even your dog."

Sam knew pretending he was not involved was pointless. *Even if I'm not the target*, he figured, *I'm a witness, probably the fall guy*.

The dreadlock-wearing quartet split up. Two pulled sharply pointed objects from their pockets and continued slowly toward the retreating gangster.

The others turned in Sam's direction. Both smiled confidently, displaying numerous gold-inlaid teeth as they produced their own shanks.

"*Dis* telling your *daddy*, *mon*, dat da Kingston Yardies is in it *ah d'way*," said one of Deluca's would-be assailants with a distinct Jamaican accent.

Observing the casual nature of his own attackers' approach, Sam surmised they knew nothing of their quarry, since he was new. *That'll cost you*, he thought.

He opened his eyes wide and remained motionless, feigning a fear-frozen state, until both Jamaicans came within five feet of him.

He moved too fast for the startled duo to counter, driving the bottom of his left foot into the closest assailant's kneecap. The blow produced a sickening crack as the leg snapped rearward, taking on the oddly jointed shape of a grasshopper's rear limbs.

Half a second later, he punched his other attacker in the larynx just hard enough to incapacitate him. Spinning around, he slammed an elbow into the choking man's temple, sending him to the concrete floor, unconscious.

As the thug plopped down, Sam leapt atop the other already there. His powerful arms slipped around the wailing man's neck, squeezing and temporarily stopping blood flow to the brain. The man's struggling ceased. To ensure he stayed out, Sam elbowed him in the face, knocking out several glimmering gold teeth and dislocating his jaw.

Unwisely, Deluca's attackers never looked over, perhaps thinking the scream they'd heard was Sam's dying yelp. If they had, they would have seen him approaching at their backs.

He viciously crippled both without warning and then pulled the insensible cohorts to the center of the enclosure. He laid their now bent and blunted weapons atop the pile and moved to the wall opposite Deluca.

"That was fucking awesome," the mobster exclaimed. "How'd you learn to do shit like that, kid?"

Sam held a finger to his lips as the door cracked open. A guard peeked in, and Sam called out, "Hey, those fellas opened up a big ol' can of whoopass on each other."

The door opened wider, and the guard raised his radio and made an announcement Sam couldn't hear over Deluca's roaring laughter. Moments later, a flood of uniforms rushed in and roughly dragged him and Deluca out.

Sam knew the incident was mob business, but figured his role would likely bring some form of retribution his way. He was not wrong. He had no idea where Deluca was taken, but he was placed in an isolation cage he could only stand inside. Just before its mesh door closed, a guard nailed him with a stun gun.

The sadist held the trigger down until another advised, "You'll give him a heart attack if you don't let up. I don't give a shit, but that's a lot of paperwork, and they'll drug test us."

The guard ended the jolt. "You got any idea what Deluca's old man's gonna do to us because of this asshole?"

"I ain't gonna wait to find out," the other replied. "I'm getting outta town tonight."

Sam remembered standing in the cramped space for

hours before the warden ordered him transferred to the maximum-security cell block. He could still hear the man's lie. "I'm doing this to protect you, Calder. You won't live to see tomorrow if I leave you in general population."

Since that day five years ago, with the exception of a five-minute supervised shower every third evening and forty-five minutes each morning in a fully enclosed exercise pen built inside the cell block, the sixty-three-square-foot cell had been the extent of Sam's world.

The only windows in the entire block were small slats high up the wall opposite the cells, but all he could tell from them was whether it was day or night. *Still, the warden may have been right*, he thought. *Maximum-security may be mind-numbingly monotonous, but it's relatively nonthreatening. Of course, I still have to sleep with one eye open as long as Bucher's around.*

His reverie ended when a gruff voice outside the door ordered, "Assume the position, Calder."

CHAPTER 2

Army Lieutenant General Thomas Devlin, the Defense Intelligence Agency's director, enjoyed arriving at his Fort Meade office before the rest of the masses. It gave him time to savor a cup of Columbian roast and read the overnight hot sheets covering events that had happened around the world while he slept. Of course, he knew the night duty officer would have notified him if anything of significance had occurred, so the morning's read was never earth-shattering.

His secretary stuck her head in. "General, the president's chief of staff called. He said the president wants to speak with the senior cabinet and National Security Council principals at nine this morning. He claimed he didn't know the reason for the meeting, sir."

"Have my car readied."

"Yes, sir."

I'll bet I know the reason, Devlin thought as he flipped to the end of the hot sheets, where the most recent events were posted. *There it is.* He began reading the blurb about U.S. Ambassador Thaddeus Cardwell dying of an apparent heart attack during the night.

౭ఎౕఎ

Devlin, already seated, watched as the cabinet secretaries and other senior NSC members entered the White House conference room in ones and twos. Most carried on muted conversations with each other or spoke into their cell phones. He glanced over at the chairman of the Joint Chiefs. The Marine four-star was talking amicably with Jeff Campbell, the president's national security advisor. Devlin knew Campbell had been a Navy admiral. The sight of the two four-stars brought to mind the time he'd approached them at another function and was not-so-politely ignored by both men.

That humiliating snub will soon cost you, he thought as he turned his gaze away, looking now at his only intelligence counterpart in the room, CIA Director Calvin Stone. Devlin considered the presidential appointee in the same light he saw the Joint Chiefs chairman and Campbell: anything *but* a friendly colleague.

None of you deserve to be where you are, he thought. *I can't wait until—*

His menacing thought was interrupted by the entrance of the immaculately attired president, who waved everyone to sit as he walked to his chair.

Devlin jealously stared at Robert Longwood, thinking that he looked as if Hollywood had cast him for the role of chief executive: six feet tall and handsome still, even though Devlin knew the man was nearing sixty.

He saw Longwood pause before taking his chair and glance across the table at his recently deceased VP's empty seat. *An aneurism in her sleep last month*, Devlin recalled as a smile creased the edge of his lips. He caught himself and quickly placed his hand over his mouth, pretending to stifle a yawn as he scanned faces to see if anyone had noticed.

He had been surprised to learn that the Constitution did not require the president to immediately nominate a new vice president. That was how he'd discovered that the office had actually been vacant several times in history, sometimes for years. He suspected Longwood intended to leave the seat empty until he ran for re-election next year and needed someone to fill out his party's ticket. *That mistake's gonna bite you in the ass*, he thought as Longwood sat.

He knew the man didn't call meetings just to chew the fat. He liked that Longwood didn't waste time with idle chitchat either. *He probably won't even say hello before beginning*, he thought.

"I know how busy you people are, so I'll get right to why we're here this morning," Longwood said. "As I'm sure you're all aware by now, Thad Cardwell died in his sleep last night of an apparent heart attack." He paused as scattered murmurs of sadness were voiced. "As you all know, Thad has been in Denmark mediating the discussions between Israel and the Palestinian Authority. What you may not know is that for the first time in decades, it actually seems that a peace accord might be reached."

Though several voiced their well wishes, the mere thought of it made Devlin cringe.

"Unfortunately, Thad was seventy-seven and had a pacemaker that was apparently giving him some trouble, so he flew back here yesterday and checked into Walter Reed for a quick replacement procedure scheduled for this morning." He paused again, letting the obvious go unsaid. "Not to seem uncaring, but we need to replace him at the negotiations as soon as possible."

"We're putting together a list of candidates now, Mr. President," said Secretary of State Elizabeth Langford.

"Thank you. I asked you all here this morning because I didn't want to say anything about this in a White House email that might somehow find itself in the newspapers tomorrow. It's imperative that each of you reiterate to your staffs that if anyone is asked by the media to comment on Thad's passing or his work, no information about the talks is to be mentioned. Premature disclosure would almost certainly lead to violence from those opposed to a peaceful resolution."

Devlin knew how difficult it was to keep anything secret in Washington, D.C., and he also knew there were some seated around him who suspected he did not support the president's ambitious foreign policy endeavor— the CIA director being one.

He glanced Stone's way again. Though he and Stone were about the same age, it irked him that the agency spook looked ten years younger. Devlin stared jealously at Stone's thick, wavy, brown hair, noting only a hint of gray at the temples. He unconsciously ran a hand through his thinning gray comb-over.

That he and Stone were not friends was no secret. Stone always attempted to steal the show when NSC discussions involved intelligence matters. Devlin knew he was merely grandstanding. Almost smiling again, he thought, *That hasn't worked out very well for you lately, has it, asshole*?

With the prohibition against CIA interrogations following accusations of torture and rendition deaths, Devlin had unilaterally assumed proprietorship of all enemy captives until he deemed it in his interest to turn them over to the FBI's High-Value Interrogation Group. He considered the HIG useless, since they began every questioning with an advisement of the captive's right to remain silent, which the captive always then exercised.

He recalled someone on his staff asking how the DIA got answers when the HIG could not. He had explained, "It's quite simple. We keep the bastards locked up aboard ships kept at sea. It's like our own private Guantanamo, a sort of interrogation purgatory. They either talk, or else."

Devlin's musings ended when Longwood concluded the meeting as abruptly as he had started it. The president stood and walked out with a wave. "Thanks for coming by, folks. Let's all go back to work now, and remember to keep this under your hats."

Outside, Devlin ordered his driver to take him to the Friars Country Club and raised the front seat partition for privacy. He needed to ponder how best to use what he'd learned in the meeting. Longwood's claim that he wanted the peace talks to resume as soon as possible caused him some angst, but he knew that wouldn't matter soon. He pulled his secure cell phone and hit speed dial number one.

"This is Armstrong, sir."

"What's your status?"

"We just landed, sir. We'll be moving to the base camp within the hour. How did Crowley do at Walter Reed?"

"He got the job done."

"Is he coming out here now?"

"No. I may need him here."

"Good. I don't. The guy freaks me out."

"Whatever. I'm meeting with Mandrake and Branson in a few minutes. How did your meeting with Jackson go?"

"He bought it all. I'll be meeting him and the other seven again tomorrow night at the logging camp to make sure they're on track."

"Did you get his cell phone number?"

"Yes, sir."

Devlin noted the number Armstrong gave him and disconnected, then he hit speed dial number two.

"This is Crowley, sir."

"Armstrong doesn't need you out there, so your team's staying here in case something comes up at this end." Devlin disconnected before hearing Crowley's acknowledgement.

He needed Lloyd Armstrong and Frank Crowley, but had never liked either man. They were co-leaders of a two-squad cadre of former soldiers and Marines he secretly employed using off-the-books DIA funds. Each of the mercenaries he retained for this illicit force had left his respective branch of the armed forces under less-than-honorable conditions. While none was the sort to make it through special operations training, they were men without allegiances and willing to do anything for money or to support their own peculiar depravities. Only Armstrong and Crowley knew who their real employer was. The rest believed they were legitimate government contractors working for the military.

Devlin thought it laughingly ironic that the taxpayers funded his little cabal of sociopathic miscreants, especially since the majority of their activities were illegal, if not outright seditious. Still, even with House and Senate Intelligence Committee oversight of black ops programs, he had no difficulty hiding the true nature of his private legion. He had long understood that elected officials sitting on those political bodies did not really want to hear the details of America's back-alley doings. Most politicians—and senior military officers, for that matter—preferred a buffer of deniability in the event that something truly nasty became public knowledge.

He knew that was why debacles like the Abu Ghraib prison incident and the Benghazi consulate massacre never resulted in blame placed on anyone of import, and he had no compunction against using their cowardly failings to his advantage. He also enjoyed that, as the DIA's director, he was unaccountable to anyone else at his agency and—through misuse of the proverbial need-to-know tenet—was even able to rationalize denying access to those meddlesome four-star chiefs over in the Pentagon.

He glanced out the car's window as it moved down Pennsylvania Avenue and spotted Calvin Stone riding in the back seat of a Town Car in the next lane. He briefly considered ordering his driver to run the CIA chief off the road, but he understood that Stone—like Longwood's peace plan—was not going to be a problem much longer.

He next phoned Donna Jones, a reporter with *The Washington Post*. When it served his purposes, he leaked information to her, and she always attributed it to an unnamed but highly placed source in the administration.

"Hello, Tom. It's always nice to hear from you."

"I was just thinking about you, my dear. I hoped we might get together tonight for dinner."

"That sounds wonderful. Should I bring my laptop?"

"Why, of course. I'll see you at eight."

After he hung up, he considered how unattractive she was and whether he should make a sexual overture after dinner. He knew his pockmarked face put most women off, but she might be as desperate as he was. That thought triggered the memory of his deceased wife, Margaret.

A colonel when he met her, Devlin seduced and married the frumpy, middle-aged spinster-to-be after the Army awarded her father his fourth star. Margaret's mother wasn't about to have her only child stuck living on a colonel's salary, so Devlin's first three stars came easily enough thanks to her persistent badgering of her husband on her son-in-law's behalf.

Devlin knew he would never see his fourth star after Margaret's father suffered a massive heart attack in his Pentagon office, dying en route to the hospital. After that, Margaret became nothing more than a useless and repugnant burden, then a threatening menace at the end.

Two years ago, she had surprised him in his hotel

room during a supposed official trip to Thailand and discovered his proclivity for pre-adolescent girls. Storming from the room, she ranted about his degeneracy and threatened to expose him immediately upon her return to Washington.

Following a woefully inadequate forensic analysis, Thai investigating authorities determined that Margaret's alcohol and prescription drug-induced drowning in the hotel's pool that night was an unfortunate accident. They saw no need to delve more deeply, since the grieving husband made it clear he planned no protest of their findings. In fact, Devlin so fully supported their deduction that they turned her body over to him for immediate cremation and closed their case. Weeks later, Margaret's three-million-dollar life insurance payout was a comforting consolation for his loss, though half went to the Thai chief investigator.

A sneer ticked at the corner of his mouth as he glanced over and saw Stone's car veer away toward Langley. *In a matter of days, weeks at most, you'll bow to my will—maybe even to my wrath, like Margaret did.*

CHAPTER 3

The cell's solid door—designed to prevent the depraved from throwing fecal matter or grabbing at passersby—featured a half-inch-thick plastic viewing port at eye level and a lazy susan opening at the bottom where paper trays and cups were rotated in and out. A buzzer sounded, and metal on metal clanked as the door's electronic locks released.

The barrier slid aside, revealing three male guards. One held a dangling chain, one carried nothing, and the third had a two-handed grasp on a Taser pointed at Sam's chest.

"On the wall," Chainman ordered.

Sam moved according to rote muscle memory. He turned ninety degrees to face the wall, spread his legs, and leaned forward, placing both palms flat against the cement.

He remained absolutely still, knowing the guards would deem any twitch an attack. He remembered how he had made *that* mistake a few times in the beginning. Each had resulted in a painful incapacitation by Taserholder, followed by loss of his exercise privilege. It was not fear of the electricity that coerced obedience. Most there, including him, were inured to it. Rather, it was the threat of losing those precious moments away from the cell's confines that compelled men to kowtow.

Though state incarceration rules mandated that maximum-security inmates receive a daily exercise period out of their cell, Bucher remained motionless. He never took advantage of the opportunity—no doubt one reason for the man's physical condition. Sam, on the other hand, had always been physically active and relished his time in the exercise pen. In fact, he sometimes thought its calming effect was all that kept his repulsive cellmate alive.

The empty-handed guard stepped in and went through the motions of frisking him before stepping back so Chainman could wrap Sam's waist with the half-inch-thick steel links. Each wrist was brought off the wall, and a handcuff snapped shut around it.

"Close your feet, asshole."

Sam obeyed, and an ankle cuff went on each leg, hobbling him.

"Let's go. It smells like shit in here."

Sam turned to follow, waddling as quietly as the clinking metal would allow. Chainman pulled at the three-foot length of chain attached to Sam's waist as if it were a leash. Taser-holder was at his back now, with the third man following him.

Sam glanced up at a window slit and saw only darkness. *Early for the exercise pen*, he thought. He wanted to know what time it was but hesitated to ask.

The gravity with which his guards carried out their duties had puzzled him in the beginning. "You'd think I was headed for execution," he recalled saying the first time. That brief breach of maximum security's mandatory silence protocol was all Taser-holder needed to send him to the deck twitching and jerking before the other two laughingly dragged him back into his cell.

He had not lost consciousness but suspected that if

Bucher saw how weakened he was, things might not go well for him in the next few minutes. He concentrated on not grimacing or giving away his true condition as he pulled himself to his feet and the cell door slammed closed. Once up, he shook like a dog shedding water and declared, "Now *that* was fun!"

Bucher, he saw, was indeed watching him closely and then rolled away.

Tolerance, even common civility, was not something any guard had ever shown him. They had made it clear that they were aware he was there, in part, because he had severely injured several of their law enforcement brethren. The memory brought on a pang of heartache, followed by the usual regret that he had not killed the three detectives.

As he and the three guards neared the hallway leading to the exercise pen, the guards unexpectedly turned left instead of the usual right. Sam tensed for a shock and asked, "Where are we going?"

Surprisingly, Taser-holder didn't pull the trigger.

Why not? Sam wondered.

Chainman answered brusquely, "You're going to your first parole hearing."

Sam remembered his dead mentor telling him he might be eligible for such a deliberation but had convinced himself that the handball court fiasco that put him in maximum security had cost him the opportunity. Now, though, as he shuffled along a hallway he had never been in before, a tiny spark of optimism ignited deep within.

"Don't bother blowing anyone a goodbye kiss, Calder," Taser-holder snidely remarked at his back. "You ain't gonna get paroled, ever."

Sam did not respond to the goading. Instead, he stared straight ahead, trying to focus on what he could say that might sway the board members. He feared that if they inexplicably chose to release him, the guards would immediately move him back to general population. Though there was no rationale for such a transfer, he suspected they would do it, hoping he would get into some sort of trouble they could use to deny his freedom. *They might even instigate it*, he thought.

They passed into a section of the prison he had never visited and entered a bleak room without windows, where Chainman ordered him to sit on a metal chair at the end of a long table. Once he was down, his wrist cuffs were connected to a fastener welded to the steel tabletop, and then his ankle shackles to the legs of the chair bolted to the floor. With him secured, the three guards flanked him, a step back.

Though he had never been through this before, Sam realized they were taking no chances that he might try to harm someone when they gave him the disappointing news they expected. Still, he hoped for a different outcome.

Another table had been placed perpendicular at the opposite end of the table. He saw three chairs along its far side. A few silent moments passed before a door opened and two middle-aged white men and a thirty-something black woman entered and sat.

Silently staring at him, their faces were void of any emotions Sam could discern. He assumed they were assessing his demeanor, and he forced the first smile he could remember making in years. He hoped it did not look as counterfeit as it felt.

After a quiet period, the man in the center of the trio slipped on a pair of thin reading glasses and made a show of opening and studying a folder before him. He seemed bored when he finally looked up over the top of the frames and announced, "We are members of the New York State Parole Board, Inmate Calder. As such, it is our duty to make a determination regarding the continuance or termination of your incarceration in this facility." He glanced down again at the file. "Your conviction on the charge of contributory manslaughter in the first degree, a Class A felony with special circumstances because the victim was pregnant, carries a sentence of five years to life."

Sam's forced smile faded as his head bowed. His heart ached at the memory the man's words evoked. After an anguished moment, he looked up again impassively.

"Furthermore, your additional conviction on three counts of aggravated assault against police officers carries added concurrent sentences of two to ten years on each count." The man paused again and removed his glasses before looking directly at Sam. "Though you have met the five-year minimum-time-served requirement to warrant this hearing, according to your file, you have yet to admit guilt for those crimes for which you were convicted. Are you aware that such an admission is a prerequisite for parole consideration?"

Stone-faced, Sam nodded once, though he actually had not known of that precondition. He suspected what was coming next and held his breath.

"Do you wish to rescind your claim of innocence at this time?"

Sam stared at the man, not responding with as much as a facial tic.

"I see," the man concluded with a tone of arrogance. "Well then, based on your unwillingness to acknowledge the heinous nature of your criminal behavior—"

Sam's heart pounded in his chest as despair overwhelmed him. He stopped listening to the man's condescending admonishment. Still, he refused to let those present see his angst. He sat there like a statue, his face a chiseled mask of uncaring acceptance.

At some point, a guard's hand roughly shook his shoulder, bringing him back to the moment. Someone new—a woman's voice—was speaking. All Sam's dispirited mind caught was "hearing is terminated" before he realized the parole board members were walking out and the guards were readying him for movement. He could not even recall standing.

Sam trudged down the hallways with his eyes fixed on his chained feet, his earlier fragment of optimism now only a deepening disheartenment. *Once again*, he thought, *life has teasingly paraded a glimmer of hope before me, only to replace it with more misery.*

As he shuffled along, a seething anger joined his despondency. He considered killing Bucher the moment his cell door closed. *If I'm to remain here the rest of my days*, he figured, *I might as well deserve it.*

He finally looked up when they stopped moving but found he was not in his cellblock. Instead, he was standing before the warden's office door. It was open, and Taser-holder nudged him forward.

Sam stopped in the center of the room when Chainman yanked on his leash.

Another guard came in and dropped a paper sack on a table by the wall.

The warden was seated at his desk. Another well-dressed man stood behind him, near a large window.

Sam looked out and saw that it was raining. He had not even seen rain since being transferred into the maximum-security cell block and had resigned himself to the likelihood that he never would again. His melancholy deepened as he gazed longingly through the glass.

"Remove his restraints," the warden ordered.

"Calder's a class-one inmate, sir," Taser-holder cautioned.

"Do as I said."

As the heavy manacles came off, the warden added, "You guards may leave."

Sam remained motionless, but his eyes caught the uniformed men glancing at each other uneasily as they complied.

"I had your possessions gathered up from your cell, Calder," the warden said, tipping his head toward the brown paper bag.

Sam glanced at the nearly empty sack. *Pitiful testament to twenty-eight years of life*, he thought. Then it dawned on him that the bag's presence meant he was not returning to his cell.

He assumed that he was about to be returned to general population or possibly even moved to a different prison.

"You lucked out, Bucher," he whispered to himself.

"What was that?"

Sam shook his head and quietly replied, "It doesn't matter."

The man at the window stepped forward and handed Sam a sealed envelope. "Mr. Calder, my name's Charles Finlay. I'm with the state attorney general's office."

Sam held the envelope unopened. "What's this?"

"This will undoubtedly come as a shock, sir, but irrefutable evidence has surfaced clearing you of the charges for which you were arrested. Moreover, the guilty verdicts on all counts of your conviction have been set aside, your record has been expunged, and the court has ordered your immediate release from this institution."

Dumbstruck, almost panting, Sam stared at Finlay, half expecting him to laugh and say he was just kidding. Instead, the man said nothing, so Sam asked, "What evidence?"

"There was a camera over the door of that restaurant that recorded—"

Sam angrily interrupted. "The cops said that camera didn't work."

"Well, frankly, they lied. I imagine they did so because what it recorded clearly shows the three detectives assaulting your wife, exactly as you claimed at trial. It also proves that you were not, in any manner, responsible for her death."

Sam continued to stare at Finlay, waiting for more.

"I'm certain the detective who hid the video had every intention of destroying it. Fortunately for you, he died before he was able to do so. The DVD, however, remained hidden until a recent renovation of his apartment. The individual who discovered it took it to the district attorney's office, and the DA who reviewed it recognized the crime scene. The end result is that you're a free man again, Mr. Calder. Furthermore, you are entitled to financial remuneration under New York's Wrongfully Imprisoned Compensation Program. That recompense will be based on your income prior to confinement and your time here, and it will undoubtedly include an added amount for your pain and suffering while incarcerated."

"What about those cops?"

"As you may recall, Detective Flanders died in an automobile accident shortly before your trial. He was the one who hid the video. Detective Hardesty died last year following a heart attack, and Detective Dugan committed suicide two nights ago, apparently after receiving word he was to be arrested. I should also add that the restaurant owner's wife claimed she was coerced to testify against you by those same detectives and has confessed to giving the video to Detective Flanders after breaking the camera. She and her husband were in the country illegally and have both been turned over to ICE for deportation processing."

There was a long moment of silence before Finlay

asked, "So, where would you like to go, Mr. Calder?"

Sam's mind was reeling. *I spent five years dreaming of getting my hands on those detectives. Now what?*

"Do you have somewhere to go, Calder?" the warden asked.

"I want to go home."

"I'm sorry," Finlay said, "but the bank foreclosed on your condo after your conviction. Of course, you'll be compensated for that, as well."

"Not *that* home."

CHAPTER 4

The Friars boasted the most exclusive membership among Maryland's elite country clubs: current and former members of both houses of Congress; Supreme Court justices and federal judges; senior, active, and retired military officers—nothing less than four stars received an invitation to join—and anyone powerful enough to have unhindered access to the White House.

Tom Devlin had never been to the club until his appointment as the DIA's director. Though the three-star was still not offered membership, others who were and hoped to garner something of political value now routinely invited him for nine holes of gossip-filled golf, usually followed by free food and drinks in their elegant clubhouse.

Today, he was to brunch with the three-hundred-pound Speaker of the House, Philip Mandrake, a man of immense girth and influence. Devlin knew Mandrake was also Longwood's political nemesis, though in the same party.

Devlin did not consider Mandrake a friend. The rotund senior congressional representative was merely a means to an end, a pathetically flawed man whom Devlin planned to toss aside after he got what he wanted from him. Mandrake's weakness was not his well-known arrogance or even his obesity. It was that he was an over-the-top Christian fundamentalist known for a near-fanatical belief in the prophesied Second Coming of the Messiah. After first meeting him, Devlin wondered how Mandrake had managed to stay in office for twenty-five years, giving him the seniority to become the Speaker. That was before he discovered that a fair-sized faction of like-minded supporters populated most of the fat man's Montana congressional district.

On the other hand, Devlin knew any higher political aspirations Mandrake might foolishly entertain would never come about, at least not without *his* help. The majority of America's electorate simply did not share in the core tenet of the Speaker's religious dogma: a fierce battle between Jew and Arab, Armageddon was inevitable, but God would return for the most faithful of Christians beforehand.

When his scheme dawned on him after the vice president's demise, Devlin began looking for an inroad with Mandrake, and quickly recognized how offensive Longwood's Middle East peace accord must be to the man's theological vision. For his purposes, Devlin needed Mandrake dependent on his counsel and continuously reassured him that he would do whatever he could to foil Longwood's vile peace intentions. He wished he could tell him about Frank Crowley's handiwork at Walter Reed but feared that might be too much for the sanctimonious zealot. *After all*, Devlin thought as he approached the portly House leader, *he believes I'm one of the faithful, too.*

Mandrake extended his plump, soft hand. "It's good to see you, Tom." He raised his other hand to a silver-haired man stepping up at his left. "I'd like you to meet Ben Branson. Ben's a big supporter from back home."

Devlin knew the Montana billionaire quite well but responded, "How do you do, Mr. Branson?"

"Please, call me Ben," Branson said, taking Devlin's hand as if for the first time.

"Gentlemen, why don't we sit on the veranda today?" Mandrake suggested. "The weather's nice, and it's a bit more private out there."

The trio stepped to an isolated table on the wide, stone patio overlooking several plush fairways. They waited until their server finished filling their water glasses and disappeared, and then Mandrake began.

"So, Tom, how are things going in the Longwood camp?"

"Well, you know I can't divulge state secrets, Mr. Speaker, but I have a source who tells me Donna Jones will be publishing an exposé on the peace talks in tomorrow's *Post*."

Mandrake chortled. "All hell's gonna break loose when those A—rabs get wind of what Longwood's trying to pull over their rag-headed eyes."

"Yes, it certainly will," Devlin replied as he began staging his next lie. "As to your question, though, I must admit that Longwood can be frustratingly obstinate. It's just that he's not much of a God-fearing man, you know, and I find that unsettling. After all, he is the president of a nation built upon God's plan." Devlin knew Mandrake could not resist the draw of that statement.

"You're absolutely right, Tom. This nation must have a man of faith leading it, or we're sure to suffer the Lord's wrath."

Devlin sipped water to hide his grin. He caught a nod from Branson and suspected what was coming next.

"Tom, this is still a secret," Mandrake said, "but I'm considering challenging Longwood for the party's nomination next year. In fact, Ben here has offered generous financial support if I should choose to do so. I'd like to know your thoughts on that."

Devlin knew Mandrake had about as much chance of beating Longwood for the nomination as he had of winning a marathon. For effect, though, he stared at the Speaker as if seriously pondering the possibility and then smiled broadly. "That's a truly wonderful idea, and you'll have *my* full support, too. You know, trying to overturn a sitting president can be difficult, but a faith-based platform might just make it feasible in these trying times."

Right on cue, Branson leaned in and said quietly, "You don't want to jump the gun though, Phil. I'd suggest you hold off on an official announcement until the party's platform committee meets. Besides, we don't want to upset our plans for tomorrow."

Devlin wanted to laugh aloud at Branson's words, since the two of them had carefully scripted the entire conversation days ago.

Mandrake's cell phone rang, and he excused himself to answer it in private. As soon as he was at a distance, Devlin asked, "Has the advance team left?"

"Not yet. My staff says they're wrapping up today and are expected to move to their temporary command center this afternoon."

"Where's that located?"

"They set it up at the Thompson Falls Airport. It's close by, but too small for Air Force One. They brought in one of those Marine One helicopters to fly him from the Missoula airport to my place."

"Remember to call me the moment you hear the advance team has left the area."

"Okay."

"When are you heading back?"

"I'm leaving right after this meeting. My jet's waiting."

"Is Mandrake going with you?"

"No. He's been invited to fly out on Air Force One with Longwood." He paused a moment. "By the way, I have a question. Why is it so important that Phillip not be with us on day two?"

Devlin couldn't share the true reason, so he responded, "I just think it would be best if he wasn't there. You know, in case he loses it or something. We can't have the media pick up on something like that."

"I understand. I've got some sedatives I can slip in his drink tomorrow night. They'll keep him out for about twelve hours."

Devlin handed him a small piece of paper. "This is Howard Jackson's cell phone number. Once Mandrake's out, use his cell phone to call it. If Jackson answers, say you got the wrong number and hang up. I just need a record of the call on the phone."

Branson nodded and slipped the paper into his pocket.

"So, did he offer you a cabinet post or an ambassador-ship for that promised financial support?"

Branson shrugged. "Nothing directly, but he hinted at some type of payoff."

Devlin saw Mandrake returning. "He's coming back."

Mandrake plopped down, his enormous belly jarring the table and sloshing water out of glasses. "Oops. Sorry about that. What'd I miss?"

"Actually, Ben was just telling me how it was your idea to invite Longwood on that fishing trip tomorrow. I have to say, that was a pretty clever move."

"What d'ya mean?"

Branson answered, "He means it'll give you more in-sight into Longwood before he even knows you'll be his opponent next year. Moreover, anyone hanging out with the President of the United States gets a lot of media at-tention. That can't hurt, either."

His mood upbeat, Devlin glanced at his watch. "I'm afraid I'll have to take a rain check on brunch, Mr. Speaker. Something has come up."

❧❧❧

Robert Longwood glanced at his reflection in a decorative mirror hanging on a wall of the Oval Office. "Do you remember when I came into office three years ago?" he said. "My hair was dark brown. Now it's almost all gray, and yours is still dark, even though we're the same age."

He didn't say his next thought aloud. *I know it's partly from job stress, but mostly from losing Cynthia before I took office.*

Jeff Campbell, Longwood's best friend since college, chortled. "Quit whining. The gray suits you. I just come from a younger-looking gene pool."

Longwood laughed. "Maybe I should grow a beard. I might look more statesmanlike . . . wise."

"Yeah, like Gandalf the Grey or Rasputin."

Secretary of State Langford, the only other person in the room, made a forced coughing sound. "Mr. President? Have you come to a decision? About the mediator position, I mean?"

Longwood faced her. "As I see it, Elizabeth, our choices are down to Charles Thompson or Sarah Michaels. I've heard the arguments for both, and I choose Charles."

"But Mr. Pres—"

Longwood raised a hand. "I'm aware he hasn't had as much experience as Sarah. Unfortunately, she's seventy-five, and politically incorrect or not, frankly, I think she's too old for this."

"I can't believe you'd yield to age discrimination, Mr.

President," Langford replied in her most indignant tone. "Thad Cardwell was seventy-seven."

"And look what happened. He died on the job. The last thing we need is to lose another mediator before this thing gets settled. Regardless of what we've accomplished to this point, it may take some time before we actually get signatures on paper. Thompson's only sixty-two and, according to his file, in perfect health."

Langford gathered her papers and stood. "I suggest you call Prime Minister Levin and President Abasad right away to make sure their representatives don't get restless while Charles is being brought up to speed."

"I'll do that. Thank you."

At the door, she turned back and added, "Not that it's any of my business, but there hasn't been a bearded president in this country in more than a century."

After the door clicked shut, Campbell said, "By the way, are you still planning on leaving tomorrow to go fishing with that asshole Mandrake?"

"Is that any way to refer to the Speaker of the House? But to answer your question, yes, I still plan to go fishing with that asshole. In fact, I invited him to fly out there with me, and you're coming along."

"Why?"

"In case you haven't seen the weather reports, Hurricane Betsy's approaching the Caribbean and forecast to turn north along the eastern seaboard in the next week. I'm going to have to be here when that happens, but frankly, we could both use a break and some fresh air before then. We're only talking about two days. Besides, I have to go to Thad Cardwell's memorial out in California, and it's scheduled for the day after the trip. Being in Montana, we'll be halfway there."

"I understand, and I know how much you love to fish, but why go all the way out there with that fat son of a bitch? You know he spends half his time trying to push through bills he knows you'll never sign, and I've heard rumors he's been talking about running against you next year."

"Yet another reason to go fishing with him."

"What do you mean?"

"Paraphrasing the ancient Chinese strategist Sun Tzu, I need to keep my friends close and my enemies even closer." He chuckled. "Maybe we'll get lucky and he'll get eaten by a bear."

"It'd take more than one."

CHAPTER 5

Sam left the meager contents of the paper bag behind and slipped the letter of exoneration into the inside pocket of the now rumpled and musty suit he had been wearing when they brought him to Attica straight from the courthouse five years earlier. He wore no tie. His jailers had taken it from him when he was booked, as a precaution against suicide. His shoelaces and belt were missing for the same reason. The last gate buzzed open for him, and he continued through without looking back or acknowledging the escorting warden's parting farewell.

The early summer air felt cool, and—regrettably to him—the rain had stopped. With the sky still darkly overcast, he thought it probably seemed like a dreary day to most. It felt glorious to him. He was almost giddy as he strode toward the end of the puddled sidewalk, where he was to wait for Finlay to pull up from the visitor's lot. The state attorney had offered to drive him into town, even giving him a five-hundred-dollar cash advance on the compensation he was to receive as soon as he got a new bank account and driver's license.

As he stood at the curb, Sam looked down at his old shoes, their tongues flopping loose. He had worn only prison-issued slippers for years, and the hard soles felt odd. He gazed at a forested hillside in the distance. He remembered arriving at night, unable to see what Attica's grounds looked like in the glare of so many spotlights. He gazed about now and saw that all around him was clear-cut and paved, dominated by high, gray concrete walls surrounded by two separate rows of twenty-foot-high chain-link fencing topped with glistening razor wire. *This place really is a fortress of dread*, he thought.

He felt an urge to remove his slack shoes and run for those far-off trees in his bare feet, as he had fantasized so many times in the exercise pen.

A part of his mind warned that one of the sentries glowering at him from the corner parapets would likely shoot him in the back, later claiming he mistook him for an escapee.

The guards had made it clear they did not care that he had been proven innocent. From their myopic viewpoint, he had harmed fellow lawmen and should not get away with it, no matter the reason.

The rain began to fall again. Sam pushed thoughts of prison aside and turned his face up, delighting in the feel of the cool drops. At the sound of an engine, he glanced back down and caught sight of a black car approaching along the main road. *That can't be Finlay*, he thought. *Not from that direction.*

As it neared and slowed, he saw that it was a limousine. The luxury vehicle pulled to a stop directly in front of him, and a heavily tinted rear window slid down.

Tony Deluca smiled at him. "*Buongiorno*, Mr. Calder."

Surprised, but unaccustomed to showing it, Sam casually responded, "I haven't seen you in five years."

"Yeah, I got paroled right after that little incident. By the way, my father's people dealt quite effectively with the Kingston Yardies, and they also caught up with those two guards who took their money."

Not wanting to hear more, Sam asked, "So what're you doing back here?"

"I came to offer you a ride away from this shithole and a job."

A large older man stepped out from the front passenger seat and opened the limo's rear door.

Sam looked around, spotted Finlay's government sedan approaching, and climbed into the limo. "Thanks. I'll take you up on the ride, at least."

As the limo driver maneuvered a U-turn, Sam looked over at Finlay pulling to the curb. The state attorney was staring at the departing car with a bewildered look. A smile widened across Sam's face. The sensation felt strange.

"So, how'd you know I was being released?"

"Hey, we pay good money to know what's happening at the attorney general's office," the gangster boasted. He pulled a dark bottle from a built-in bar, poured a small glass, and held it out. "I'm actually a Scotch man myself, but my old man flies this privately-blended stuff called Sambuca in from Sicily. You gotta try it."

Sam took the glass and sipped. "Tastes like licorice."

Tony laughed huskily and reached across to slap him on a knee. "You know, you're right. It does." In a boisterous voice, his Bronx brogue emerging, he asked, "So, do you have somewhere you would like to go first? Is there someone special waiting? A woman, perhaps?"

A curtain of grief slid across Sam's face as he turned to the window and quietly answered, "Yeah, there's a woman I need to visit."

❦❦❦

A gentle rain continued to fall as the mobsters waited

in the car and patiently watched Sam from a distance. It took him nearly an hour to locate the marker, since he had not been permitted to leave the jail at Rikers Island to attend the funeral. Now, standing above Judith's grave for the first time, he paid no attention to the chill dampness of his suit or the rain blending with his tears. The only thoughts flooding his mind were memories.

Judith had been the center of his world during their short time together. Before her, his SEAL team had occupied that spot, but her unexpected entrance into his life had changed that almost overnight. While he had still relished the team's camaraderie and the challenges of his duties, Judith's happiness became much more important to him, and his job scared the hell out of her.

They had married just two months after meeting, and their first separation came only weeks later when he had to leave on a two-month special operations mission. While Skyping from a ship off the east African coast six weeks into it, Judith had revealed her pregnancy. Sam remembered how thrilled he had been that night, but after nearly dying on a mission the following day, he'd found himself facing a difficult decision. For advice, he went to the ship's chaplain, whom he'd confided in before.

"I don't want to let my team down, but I can't do anything that might risk losing Judith and the baby."

"Sam, you and I have both known SEALs who sacrificed everything to stay on the team, in the action. Then later, to ease the pain of those lost wives and children, many of those men succumbed to alcohol abuse, or worse."

"I've always known that no man can stay on the team forever. Age alone will force you out. It's inevitable."

"Your new family won't push you out, and they might even be the answer to getting your father to welcome you back."

His decision made, Sam had gone to his commanding officer the following day and requested his discharge from the Navy once their deployment ended. The request surprised his teammates, even angered a few.

As it always did during these reminiscences, Sam's mind unwillingly took him next to that unspeakable night a week after the team returned to their Virginia base. Unable to bear the painful recollection, Sam knelt, kissed two fingers, and touched them to the bronze marker. His heart ached as he stood and walked away, unable to look back. He accepted a blanket offered by the large man who held open the car's rear door.

"Sorry about getting your seat wet," he said to Deluca as he climbed inside the limousine.

"F'get about it. Let's go to my place now and get you some dry clothes to wear. My old man wants to meet you."

"Why?"

"Hey, you saved my ass that day. I ain't someone who ignores a debt like that, and my old man ain't, either."

"You don't owe me anything, Mr. Deluca. Besides, I didn't have much choice."

"Yeah, maybe not, but I figure I owe you anyway. And call me Tony."

∽∾∽

The limo pulled to the curb in front of an elegant Manhattan skyscraper, and a uniformed door attendant pleasantly greeted Sam, Tony, and the large man from the front passenger seat, introduced as Louie. The three stepped into an elevator and rode it to the seventy-fifth floor.

Tony's penthouse filled the entire floor, and the private lift opened directly into it. The mobster took a few minutes to show Sam around the stylish, multimillion-dollar residence, sounding especially proud of its exceptional views. After that, he left him in one of its five lavish bathrooms for a long, hot shower.

Sam relished being free to stand under the hot water without a time limit and did not emerge until he noticed his fingertips had pruned. When he returned to the bedroom, he found his drenched suit missing and a new one bearing an Armani label set out. Beside it were packages containing underwear, socks, and expensive new shoes that, amazingly, fit. After several failed attempts at trying to remember how to fashion a decent tie knot, he gave up and stared at himself in a full-length mirror.

Did I really wake up in prison this morning? He asked himself, shaking his head.

He found Tony and Louie lounging in the living room with the limo driver. "Thank you, though I'm not sure I'm an Armani-wearing kinda guy."

"Hey, you look great. Now let's go to my father's place. You'll love the food."

∽∾

Sam looked around as Tony's limo pulled to the curb, seeing nothing that looked like a restaurant. There was only a door with a curtained window in its upper half. "I thought we were meeting your father at a restaurant."

"It's more like a social club that serves dinner to my father's associates," Tony replied as he climbed out and started across the wide sidewalk toward the closed door.

Sam noticed someone peeking out the door's curtain as he followed Tony.

The door opened, revealing a large, muscular man wearing a shoulder-holstered pistol. He stepped aside for them to enter and closed the door behind them, locking its deadbolt.

Definitely not a restaurant, Sam thought.

Tony continued toward a large, round table in the back of the narrow room. An older man in an expensive-looking suit was seated there.

"Pop, meet Sam Calder."

Sam accepted a surprisingly firm handshake from the elderly mob boss, noting the familial resemblance between Tony and his white-haired sire. The old man had stood to greet him, too. *That's probably something he doesn't normally do*, Sam thought. "How do you do, Mr. Deluca?"

The crime lord motioned toward a seat. "Please join us for supper, Mr. Calder. I've been looking forward to meeting you."

Sam glanced around as he pulled a chair out. He and the two Delucas were the only ones at the table, though there was a fourth plate set out. Six other suited men were scattered about the room, and the doorman repeatedly glanced out the curtained front door window. He was wearing a set of headphones now.

"The guy at the door is keeping an eye on a bunch of feds across the street," Tony said, as if he had read Sam's mind.

"What are feds doing over there?"

"The FBI has an organized crime surveillance team in the Excelsior Hotel. They don't know we own the place. They're actually paying us for the room—through a dummy corporation, of course." He laughed. "Mostly we just like to screw with 'em. We got their suite bugged, so we know everything they're up to. Charlie's listening to everything they say. That way we don't give them any cause for so much as a parking ticket."

Louie, behind the bar, added, "They take pictures of everyone who comes and goes from this place. Probably got you in their facial recognition program right now."

"Maybe we should leave through the tunnel," Tony suggested. "That'd mess 'em up."

"You have a tunnel?"

"Hey, this is New York, Sam. There are tunnels everywhere. One in the basement here leads to the building next door, which we also own. From there it branches across the street to the hotel's basement. Those feds have no idea who or what actually comes and goes from here."

Sam shook his head, chuckling.

Three men appeared from the kitchen then, one much older than the others and wearing traditional chef's whites. He pushed a cart laden with covered platters.

"If your food ain't any good," Tony announced with a grin, "feel free to shoot the chef."

The old cook shook his head as he stopped the cart next to their table and sarcastically responded to Tony's jibe. "You'd better watch your mouth, kid, or I may never stop spitting on *your* food."

Every man in the place, except Tony, chuckled at the old man's comeback.

The chef took the fourth seat at the table, and the elder Deluca said, "Mr. Calder, this is my younger brother, Luigi."

Sam shook the mobster cook's hand, now thinking the reference to the Mafia as *la famiglia* more telling than he had appreciated.

One server ladled portions of steaming chicken cacciatore along with roasted baby potatoes and steamed asparagus tips onto Sam's plate, while the other poured a white wine. Sam couldn't help thinking back on the cold powdered eggs and burnt toast he had devoured just that morning.

"I hope you enjoy your meal, Mr. Calder," Salvatore said. "Our family is in your debt."

"You don't owe me anything, Mr. Deluca. I just want

to get on with my own life, as far from New York as possible."

"Hey, we got a nice place down in the Caribbean," Tony offered. "You can go down there and stay as long as you want, chase women and stay drunk."

"Thanks, but I've got family out west, in Montana. I haven't seen them in a long time."

Salvatore Deluca wiped his mouth with a napkin and pulled a business card from his jacket pocket. He handed it to Sam. It was blank except for a phone number. "Call that number should you ever require our assistance, Mr. Calder."

Sam nodded his understanding of the gesture, but could think of nothing that could make him call the number.

"Are you sure I can't get you to reconsider, Sam?" Tony asked. "We could really use a guy like you around here."

A prison-inspired part of him briefly considered Tony's offer, but the painful memory of what had happened in that city was too overwhelming to ignore. He realized living there would be impossible. He shook his head. "Thanks, but no. I'm headed to Montana."

"How're you getting there?"

"Can you give me a lift to a bus station?"

"You wanna take a three-day bus ride?"

Sam shrugged. "I need some time to think through what I'm going to say when I get there. My dad and I had a falling out a long time ago."

"I can do you better than a bus ride all the way across the country." He stood and stepped away to make a call on his cell phone.

When dinner was finished and they had bid Salvatore and Luigi farewell, Sam, Tony, and Louie climbed back in the limo, and Tony instructed his driver to head to the Teterboro Airport.

"I've got the cash for an airplane ticket," Sam said, "but I don't have a driver's license or any other type of picture ID. That's another reason the bus seemed like a good idea."

Tony guffawed. "F'get about it. You're taking our jet home. You ain't gonna need any picture ID. I called the pilot, and he said he can get you to some town called Missoula. Is that near your home?"

"Yeah, it's about two hours south of our place."

"Okay, then, you can catch that bus you wanna ride in Missoula, but at least you'll be there tomorrow instead of three days from now."

At the New Jersey airport, Tony escorted Sam to the stairs of a Gulfstream G6 luxury jet parked in a private hangar.

"*Ciao*, my friend, and don't lose that card," Tony said, grinning, as they shook hands. "You never know."

"Goodbye, Tony, and thanks again." Sam climbed the steps, turned, and waved to Louie standing at the limo. The gangster returned the gesture.

Inside, Sam found himself alone with eight luxurious leather seats to choose from. He took one and hooked its lap belt as one of the pilots came toward him from the small cockpit.

"Sir, we'll be taking off shortly and should have you on the ground in Missoula in about three hours. It'll be the middle of the night there, but it's the best we can do. They're closing the airport at five a.m. for some VIPs scheduled in there tomorrow."

"That'll be fine, thanks. I'm just gonna catch a cab downtown to the bus station, and they probably won't leave until morning anyway."

The pilot turned away, closing and latching the aircraft's door on his way back to the cockpit.

They were airborne fifteen minutes later, with Sam staring out the small window at a sea of lights below. The jet entered a cloud layer, and his view disappeared. He pressed a button on the armrest and pushed back. As his seat reclined and his legs were lifted, he closed his eyes, hoping the nightmare would not come.

CHAPTER 6

Tom Devlin stared at the satellite image of Ben Branson's estate at the base of the elongated mountain. The range reached more than 6,000 feet at its northern end, but the lodge sat in the much lower foothills at its southern tip, just outside the national park's boundary.

A small lake lay midway up the mountain, with its drainage running through Branson's property. This was the stream where the president would be fishing tomorrow. Devlin studied the image for several minutes, zooming in for detail of specific areas, and then pulled his secure satellite phone. When Lloyd Armstrong answered, he asked, "Is Jackson all set?"

"I went up to that old logging camp where they're staged. Jackson brought seven guys with him, and they assured me they told no one where they were going."

"Were they all wearing MSM patches?"

"Yes, sir. They're a nasty-looking bunch. Two had shaved heads, and all had long beards. I'm pretty sure most of them were drunk, too."

"I don't give a shit, as long as they show up where they're supposed to, when they're supposed to."

"They know the route they're to take to the lake, and

Jackson assured me they would be there on time. I still can't believe he actually thinks they have federal authorization to carry rifles into a national park and sneak up on the president as part of a Secret Service exercise."

"I told you they were idiots. Is the netting in place?"

"It is, sir. As soon as you told me the advance team was gone, we went up there and put two rows across the stream just below the lake, exactly as you instructed. Then we shocked the water and pulled out everything that popped up, buried nearly a hundred fish."

"Okay, if they take the bait, I'll notify you when the chopper they send in to clear the area has departed and I get the Predator out of there. You should have plenty of time to get into position."

"We'll be there. But what if they send in some Secret Service on foot ahead of time?"

"If they do, you'll have no choice but to abort and get out of the area unseen. They shouldn't need to send people in, though, not after the Blackhawk verifies there are no life signs in the area and I follow up with my own assurances. Did you double check the ghillie suits?"

"Yes, sir. All of them are working perfectly."

"Good. No infrared imaging will be able to pick you up wearing those."

"We're ready, sir."

Devlin hung up and took his private elevator to the DIA's underground command center. The duty officer called the room to attention when the three-star stepped into the room.

"Is everything on track for the exercise, Lieutenant?"

"Yes, sir. They're fueling the Predator now, and the pilot and technician are on standby."

"Have you briefed the command center staff?"

"No, sir. I was waiting for your go-ahead."

"Okay, people, listen up," Devlin called out to the other young officer and half-dozen enlisted persons at various consoles. "We're about to begin a two-day exercise using an unarmed MQ-2 Predator surveillance drone in support of the Secret Service while the president is fishing in Montana. This will be a classified exercise involving presidential activities, so you are not to discuss any aspect of what occurs here outside this room. Are there any questions?"

No one spoke up, as expected. Devlin had personally ensured that each person assigned there for this operation was new to the job and suitably intimidated by his presence. Nonetheless, he had also forced everyone there to sign a nondisclosure agreement threatening court-martial and a long prison term for disobedience.

CHAPTER 7

S am allowed himself to doze but not sleep during the three-hour flight, hoping to avoid the nightmare. He was fully awake when the Gulfstream's wheels squeaked on the runway at the Missoula International Airport.

As the jet taxied to the transient aircraft area, he noted that there were no airliners at the terminal they passed, but he did see the familiar silhouette of a large helicopter parked far out on the tarmac.

There seemed to be an overabundance of security vehicles around it. He set his curiosity aside as the G6 came to a stop and its engines began winding down.

The pilots emerged from the cockpit a moment later. "Welcome to Missoula, sir," said the older one. "I radioed ahead to have a cab waiting for you."

"Thanks," Sam replied as the younger pilot opened the aircraft's door and lowered the short steps.

Outside, several airport maintenance men were already busy prepping to refuel the jet. The pilots joined them.

A white car with a taxi logo painted on its passenger door pulled up, and Sam started toward it.

The cabbie met him halfway, asking, "No luggage?"

Sam realized how inappropriately dressed he was for his new environment. "Is there anything open this late where I can get some clothes better suited for Montana?"

"There's a Wal-Mart on the way back into town. It's open twenty-four-seven."

"That'll do," Sam said as he slid onto the rear seat with a sudden flashback to the last cab ride he remembered.

To his relief, the driver diverted his thoughts as they pulled away. "Are you some kinda celebrity?"

Sam chuckled. "No."

"That's a pretty airplane you got there. Are you here on business or something?"

"No."

His reticent manner must have convinced the man to stop asking questions, because the rest of the ride to Wal-Mart passed in silence. "Leave the meter running," Sam said as he climbed out. "I'll be back as soon as I get a few things."

"Take your time, pardner."

Inside, Sam walked to the men's clothing section and purchased a pair of prewashed blue jeans, a long-sleeved denim work shirt, leather work boots, heavy socks, and a wide leather belt. He took everything into a changing room and removed his Armani suit.

As he slid back into the cab, he draped a garment bag he had purchased for the suit on the seat. "Okay, how about dropping me at the bus station."

"You sure you don't wanna go to a hotel? There ain't any buses out until tomorrow morning."

"I'll wait," Sam replied. "I'm used to it."

დოდ

"We got a bus leaving for Boise at five," the Travelways agent said. "The driver can drop you in Lonepine on his way past there."

"Thanks," Sam replied as he paid for the forty-dollar ticket.

Last to step aboard as the sun began to brighten the eastern sky, Sam saw twenty or so other passengers scattered about, most alone. None made eye contact with him as he moved down the aisle to a seat near the rear but far enough away from the onboard toilet to avoid the unpleasantness his prison cell had forced him to endure. He dropped the garment bag onto the seat next to his to discourage anyone from sitting there and starting what could turn into a long and unwelcome conversation. He wanted privacy, not companionship.

He couldn't contain a smile when he glanced out the window two hours later and saw a sign announcing they were entering Sanders County. But his trepidation began to mount as he looked out at rail-fenced pastures on both sides of the nearly empty highway. He had grown up in this wide valley between two mountainous national parks, and had hoped to bring Judith and their child there. Instead, his unannounced homecoming today felt hollow and unwelcome.

While the landscape had not changed since he had last seen it nearly a decade before, Sam knew he had and feared not for the better. Fighting an unrelenting enemy that never seemed to diminish in numbers had undeniably hardened him. However, it was what followed that made him worry that he was unsalvageable now. Though the nightmare of prison was over, those five years of angst-filled days and memory-tormented nights might have altered him in some irreparable way. He wondered if he could ever be the man he once was, the man his family had known.

Will they turn me away again? His thoughts were already creating a crushing anxiety within him when he caught sight of a man walking along the highway's shoulder, and his mind leapt back to when his exile began.

Sam had waited until his eighteenth birthday so he would not need his father's permission when he hitchhiked to Missoula to enlist in the Navy. He felt he had no choice. He was certain his father's consent would not have been forthcoming, and even a request for it would have set off a battle.

Sam knew his father, Jeremiah Calder, had one drive in life: to run the family's hundred-year-old horse ranch. World affairs might be something to jaw about around the kitchen table, but it was not something his father would have believed warranted abandoning the family's heritage. Nonetheless, unlike his father and older brother Mark, Sam had developed a yearning to take up the fight against his nation's attackers and had left, knowing the ranch would run just fine without him.

His different take on things, in Sam's view, had been born ten years earlier with the loss of his mother at the hands of a drunk driver. The wealthy alcoholic responsible escaped serious punishment with the aid of several high-priced lawyers and a judge rumored to be a close friend. While his father and brother grudgingly accepted that outcome, then eight-year-old Sam had seen it as justice denied, and his need to fight such wrongs took root.

After Nine/Eleven, it seemed just as abhorrent to him that the supporters of those men who had taken so many innocent lives might escape unscathed. Several years later, after watching a Navy SEAL recruitment video on the Internet at school, Sam decided on his course of action.

It all seemed so simple back then, he thought now.

He remembered calling his father from the recruiting station moments before he boarded the bus for basic training, only to hear the old man condemn what he had done and hang up. Three years later—the first two spent in SEAL training and the last in Afghanistan—Sam had returned to the ranch on leave, hoping time would have eased his father's ire. Painfully, he remembered, it had not.

Mark had greeted him warmly, but his still-smoldering father left for a week-long trip in the mountains moments before he arrived, and returned only minutes before he had to depart for his flight back to his SEAL team's Virginia base. He could still hear the old man's terse words as he passed him in the doorway, not even glancing his way. "See ya around."

Although it was heart-rending, Sam had stubbornly refused to show it. Ignoring the old man's acerbic words, he grabbed up his duffle bag and stomped out.

Another combat tour and several black ops missions followed, but Sam stayed on the East Coast when not deployed. He knew it was obstinacy, but he refused to submit himself to the distress of another rebuff. The last had left what felt like an unhealed hole in his soul.

Two years passed. The holidays, spent in solitary hotel rooms, were especially painful. After Judith entered his life, his attitude softened, and he soon saw a possible way back into his father's heart—through a grandchild.

Then New York City happened, and all hope of a renewed bond was lost as he disappeared into the penal system. He never wrote to let his family know what had happened or where he was. He felt that if he was to live out his days in a penitentiary, they were better off not knowing.

His depressing daydream ended when the bus pulled to a stop in the dirt lot of the Lonepine Motel and Tavern.

"This is where you get off, young man," the driver said. "None of these mountain towns have a regular station."

The moment Sam stepped off, the door slammed shut

and the bus pulled away, dragging a dust cloud with it. Sam suddenly wished he had called before leaving New York. *Maybe I made the trip for nothing,* he fretted. Blinking away grit, he walked to the motel's office and asked to use their desk phone for a local call.

He dialed the number he'd never forgotten but hadn't used in a decade. *If this doesn't work,* he thought, *I guess I can just get a room for the night and catch the next bus that passes by.*

After several rings, Mark's recognizable baritone voice answered, "Hello?"

"Hi, Mark. It's me, Sam."

A long pause followed before his brother quietly asked, "Where are you?"

"I'm here, at the Lonepine Motel. I just got off the bus."

"Thank God," Mark said. "I'll be there in fifteen minutes."

Sam's heart leapt.

CHAPTER 8

President Longwood saw his billionaire host standing a hundred feet away as the Marine One helicopter set down on the rich man's private helo pad. As always, Longwood was the first to exit.

"Welcome to my home, Mr. President," Ben Branson said, extending his hand.

"Thank you, Ben. I can't tell you how thrilled I was to receive your kind invitation."

"Oh, it's my pleasure, sir. But to be honest, it was Phil Mandrake's idea."

Mandrake and Campbell joined them, and Branson escorted the three into his multimillion-dollar log home as the rest of the Secret Service and accompanying White House staffers hurried elsewhere.

Inside, Longwood stood in front of a thirty-foot-wide floor-to-ceiling window with a view of Branson's huge pool, nine-hole golf course, and the majestic mountain beyond.

"Ben, you've got a magnificent place here."

"Thank you, Mr. President."

"And you won't believe the size of the trout around here, Mr. President," Mandrake said.

"I hope they're at least that big," Campbell said, point-

ing to a large fish mounted over a fireplace on the opposite wall.

"I assure you they are," Branson responded. "And my
chef excels at several trout dishes."

"That sounds terrific," Longwood said. "I can't wait."

"Well then," Campbell said, "I suggest we get to it. I
have all the gear you'll need set up out on the veranda."

സൗസ

Sam left the hotel office and stepped back out under
the hot sun, feeling his empty stomach gurgle. He looked
over at the attached tavern. Though it was still early,
there were a couple of pickups parked in front, implying
the place was open. He had never been inside—he'd been
too young when he lived here—so he decided to wait for
Mark there instead of the shadeless parking lot. *I should
have time for a burger and a beer*, he thought.

The moment he entered, he realized he had not missed
out. The place reeked of stale smoke, and a cloud of it
hung below the stained and broken ceiling tiles. Lighting
was minimal once the door closed behind him, but he
made out a dozen small round tables arrayed near a tiny
dance floor in the center of the room. On his left was a
twenty-foot-long bar with a dozen tattered stools alongside, and in a far corner, a well-used pool table stood near
a badly scarred dartboard on the wood-paneled wall. A
female voice Sam didn't recognize was bellowing a
catchy country tune from a jukebox.

*It's probably dark to hide stains and the true appear-
ance of the women who hang out here*, he thought. He
saw two there now, seated on stools at the far end of the
bar, with two men hovering over them. They laughed at
something the men were saying, or doing, to them.

Sam set his garment bag down and took a seat at the

end of the bar closest to the door. After catching the bartender digging for something in his nose, he elected to
skip the burger and only requested a beer. When his beverage arrived, he took a sip of the semi-cold liquid and
tipped the bottle toward an unmarked hallway, asking,
"Restrooms down that hall?"

"Yep, but the toilet overflowed again. Just go out in
the parking lot. No one's gonna see ya."

After five years of doing his business in front of
Bucher, Sam was not about to use the open lot, especially
at this time of day. "What do your female customers do?"

"The ladies' toilet works just fine, but you can't use it
cuz I got lady customers here now. Just go outside, like I
said."

Sam began walking toward the hallway. "Tell you
what—I'll lock the door."

A *thunk* at the back of the room caused him to pause
halfway there. The source of the sound was a large knife
that now protruded from the wall a foot left of the dartboard.

One of the two men toying with the women had
thrown it, and all four were now staring at him.

The one with an empty knife sheath on his belt boldly
stated, "We don't take kindly to faggots using the ladies'
toilet."

"I promise to put the seat back down, ladies," Sam
said as he started toward the hallway again.

At that, Knife-Thrower stepped back from his stool,
cutting off Sam's route. "You ain't listening. Now you
don't even get to finish yer beer, asshole. Go on, get outta
here."

The other man joined his friend, the pair standing side-
by-side in front of Sam. Knife-Thrower had his fists knot-
ted, and the other was toying with the handle of his own
blade, still in a scabbard at his belt.

Sam thought the two were probably goading him as part of some macho role-playing for the women.

With a lit cigarette hanging from her lips, one plump woman around fifty years old said, "You know, he's good look'n, Joe Bob. Maybe you otta axe him fer dat blowjob you been whining fer."

"Shut the fuck up, Mary Beth," Knife-Thrower answered. "I ain't queer."

The men looked to be in their mid-thirties with missing teeth and bad haircuts. Both wore blue jeans, sneakers, and an old-style woodland camouflaged BDU top with a large patch sewn on the left shoulder where soldiers wore their unit insignia. Both patches read, *Montana State Militia.*

Sam could tell that neither paunch-bellied antagonist had any training in close-quarters combat, as they had placed themselves in a vulnerable position directly in front of an unknown adversary. *Still, they might be vets*, he thought, and decided he would wait for Mark outside to avoid having to harm them.

As he started to turn away, he caught the second man beginning to pull his knife from its casing and realized his acquiescence had only inspired more aggression, as it had once done with Bucher. To feed their own vanities and bolster their image with the women, they would not allow him to leave now without complete humiliation, probably even injury.

Sam's instincts, training, and experience took hold. It was easy with them standing as they were, though he aimed for minimal damage. First, he punched the closest one in the solar plexus. As Knife-Thrower bent in half, sucking for air that would not come, Sam gave the other one, who froze for that half second, an elbow to the jaw.

Both incapacitated bullies collapsed to their butts on the floor, dazed and hurting, but very much alive and unbroken. Sam's punishment had taken only two seconds.

The women stared, their mouths slack, but the bartender moved toward something concealed under his counter. Sam shook his head in warning.

The man stopped and blurted out, "You'd better hightail it outta here, mister, or they're gonna kill ya."

Sam bent over the duo still not quite alert. "Is that true? Because I gotta tell you, fellas, I'm not real impressed so far." He knelt, pulled the second man's knife from its scabbard, and threw it backhand with tremendous force. It stuck in the dartboard's center.

At that moment, the door opened, filling the dark room with bright sunlight. A uniformed deputy sheriff stepped inside.

Sam stood straight and raised his hands to show he had no weapon. The two on the floor remained there, neither yet able to speak or stand.

"Is there a problem here?" the deputy asked, his right hand on his holstered pistol.

The bartender immediately began yelling about assault charges and customer injuries.

The deputy let the door close and approached, calmly scanning the floored men with a flashlight in his left hand. Then he lit Sam's face up. "Well, I'll be. It's been a long time, Sam."

Seeing past the mustache that disguised the deputy's face, Sam recognized his high school classmate, Pete Flynn. "Hey Pete, how ya been?"

"I've been good. Say, didn't you go off and join the military or something?"

"Yeah, I was in the Navy. I'm out now. I just came back into town on the bus. Mark's on his way over to pick me up."

"That's good to hear. I'm sure your dad can use your help around the ranch about now."

The pair on the floor began whining then. Flynn ignored them and pulled Sam aside. "Are you aware those two idiots are with the MSM?"

"I don't know them. What's the MSM?"

"Oh, it's some foolish group that formed up after the National Guard got shipped over to Iraq. Mostly they're just drunks and nut jobs, but they might make trouble for you. Why don't you leave this to me and go on home. I'd recommend you stay outta this place, too."

"Thanks, Pete." Sam dropped a five-dollar bill on the bar, grabbed the garment bag, and walked out. The moment he stepped into the sun again, the same beat-up quad-cab pickup he remembered pulled into the lot and stopped behind Pete's patrol car. Sam noted how the pickup's once dark-blue paint was now sun-faded. He tossed the garment bag into its cargo bed and jumped into the front passenger seat.

The siblings stared at each other for a long moment before Mark's hand reached across. "My God, it's good to see you, little brother."

Sam eagerly shook the hand. "You, too, Mark."

Two years older, an inch taller, and twenty pounds heavier than Sam, his brother had not changed in Sam's view. His huge hand felt rough, and his grip strong. Sam remembered when his had been the same—the product of a lifestyle he hoped to once again enjoy, maybe.

"You look fit. Are you still in the Navy?"

"No."

Mark stared at him a moment longer before asking, "Does that mean you're home to stay?"

"That depends. Does Dad know I'm here?"

Mark's face became a mask of sad reluctance, and Sam's heart sank. He feared his father was already making for the hills. After a moment, Mark slowly pressed the gas pedal. "Yeah, he knows, Sam." He paused and took a deep breath. "Look, there's only one way to say this, so I'll just spit it out: Dad's dying."

Sam stared unseeing through the windshield as Mark explained about their father's yearlong bout with lymphoma. When he was finished, both stayed quiet for the remainder of the ride. Sam couldn't bear to hear more and was too stunned for idle chitchat. *I worried about so many things on the way here*, he thought, *but I didn't see this coming.*

Ten quiet minutes passed before they turned off the highway onto a wide, gravel road that ran a straight eighth of a mile through rail-fenced pastures. Sam saw horses grazing in the foot-tall grass on both sides and felt a mix of emotions: comfort at the familiar sights and smells, and dread at what he feared was coming. The gravel road ended at a massive and beautifully hand-hewn log home sitting in the midst of more pastures just a quarter of a mile from the base of a thickly treed mountainside.

Sam spotted a smaller log dwelling near the barn behind the house. *That's new*, he thought. Before he could ask about it, the truck pulled to a stop in front of the wide porch that spanned the entire width of the home's front. His father opened the screen door in its center.

Sam immediately noted a smile on the recognizable but gaunt face. Before the old man slid on his Stetson, Sam also saw that his father's hair—previously as thick and wavy as his own—now consisted of thin, white tufts. He looked emaciated, smaller, and his arms seemed to have lost their musculature.

"The chemo and radiation treatments are a bitch, but he's holding his own," Mark said quietly.

As he climbed out of the truck, Sam's eyes moistened, both because his father was there to greet him and at seeing the man so obviously frail and unwell.

Jeremiah Calder did not walk down the four steps to meet him. He waited at the door, holding his smile, until Sam towered before him. The old man nodded several times before reaching out to him with tear-filled eyes. "Welcome home, Sam."

His father's voice sounded weak, not like Sam remembered. Unable to speak, he gently hugged his withered father for the first time in more than a decade, his own tears sliding unabated down his cheeks.

Mark shoved past with Sam's garment bag, apparently trying to keep the moment from becoming too maudlin. "Come on inside, you two. I need a beer. Sam?"

Sam's voice was on the edge of cracking as he answered, "You bet," and released his father.

Sam stepped into the rustic great room and immediately saw the familiar antlered elk head hanging over the fireplace mantle above the century-old, double-barreled shotgun he hadn't been able to lift until he was thirteen. The furnishings had not changed since he had last been in the room.

Mark dropped Sam's bag at the base of an open staircase leading to four bedrooms and a large bathroom off a second-floor hallway. He then disappeared into the kitchen as Sam dropped onto the same sofa he remembered lounging on through countless TV programs, movies, and football games. *Nothing has changed*, he thought. *Well, almost nothing,* he corrected himself as he watched his father carefully make his way to a familiar chair.

Sam sensed that the two men living there, without the help of a woman's touch, probably struggled just to keep the place from falling apart, especially now. *Updating the furnishings would never dawn on either of them unless someone's butt fell through the bottom of a chair*, he thought. His own sank deeply into the threadbare sofa and he thought that might happen at any moment.

Mark returned and handed him a long-necked bottle as he laid a plate piled with cold fried chicken on the cluttered coffee table. "Hungry?"

Sam snatched up a leg with his free hand, noticing that Mark had not brought his father a beer.

"I can't drink booze while I'm on chemo," the old man said flatly. "So, where you been all these years?"

Sam had no desire to recount the truth and saw no reason to burden his father with it now. "In the Navy, mostly, but that's over now. I came home hoping I might be welcomed back. I don't really have anywhere else to go."

His father glanced at Mark, who was smiling, before turning back to him. "You know, Sam, I wanted to see you again before…well, anyway, I wanted to apologize for how I behaved the last time you were home."

"It was my—"

Jeremiah cut him off. "No. I was bullheaded and wrong to take off like that. I'm sorry, and you are definitely welcome here."

Sam's heart swelled as he took several deep breaths and blinked back the wetness filling his eyes. He still felt that his life had little purpose, but at least he had a family again, and a home. *Maybe if I get that dishonorable discharge off my record, I'll be—*

His thoughts were interrupted when Mark reached over and slapped him on the shoulder. "Well, now that that's settled, do you still remember how to ride?"

"It's been a while, but I'm sure I can manage. By the way, what's with that house I saw out there past the barn?"

His father said, "Oh, that. Well, back when the economy started going bad, people pulled away from buying horses, and we needed to find some way for the ranch to make enough money to get by. That's when Mark here saved the day."

"How'd you do that?"

"I happened to be in town one day and overheard this fella going on about being on his way home from a week's vacation on a cattle ranch down in Wyoming. It gave me an idea, so I did some Internet research over at the library in Hot Springs and found out there was a growing market for outdoor vacations at places just like this. After I convinced Dad, we built that guesthouse out there and had an outfit put up a website offering a week-long dude ranch vacation package. Within a year, we had folks calling for reservations two years out. We not only survived the downturn, we were doing pretty darn well, until Dad got sick.

Jeremiah stepped in. "We show 'em how to saddle and ride a horse and then have 'em help with a mock round-up. They never quite seem to catch on that the horses will walk back to the stable on their own if you just whistle for 'em. Anyway, halfway through their week, we take 'em up onto the mountain, where we built a cabin. After a day or two up there, they think they're real cowboys and mountain men. I've even had a few ask me for a job here afterward."

"How'd you get permission to build a cabin on national park land?"

"We just had to promise to leave it unlocked and stocked as an emergency shelter, and the Forest Service approved it," Mark replied. "It's even marked on topographical maps. No one has ever used it that I know of, though. It's probably too high up and isolated. In fact, I'm riding up there tomorrow to make sure it's ready for the coming dude season. You're welcome to join me if you're up to it. I could use the help."

"I usually go up there with him," Jeremiah said, "but I ain't quite up to it this time."

"I haven't been on a horse in a while, but I'm game. What do we need to do up there?"

"We had a bear break in last spring and tear the place up," Mark said. "It apparently liked Spam."

That brought a chuckle from all three.

"I can see how this place would appeal to city folks, at least for a while," Sam remarked.

"That's cuz they ain't ever spent a winter here," Jeremiah responded, laughing. "And sometimes they get kinda cranky when they find out we ain't got all the creature comforts they're used to in the city, especially the teenagers."

"What d'ya mean?"

"Well, you and Mark were never into 'em, but this place is too far out for cell phones, and that makes the kids trying to send them text messages to their friends crazy. We have the house phone, of course, and we have a satellite dish for TV. At least, we used to."

"Uh-oh, what happened to the dish?"

"A storm took it down last month," Mark replied. "It'll probably be another couple of weeks before someone comes up from Missoula with a new one." He chuckled. "Until then, you know Dad—it's a different John Wayne DVD every night."

CHAPTER 9

Longwood watched the clear, icy-cold snowmelt and rain drainage flow smoothly over a base of rounded stones, but no fish swam by. They had been throwing their lines out all afternoon without a nibble. "I admit it's a beautiful stream, Ben," he said, "but I'd sure like to know where the fish are hiding."

"I can't understand it, Mr. President. This is usually one of the hottest spots around."

Campbell, waist deep in his insulated waders thirty feet downstream, said, "I hope your chef knows how to cook something besides fish."

Even the members of the president's security detail, spread out along the stream's banks, looked bored to Longwood. They held their positions as the monotonous hours passed with nothing more interesting to watch than a curious rabbit or squirrel.

"Why don't we try moving upstream some?" Campbell suggested.

"I agree," Longwood seconded.

With that, all four anglers turned and began making their way across the wide stream's slippery stone bed. Mandrake didn't make it. He slipped and went fully under, releasing the expensive fly rod Branson had loaned him. It disappeared, swept away by the current.

As the obese man struggled to get back to his feet, Longwood realized Mandrake had not fastened the belt around his chest waders. At his first slip, they had filled with ice-cold water and now acted more like a sea anchor. Though it was barely waist deep where Mandrake thrashed, the portly amateur outdoorsman could not keep his footing. He repeatedly stood and slipped back under until it became clear he was likely to drown if someone didn't come to his aid. Campbell was closest.

"You'd better help him, Jeff," Longwood said.

By the time Campbell reached him, Mandrake was frantically flapping his arms and squealing gurgled, unintelligible sounds each time his head popped up. The retired four-star admiral, holding his own fly rod in his left hand, reached under the surface with his right, grabbed Mandrake's collar, and pulled his head out of the water.

Mandrake seemed to panic then and grabbed at Campbell's arm with both of his, threatening to yank his rescuer off his feet. But Campbell let go and jerked his arm free. He grabbed at a flailing ankle instead and pulled Mandrake toward the bank only ten feet away.

Three feet from dry ground, with Mandrake thrashing and gagging, Campbell let go and ordered, "Stand up, man! You're only in a foot of water now. Don't you feel the rocks on your backside?"

Longwood was having a hard time squelching a laugh as he watched Mandrake maneuver to his knees and struggle to stand.

Two Secret Service agents managed to pull Mandrake atop the bank, and he slipped off the suspenders holding up his waders. Gallons of water poured out.

"Maybe you should check those for our missing fish," Longwood teased. Everyone laughed except Mandrake, who was shivering and retching.

"Well, let's head upstream," Longwood said.

"No more fishing for me," Mandrake declared. "I'm going back to the lodge, change clothes and spend the rest of the afternoon on that golf course." With that, he abandoned his waders and stormed off.

As it turned out, the next spot where the three remaining fishermen tried their luck mirrored the first spot's disappointment. It was certainly not for lack of trying.

Campbell was second to give up and sat down on the bank shortly after Branson figuratively threw in his own towel, saying, "I just can't understand it."

As the sky began to darken, the group returned to the lodge, tired and dejected.

Longwood accepted a cold bottle of beer and dropped onto a patio chair. "Well, that was a thoroughly relaxing and absolutely frustrating afternoon."

Branson immediately began apologizing again, but Campbell interrupted him. "Ben, you can't make fish bite. Shit happens."

Branson excused himself to make a call and left the veranda as Mandrake stumbled outside and nearly collapsed a lounge chair as he fell onto it. "Why don't I smell fish? Don't tell me you boys got skunked again."

Longwood and Campbell exchanged looks, but neither responded to the man's slurred words and sarcastic tone. It was apparent that the House Speaker had not played golf.

Based on his garbled speech and mustard-stained shirt, he had likely lounged through the afternoon, eating and drinking to excess.

Branson returned then and made himself a drink at an outdoor bar. He made a second and handed it to Mandrake. "Here, Phillip. Give this hundred-year-old Scotch a taste."

Mandrake took the glass and swallowed its golden-brown liquid in one gulp. Without comment, he held out the empty for a refill.

"Are you sure you want to keep drinking like that, Phillip?" Longwood asked. "You seem to have had quite a few already."

"I'm fine," Mandrake responded, his words indistinct. "At least I didn't waste the whole day trying to catch fish that ain't there."

With that, Longwood had had enough. "I'm afraid I'm going to have to cut this trip short, Ben. I know we still had another day scheduled, but—"

"That's a shame, Mr. President," Branson interrupted, "because I just spoke with a friend who said he was up at Pointer Lake this morning—that's barely a mile upstream from here—and the trout were jumping out of the water." Before Longwood could respond, he added, "I didn't mention this before, but that big fella on the wall in there came from Pointer Lake. There isn't any pressure on them up there, so they grow to be monsters."

"It wouldn't hurt to try out the lake for a couple of hours in the morning," Campbell said.

Longwood stared through the window at the huge trophy on the wall. After a moment, he pushed aside his displeasure with Mandrake and gave in. "Okay, we'll give the lake a shot."

Mandrake let out a loud snort. He had passed out.

Secret Service Agent Angel Washington, standing off to the side, faced the president and said, "I think going to that lake would be unwise, sir. We don't have time to do a proper advance of the area, and it's already dark."

Longwood shrugged. "Unless there's some wacko living on the lake who's bent on killing anyone who shows up, I really can't see the harm in a quick run up there. We chance more every time I get out of the car to mingle with a crowd at an event."

"No one lives anywhere near Pointer Lake," Branson said. "The entire mountain is a national park, and the lake is several miles in from the nearest road. Folks generally won't hike that high or far when there are closer places to fish."

"Still, sir, I believe Agent King will advise against it. We studied satellite shots of the entire area before coming, and we can't land a helicopter anywhere near that lake because the trees go right up to its banks. That would mean a limited security presence, too, since you'll have to use the golf carts to get up there, and there are only four of them. What about Major Johnson and the football, sir?"

Longwood smiled at the woman's persistence, but declared, "I'm going, Angel. I'll be all right. Tell Chris to do whatever he has to do to make it happen." He paused, realizing that he would have to keep the nuclear execution codes close by at all times. "Major Johnson can tag along, too."

☙❧

Angel left the veranda and used her wrist mic to call together Chris King, the protective detail's senior agent, and the other three team leaders so she could brief them on the president's intention.

"It should be okay, since nobody knew about it until a few minutes ago," King told her when the foursome met in the kitchen.

"We should at least get someone to do an infrared sweep of the area tonight," Angel suggested. "Doesn't the National Guard have a chopper on call at the command center?"

King nodded. "Yeah, I'll take care of that. You call the DIA. They're running a counterterrorism exercise while we're here, and they have a Predator available. As for tomorrow's coverage, with only the four golf carts for Alpha and Bravo teams, Charlie and Delta will have to stay here."

Washington thought her expression must have given away her displeasure with that decision, because King added, "If something goes down, your team's the only one capable of getting up there on foot in a hurry. That's why you guys do all the jogging with him."

"Yeah, I know."

Before they broke up, King contacted the temporary command center at the tiny Thompson Falls Airport and requested they get the Montana National Guard to send a helicopter in for an infrared sweep of the lake and its surrounding woods. "Report anything bigger than a rabbit. I don't want the president having to wrestle a bear over a fish."

While King coordinated the chopper, Angel called the DIA command center and requested their Predator lend a hand after the Blackhawk cleared the area.

"Our drone will take up surveillance the moment the chopper finishes," General Devlin personally assured her. "And it'll remain over the area all night."

Lastly, Angel suggested sending in her team on foot ahead of time but was denied permission.

"Those woods are too dark to safely navigate now," said King. "We'd likely spend most of the night recovering injured agents."

"Don't forget," the Bravo Team leader added, "the furry critters with big teeth and claws come out looking for dinner at night."

❧❧❧

After the National Guard chopper had finished its infrared scan of the woods around Pointer Lake and headed back to base, Devlin asked, "What's the fuel status on the bird?"

"It's at forty-five percent, sir," a sergeant answered.

"How long would it take to return it to base, refuel it, and get it back over the lake?"

"Four hours, sir."

"Okay, do it. Have it keep watch until I say differently. I want all calls to and from the Thompson Falls command center to go through my office first. I'll be there all night."

Knowing Armstrong had more than enough time to get his men into position before the Predator returned, Devlin went to his office and called the mercenary on his satellite phone. "You have a green light. You've got four hours before the Predator gets back."

"We're on our way, sir."

He then called Ben Branson. "Did you give Mandrake the sedative?"

"He's already out. It took four Secret Service guys to carry his fat ass to bed."

"Did you make the call to Jackson's cell phone yet?"

"Yes. Jackson answered it, but I hung up and turned the phone off so he couldn't call back. It's on the nightstand next to Mandrake."

After hanging up, Devlin reflected on how well things were working out. The Blackhawk crew had reported spotting the MSM's encampment to the northwest, but he had expected that and informed the Secret Service that it was a logging camp several miles from the president's intended fishing spot.

Everything's in motion now, he thought. *I just need to be patient.*

CHAPTER 10

S am woke before dawn, feeling refreshed and smiling at the well-remembered comfort of his old bed. He realized he had not woken that way in longer than he could remember. This was his first sleep in years that had not been continuously interrupted by his usual nightmare, Bucher's shifting bulk, someone's night-terror screams, or the incessant clanking of metal as guards noisily moved through the cement and steel structure at all hours.

He once again savored the freedom to stand in the shower until the water went cold. He chose not to this time, though, remembering how Mark had reacted whenever his little brother used up all the hot water. He chuckled as he recalled a winter morning years back when Mark had picked him up and tossed him into a nearly frozen horse trough in punishment.

He stared at his clean-shaven face in the bathroom's mist-covered mirror. "Good thing you didn't kill Bucher after all," he said quietly and wondered if he would ever be able to put the memory of that repulsive man out of his mind.

As he stepped to his bedroom door after dressing, he saw his old black Stetson hanging on the peg where he had placed it ten years earlier. He pulled it off, smacked the dust off, and slid it on his head. *Damn, that feels good*, he thought.

Moments later, he was sipping fresh coffee at the kitchen table and listening as Mark explained where they were headed on their upcoming ride up the mountain behind the house. Sam had hiked and ridden all over the 6,000-foot-high range as a youth and was excited about doing so again.

"Our first guests are scheduled to arrive in a few weeks," Mark was saying, "so we need to get up there and check that the trail's okay for the horses and all is well with the cabin. Those city-dwellers might enjoy pretending to be cowboys and mountain men, but they don't actually want to split their own firewood or get the blisters that come with it. We need to make sure there's a healthy supply at the ready and fix anything busted in the cabin during the winter."

"So how long will we be gone?"

"We should be at the cabin in about two hours, and if we don't run into any big problems, we should be finished before lunch and back here by mid-afternoon."

"Will Dad be okay?"

"Yeah, I'll be fine," Jeremiah answered as he stepped into the room, snapping his wide suspenders over his shoulders. "I'm only out of it for a couple of days after the chemo. I'm already feeling stronger, and I'm hungry this morning."

Mark jumped up and reached past his father for a basket filled with just-gathered eggs. "I'll get some breakfast going. Why don't you sit down and have some coffee, Dad?"

Jeremiah took Mark's seat. "He's kinda like a wife, ain't he?"

Sam chuckled again. "You know, Mark, now that Dad

mentioned it, I was kinda surprised you aren't married."

"Oh, he's got a gal on the line. He's just taking his time getting around to ask'n her."

"Do I know her?"

"Yeah," Mark replied. "I've been seeing Becky Miller."

"I remember Becky. We had some classes together in high school. How'd you two get hooked up?"

"Remember I told you how I used the Internet over at the library? Well, she's the librarian. She's divorced and has a six-year-old boy, Toby. He's a great kid and loves to ride."

"By the way," Jeremiah interjected, "with the warm weather, the bears are likely up and about on the mountain, so you'd best keep an eye out."

"We can't take guns up there," Mark answered, "but I'll pack some bear spray."

There was a gleam in Jeremiah's eye as he said, "I got a favor to ask, though I doubt you two will consider it much of a burden."

"What d'ya need?" Sam asked.

"I got a hankering for some fresh trout."

Both brothers smiled.

"Pointer Lake," said Mark.

Sam recalled numerous fishing trips to the small, pristine mountain lake brimming with huge trout. "That'll add a day, though," he said. "We can't ride down the mountain after dark. Are you sure you'll be okay by yourself until tomorrow?"

"Damn straight I'm sure, especially for fresh trout."

"How about fishing gear?" Sam asked.

"We keep a few rods and some tackle at the cabin for guests who like to fish," said Mark. "If everything's okay at the cabin, we should be on the lake before noon."

After breakfast, the brothers saddled two large mares.

"These two have made the trip up the mountain so many times," Mark said, "they could probably get us there asleep in our saddles."

Mark's horse had two propane canisters strapped to her haunches. He also had a heavily burdened packhorse in trail. "This fella's gonna haul up a couple dozen plastic gallon jugs of water and a supply of canned goods that can last the summer without refrigeration."

Strapped to the rear of Sam's horse was a cooler filled with ice, along with a few cordless power tools in case they had to make repairs. "Is this all I have to bring?"

"Yeah, and don't spill that cooler, or we'll have no way to keep the fish fresh. We both have a couple of sandwiches in our saddlebag for lunch, too."

After a quick farewell to their father, the brothers took off across the pasture behind the barn just as the sun peeked over the eastern horizon.

Sam gazed up at the looming mountainside before them, knowing from experience that the broad slope of imposing, hundred-foot pines belied the challenge ahead. Still, he was eager.

Once they began their ascent, the two almost continuously had to duck low branches and maneuver around trees and large rock outcroppings. Two hours in, they had to dismount and walk when the steepness of the slope caused the horses to lose their footing.

Not a pleasant outing by any standard, Sam thought as he wiped his sweaty face and slapped at a mosquito that wouldn't give up trying for his blood.

℮℈℮℈

When they finally came out of the trees into a level clearing about a thousand feet below the summit, both were soaked with sweat from their ordeal.

Sam was also painfully aware that the years away from a saddle had softened parts of him, but he had no intention of confessing that to his brother. "You actually have people pay to do that, huh?"

Mark laughed. "Hard to believe, ain't it? They call it an eco-adventure."

As they approached a log cabin set in the center of the clearing, Sam noted a fenced corral and covered tackle shed attached at one side, and an outhouse about fifty feet to its rear. "I hope we don't have to clean that thing out."

"We dug a new hole for it last year. It should be fine. We just have to stock it up with biodegradable toilet paper and drop a can of poop-eating algae in the hole."

After unsaddling the horses in the corral and giving each a bucket of oats, Mark filled their water trough from a jug off the packhorse. "Okay, let's check out the cabin."

They first pulled out six wooden Adirondack chairs stored inside for the winter and set them around a stone-lined fire pit out front. Back inside, Sam saw that his father and brother had outfitted the place with a long picnic table with bench seats, six wooden single beds designed for air mattresses and sleeping bags, a woodstove for heat, and a small kitchenette that required propane to operate a camp stove and a percolator coffeepot. Sam felt pride at how well constructed and comfortable the place was. *It'll probably stand for a hundred years*, he thought.

They spent the next hour splitting firewood, which left them sweat-soaked and muscle-sore. Sam was grateful he had maintained a demanding physical regimen in prison. Once the wood was stacked, they plopped down on chairs next to it and enjoyed their sandwiches. They also found two cold beers their father had slipped into the ice-filled cooler.

Afterward, Mark retrieved two fly rods, a couple pairs of waders, and a tackle bag from the cabin. They saddled their horses again and strapped the cooler down behind Sam's saddle.

"If I remember right," Sam said, "the best route is south along that ridge over there for about a half mile. That takes us down into the northeast corner of Pointer Valley."

"Yep, you remember right," Mark replied as he climbed onto his horse. "It should be a pleasant hour-long ride today."

ॐ

Longwood walked into the lodge's huge kitchen, where he found Chris King briefing his four team leaders about their upcoming day's security responsibilities. "Are we all set, Chris?" Longwood asked.

"Yes, sir. Alpha and Bravo teams will go with you, along with Major Johnson. Charlie Team will remain here and respond on foot, if necessary. Delta will remain in reserve."

"Sounds good," Longwood said as Campbell and Branson joined them.

"Has anyone seen Phillip?" Longwood inquired. "I hope he's up and ready. We're already running late."

"I checked on him a few minutes ago," Branson said. "He was still asleep, and I couldn't wake him. I think he may have imbibed a bit too much last night."

"Well, he's probably better off staying here anyway," Longwood said. "I wouldn't want to see him take another spill."

Branson's chef had set out a breakfast buffet in the dining room. After eating, they walked out onto the patio, where four electric golf carts were lined up, ready for riders. Longwood and Campbell climbed aboard one, with Branson driving, since he knew the route.

Chris King rode with them.

The remaining agents shared the other three carts, accompanied by Major Johnson, who brought with him a black case containing the president's nuclear execution codes. One of the Secret Service men was a sniper carrying a portable tree stand in a backpack, while the others carried Uzis concealed behind light jackets.

Once they started off, the electric vehicles were slow and nearly silent in the quiet forest, allowing their riders to talk comfortably. The journey snaked through pines for nearly an hour. When they finally emerged at the south end of the small lake, the sun was high in the sky, flashing through the tall forest canopy. The carts stopped only feet from the water's edge, and Longwood looked out. "My God, it's beautiful."

"It's a bit tricky at this end," Branson warned. "You can wade out maybe a hundred feet from the bank here, and it'll never go over your waist, but if you go past that marker over there," he pointed at a red-painted post, "the shelf drops off and slants down several hundred feet at the south end."

"This little lake is that deep?" Campbell inquired, sounding astounded.

"Yep, it's actually a canyon. It must have filled after an avalanche closed this end off eons ago."

The group dismounted and approached the gently sloped three-foot embankment at the water's edge, silently staring out at the tiny lake only a hundred-meters wide and three-hundred long. There was not a ripple to be seen on its flat surface, which mirrored the brightening blue sky above.

Suddenly, a huge trout jumped out of the water barely fifty feet from where the group stood. It flipped itself madly as it swallowed whatever insect it had attacked and fell back with a loud splash.

"Now that's what I'm talking about!" Longwood exclaimed.

"As promised, Mr. President," Branson said.

The Secret Service spread out among the trees along the bank, trying to see through the maze of trunks.

The sniper, who had already climbed thirty feet up a tree at the water's edge, radioed, "Crow's Nest has no clear line of sight in any direction except out over the water."

As Longwood put on his waders, he overheard King answer, "Okay, just keep the president in sight in case he gets too near that drop off by the red post."

Longwood fastened his chest belt and grabbed his rod.

Moments later, the three anglers were waist-deep and a hundred feet apart. The president was first to cast out to where the leaping monster had shown itself. On his second toss, he yanked back on the long rod and set the hook deeply into a fish's lip while gleefully yelling, "It feels like an eight-pounder!"

CHAPTER 11

Devlin was waiting for the call from his command center and lurched for his desk phone at its first buzz. "Yes?"

"Sir, the Predator just picked up eight figures northwest of the lake. They're moving south on foot toward the president's location."

Feigning concern, Devlin ordered, "Bring them up on the big board. I'll be right there."

Thirty seconds later, he stared at the five-foot-wide wall screen showing a picture of thick forest in black and white. There was nothing to see except treetops.

"Switch to infrared," the lieutenant directed a sergeant.

The picture changed. Trees and ground became muted shades of gray with tiny white blotches flickering in and out amongst them. "There they are."

"Zoom in and see if they're armed," Devlin ordered, already knowing the answer.

The state-of-the-art camera a thousand feet above the forest focused on the intermittently visible line of figures, and it was easy for all there to see that each carried a rifle.

"Sir," the lieutenant said, "weapons aren't permitted on National Park land. Should we notify the Secret Service?"

"Yes. Notify them of the unknown force's size, location, direction of movement, and that they're carrying long guns. How far are they from the lake?"

"They're five hundred yards from the northwest corner of the lake, sir, closing slowly. The president's at the southeast corner."

"Very well," Devlin continued, on script. "At that distance, the Secret Service can easily intercept them before they ruin the president's fishing. They're probably poachers in for a real surprise and a large fine. Good job, people."

"Sir, it's probably nothing, but when the Predator was inbound, it also picked up two men on horseback northeast of the lake."

The unexpected news unsettled Devlin. "Where are they now?"

"The last time we saw them, they were just mounting their horses outside a cabin. There was a third horse in the corral there, too."

Knowing the fateful moment he had so eloquently manipulated was nearly upon them, Devlin was not overly concerned about the unknown riders. "Forget about them," he said and turned away.

"Sir, the bird's almost at bingo fuel. The pilot says he won't be able to stay over the lake for more than another three minutes and still have enough fuel to get back to base."

Devlin did not turn around as he said, "Return the bird to base. That thing cost two million dollars. The Secret Service can handle the intruders. The exercise is terminated."

℮⁓℮⁓

Sam had thoroughly enjoyed the ride to the valley

where Pointer Lake was situated. The dense trees along the ridgeline required constant maneuvering, but the slope was gentle enough that the trip went easily for both man and horse. Fallen pine needles covered the forest floor, cushioning the mares' quiet steps. The only noises Sam heard were chirping and whistling birds, squirrels squawking warnings of trespassers, and the squeaking of their leather saddles. He felt the day had been perfect so far, though his blistered posterior reminded him how long it had been since he had ridden so much. That thought brought the inevitable painful memory of why it had been so long.

Thankfully, Mark distracted him. "I see water through the trees down there."

"Yeah, I see it, too."

Movement across the northern edge of the lake thirty feet ahead caught his attention. He saw what looked to be a half dozen men running uphill through the trees, then two of them suddenly tumbled back down. Before his mind resolved what he was looking at, a familiar sound disrupted the forest's quiet like a slap to the face.

"What the hell's that?" Mark asked, reining his startled horse to a stop.

"Uzis," Sam declared. "Stay back here in the trees, and don't let your horse run off. We may need to hightail it outta here in a hurry."

"Guns aren't allowed up here."

Sam plucked a pair of binoculars from his saddlebag and scanned the area where he had seen the two men fall. All six were down now. "What the hell's going on?" he whispered to himself.

He was still staring at the somber scene when a loud explosion to his left reverberated across the lake. Both brothers' heads snapped in the direction of the blast as the second of several occurred in rapid sequence.

Though he was thoroughly confounded at this second incomprehensible sight, Sam recognized what was happening several hundred yards to the south. Mortars were landing amongst a group of men. Some were riding through the trees on what looked like golf carts. Others were scrambling to get aboard other carts. Sam could not fathom this bizarre scene in such a pristine location.

With both frightened horses pulling at each detonation, the brothers held tight to their reins.

Sam swung the binoculars south and watched one of the crowded carts take a direct hit. Everyone aboard was blown into scattered pieces of gore. Several of the men aboard the carts were also holding Uzis.

Another mortar landed just behind a moving cart, flipping it into the air and tossing its occupants in different directions. One landed in the water face down and quickly sank out of sight. Another lay on his stomach against the bank, his lower half in the water. The other passengers had disappeared amongst the splintered and burning trees. It looked as though every pine in the area was on fire or felled or both, and yet even more mortars rained down. *Someone really wants those guys dead*, Sam thought.

The air at the south end of the lake became a brownish-black fog of flying dirt and smoke. Jagged, broken tree stumps made it look as if a tornado had come through, but the downed pines were on fire, some leaning into the water, some floating.

"This is insane!" Mark declared.

Sam pointed to the thickly treed hillside directly west of the lake. Smoke was visible coming through the tree canopy. "There! That's where the mortars are coming from."

Sam spun back to the first group they had spied. Again, movement in the trees on the hillside caught his attention, and he raised the binoculars that way. At first he saw only one figure, and then a second, then more. "What the hell?" he muttered once more as he watched camouflaged bodies rising up like zombies crawling from their graves. He counted eight.

"What do you see?"

Sam handed Mark the binoculars. "There are eight guys moving down that hill through the trees, and there are more bodies on the hillside between them and those six at the base. The ones at the bottom are in civilian clothes, and those above them are in camouflage shirts and blue jeans, but those eight coming down from the top are wearing high-tech military ghillies and carrying suppressed sniper rifles."

The brothers stood frozen, their faces hardened at the slaughter they had witnessed. Armed only with bear spray, Sam knew they would stand no chance against the larger and better equipped force.

"Who shot who?" Mark asked.

Sam took the binoculars again and watched as the ghillie-suited figures put their sniper rifles into the hands of the blue-jeaned corpses and squeezed the triggers. He could see their actions, though he could not hear the sound-suppressed rifles firing. Still, he realized they were ensuring the dead men's prints were on the weapons and each corpse had gunpowder residue on its hand.

That done, they swapped out their sniper rifles for the bolt-action hunting rifles lying next to the bodies, and all eight faded into the woods, moving west.

Sam jumped up into his saddle. "Let's follow them."

"Are you nuts? We need to get the hell out of here."

"We can't let them get away with this. We'll grab a couple of those sniper rifles."

Mark reluctantly followed.

Sam wheeled his horse around to give chase, but then

heard a helicopter approaching. "Wait! Stay hidden. I don't want some helicopter sniper to think we had anything to do with this and plink us."

A Blackhawk came in and hovered near the mortar battleground to the south. Sam stared at it through the binoculars. "That bird's got FBI painted on its boom." He watched as six ropes dropped from its belly, followed immediately by six figures clad in black simultaneously sliding down the ropes.

Only seconds after they disappeared into the smoke, two consecutive mortars landed where they had vanished. A third and fourth followed quickly, and Sam watched the helicopter speed off with the empty ropes dangling below it and smoke trailing from its tail rotor.

Sam knew the FBI men had to be dead. After a few moments passed without another explosion, he said, "The mortars are finished. They probably bugged out, too. Let's go that way instead. There's a slim chance someone might still be alive over there. That's more important than following those other guys."

The brothers turned their horses and raced south along the eastern shoreline with trees tight on their left, the water on their right.

As they closed on the macabre scene, Sam sensed that the flames and smoke were intensifying, and quickly realized the blaze was turning into a full-blown forest fire. Thankfully, the wind seemed to be pushing it south, away from the lake.

The first human carnage he passed was a dismembered body crumpled against the burning base of a mangled tree. A white-haired man's head lay near a decapitated torso in shredded fishing waders. A few yards away, another similarly dressed man with both legs missing lay splayed atop a splintered stump. A body lay flattened under a fallen pine, only its legs showing. Oddly, one mutilated corpse was strapped to a tree stand attached to that same pine. Shredded human limbs and golf cart debris were strewn about. *Mortar attacks leave a gruesome killing field*, he thought.

Sam coughed from smoke as his horse slid to a stop. He could see only two bodies that seemed intact in any conceivably survivable manner. He chose one near a red post at the water's edge and leapt from his saddle. Mark grabbed the reins to keep Sam's horse from running off.

Sam pulled the knife at his waist and jumped down next to the man whose fishing waders were filling with water because his chest belt had come off. Sam cut the waders' suspenders, freeing the man of the water weight that was slowly pulling him under. The waders sank out of sight. He noticed that the muddy bank and water were tinted red. Only then did he see that the man's left forearm was not tucked under him as he had thought, but had been brutally severed just below the elbow. He knew from experience that the wound was bad but survivable with proper emergency aid.

He rolled the injured man onto his back and checked for signs of life. Though he seemed dead, blood spurted from the grotesque stump. "This guy's alive!" he yelled as he whipped off his own belt and wrapped it around what was left of the arm in an attempt to staunch the pulsing flow of vital arterial blood.

After securing the horses' reins, Mark rushed over to help.

"The embankment protected this guy from most of the mortar and tree shrapnel," Sam said. "Let's get him out of the water."

Mark slid his hands under the injured man's armpits and pulled him to dry ground. He dipped his Stetson into the bloody water and poured it over the man's mud-caked face, then checked that his airway was clear.

Sam climbed out of the water and began tightening his makeshift tourniquet. He heard his brother gasp.

"I don't believe it," Mark said. "It's President Longwood."

Though he knew the name, Sam had not seen a television in more than five years and could have passed Longwood on the street and not known him. It dawned on him then that if this man really was the president, the next volley of first-responders to arrive would likely shoot first and ask questions later, considering what had just happened to those FBI men.

"We need to get him out of here," Sam said.

"Maybe we should leave him."

"Think about it," Sam said. "Those were military-equipped snipers up there to the north, and those other guys to the west were using mortars. You don't buy those at Wal-Mart. The snipers also swapped out their weapons with those dead guys on the hill. This whole thing's a setup. If we leave him here, the people trying to kill him might very well be coming in next to make sure they got him."

"Okay, okay," Mark said quickly, looking south. The forest there was a raging inferno. "Let's get the hell out of here. The wind's pushing that fire south, but if it changes direction, it'll chase us down in minutes."

"Wait!" Sam jumped up and ran to the body of the only other man who looked intact. He, too, was breathing but had several injuries Sam knew would preclude him surviving on horseback. Surprisingly, the president's severed arm lay next to him.

At first Sam thought they should take it with them, but then he looked more closely and realized there was no point. Instead, he reached down, pulled a ring from one finger of the badly mangled hand, and raced back to his brother.

"That guy's alive, but we can't move him on a horse. Let's get out of here."

Mark jumped atop his saddle. "Lift him up."

Sam hefted the president to Mark's lap and draped him over the saddle. "Walk the horses back onto ground cover." He grabbed a small branch and brushed away their boot and hoof prints from the dirt and mud where they had pulled the president from the water. Sam stared back the way they had ridden in and saw that pine needles covered that approach.

"Hurry up. Let's go," Mark yelled.

Sam jumped on his horse, and they headed east a short distance, then north along the ridgeline as fast as dodging trees would allow. He glanced back every few seconds until his view of the lake was completely blocked. He worried that his hasty decision might cost the badly injured president his life, but he was convinced that someone in the government or military had just tried to assassinate the man and might very well have people headed to the lake to make sure they had succeeded. Since he and Mark were witnesses to the truth, their lives were now in jeopardy, too.

The moment Sam felt they were deep enough into the forest that no one could determine their position visually, he called for a stop. Mark gently lowered the unconscious president to Sam's arms.

"He's white as a ghost," Sam said. He lay Longwood on the ground and felt his neck. "He's still got a pulse, though, and he seems to be breathing okay."

The brothers checked Longwood for any additional injuries and found nothing worse than lacerations and splinters. The belt tourniquet had stopped the bleeding.

"I hope there's no internal damage," Sam said. "I'll bet he's got a helluva concussion."

Mark cocked his head, listening. "That sounds like another helicopter coming in back there. Maybe we should—"

"We can't stroll back in there with him now. They'd probably shoot us on sight at this point."

"Yeah, I know you're right, but do you have any idea what happens to us if we're caught with him like this? They'll think we kidnapped him."

"It doesn't matter. We have to try to save him."

"Okay, but we need to stabilize him before we can get him off this mountain. Let's get him to the cabin."

"I think he'd be better off sitting up. Can you hold on-to him?"

Mark mounted his horse. "Heave him up and take my reins so both of my hands are free."

Sam hoisted the president again, but this time they positioned him upright in the saddle while Mark sat behind with both arms around him. The president's head lolled back on the big rancher's chest.

Sam took the reins, and they moved off at a slow walk.

ℰↄℰↄ

"What happened?" Devlin asked when Armstrong called on his satellite phone.

"It went down exactly as planned, sir. Those MSM idiots marched right past our position and stopped halfway down the hill just as the Secret Service guys were coming up to intercept them. The dumb bastards even used their rifle scopes to look at the agents coming toward them, so when we plinked a couple of the agents, the others assumed they were shot by the rifles pointed at them. They dropped all eight of the MSM in two seconds with those Uzis they carry. Then we shot the other four agents, and the mortar team opened up. It was like a symphony."

"What's your confidence level on Longwood?"

"Nobody lived through that. The whole forest is on fire over there now."

"Did your men remember to douse the tubes with bleach?"

"Yes, sir, and those electric mountain bikes worked like a charm, too. They hardly made any noise and got us out of the area pretty quickly."

"Okay, stay at base camp until I call. I'll get you back here once the authorities declare it a *fait accompli* and leave the area. Good job."

CHAPTER 12

I t's a goddamn battlefield up there, Vince," the shaken FBI helicopter pilot told his boss.

FBI Special Agent Vince O'Malley, the SAIC—Senior Agent in Charge—at the bureau's regional office in Missoula, had driven up to the Thompson Falls Airport to check on his SWAT team on loan to the Secret Service. He had arrived just as his men took off for the lake and was stunned when, only minutes later, the helicopter returned with two shaken pilots and shrapnel damage to its tail rotor.

He patted the pilot's shoulder. "Okay, Stan, hang in there." He glanced around and saw another helicopter, an Air National Guard MH-60 Pavehawk. It looked to be preparing for takeoff. He pulled off his Stetson and ran to it.

"Are you guys headed to the lake?" he yelled up to three men in flight suits, busy in its belly.

One nodded his head, his face somber.

At six-feet tall and two-hundred pounds, wearing blue jeans and boots, forty-four-year-old O'Malley knew he looked more like a rancher than a seasoned federal agent. He held up his credentials. "I'm FBI. I need to go with you. I've got men in the field."

The three slid over, and one handed him a headset. A moment later, a young woman wearing a Secret Service ID tag around her neck ran up and handed two of them a pair of black boxes. O'Malley couldn't hear what she told them, but it appeared to be instructions on their use.

As the bird rose above the surrounding buildings and the command center's huge tent, O'Malley got his first good view of the burning mountain. He prayed some of his SWAT guys had survived.

The Pavehawk circled around and came in from the north to avoid the southward-pushing forest fire. From two-hundred feet above the trees, O'Malley could only stare at the inferno raging to the south.

After swooping down over a treed hillside, they hovered twenty-five feet above the center of the small lake for a moment.

Smoke obscured most of O'Malley's view to the south, but he could tell by the jagged stumps and the way the splintered trees pointed in multiple directions that explosions, not fire, had been responsible for most of the destruction.

The rotors blew the smoke away as the chopper edged closer, and O'Malley got a clearer view of the bloodbath that had occurred there. Dismembered bodies, severed limbs, and twisted metal debris lay scattered amongst the smoldering timber. He spotted an intact figure lying next to a jagged, smoking stump. "There's someone over there—ten o'clock."

"We need to get out," called one of the two Air Force Pararescue men, called PJs, seated beside O'Malley. "I've got a good signal on the football."

The other said, "I've got conflicting signals from the president's beacons."

"What d'ya mean by that?" the pilot asked, maneuvering lower and closer to the ghastly scene.

"It means his locator beacons aren't at the same location," the PJ responded before he and his partner leapt from the side door, boots first.

O'Malley stared out at body parts visible all around, and the PJ's words sadly sank in. He watched the pair swim to shore, climb onto the bank, and stare at the little boxes each carried. One took off toward a body O'Malley could barely make out through the swirling smoke. The man's torso was pinned beneath a huge pine that had crashed down, partly in the lake. He watched the PJ search the area around the exposed legs a moment, then move a few feet to the side and lift a black case, examining it.

"The football's secure," the PJ announced through his helmet radio.

O'Malley saw the other PJ at the intact body he had spotted. His heart began pounding when the trained medic waved for his partner to join him and both knelt there. *It must be the president*, he thought as he watched them performing first aid. He began to wonder if Longwood might still be alive.

"We have a survivor, but it's not the president. Drop the cradle."

"I thought you had his beacons," the pilot said as he climbed to fifty feet so he could hover directly above them without his downwash causing too much of a windstorm on the ground below.

"You'll understand in a minute."

From this height, O'Malley could see the level of destruction where the FBI pilots had told him his SWAT team descended, and he realized there was no hope. The fire had moved on, but the area looked like a nuke had detonated there. He turned away and watched the crew chief swing a litter out, lowering it on its cable.

Moments later, the badly injured survivor rose to the

Pavehawk with something strapped to his chest. The crew chief pulled the litter inside.

"We'll stay down here and try to locate the president while you get the survivor to medical."

"Roger that," a pilot answered.

As the helicopter pivoted for its departure, O'Malley was looking at where his men had been lost when he caught sight of an apparition staggering out of the smoking ruins of the forest. "There's someone alive down there!" he yelled, pointing.

The PJs rushed toward the person, who collapsed at their approach. One announced, "It's a female. Secret Service, I think. She's unconscious, but her injuries don't appear life-threatening."

The crew chief dropped a second litter down the cable as the helicopter slid over to where she lay. Once the woman was on board, the pilot gunned his throttles for the Thompson Falls Airport as the crew chief strapped an oxygen mask to the woman's face. O'Malley saw that she was a black woman, but that was all he could discern. She was soot-covered and unconscious, and the legs of her pantsuit were burned.

He turned back to the injured man. "What's that?" he asked the crew chief, who was lifting the object from the man's chest.

He uncovered it.

"Oh, shit!"

The Pavehawk set down at the airport only long enough for a doctor to climb inside and tend to the injured until they reached the nearest hospital.

O'Malley took advantage of the brief stop and jumped off. He entered the command tent and stood near the communications table, listening as another helicopter pilot radioed that he had just dropped off a team of Secret Service agents at the north end of the lake.

It wasn't long before he heard that team's leader call in. "Central, Delta Team has located Bravo Team. All are down. We have eight unknowns down here, too."

"Can you reach the south site from your position?"

"Roger that."

"Take half your team to assist PJs trying to locate the president, and send the other half to search the woods on the hillside west of the lake. That's where the FBI pilots said the mortars were coming from."

"Roger that. Do the PJs have the president's beacons?"

The agent paused before answering, "Affirmative."

An agonizing fifteen minutes passed before O'Malley heard, "Command, Delta—no other survivors located, and we're still missing one agent from Alpha Team."

Another agent standing next to the one operating the radio grabbed the microphone and asked, "What about the president?"

"PJs reported that the arm found next to the survivor has his wristwatch beacon on it."

O'Malley saw the man hesitate, his eyes closing and his head dipping. He raised it and solemnly asked, "What about the backups? Both shoes had beacons in their heels."

The agent's voice sounded almost despondent as he somberly replied, "The other signals are coming from the lake. We'll need divers. I'll send the football down with the next chopper. We also found two sixty-millimeter mortar tubes on the hill west of the lake."

"Has anyone heard from Charlie Team?" someone asked. "They were headed to the lake on foot."

O'Malley saw the dejected look on several of the Secret Service agents' faces and heard one answer, "Angel's the only Charlie Team survivor. She's on a chopper headed to the hospital."

How the hell did she survive that fire? O'Malley wondered.

After another few moments, O'Malley realized he had heard enough and made his decision. First he walked outside the big tent and looked toward the enormous smoke cloud billowing higher and higher. He shook his head and growled angrily through gritted teeth before turning back inside to face the crowd, most talking on satellite phones or radios.

His commanding voice boomed over the chatter-filled room. "Can I have your attention?"

Most heads turned his way.

"I'm Vince O'Malley. I'm the senior FBI agent here, and I'm assuming jurisdiction over this crime scene as of this moment."

Several voices rose at that, mostly Secret Service objecting to his declaration when they had not yet located the president.

O'Malley didn't care. "The fact that an attack went down has been confirmed, and that puts this under FBI jurisdiction now." Without giving anyone a chance to argue, he added, "I want the senior Secret Service agent over here right now, along with the senior military person and the senior state trooper."

Several Secret Service agents looked around at each other, and it became apparent that the most senior of them were not there. They were either dead, searching at the lake, or still at Branson's lodge. For the military and state cops, it was easier.

A female Air Force lieutenant and a middle-aged trooper approached.

O'Malley pointed at the closest Secret Service agent. "Okay, you're it for now. Come here."

The twenty-something agent stepped up. "I'm Clay Mathis, Agent O'Malley. What do you need?"

"Lieutenant Ryan Suggs, sir," said the Air Force officer.

The trooper said nothing.

O'Malley nodded for the group to follow and walked outside again. "First off, Mathis, you make sure everyone is out of that lodge. The fire's heading straight for it."

Mathis stared up at the rising smoke cloud and exhaled loudly. "I'll call them. Marine One is still there." He took off.

O'Malley walked back inside with Suggs and the state cop. "Lieutenant Suggs, I need you to close every airport for a hundred miles and the airspace above us for fifty in all directions. We need to keep the TV helicopters from getting in our way until we can get that fire out." He liked that Suggs only nodded and turned away.

O'Malley turned to one of his pilots next. "If you're up to it, Paul, that fire's only burning down that one slope. Let's see if we can't get some air tankers in here right away and put it out before it spreads. If not, we'll be trying to run an investigation with a battalion of firefighters traipsing all over our crime scene." He paused for a second and added, "Also, check with the Secret Service guys and find out how many agents were on Charlie Team. Apparently all but their team leader are still up there. We'll need to recover them."

"I'll get right on it, Vince," the pilot replied and walked off.

O'Malley turned to the trooper. "Who are you?"

"Jim Givens. What do you need?"

"It's probably too late, Jim, but we need to seal off all the roads into and out of this area for at least fifty miles around. Can you do that?"

"We can try. There aren't that many. How many suspects are we looking for?"

"I'm not sure. They found two sixty-millimeter mortar tubes. It would take at least two men per tube."

"More likely three for a sixty," Givens said, and then added, "I was infantry."

"Okay, we're looking for six guys we have no descriptions of. The original eight suspects who started this fiasco are apparently dead."

"I'm on it," Givens stated, pulling a radio as he stepped away.

The quieter voices around him told O'Malley that people were calming and beginning to think more logically now.

Mathis returned. "Marine One is coming down from the lodge. The place is empty now."

A young Secret Service agent at the communications table called out, "The male survivor from the lake has been identified as Chris King, head of the president's detail."

O'Malley's cell phone chimed. The caller ID indicated it was his boss, FBI director Trevor Pearson. "Hello, sir," he answered, stepping away for privacy.

"Hello, Vince. Where are you?"

"I'm at the Secret Service command center at the Thompson Falls Airport. I was here when it went down, and I've assumed jurisdiction of the crime scene."

"Okay, I know you must be jumping through your ass about now, but I need an update."

O'Malley quickly briefed him on what he knew. "I'm assuming once we recover the president's body," he concluded, "it's to be shipped back to D.C. aboard Air Force One?"

"That's correct. I'm setting up an inter-agency task force here. Keep your eyes and ears open out there, Vince. We need to make certain we don't miss something."

O'Malley heard a helicopter arriving. "I hear you, sir. I gotta go."

He stepped outside again as a VH-60N Whitehawk landed and a stream of people began emerging from it. He recognized Phillip Mandrake among them. Oddly, he appeared to be wearing a bathrobe and slippers. Several Secret Service agents exited and surrounded Mandrake, pulling him away from the line of people headed away from the chopper. As O'Malley watched, the agents directed him back aboard, and they were airborne again moments later.

"Where's that chopper going?" O'Malley asked one of the people passing him.

"They're taking Mandrake to Air Force One. It's parked at the Missoula airport."

CHAPTER 13

At the cabin, Sam dismounted, and Mark lowered Longwood's inert body to him. As he turned to take the president into the cabin, Sam saw an enormous cloud of smoke to the south. "Look at that."

Mark dismounted and turned to look. "We're lucky that fire went south," he said, "or we'd have fried for sure."

While Mark led the horses to the corral, Sam carried the president inside and placed him on a bed, where he carefully cut away his filthy, bloody clothing. Mark came in and started a fire in the woodstove, then set about boiling a pot of water on the camp stove.

"We can't leave that tourniquet on much longer, Sam. The wound's dirty. It'll get infected, and gangrene will set in pretty quickly at this altitude."

"Yeah, I know. As long as he stays unconscious, I should be able to clean it up and cauterize it."

Mark retrieved a small first aid kit from a shelf and examined its contents. "He needs antibiotics and all this damn thing has in it is bandages, aspirin, iodine, and a suture kit."

"You have a suture kit for your guests?"

"It was Dad's idea, after one of them tried to whittle a

piece of firewood and sliced his hand open."

Sam walked to the kitchen area in search of a cauterizing tool. The best thing he could find was a large butcher knife. He put its blade in the woodstove's flame and set about pulling splinters from all over Longwood's body. Afterward, he cleaned and sutured the largest lacerations. The smaller wounds got iodine and bandages.

"The knife's ready," Mark said.

Sam did not relish the thought of what he had to do next. He had done it before, in combat, and much like the SEAL's injury—a foot blown off by an IED hours from help—the president's amputation was not a cleanly severed limb. The explosion had left the ends of the bone jagged and the flesh ripped, as if by claws.

Distasteful as it was, he first had to use a knife to cut away the dangling tendons and flesh before sawing at the uneven bone that protruded from the gory stump. He was grateful Longwood remained unconscious throughout his careful butchering, though he did stir and moan when the knife's searing metal pressed against the exposed tissue and nerve endings.

Once Sam thought he had heat-sealed the wound well enough, he removed the tourniquet to make sure the bleeding did not resume, then cleaned, iodized, and bandaged the remnant of the limb. "At least he's still got the elbow," he said as he finished.

Afterward, Mark dressed Longwood in clean, spare clothes kept at the cabin while Sam dropped the removed flesh and bone into the poop-eating algae under the outhouse.

"What now?" Mark asked when Sam returned.

"We've got no phone or radio up here, so either we carry him out, or one of us goes for help."

"We're still faced with the same problem," Mark pointed out. "Who can we trust? If we contact the wrong people, we might find out they have access to something even more deadly than mortars—maybe a gunship."

Sam nodded. "Okay, we have to get him out of here ourselves, then. We can use the house phone and call for help from folks we know."

"It'll take hours to get off this mountain carrying him, and I don't want to be doing it in the dark. We'll have to wait until morning."

Sam looked down at Longwood. "I hope he lasts that long."

കൗൿ

"How's King doing?" O'Malley asked the FBI agent he had sent to the hospital.

"He's still in surgery. The preliminary diagnoses included compound fractures of both arms and his right femur, plus six broken ribs and a punctured lung. He also has a bad skull fracture, a dislodged eyeball, and what looks like a thousand splinters and lacerations, some severe." He took a deep breath, exhaled, and quietly added, "He's not expected to make it, Vince."

"Okay. Let me know if his condition changes." O'Malley called his director next. "Sir, this is Vince. We have one—"

"Hold on," Pearson said. "I'm putting you on speaker-phone." There was a pause and several clicks. "Okay, Vince, go ahead."

"We have one survivor from the lake: Secret Service Agent Chris King, head of the president's detail. He's in very critical condition. At the south end of the lake, we recovered the remains of National Security Advisor Campbell and Mr. Branson, as well as five Secret Service agents, Major Johnson, and our six-man SWAT team."

"I'm sorry, Vince," Pearson said.

O'Malley sighed but did not otherwise respond to the sympathy. "The football was recovered intact and transported to *Air Force One*, along with Speaker Mandrake, who did not accompany the president this morning. We're still missing one Secret Service agent. We believe he's in the lake along with the president. At least, that's where the president's shoe locator signals are coming from. We did recover a severed left arm with the president's watch beacon on it. I sent the arm to *Air Force One*."

"Are the divers on scene yet?"

"They just arrived. They're gearing up now."

"What about the north end site?"

"We recovered the bodies of six Secret Service agents killed by gunfire at the north end of the lake—suppressed sniper rifle fire, to be specific. We recovered those rifles with the bodies of eight local males found on the hillside there."

"How do you know they're locals?"

"Each was carrying identification indicating they're from a small mobile home community near here called Noxon. I sent agents and state police to secure the place. The dead suspects were also all wearing camouflage shirts with a patch for an organization called the Montana State Militia."

"How many got away?"

"We believe six—the mortar teams."

"Do you have any leads on them?"

"No, sir. It's a pine forest with several inches of needles covering the ground. They also bleached the tubes, so no DNA."

"Okay, the president's cabinet is going to—"

O'Malley interrupted him this time. "There's more, sir. We also recovered the remains of nine Secret Service agents from the woods south of the lake in an area the fire overran. They were part of a team attempting to reach the lake on foot. There was one survivor."

"How'd he manage that?"

"It was a female, the team leader. She's in the hospital. I haven't had a chance to speak with her yet."

"What's the status of the fire?"

"It's been contained. The lake scene's a mess, though. We're working on cleaning it up now."

"Okay. You heard all that," Pearson said, addressing the multi-agency crisis action group assembled in his conference room. "We'll start with the Secret Service."

O'Malley nodded. "The director's on her way out there aboard an Air Force cargo jet with a new detail to take over security for Mandrake. That jet will return to Washington with the surviving Secret Service personnel and all of the recovered remains, with the exception of the president's."

"What's the cabinet up to?" Pearson asked.

"They're meeting in a couple of hours," a voice replied. "Some of them were out of the area and are still en route. I'm told they requested that the chief justice be ready as soon as Mandrake returns to Washington."

"Isn't that a bit premature?" O'Malley interjected.

He heard a voice he recognized as Attorney General Clive Howell. "It's the prudent thing to do. Even if the president's somewhere other than at the bottom of that lake, he's probably seriously incapacitated. Based on that, and the fact that we have no vice president, they'll have no choice but to invoke the twenty-fifth."

"Vince, what do you have on the Montana State Militia?" Pearson asked.

"The group is a paramilitary organization allowed for in the state constitution, ostensibly for use as an emergency fall-back unit during times of natural disaster or civil disorder when the state's National Guard is unavailable. However, that said, they've never been utilized, even though the Montana Guard, like most others, has been federalized and deployed overseas several times in recent years."

"Why is that?"

"Apparently most state officials are afraid of them. Several chapters are composed of heavy drinkers and somewhat outspoken anti-government types. There are even a few felons on their roster."

"How did a group like that get their hands on suppressed sniper rifles and mortars?"

"The serial numbers on the rifles came back as part of a cache stolen from the Montana National Guard armory in Billings. Interestingly, Army investigators received an anonymous tip that the MSM might have been responsible for the theft."

"How the hell did those guys not get identified during the advance?" someone asked.

"They were looked into during the preliminary," someone else responded, "but it was found that local law enforcement didn't consider them anything more than bar-fighting rabble-rousers."

"Excuse me, Director Pearson," a new voice stated. "I'd like to offer the DIA's assistance with anything you feel we can do to help."

"I don't see what a military intelligence agency could possibly bring to the table, General Devlin. This is a civilian law enforcement matter."

"I might remind you that it was *my* surveillance drone that spotted those militia men in the first place—"

Pearson cut him off. "I'm not sure where you're going with this, General, but thank you. We'll let you know if we need your agency's assistance. Okay, Vince, I want every MSM member and supporter identified and brought in for questioning. I want search warrants on all properties owned or lived at by those eight dead men. Find out who their friends and sweethearts were, who their relatives are, who they did business with, went to school and church with—find out everything about them. You need to locate those six missing mortar men quickly."

"Yes, sir."

CHAPTER 14

Sam sat up the instant Mark shook his shoulder. "I'm awake. How is he?"

"His pulse is weak, but steady. There's no bleeding, but he does feel like he's got a low-grade fever now."

"Okay, I'll take over. Get some sleep."

"Gimme two hours," Mark said as he lay down. "We should leave at sunrise. I heard choppers off and on the past hour. They were down south, but they might swing up this way, and I really don't want to be found up here with him."

"Me neither," Sam said as he stood and walked to the door. He stepped outside to clear his grogginess. Above, the clear sky was filled with stars. He was reminded that it had been many years since he'd seen any stars at all. He rubbed his hand through his hair, thinking, *How the hell can I go from that nightmare to this one in only two days? All I wanted was to be welcomed home, and when I am, what do I find? My dad's dying. Today, all I wanted to do was go fishing, but what do I run into? A goddamn scene from hell I foolishly leap into, putting Mark's life at risk, too. We could both end up dead or in prison.*

He turned back inside and spent the next two hours

wiping sweat from the president's brow with a cold washcloth he repeatedly wetted in the cooler's melting ice.

After he woke Mark, the pair ate some of the canned provisions they had brought and dismantled one of the bed platforms to use as a litter.

Mark hefted one end. "This thing is heavy by itself and a bit awkward, being so wide. We'll have to tie him down so he doesn't slide off when we get to the steeper parts of the trail."

Sam grabbed up the clothes he had cut off Longwood. "I'll burn these in case someone shows up here. No need to leave something that'll set the bloodhounds on us. We also need to clean the cabin of any obvious indications that someone was bleeding in here."

Mark went about the cleaning while Sam took the remnants of the president's bloody clothing, along with the dismantled bed parts not used, out to the pit and started a fire.

By the time the sun rose above the peaks to the east, they were ready for what Sam knew would be a long and arduous task.

He lifted Longwood to the makeshift litter, covered him with a blanket to keep bugs off his face and wounds, and secured him with rope around his chest and legs. He then tied the reins of the lead horse loosely to his own belt, with the three animals tethered together in a line at the rear.

"Let's go," he said at last.

"I sure hope he stays unconscious," Mark said, lifting the front of the litter.

Sam did the same with the aft end where the president's head lay.

⋄⋄⋄

As Devlin entered his command center, a lieutenant called out, "Sir, we have something from the Predator I think you should see."

"Why is the Predator still in use? I terminated the exercise yesterday."

"The FBI requested we redeploy it late last night, sir. They're looking for some missing suspects and asked that we scan the mountain for human life signs."

Devlin angrily stepped to the console, remembering that he had foolishly offered whatever assistance the FBI might need, though he had not actually meant it. He had only intruded on their meeting in order to find out if they had any evidence that might lead investigators to his mercenaries. "Okay, show me what you have."

The display was a taped infrared image from hours before. It showed the body recovery and evidence-gathering effort he knew was still going on at the lake and south at Branson's destroyed lodge. The lieutenant fast-forwarded the video as the drone pilot flew it north in an attempt to backtrack the path of the MSM attackers.

"That's the logging camp the Blackhawk spotted the evening before the attack, sir. The Forest Service says the logging operation shut down years ago, yet there are several pickups parked there. None have a heat signature. There were people there when the helicopter first spotted the location, but as you can see, it now appears abandoned, yet they left their vehicles."

"And what do you infer from that?"

"Well, sir, I believe that might be the staging point for those eight men. I'd like to notify the FBI."

Seeing no threat in that, Devlin replied, "Very well, do so."

"There was another anomaly, sir."

"Show me."

The surveillance film sped through several more hours

of recording and stopped at another infrared image, this one of a cabin. The place definitely showed a human presence and three horses in a corral. A man stepped out of the cabin, but only for a moment. The infrared could not provide a clear image of his features, but it was obvious that he looked up at the sky briefly before turning back inside.

"Those are just the campers you saw there on horseback yesterday," Devlin said irritably.

"That's not the anomaly, sir." The image fast-forwarded again until a campfire appeared in front of the cabin and the lieutenant added, "Here it is, sir. The man built an outside fire at oh-four-thirty hours and burned some unidentifiable items, though the infrared shows they already have a fire source inside the cabin. I just thought it a bit odd, sir."

Devlin's mouth went dry as he stared at the screen. His pulse quickening, he found himself grasping the top of the lieutenant's chair until his knuckles turned white. He knew the FBI had accounted for everyone at the lake, except for one agent and Longwood.

"Forget about them," he directed. "They're well away from where the assassins were seen, and there are three horses. You probably missed the third person yesterday. He might have been in that outhouse, and they're probably just burning something they don't want smelling up the cabin."

"Yes, sir. The Predator had to leave for refueling a few minutes ago. Should we continue to search the mountain for the FBI, sir?"

"Report that logging camp to them, and send the Predator to the lake when it returns. I want to know the moment they recover any bodies from it."

Devlin walked out of the command center and immediately dialed Lloyd Armstrong on his satellite phone.

"Listen carefully. There's a cabin on the northeast side of the mountain. I want you to take some men and get up there, but be careful. The FBI will be going to that logging camp those MSM idiots were using. I don't want you running into them."

"What are we looking for at the cabin, sir?"

"They haven't recovered Longwood yet, but they know he's missing his left arm, and they have signals indicating the rest of him is in the lake. Regardless, I want you to find out if whoever's at that cabin knows anything about what happened. The infrared shows at least two, possibly three people there. If they don't know anything, walk away. If you think they might, put them down and get rid of the bodies where they won't be found, ever."

"I'm looking at a topographical map now, sir. The cabin's marked on it, but I don't see any roads leading up there. It'll take us a couple of hours to get there on the bikes."

"Then get moving."

CHAPTER 15

"Vince, the divers are scheduled back up in ten minutes."

O'Malley roused and nodded to the young agent standing above him. He glanced at his watch and got to his feet. At least he'd managed to grab a two-hour nap in the twenty-four since the attack.

After downing a few sips of coffee to help clear his drowsiness, he walked outside the command center tent and found that the agent had ordered a helicopter readied to fly him up to the lake.

During the short hop, he stared sadly down at what had been unspoiled forest the day before, but was now scorched terrain dotted with broken and blackened spires. Passing where it had stood, the only sign of the Branson estate he could make out was the building's huge foundation and a swimming pool littered with floating debris.

As they lowered to the ground lakeside—easily done now that lumber company helicopters had lifted away enough downed trees to make a landing zone—O'Malley saw several bright lights turning off. They had flown in generators and spotlights to turn night into near-daytime at the site so work there did not slow. O'Malley knew the nation was holding its breath, waiting to hear the official announcement that they had recovered whatever was left of the well-liked president's corpse.

O'Malley blinked through a cloud of swirling ash as the helicopter settled. He spotted several wet-suited divers removing their gear. A dozen FBI and Secret Service agents were standing near a body bag on the ground.

"Is that the president?" O'Malley asked as he approached.

"No," a Secret Service agent answered. "It's our missing Alpha Team agent."

O'Malley turned to the divers. "Have you found any sign of the president?"

One pointed at a table. "All we found were those waders, sir. The signals were coming from loafers inside them."

"No sign of his body?"

"To be honest, sir, it's a long way to the bottom, and it's covered with a somewhat unsteady rock pile. There are thousands of tons of boulders stacked precariously down there, and a lot of debris from the incident ended up there, too. We found the waders easily enough because of the signals, but all we found after that were parts of golf carts, some weapons, and that agent's body. It's quite possible rock falling during the attack covered the president, sir."

O'Malley shook his head and snorted in frustration.

"There's something peculiar about the waders you should see, sir."

"What's that?"

The diver walked to the table, picked up the insulated rubber pants, and held out the suspenders. "These were cut with a knife."

O'Malley walked over and examined them. "The man had one arm and was probably unconscious. So who cut his waders off?"

"Maybe that agent did it before he went under," someone suggested.

Another diver said, "That guy has a massive head wound and two badly broken arms. He was probably dead when he hit the water."

One of the other FBI agents said, "Everyone who was here has been accounted for, Vince. The president must have cut them himself, maybe trying to keep from being dragged to the bottom."

O'Malley set the mystery aside and turned back to the divers. "Keep searching." He walked back to the helicopter and left for the command tent again.

The moment he arrived, the agent at the hospital called. "Chris King just died, Vince."

"Damn. Is that other agent awake yet?"

"Yes, she is."

"Okay, I'll be there shortly. I need to speak with her."

O'Malley grabbed another cup of coffee and a couple of donuts and got into his car to update his director in private. Once that was done, he climbed aboard the Blackhawk again and slipped on a headset. The chopper's engine noise increased in volume, and its rotors began to beat the air vigorously.

"It's about a fifteen-minute flight to the hospital," one of the pilots said.

O'Malley rolled his eyes. *Great, just long enough to get airsick.*

☾∾☽

O'Malley hurried through the hospital corridor. He didn't expect to learn much from Angel Washington, since she hadn't made it to the lake until well after the attack was over, but he had heard something interesting about her misadventure and one of her lost teammates.

She was preparing to leave when he walked into her room.

"Wow, you must heal quickly, Agent Washington."

She pulled on her jacket. "I wasn't hurt that bad, mostly heat blisters and lungs full of smoke. Who are you?"

He flashed his ID. "Vince O'Malley, FBI. I'd like to ask you a few questions."

"I need to get back to the mountain, Agent O'Malley. I have people down in the field."

O'Malley understood her mindset. She had lost co-workers, probably friends. She was hurting.

"I lost my entire SWAT team on that mountain, Agent Washington," he said. "They were all good friends of mine. I understand how you feel. All of your people have been recovered."

That seemed to ease her undeserved guilt, and she appeared to relax some as she sat on the edge of the bed and took a deep breath. "Okay, what d'ya need?"

"Tell me what happened, from your perspective."

She took a moment to collect her thoughts. "We were about halfway to the lake when a wall of fire popped up right in front of us. I knew we couldn't turn around and outrun it. The ground cover was burning, and flames were moving through the trees like a tsunami, so we made a dash for the stream the president had fished the day before." That made her pause. Her head down, she said, "I and two others made it, but a huge burning tree fell across the stream on top of them, and then Tom Riker came running out of the fire and dove in just a few yards from me. His clothes were on fire, and he never came up."

"He was recovered," O'Malley reassured her. "What do you know about that netting he was wrapped in?"

"When Tom didn't come up, I tried to find him. I thought maybe he hit his head, diving in like that, but when I found him, he was all tangled in it. How does a man drown in the middle of a forest fire?"

"How do you suppose it got there?"

"I have no idea," she said, "but the president fished that stream without a nibble the day before, and that netting was probably the reason. That was why they went up to the lake to begin with. Branson said he was told they were biting up there."

"Do you know who told him that?"

"He said a friend called."

O'Malley sighed. "His phone records don't show any calls being received the entire evening."

"I'm sorry, but that's all he said. You'll have to ask him."

O'Malley shook his head. "He was killed up there, too." He paused a moment. "The survivors and the casualties are returning to Washington aboard an Air Force C-17 that brought in a new detail for Mandrake last night. I have a chopper outside. If you'd like, I can give you a lift down there so you can go back with your people."

"Thank you."

O'Malley dropped her at the Missoula airport, and as he was about to take off again for the lake, he got a call from an agent there.

"Hey, Vince, the divers just came up again and said they still haven't found anything. They say they've scoured every inch of the bottom and insist he has to be buried under the rocks."

"Any chance they can dig him out?"

"They say the rock pile's too unstable and the boulders are too big. We could lose more people trying to dig around down there."

"Okay, I'll pass that along to the director."

O'Malley changed his mind about going to the lake and had the pilots take him to the command center instead. Once there, he walked over and grabbed another cup of coffee, noting by its taste that it was several hours old. He sipped at the bitter fluid as he answered another call, this one from his chief forensic technician in Missoula.

"I know this is going to sound crazy," said the technician, "but we've confirmed that the eight suspects recovered from the hillside were killed by the Secret Service weapons, and those six agents were, in turn, killed by the suspects' weapons."

"Wait a minute. I'm going to have a hard time selling *that* to the director."

"Gunshot residue on their hands and ballistics matches are pretty convincing evidence. I should add that we also ran a blood-alcohol screen on everyone and found half of the suspects to be legally intoxicated, and the rest were pretty close."

"Oh, that's even better. They were drunk and still managed to kill six Secret Service agents armed with Uzis in broad daylight."

"That's not the only weird thing. One of them was clearly left-handed but had the GSR on his right."

"I know a leftie who bats and plays golf right-handed. The booze thing has me concerned, though. Okay, anything else?"

"I almost forgot. There wasn't anything of interest on the three functional cell phones we got off the suspects: just local calls to each other. One phone had an Uzi round in it, so we had to send that one to the D.C. lab."

"Okay, thanks."

O'Malley hung up and called Pearson next, reluctantly telling him of the latest findings. As expected, the director sounded skeptical about the shooting analysis but seemed to accept what the evidence indicated.

"We brought everyone from the Noxon trailer park in

for questioning and testing for gunshot residue and ammonium perchlorate." O'Malley said. "None showed any signs of either. There's another aspect of this that's bothering me."

"What's that?"

"The initial sighting of the suspects came from a Predator using infrared imaging. They saw the eight MSM men moving down that hillside from the north, and that's how many suspect bodies we recovered. But if the Predator didn't spot the mortar teams, that means they either slipped past it—highly unlikely—or were already in position and were somehow able to hide from it. Now, if *they* could do that, why didn't the other eight do it, too? Why did they just come strolling in like that?"

"Maybe they were just late getting there. You did say most of them were intoxicated." O'Malley heard the director take in a breath and release it. "Look, Vince, this town's going crazy. I'm sure all of that will sort out once you find those mortar men. Right now, you need to stay focused on that and finding the president's body."

"The divers say he has to be under the rock pile down there, and it's too unsteady to risk trying to dig him out."

After a moment of silence, Pearson said, "Okay, I'll make the call: missing and presumed dead."

CHAPTER 16

Sam and Mark moved slowly down the mountain, taking extra caution to avoid dropping their heavy burden, despite the mosquitoes constantly biting their necks and faces. The slog had become a punishing ordeal.

"Let's take another break and see how he's doing," Sam suggested, breathing heavily.

After checking Longwood's vitals, Mark announced, "No change. I'm glad he's still unconscious. That severed arm is going to bring a lot of pain, and we don't have any way to deal with that up here."

Sam stretched, trying to ease cramps that came from holding the heavy makeshift litter as steady as possible on the tricky slope. He pulled off his Stetson, swiped his forearm across his forehead, and glanced up through a wide opening in the treetops as he rotated his head to stretch his burning neck muscles. He spotted a circling aircraft as it flashed in the sun. *It's low*, he thought. "Hand me those binoculars, Mark." Sam peered up through the ten-power lenses, noting the aircraft's long, thin, glider-like wings and slender fuselage. He recognized the make. "That's a Predator."

"What kind, Eagle or Hawk?"

"Neither. It's a military surveillance drone."

"Oh, shit. I hope it's not looking for us. We'd better keep moving."

☙❧

"General, we brought the Predator back to monitor activity at the lake as you requested, but on the way we detected some heat signatures on the east face of the mountain and got a good visual on the individuals who were at that cabin."

Devlin leapt from his chair. "I'll be right there."

After learning that divers had recovered the missing agent from the lake but only Longwood's waders, Devlin worried that the people at the cabin may have witnessed what really occurred and somehow managed to remove Longwood from the scene. At the command center console, he stared at the clear black-and-white visual image, his heart pounding. "What are they doing?"

"We caught a momentary glimpse of them through a gap in the trees a few minutes ago, sir. It appears that they're bringing someone down the east face of the mountain on a litter. The three horses are trailing behind them."

"It must be the third rider, then," Devlin said hopefully.

"I don't think so, sir. Only two horses have saddles. I think the third one's a packhorse."

His heart pounding, Devlin asked, "Is it a man or a woman on the litter?"

"We can't tell, sir. They have a blanket fully covering the individual. That may mean it's a body, but I'd think if that were the case, they'd just drape it over a horse rather than carry it. Most likely, they're trying to keep insects off."

Devlin could clearly see the two men's features in the daylight and was surprised when one raised a pair of binoculars directly toward the Predator. Moments later, they disappeared into the trees. *They wanted out of the Predator's view*, he thought. *They're running.*

Devlin did not want the command center spotting Armstrong's group. "Okay, forget about them. I want the Predator to stay on the lake scene. Let me know if they pull out any more bodies or the divers pack up."

A sergeant at another console said, "Sir, CNN just announced that the FBI has officially declared President Longwood missing and presumed dead. They're ending their search."

Devlin was disappointed. "Okay, send the drone back to base. We're done here."

In his office, he felt sweat forming on his hands and had to concentrate to get his breathing under control as he called Armstrong on the satellite phone. "How far are you from the cabin?"

"I can see it ahead."

"They aren't there anymore. They're moving down the east side of the mountain with a litter, and the divers never found Longwood's body. They're ending the search for it."

"Do you think he might be on that litter?"

"It's not inconceivable. Now move it."

"Yes, sir. Do you want me to check out the cabin real quick?"

Devlin sensed he might be losing control of the situation. He didn't think it likely, but he knew his entire scheme could be in jeopardy if those two men had a living Longwood on that litter. Even if they were just bringing down his corpse, it would mean they had been at the lake and had likely seen what happened. "Yeah, but make it quick. I'll stay on the line."

Seconds of silence, then, "We're inside now, sir. There are a few fly rods leaning against the wall and some dishes in a rack next to a large plastic bowl apparently used as a sink. I see plates and silverware for two, not three."

"That could mean the third person didn't eat because he or she was sick or injured."

"Sir, I found a letter stuck to the back of the door. It has a Forest Service letterhead and says the cabin is open to the public for survival purposes. There's an address and phone number for a Jeremiah Calder, who's apparently responsible for repairing any damage to the place."

Devlin had already brought up the mountain on Google Maps and was staring down at it. He studied the adjacent valley to the east. There was a ranch symbol directly below the mountain, and a second about a mile north of that one. "Is there an address for Calder?"

"Yes, sir." Armstrong read the address.

Devlin typed it into Google Maps. "Okay, the Calder ranch is at the base of the mountain."

"The eastern face is too steep for the bikes, sir. We'll have to chase 'em on foot."

"Then get moving!"

CHAPTER 17

Seven hours after they had begun their trek, the brothers walked out from under the trees at the base of the mountain.

"Let's rest a minute, Sam. I'm about done in."

They set the litter down and began stretching their aching and cramped muscles.

Sam knelt and felt the president's pulse. "He's hanging in there." He looked up then and saw nothing but blue sky above. "That Predator's gone. I hope it didn't spot us."

"You know, if they're looking for him and he ends up dying on us, we'll be in some deep shit."

"That can't be helped, Mark. We're committed now, no matter what."

After a few moments of rest, they switched ends and were about to pick up the litter again when Sam spotted the ranch truck rushing toward them.

It slowed to a stop, and Jeremiah bailed out. He halted in his tracks when he looked down at the litter. "Who the hell is that? Is he dead?"

"No," Sam said, dropping the tailgate. "He's hurt bad, though. It's a long story. We need to get him to the house and call for medical help."

Mark removed the saddles from the horses and let all three loose in the pasture there. They walked off and immediately began grazing as the brothers climbed into the cargo bed with the litter and saddles. Jeremiah turned the truck around and sped for the house.

He held the screen door open as Sam and Mark moved into the great room. They kicked the coffee table aside and set the litter on the floor. Sam lifted the blanket from Longwood's face.

"You know," said Jeremiah, "that fella looks a lot like—" He paused and leaned in for a closer look. "Oh, shit. It is him."

"Yeah, we know," Sam said as he lifted the blanket farther, exposing Longwood's injured arm.

"Oh, please tell me you fellas didn't do that to him."

"Of course we didn't do it," Mark answered.

Jeremiah knelt and felt Longwood's neck. "His pulse is really shallow."

"He needs a hospital," Sam said. "He lost a lot of blood."

Jeremiah moved for the telephone. "I'll call for the paramedics."

"Don't tell them it's the president," Sam instructed.

"Hell, they probably wouldn't believe me if I did," Jeremiah said as he dialed nine-one-one. "This is Jeremiah Calder off Route One. I need paramedics out to my place right away. I got a fella here who's been injured."

"What kind of injury?" the dispatcher asked.

"The kind that needs a paramedic," Jeremiah responded brusquely and hung up.

No more than three minutes passed before Sam heard a siren approaching. He looked out a front window and spotted a sheriff's patrol car coming fast down the gravel drive, its overhead lights flashing, dust trailing. He wondered if it was his high school chum, Pete Flynn, but recognized the elderly county sheriff, Tim Rafferty, climbing out of the car after it slid to a stop at the base of the porch. Jeremiah had gone to high school with him and met him at the door.

"You're looking better, Jeremiah," Tim said. "Is Mark hurt?"

"Nope, but you ain't gonna believe who is."

The white-haired sheriff removed his Stetson as he stepped into the house. He nodded to Mark and looked at Sam. "Well, I'll be. When'd you get home, Sam?"

"I just got into town a few days ago. How far out are the paramedics?"

"They're coming from Hot Springs, so it'll probably take them another ten minutes or so. I just happened to be out this way when the call came in."

The thick-mustached lawman walked to the president's feet and stared down at his face for a moment.

"Oh, shit!" He drew his huge revolver and shakily pointed it at Sam, then Mark, then Jeremiah, and back to Sam. "Don't move, any of you!"

Sam and Mark put their hands up as Jeremiah stepped forward. "Hold on, Tim. Hold on. We didn't do this."

Rafferty looked uncertain how to handle the situation. He held his gun on the trio but asked Sam and Mark, "Is that true? You fellas weren't a part of this?"

"No, we weren't," Mark stated. "A bunch of fellas in military outfits attacked him up at Pointer Lake. They killed a whole lot of other folks up there, too."

"What?" Jeremiah blurted out.

Rafferty slowly lowered his revolver and holstered it. "Don't you watch the news, Jeremiah?"

"Our dish is down."

"Well, he was up there fishing with that billionaire Ben Branson and Congressman Mandrake. A bunch of them Montana State Militia fools attacked 'em. The

FBI's been searching Pointer Lake for his body. They declared him dead just a few hours ago."

"I didn't see Mandrake up there," Mark said. "His fat ass would've been hard to miss, even blown up."

"Yeah, well, he wasn't there when it happened. The news folks are saying he's gonna be sworn in as president."

"I doubt that's gonna happen now," Jeremiah said. "This one ain't dead yet."

Sam cut in. "He may be alive, but he's not able to perform his duties. They'll have to make the vice president take over until he's fit again."

"There ain't any vice president," Rafferty said. "Jeez, you fellas really need to watch the news sometime. She died last month, and they ain't replaced her yet. That's why they're saying Mandrake will get the job. He's next in line."

Not wanting to explain why he hadn't known about the vice president's death, Sam knelt at Longwood's side. "We need to tell you what *really* happened up there, Sheriff."

"What d'ya mean by what *really* happened?"

While they waited for the paramedics, Sam and Mark told Rafferty what they had witnessed at Pointer Lake.

The sheriff repeatedly shook his head throughout their tale, saying nothing. When the brothers finished, he said, "The feds are claiming the Secret Service killed them MSM fellas but got themselves killed doing it. I thought that sounded like bullshit. I've arrested a few of those MSM idiots, and they're usually too drunk to change a tire, let alone pull off something like that."

The paramedics arrived then, both rushing to the porch as Jeremiah held the door open.

"Holy shit," one blurted out as the pair knelt at each side of the litter.

The other only managed to say, "Hey, isn't he—" before Rafferty interrupted him.

"Yep, he sure is, and I strongly recommend you two young fellas not screw this up."

☙❧

The paramedics finished giving the unconscious president a second intravenous infusion of Lactated Ringer's solution, a protein-rich fluid designed to strengthen a victim after severe blood loss more effectively than standard saline.

"I'll get the gurney," one medic said as the pair stood. "We need to get him to the hospital now."

"I'll need you and your boys to come into town with me," Rafferty told Jeremiah. "I'm sure a shit storm's gonna fall on this place when this gets—"

When Rafferty stopped mid-sentence, Sam noticed the sheriff's face take on a puzzled look. He turned to look at the window where Rafferty was staring.

A darkly dressed man carrying a suppressed assault rifle moved across it.

At that same instant, another suppressor-equipped weapon opened fire from the screen door and the sheriff flew back against the fireplace six feet behind.

Rafferty managed to draw his revolver, but nothing more. His unfocused eyes and the bleeding holes in his shirtfront spoke volumes.

Everyone in the room, except Sam, froze in place.

Sam dove for the floor next to Rafferty and pulled the huge revolver from the dead man's hand. In one fluid motion, he swung it around and fired a single shot, striking the man who stood at the screen door.

Unlike the suppressed assault rifle, the sheriff's .44 caliber six-shooter was deafening inside the house as the huge bullet blew off the top of the killer's head, knocking him backward into the man who had passed by the window a moment earlier. That gave Sam a half-second to put the next round into that man's face, dropping his now-headless corpse onto the front porch.

Sam spun back toward the awed group—still unmoving in the center of the room—just as multiple suppressed bullets coming from the kitchen door struck the standing paramedics.

One of them, his back riddled with wounds, collapsed atop the president. The other took several rounds in the chest and fell against Jeremiah, who stood behind him. That saved Sam's father as the two shooters coming from the kitchen next fired at him and Mark.

The one firing at Jeremiah hit the medic again, which allowed time for Sam to respond with a round into that shooter's right ear. But while he did that, the other attacker swung the barrel of his rifle toward Mark's tall frame.

Two of his bullets struck their target, knocking Mark to the floor just as Sam fired a round into the gunman's temple.

Jeremiah dropped the dead medic and leapt to his oldest son, who lay sprawled on the floor, motionless. "Oh my God, they killed Mark!"

Sam heard his father's painful declaration and saw that his brother had suffered shoulder and head wounds. But he knew the rest of them would likely be dead soon, too, if he hesitated. Realizing the sheriff's revolver had only two rounds left, he rose and rushed to the front door. He dropped the handgun and pulled the unfired assault rifle from the grip of the second man he had killed, then spun around just as a fifth attacker entered the back door, which he could see through the doorway leading into the kitchen. Sam fired the rifle once, and the man's skull exploded. His body tumbled out the door he had just entered.

As Sam glanced out the front windows, watching for more assailants from that direction, his father stepped to his side.

"Sam, you have to get the president away from here."

The pickup sat in front of Rafferty's patrol car, but Sam knew neither vehicle would offer the protection the paramedics' van could. He also knew there were medical supplies in it that Longwood desperately needed. "We might have a chance if we can get him to the van."

Firing through the screen door, Sam shot both tires on the driver's side of the sheriff's car and the pickup to ensure the attackers could not pursue them with either vehicle.

Jeremiah pulled at Sam's rifle. "Gimme that and I'll cover you. You have to carry him."

Not knowing how many more attackers there were, but assuming there were more, Sam moved quickly. He released the assault rifle to his father and rushed to move the dead medic's body and lift the president over his shoulder. As he turned, he saw his father staring down at Mark.

"I'm sorry, Dad."

A tearful Jeremiah faced him. "You aren't responsible for this, Sam. Now go!"

"Wait a minute. You're coming, too."

Jeremiah shook his head. "No, I'm not," he said stonily. "I was about to die very slowly and badly from this damn cancer. I'd rather go out right here, standing up with my boots on next to my boy."

Sam's heart was breaking. He knew his father was determined to make a stand, but he could not leave the man who had just come back into his life. He bent to lay the president down.

Jeremiah grabbed his free shoulder. "No, Sam. Look, I didn't support you going off to fight other people's battles before, and I should have. Now they've come to our home and done this. I want you to get the president to safety, and promise me you'll make the bastards responsible pay for all this."

Sam stared at his father's pained face and nodded. "I will, Dad. I promise."

"I love you, Sam. I always have. Now go!"

"I love you, too, Dad," was all Sam could marshal as he reluctantly turned for the front door.

As he went through it at a run, several bullets struck its frame, barely missing their targets. Sam continued forward as Jeremiah stepped onto the porch and sprayed the corner of the house where the bullets had come from.

Sam reached the van's already-opened back door, heaved the president's limp form to the floor there, jumped over him, and slammed the door closed. As he leapt to the driver's seat, more bullets struck the van's metal side, and one punched a small, round hole in the driver's door before tearing apart a large section of the dashboard.

He started the engine and dropped the van into gear, expecting someone to shoot out its tires. Surprisingly, no one did.

As the van turned away from the house, its spinning wheels throwing gravel, Sam glanced at the passenger side mirror and saw his father wheel about and fire the assault rifle into the house from the front door. Sam's mind painfully told him he would never see the man alive again.

Then he was racing down the drive, a dust cloud behind obstructing his view of the gun battle.

ℰℬℰℬ

Devlin answered his sat phone the instant it chirped. "Did you get them?"

"Not all, sir."

"Shit! What happened?"

Armstrong explained the sequence of events. Devlin could not understand how civilians could cut down six men. *The only real threat should have been the sheriff,* he thought, *and they took him out first.*

"That old man shot one," Armstrong said, "but he didn't shoot the others, sir. They all took single head-shots. That's the signature of someone with skills way beyond even a regular soldier, let alone a rancher. The one who got away was probably that shooter."

"Are you telling me one man did all that and you let him get away?"

"We couldn't chase them. They shot out the tires on the patrol car and the pickup."

"Did you see Longwood?"

"No, but Tillman yelled out that the guy running to the van was carrying someone over his shoulder."

"Ask Tillman if the one being carried was missing an arm."

"I can't. He's the one the old man got."

"So we don't even know if we're on the right trail or not. Shit!"

"We're cleaning up here now, sir, but we'll have to leave the six men we lost."

"Pull all the bodies into the house and gather up the dead guys' weapons, pistols included. Then torch the place and get the hell out of there before more cops show up. You can bury the guns on the mountain on your way back up for the bikes. Don't worry about leaving the bodies. I deleted all your military DNA files and fingerprint records long ago."

"It'll take hours to get back to the bikes on top of the mountain."

"Then get moving, and make sure you hide those dead men's bikes, too. I'll try to figure out some way to find the bastard who got away." He hung up.

His heart was racing, and he felt short of breath. *How the hell can this—*

The thought was cut off as his secretary knocked at his office door.

"What?"

"Sir, Secretary Langford just called. She said the cabinet is meeting at the White House in an hour and would like the NSC principals to attend."

CHAPTER 18

S am sped north on the isolated roadway, unsure if the attackers had access to another vehicle. He wanted somewhere to hide just in case and then remembered what could be a good spot. *If it's still standing*, he thought.

Relieved to see that it was, Sam pulled into a remote gas station five miles from the ranch. Abandoned decades before, it no longer had any pumps under its portico and most of the windows had been broken out and covered with plywood. Fortunately, its bay door was intact, unlocked, and opened easily. Inside, he saw no indication of the garage's original purpose, but empty beer cans and pizza boxes hinted at its latest use.

Sam focused on caring for the president, trying not to think about what was happening at the ranch. He had yanked the intravenous lines out when he lifted Longwood off the floor, so he moved him to the van's gurney and administered a new drip, adding an antibiotic he found in the medical supplies. Next, he wrapped the president's head in bandaging, leaving only his eyes, nose, and mouth clear. *Just in case someone stumbles on us*, he thought.

With his patient's pulse weak but steady, Sam stepped

outside and brushed away the tire tracks from the dirt lot with a small whiskbroom he found below the driver's seat. As he did so, he glanced down the valley and froze. Black smoke was rising against the blue sky from the direction of his home.

Heartbroken, Sam could only stare at the rising column. He then realized that first-responders would know someone left the scene in the paramedic van, so after noting his position on it, he disabled its GPS. *That might give me some time*, he thought, *but I can't drive around in this thing.*

He had no options. If he went to the authorities, they would likely arrest him for any number of things. *At the very least, I'll be charged with kidnapping when they find the president.* Worse yet, he feared the assassins would then have an opportunity to complete their seditious deed, and his family would have died for nothing.

Now that he was the only living witness to what really happened at the lake, the assassins would want him dead, too. That thought brought back another memory, one that suddenly gave him an option. Searching his wallet, he found Salvatore Deluca's card. "Now I just need a phone."

The adrenaline dump from the gunfight and escape was wearing off, and Sam felt drained. He knew he had no choice, though. He had to return to the ranch. That was the closest place he could think of where he might be able to find a phone. He knew he would have to be very careful, and lucky. *If I'm not*, he thought, *I'm going back to prison, or the morgue.* Then he realized something else. *If I die tonight, no one will know where to find the van, and the president will likely die, too.*

He found paper and a pen in the glove box and wrote down what he had witnessed at the lake and what happened at the ranch, including where he had hidden the van. He signed it and shoved it in his pocket.

As darkness fell and he was preparing to leave, Sam saw Longwood beginning to stir toward consciousness and knew he could not let that happen. He was going to have to leave him alone, and the man would undoubtedly be confused and in pain when he woke. Instead, he pulled a vile of morphine from the van's narcotics locker and added it to Longwood's intravenous drip, sending him into a drug-induced slumber.

After he was satisfied that the president was sleeping comfortably, he set off on foot, moving along the road-side shoulder. He paced himself for the nearly five-mile jog. When he got within sight of the ranch's gravel drive, he noted several patrol cars and ambulances parked along its length and thought one was sure to have a satellite phone in it, since cell phone reception was so spotty in this part of the valley. He slipped into the adjacent pasture. Though several horses whinnied at his passing, darkness concealed his run across the open space.

Near an idling fire truck, he slipped through the fence rails again and crawled into shadowed bushes, staring sadly at a half-dozen firefighters surrounding a huge, smoldering debris pile that had been his family's home for more than a century. He couldn't fathom what they were going to make of what they would discover in the ash.

Heartsick at what he was seeing, Sam was about to begin his search of the vehicles when the fire engine's diesel quit and he heard a voice he recognized.

"Hey, Tom, the tires on the driver's side of the sheriff's car and the pickup have been shot out."

Sam watched as two uniformed deputies came together. One was Pete Flynn, whom he had spoken with after his scuffle in the tavern. The other was Tom Craftman, another high school chum, Mark's age. Then headlights turning onto the gravel drive caught Sam's attention.

The new car parked at the back of the long line, and a tall man wearing boots, blue jeans, and a Stetson climbed out. Sam noticed a .50 caliber Desert Eagle holstered at the man's hip as he strode past Sam's hiding spot and approached the deputies. He pulled out identification and said, "Vince O'Malley, FBI."

"Howdy. I'm Tom Craftman. This here's Pete Flynn."

"Tim Rafferty was a friend of mine. I heard someone may have killed him. Is that true?"

"We're not sure yet. The ash is still too hot to dig in, and it's too dark to see clearly. His car's over there with bullet holes in both tires on the driver's side."

"What was he doing here?"

"There were two paramedics dispatched here for someone with an unspecified injury. Their van's missing, and we haven't found any sign of them yet, either."

"Does the van have a GPS locator?"

"Yep, but it ain't responding."

Sam wanted to hear more, but the fire truck started up again, forcing him back to why he had come there in the first place. He backed away and crawled amongst the line of vehicles scattered along the gravel drive, carefully examining their seats and glove boxes until he found what he needed.

A satellite phone lay on the front seat of the FBI man's car. He snatched it up and sprinted into the dark field, hoping the federal agent continued asking questions a while longer.

His call was answered on the second ring. "Who is this?"

"This is Sam Calder. I need help."

"Hold on."

There was a nearly thirty-second pause before a recognizable voice asked, "Sam, what can I do for you?"

"I'm in Montana, and I need to be somewhere far away as quickly as possible and without anyone knowing about it."

Without hesitating, Tony responded, "Tell me where you are, and I'll make that happen, my friend."

Sam explained where he was hiding, giving Tony the coordinates he had taken from the van's GPS. "Don't call this phone back," he added. "I sorta borrowed it from the FBI."

"We'll help you as soon as we can set things up. Be patient and remove the phone's sim card." The line went dead.

After breaking the phone's card and tossing the pieces into the dark field, he darted back to the government car and threw the now-useless machine onto its front seat. He quickly crossed the pasture again and headed north on his way back to the garage.

∽∾∽∾

Devlin glanced over at Secretary of State Langford in her normal White House conference room seat to the right of the president's. She was staring at his empty chair. She then looked across the table to the vice president's seat. Though every other chair had an occupant, Devlin figured the touchy-feely Langford likely felt abandoned.

"May I have your attention, please," she stated to the jabbering crowd.

The noise level decreased dramatically as faces turned her way.

"Thank you. Now, we need everyone, with the exception of the cabinet secretaries, Attorney General Howell, and the NSC principals, to leave the room."

When the doors clicked shut, she announced, "You've

all been briefed on the latest that we have. The divers were unable to locate President Longwood, but his appendage was recovered, and he has been declared missing and presumed dead."

Devlin saw heads droop around the table.

"Where's Mandrake?" asked the secretary of defense, George Alvarez.

"He's been aboard *Air Force One* since shortly after the incident yesterday," Langford answered. "He'll be here in less than an hour."

Alvarez continued with exactly what Devlin wanted to hear. "We must invoke the twenty-fifth and have the chief justice on hand so we can get it over with as soon as Mandrake gets here. We need the National Command Authority reestablished as soon as possible. I cannot stress the importance of having control of the nation's nuclear arsenal in presidential hands."

"Are we certain Philip Mandrake's the right choice?" Langford asked.

Devlin figured she might balk. *Mandrake's well-known religious zealotry is undoubtedly troubling her*. He held his breath.

"We have no other option, Elizabeth," answered Alvarez. "As Speaker of the House, he's third in the constitutional line of succession and must be named president, unless you're aware of some reason he might be considered unfit."

Before Langford could voice any concern, the attorney general spoke up. "Madame Secretary, I strongly urge you to recuse yourself from these proceedings if this body is determined to pursue that particular line of discourse."

"Why?"

"If Mandrake is deemed unfit, Senator Carlson, president *pro tempore* of the Senate, is next in line. However,

as I'm sure you're aware, he's eighty-four and hospital-
ized with end-stage pancreatic cancer. That leaves *you*
next in line, Madame Secretary, and that makes your involvement in such a decision a grievous conflict of interest."

"I see," Langford acknowledged. "If someone wishes
to pursue the matter, I will recuse myself."

No one voiced anything, so after a quiet moment, Alvarez said, "I propose we notify Chief Justice Reinhardt
that we are prepared to invoke the twenty-fifth amendment and appoint Phillip Mandrake president."

Heads began nodding around the table, and Devlin exhaled, relieved.

"Should we appoint a vice president, too?" someone
asked. Devlin stifled a gasp.

The attorney general said, "The new president may
nominate a vice president for approval by a simple majority vote in both houses of Congress, or he can leave the
position empty until next year's election. That will be up
to him."

იარ

Forty minutes later, Devlin stood on the south lawn of
the White House and watched as the Marine One helicopter landed. The moment the forward door opened, a Marine passed a box marked BIOHAZARD to a pair of Secret Service agents. Devlin knew they were taking it to
Walter Reed's pathology lab for DNA verification that it
was, in fact, Longwood's severed arm.

Mandrake stepped out of the helicopter next, sweating
and out of breath. He plodded across the lawn amidst an
entourage of Secret Service agents. Devlin was surprised
when Mandrake cheerily waved at the throng of cameras
and solemn-looking reporters standing in silence a hun-

dred yards away. Mandrake glanced his way and turned to him with a broad smile. Devlin maintained a more serious expression but greeted him with an outstretched hand. "Hello, sir. I'm glad to see you're okay."

"Only by God's grace am I standing here with you now. Is my family here?"

Devlin released the fat man's sweaty hand and gestured toward the doors. "They're waiting for you in the East Room, sir."

Inside, White House staff ushered them to the large room where the cabinet, senior leaders from the House and Senate, and Mandrake's family and House office staff were waiting. A lone television camera was set up in the back of the room. Devlin knew all the networks would use the same feed.

He saw understandably somber looks on the faces of those from the Longwood camp but also noted smiles flickering on several of Mandrake's people, especially his smarmy chief-of-staff, Preston Maddox. *Big promotion for you*, Devlin thought. He wondered how the television networks would portray the contrasting emotional images.

Mandrake greeted his wife and two adult sons perfunctorily as Devlin observed that obesity seemed to be the family's common denominator. Accompanied by them, Mandrake stepped onto the small stage normally used for private concerts and award ceremonies.

Chief Justice Reinhardt was already there, a Bible in hand.

Five minutes later, President Phillip Mandrake stepped up to a dozen microphones set up on a nearby podium and faced the lone television camera. "My fellow Americans, I have assumed the mantle of leadership today, humbled by God's great plan…"

CHAPTER 19

The tension and terror of the past two days had not given Sam time to think about what was happening. He could only react. Now, waiting out the night in the garage seemed never-ending. *If I had listened to Mark and ridden off*, he told himself, *none of this would have happened. Now I've lost everything that meant anything to me, again.*

Unable to stop thinking about his last days with his brother and father, Sam's anguish dragged him down a well of grief he knew too well. *It's just like it was with Judith and prison*, he thought. *Life taunts me with something good and then rips it away.*

After wallowing in his sorrow and self-pity for hours, he suddenly found himself becoming more angry than despondent. That spark of resilience that had always helped him to persevere when others faltered seemed to have ignited again. In that moment, he knew if he were to survive and save Longwood as he'd promised his father, he would have to draw upon that part of himself he had used to survive all the other horrible moments in his life, no matter the cost.

Longwood was still sleeping under the influence of the morphine and seemed to be stable. Sam feared the man might have some type of internal injury that a doctor would recognize and properly deal with, but he also knew that turning him over to the authorities, even dropping him off at a hospital, would give the killers the opportunity that the attack at the ranch proved they wanted. That turned his thoughts back to the ranch assault but not his losses. Instead, he focused on what he could deduce about the enemy.

The weapons and ghillie suits at the lake definitely connect them to the military, he thought. He also suspected they had used the Predator to track them to the ranch. That reinforced a military connection. He thought it incongruous that they had access to such high-tech equipment yet had such lame tactical skills.

He began to think about that. *One walked in front of a window in daylight. That single error alone was the only reason they weren't able to kill everyone in the room before I could kill them. And their timing was off. The ones from the back entered several seconds after those at the front.* Sam knew from experience how critical simultaneous entry was in order to surprise and confuse one's targets in those precious first seconds.

They also fired their weapons on full auto and at center mass. That means they had little or no significant field experience. Regular infantry, he knew, tended to spray bullets in a firefight, often not even aiming at a specific target. Special ops-trained fighters, on the other hand, aimed, fired once, and moved on to another target. A bullet in the brain would shut a man off instantly, but body hits could be defeated by armor or even sustained long enough to get some rounds off in return.

Hunger pangs distracted his thoughts then, but he knew it was only an irritant at this point. On the other hand, he knew his growing thirst was a warning of more dire things to come. Since there was no running water in the garage, to avoid dehydration he had no choice but to intravenously administer himself a couple bags of saline solution. He sat quietly as the fluid dripped into his vein, and noticed it was getting light outside. Unintentionally, he closed his eyes and drifted off.

🙟🙠🙡

The new satellite phone O'Malley had picked up chirped, and he glanced down to see *FBI* on its screen. He almost ignored his director's call, as he was just pulling into the Calder drive again, but changed his mind and picked it up instead. "This is Vince, sir."

"Hey, Vince, I need you on a teleconference at five p.m. your time for a task force update."

"Okay, I'll be back in the office in about two hours. I'm just stopping by another crime scene for a minute to check on something."

"Is it connected with the assassination?"

"Nah, it's personal. The local sheriff may have been killed. I knew him."

"Sorry to hear that. I'll talk to you later." The line went dead.

O'Malley climbed out of his car, slipped his Stetson on, and walked toward where he could see the two deputy sheriffs he had spoken with the night before, leaning against a patrol car. Their faces and uniforms were soiled, which meant they had finally been able to search through the blackened ash and debris pile behind them. Both were gulping water from plastic bottles.

"Good morning," O'Malley said.

The deputies returned the greeting, and Craftman added, "I tried to call you a while ago, but that sat phone number you gave me is out of service."

"That damn phone went kaput on me," O'Malley answered. "I'll give you a new number in a minute. What were you gonna call me for?"

"Once it cooled off, we found the sheriff's remains in there, along with nine other people, and—"

O'Malley cut him off. "Are you serious?"

"I wish I wasn't. We've never had anything like this around here. We found the sheriff's .44 caliber revolver, and only two rounds had cooked off in the fire. The other four casings in it had firing-pin indentations, and five of the corpses had their heads blown apart."

"Were they killed execution style?"

"No. One of them was found at the back door inside the kitchen, and the others were found in the living room. I don't think the sheriff shot any of them, either. He was the worst shot in the department, and we found his gun at the front door, but his remains were twenty feet away. We know it's him because his badge and handcuffs are there."

"So, who could've been the shooter?"

"At this point it's still conjecture, but there may be a connection between what happened here and that MSM bunch you're looking for."

O'Malley was shocked. "You think so?"

"The old man who owned this place, Jeremiah Calder, had cancer and wasn't expected to last much longer. His oldest son and I were high school classmates and friends. He's the fella we told you about last night, the one the firefighters found alive out here."

"How is he?" O'Malley asked.

"It looks like he's gonna make it," Flynn answered, "but the other round just clipped him on the side of the head. He must've come to and managed to crawl outside before the place went up. The doc says he's in a coma now, though, and could come out of it tomorrow or next year, and he may or may not remember anything."

"So what's the connection with my case?" O'Malley asked. "Were they affiliated with the MSM?"

Again, Flynn answered. "I've known the Calders all my life, and there's no way any of them would have anything to do with those idiots. Jeremiah's other son, Sam, has been gone for years, but I ran into him just the other day. He got into a scuffle with a couple of MSM guys over at the Lonepine Tavern."

"Hang on a minute," O'Malley said. He went back to his car and returned a moment later. "I just ran Samuel Calder through NCIC, and he came back with a Department of Defense block on his background. I'll have to get Washington to call the Pentagon."

"He was in the Navy," Flynn said.

"Could he be one of those bodies you found?"

"Maybe, but it'll be a while before we get DNA identifications or dental matches, unless you can help speed that up."

"I can try. Send the remains that you can't identify down to our pathology folks in Missoula. I'll call and set it up."

"Thanks."

"Have you located that paramedic van?"

"Not yet."

❧❧❧

Sam woke from a troubled rest, pleasantly surprised that he hadn't had the nightmare. It seemed to be almost midday. He immediately checked Longwood, finding him still sleeping soundly, his breathing steady. He administered another bag of Lactated Ringer's and gave himself another bag of saline, trying not to think about his own growling stomach.

He spent the next hour wiping down every surface in

the garage and van he might have touched before he put on surgical gloves.

Mid-afternoon, Longwood began to stir again. His eyes opened briefly, then closed, and he moaned. Sam was wiping the man's forehead with a paper towel when he heard a vehicle pull around the back of the garage. Fearing discovery, he leapt from the van and peered through a crack in the plywood covering a rear window, his heart pounding.

The sight of Tony's man Louie climbing out of a dusty Hummer was a tremendous relief. Sam's quickened pulse calmed as he unlocked and opened the garage's rear door.

"I thought you might be hungry," the big Italian-American said, holding out a bag. "I brought you a pro-sciutto sandwich and some cannoli."

Sam accepted the bag and shook the man's hand. "Thanks, Louie. I'm starving."

"F'get about it. Let's go."

Sam gulped a bite of sandwich and said, "There's someone else here who has to go with us. Give me a minute. He's injured."

"Okay, I'll drop the back seats down," Louie said as he turned to the SUV.

Not wanting the president waking during the trip, Sam put the sandwich aside and gave Longwood another dose of morphine before wrapping him in blankets to conceal the missing arm.

Louie saw the bandages and asked, "What happened to his head?"

"He was burned," Sam lied.

After moving Longwood to the SUV's now-flattened rear seats, Sam removed the sheets from the gurney, wiped it down, and pushed it back into the van. He grabbed two plastic bags before shutting its rear doors. One contained medical supplies he'd prepared earlier, and the other held the waste he had created. He shoved the sheets into the garbage bag. He did not want to leave any evidence that might lead someone to discover Longwood had been there.

Sam climbed in next to his patient and began eating again as the SUV pulled onto the roadway and headed north.

"It took me some time to get here because the cops have all the roads and airports locked down. That's why I rented this thing, under a fake name, of course. We'll be taking a shortcut now."

With that, Louie turned onto a dirt road that headed into the trees. "This thing has GPS, and all I had to do was put in the coordinates you gave Tony and tell it to use non-paved roads to get there. It gave me all the roads the lumber companies made through these woods. Downed trees blocked a few. That's why it took me so long. The trip back should be quicker."

ဢၣၔၣ

The dirt road emerged from the trees and joined a paved one ninety minutes after they began their occasionally rough, cross-country journey.

There was no traffic in sight on the road, and Sam noticed the asphalt was broken in spots, with weeds growing through cracks.

Louie seemed to read his mind. "Apparently this old road ain't used much anymore because of the interstate, but it was perfect for our needs today. Mainly because it's outside the area the cops have locked down." He pulled a hand-held radio from the glove box. "I can't believe cell phones don't work around here. It's uncivilized." He keyed the radio and transmitted, "We're ready."

A voice responded, "Roger that. I'll be there in a few minutes."

They sat chatting about Montana's remoteness and other unimportant things while they waited. Finally, Sam saw a single-engine airplane turning low above the trees. It maneuvered to line up with the road, landed smoothly, and came to a stop fifty feet away. The pilot remained at the controls and kept the propeller turning while a young man climbed out and waved.

Louie drove closer. "That's Mario, my cousin's boy. He'll drive this thing to Chicago and leave it in the long-term parking lot at the airport."

Louie looked pale and fidgety as he climbed into the copilot seat.

Sam took the rear one, and Longwood was positioned on the floor at his feet, still covered in blankets. "Are you okay, Louie?" Sam asked, though he clearly was not.

"I like Tony's jet," Louie replied. "It's waiting at an airport over near the North Dakota border. That was as close as we could get it without the feds asking questions."

The Cessna 172 lifted off, leveling no more than a hundred feet above the trees. The pilot explained that he was flying under visual flight rules and wasn't under radar control because he hadn't filed a flight plan with the FAA. "There ain't much radar in this part of the country anyway, except around the cities."

After a short while, they were circling a small airport. The place appeared abandoned, and Sam spotted only one aircraft sitting on its empty tarmac: Tony's sleek Gulfstream.

After landing, Louie gave the smiling Cessna pilot a thick stack of bills and helped Sam load Longwood aboard the luxury jet.

As the pilot and copilot started its engines, the phone

on the wall next to Sam's seat rang. He picked it up. "Hello?"

"Glad you made it," Tony said.

"Thanks. You saved my ass."

"F'get about it. They're flying you to our place on Antigua, down in the Caribbean. No one will bother you there, and you can stay as long as you want. Louie will help you get settled."

Sam stared at the president's bandaged head. "Is there someone there I can trust to provide medical attention to an injured friend I brought along?"

"Yeah, there's a doctor there we use all the time. He's good with bullet wounds, too, if that's what your friend has."

Not wishing to clarify the nature of Longwood's injuries and assuming a doctor who dealt with gunshot victims was sufficiently skilled in trauma, Sam only said, "Thanks."

"*Ciao*. I may come down for a visit." Without saying more, Tony hung up.

The jet lifted into the air moments later, and Sam sat back. He was tired, depressed, and apprehensive of what the future might bring. Staring out a window, he numbly watched as the forested mountain terrain below slowly transitioned to flat, sectioned-off farmland, and finally just scattered lights as the sun sank lower in the west.

He barely noticed any of it as his mind remained focused on the past two days' events. Just days earlier, he'd been in prison. Now he was secretly dragging around the nation's unconscious and battered chief executive while being stalked by a ruthless faction of the government. He could only predict a dire outcome.

My life sucks, he thought.

CHAPTER 20

Devlin was agitated as he entered FBI headquarters wearing a civilian suit. He was upset that the bureau had given up the search for Longwood's body, and more so that Lloyd Armstrong had been unable to confirm that the man who escaped the ranch debacle had Longwood. *At least Mandrake is now president*, he thought.

Director Pearson had set up an assassination task force update briefing this evening, and he wanted to attend, though he was not invited. He knew the investigation had expanded to include hundreds of federal, state, and local law enforcement personnel, but not the military. He knew why, too: the nineteenth-century federal Posse Comitatus Act prohibited the use of federal military assets to enforce civilian laws. Still, he figured no one would even notice his presence.

Dozens of senior law enforcement executives took seats near the front of the large room, while the more experienced investigators meandered around trying to find a seat or a place to stand. Devlin moved to the back with them as Pearson entered from a side door and walked to the podium.

"Ladies and gentlemen, we'll begin with a teleconference briefing from the special agent in charge of the Montana crime scene."

The large screen behind Pearson was already on, and a man wearing a suit stepped into the picture. He looked uncomfortable.

"For those of you who don't know me, I'm Vince O'Malley. I'm the SAIC at the bureau's Missoula office. First off, I'm sorry our efforts to recover President Longwood proved unsuccessful. I can assure you that the divers scoured every inch of that lake before determining that the president must be under the thousands of tons of rock that fell from the walls of an underwater canyon during the attack. Unfortunately, the body has been deemed unrecoverable because of the extreme danger of additional landslides."

O'Malley paused a moment, as if waiting for any comments or questions, then continued when none were voiced. "While the original eight suspects are dead, we still have an ongoing search for the mortar teams. We detained every adult male and female from Noxon associated with the Montana State Militia. That's the small mobile home community where the dead suspects resided. We accounted for every person living there, and none had ammonium perchlorate residue on their person. Firing mortars would certainly have left behind such physical evidence detectable by our equipment. If the mortar teams were from Noxon, they're very good at concealing that, and I didn't find any of those individuals to be bright enough to do that. We also investigated every aspect of their lives—finances, criminal records, military history, school records—everything was examined. We even polygraphed them. Aside from generally being ignorant anti-government types, none appear to know any more about the assassination than the general public, and none were even aware that their eight dead friends were involved."

A black woman wearing a windbreaker with *Secret Service* stenciled on the back stood and asked, "Excuse me. If those missing suspects didn't come from Noxon, do you have any other leads on them?"

"Good to see you again, Agent Washington, and yes, we do. I was just getting to that. There was a gunfight at a ranch in the valley east of the lake yesterday. I should first say that such an event is uncommon in these parts. Even more uncommon was that ten people were killed and the place was burned to the ground afterward."

"Did you say *ten* people were killed?" Pearson asked.

"That's correct, sir. The thirty-year-old son of the rancher survived, though he's in a coma, so we haven't been able to talk to him. As far as the bodies recovered at the scene, we had to use dental records for identification because of the intensity of the fire and the destruction of the remains that occurred when the home collapsed. We were only able to confirm the identities of the ranch owner, the local sheriff, and two paramedics who responded after a nine-one-one call from that rancher. The other six bodies remain unidentified. None has a fingerprint, DNA, or dental record on file."

"That's quite unusual," Pearson interjected, "especially for the type of individuals who get in gunfights. What connects this shooting to the assassination?"

"Well, to be honest, the connection's a bit tenuous." O'Malley paused again. "Let me explain. We recovered 7.62mm bullets from each of the four bodies we were able to identify, and though we did recover the sheriff's .44 caliber revolver, someone removed the weapons that fired those 7.62mm rounds from the scene before the fire was set. As I said, six of the remains are still unidentified, and a single head shot from the sheriff's revolver killed four of them, and not execution style. That handgun was found twenty feet from the sheriff's body, and his own men admitted he was a terrible shot, so it's unlikely he killed those men. One unidentified body has a single 7.62mm head wound, and although 7.62mm rounds also killed the sixth man, they were all in his chest."

"So the link to the assassination is the ammo," someone stated.

"It was the same caliber that was used against the Secret Service agents at the lake the day before."

"Earlier, you mentioned the rancher's son survived," said Pearson. "Is it possible he's one of your missing mortar suspects?"

"I don't believe so. He, too, suffered a 7.62mm round in the shoulder and a glancing head wound. He apparently came to and managed to crawl out of the house before the fire engulfed the place. Now, someone took the paramedics' van and deactivated its GPS locator. That's not an easy thing to do. Sheriff's deputies discovered that van two hours ago in an abandoned garage a few miles north of the ranch. The lab folks were unable to recover any fingerprints or DNA from it, but it did have several bullet holes in it, and a 7.62mm round was found in its dashboard. We also found two sets of shoe prints in the dirt leading from the back of the garage to an off-road vehicle. Additionally, there were tracks in the dirt from the van's gurney, indicating a third person was there and unable to move on his or her own. The off-road vehicle's tire tracks left that garage headed north and turned off the paved road again a few miles up. It then traveled lumber company roads to an old highway, where it vanished."

"Do you think the rancher might have been involved in what occurred at the lake?" someone asked.

"Maybe, but the local authorities know the family well and are emphatic that both father and son were not the type to associate with the MSM. However, the rancher had a second son, and we learned that he was in an alter-

cation with two MSM members a few days ago."
O'Malley punched an unseen button, and a face appeared
on a separate screen.

Devlin's pulse raced at the sight of the man he had
seen staring up at his Predator from the mountainside.

"This is the other son, Samuel Calder. He's twenty-
eight years old, and—"

A new voice interrupted O'Malley from the back of
the room. "Excuse me. I'm Special Agent Nick Peppers.
I'm normally assigned to the New York Organized Crime
Task Force. I saw that man on a sidewalk in New York
City four days ago. He was in the company of Anthony
Deluca, the son of mob boss Salvatore Deluca."

Every person in the room, including O'Malley,
seemed stunned or confused at Peppers's statement.

"I tried to identify him," Peppers added, "but the facial
recognition program had a Pentagon block, and I was
transferred to this task force before I could pursue the
matter."

O'Malley considered this for a moment. "To be honest, I'm at a loss as to any connection Samuel Calder
might have with the mob. However, Calder did do five
years in Attica on a felony assault and manslaughter conviction. They released him last week. Before he went to
prison, though, Calder was a Navy SEAL with several
combat tours, including some black ops stuff. His identity
was blocked by the Pentagon a long time ago because of
his involvement in those covert operations."

Devlin was almost panting. He now knew exactly who
his enemy was and that he had a prison record and some
type of connection to the New York mob. He also knew
that many in the room were undoubtedly assuming that
Calder—possibly the Mafia—was likely involved in the
assassination. *How quickly things change*, he thought,
pleased with this strange turn of events.

O'Malley went on after a brief pause. "I'm certain Samuel Calder is somehow mixed up in all of this, and it's not entirely inconceivable that he could be one of our missing mortar men. He would definitely know how to use one. I must point out, though, that New York *released* Calder from prison. They didn't parole him. The court vacated his conviction and not because of some loophole. According to the New York attorney general, a recovered video proved the cops involved in Calder's arrest lied to cover their own asses after they molested Calder's pregnant wife and one of them drunkenly shot and killed her. Calder did five years of very hard time on a frame job."

Someone called out, "Maybe he's one of the six bodies you can't identify, since his identity was blocked."

O'Malley's head shook. "No, Calder's DNA was made available to us by the Pentagon. He's not one of the six. I also find it difficult to believe that a highly decorated Navy SEAL, even one with Calder's prison history, would associate with a group everyone seems to dismiss as drunkards and idiots. Remember, Calder was in an altercation with two of them, and the deputy involved stated that Calder said he didn't know them and had returned to the area just that day. Frankly, I can't prove it yet, but I think the six unidentified bodies are our missing mortar men, and based on the way five of them died—a single gunshot to the head—Calder was likely responsible for killing them and took off in the van."

"You said the rifles that fired the 7.62mm ammo were missing," said Pearson. "Do you think Calder took those weapons?"

"I don't believe so. Assuming he was there, I think he left before the fight was over. The local cops swear Samuel Calder would not have left his brother lying in the yard injured or burned his own home down. In all likelihood, Calder thought his father and brother were dead when he took off in that van, and someone else still there scooped up the weapons before torching the house. Remember, the cops pulled a 7.62mm round out of the van's dashboard, indicating those weapons were likely shooting at him as he left."

"That's a lot of conjecture, Vince," said Pearson, "but if that's the case, you have at least one more suspect than you thought: whoever shot at the van and took the weapons. In addition, if Calder wasn't involved in what happened at the lake, why is he hiding? Why didn't he go to the authorities after he escaped the ranch?"

"I have no idea, sir. That's why we need to find him. We could have this all wrong. We also have no idea who was on that gurney or driving the off-road vehicle."

Devlin's overall impression was that the FBI did not have any evidence that could lead to his mercenaries' involvement. But he suspected the Calder brothers might be able to provide that evidence if they were, in fact, at the lake.

When the briefing ended, Devlin pushed his way through the departing crowd. He wanted to get to Special Agent Peppers before the FBI man made it aboard one of the quickly filling elevators. He did, but Peppers was on his cell phone throughout the ride down.

As the lift reached the main floor, he hung up, and Devlin maneuvered closer. "Agent Peppers, I'm Tom Devlin, DIA. Got a minute?"

"Sure," Peppers responded affably and stepped aside as the elevator crowd departed.

"I was wondering if you had any idea what Calder might have been doing with a New York mobster."

"After O'Malley identified him, I called one of my people and had her check out his prison record. Deluca did a stretch in Attica at the same time Calder was there.

That has to be how they knew each other, though Calder did his entire time there in maximum security."

"Is your task force still in effect?"

"I wish, but no. My supervisor shut it down when I transferred to this task force. I am going to keep an eye on Tony Deluca when I get back, though, in case Calder reaches out to him again."

Devlin shook the agent's hand. "Well, thanks for the info."

From the back of his staff car, Devlin pulled his satellite phone and called Armstrong. "You said there were no survivors at that ranch except the two who escaped."

"That's right, sir."

"You're wrong. They have one at the local hospital. It's the older of the rancher's two sons. I'd wager those brothers are the two from the mountain. Get someone over to that hospital and get rid of him."

"Before we do, do you want us to find out if that really was Longwood the other one carried off?"

"You can't. This guy is in a coma. Just kill the son of a bitch before he comes out of it and starts talking. We can't risk it."

"Okay, I'll send a man over right away. We'll have to steal a vehicle, though. None of us have a Montana driver's license, and I don't wanna chance a cop stopping an unlicensed electric dirt bike with my guy carrying a silenced pistol."

"Just get it done. The guy's name is Calder. The other brother's the one who got away, but I have a lead on how to find him, too. Now that the FBI has called off their search at the lake, as soon as your man is done, I'll arrange for what's left of your team to get back here."

Next, Devlin called Frank Crowley. "Get your men together. I have a snatch-and-grab I think you might enjoy, but you'll need to move quickly or the FBI may beat you to it."

CHAPTER 21

How's he doing?" O'Malley asked the nurse.

"With comas, you never know. I've seen people open their eyes and smile, then go right back into it. What are you testing for?"

Tom Craftman had accompanied O'Malley to the Sanders County Hospital. "He's testing for ammonium perchlorate." O'Malley answered as he swabbed Mark's hands. "It's a residue left after firing munitions."

O'Malley examined the swab and dropped it in an evidence bag. "I'm not expecting to find anything. I'm just covering all the bases so I can rule him out as a suspect."

Craftman touched a tube snaking under the covers, and the nurse said, "That's a feeding tube."

"Has anyone come by or called about him?" O'Malley asked.

"No."

"Well, his brother's missing, and we think he may have been at the ranch when all this happened. He's only a person of interest right now, but please call nine-one-one right away if he shows up."

"Okay." The two lawmen left the private room as the nurse began to check the machines connected by wires to Mark's still form.

Outside, Craftman said, "I gotta get home. My wife's probably pissed at me being so late, especially after an all-nighter."

"I hear ya. I gotta drive all the way back to Missoula."

As Craftman slipped behind the wheel of his unmarked sheriff's car, parked next to O'Malley's, the FBI agent dropped his keys. He bent down for them just as a set of headlights pulled into the small lot.

Craftman said, "Hey, O'Malley, it's too late for visiting. Maybe it's Calder."

O'Malley found his keys but stayed down when he heard Craftman whisper, "What the hell?"

The arriving vehicle was a pickup with one man inside. O'Malley watched him exit the truck and toss a cigarette as he headed inside.

"That's not Calder, and he didn't seem injured," O'Malley said.

"I didn't recognize him, but I do recognize that pickup, and he ain't its owner. It belongs to a friend of mine who owns a chicken farm over by Noxon." Craftman pulled his satellite phone as O'Malley stood and joined him.

"Jim, this is Tom Craftman."

O'Malley heard an indistinct male voice respond, then, "Yeah, I know it's late. Sorry about that. I need to ask if you've sold your truck."

There was another undecipherable response, and Craftman exhaled in frustration. "Is your damn truck in the yard, Jim?"

O'Malley heard cursing coming through the phone.

"I'll call you back in a few minutes. Your truck's right here in front of me."

Craftman hung up, and the pair walked back into the hospital, guns drawn.

"I didn't see which direction he went," Craftman said. "I'll check the nurse's station."

"I'll check the pharmacy," O'Malley said and headed down the semi-dark hallway.

The pharmacy lights were off and its door secure, so O'Malley headed for the nursing station.

There was nobody around, but as he scanned the empty hallway, he heard *muted pop* and something thumped against the wall directly across the hall in Mark Calder's room.

O'Malley rushed toward the door as a woman's voice started to scream and a second *pop* sounded and she fell silent.

He slammed the door's lever-action handle down with one hand and pushed into the door's widening gap with his pistol pointed forward.

His first sight was the nurse lying on the floor, a pool of blood spreading beneath her white uniform. A millisecond after, he spotted the stranger standing at the foot of Mark Calder's bed, a suppressor-equipped pistol gripped in both hands. The stranger's face and weapon started turning his way.

Boom!

The stranger's body flew back toward the windows, and slumped to the floor. Stepping inside, O'Malley found Craftman sitting against the wall behind the door. O'Malley knelt at his side, found a pulse, and located a vest under the bullet hole in the deputy's shirtfront. He heard someone calling a woman's name outside the room.

"In here!" he yelled.

The door burst open, and the night orderly and staff doctor rushed in. The orderly froze in place while the doctor quickly knelt next to the nurse.

"She's dead," the doctor announced as he looked up at

O'Malley's still-smoking pistol. "What the hell did you do?"

"Holy shit," the orderly blurted out.

The doctor looked up at him, and then to where he was staring. He jumped up and approached the obviously dead man still holding his suppressed pistol in one hand. "Who the hell is that?"

"I have no idea," O'Malley answered.

Craftman moaned, and the doctor went to him. A few moments later, Craftman was struggling out of the Kevlar that had saved his life. "Now my wife's really gonna be pissed."

ぐぁぐぁ

"That's right, nothing," O'Malley told Craftman on the phone the next morning. "The guy's a ghost, like the six from the ranch. There was no DNA match from the military or the national prison registry, and no fingerprint match from NCIC. We even tried Interpol, and we can't do dental because I blew his damn head apart."

"What about his weapon?"

"The serial numbers were etched out with acid."

"Well, I'm stumped, and I got a helluva bruised chest. I didn't have time to see his face, just his gun turning on me. I confirmed he stole the pickup from Jim Mason's chicken farm. Jim leaves the keys in it so he doesn't lose 'em. There ain't anybody else living anywhere near there, though, so if he ain't from Noxon, where'd he come from?"

"Well, he definitely isn't from Noxon. We've accounted for every resident there."

"I guess we're just going to have to wait for Mark Calder to come out of the coma and hope he can shed some light on all of this."

"We need to put him in protective custody and move him down here," said O'Malley. "I don't know what his role is in all this, but the fact that someone tried to kill him at his home and again in your hospital tells me he's definitely involved in more than ranching."

"Okay, I'll have him moved down there right away. Take care of him."

"You have my word."

CHAPTER 22

Sam snapped awake at Louie's touch on his shoulder.

"We're almost at the island."

"What time is it?"

"The pilot says local time is four-thirty a.m."

"What about customs?"

"That ain't a problem," the big thug said as he swung on a shoulder holster. "Half the island works for Salvatore, and the other half wants to."

Sam glanced out a window and saw only darkness and a smattering of lights as the jet banked toward a runway that suddenly lit up. They touched down with a squeak of the tires, and taxied toward a hangar at the far end of the airfield. As they moved across the tarmac, the runway lights went out, and no lights were on in any other structure. Even the small terminal building was dark.

Louie opened the side door as the engines quieted. The first thing Sam noticed was warm air and the smell of the ocean. *Long way from Montana*, he thought as a cargo van pulled into the hangar. Its driver climbed out and opened a sliding side door, revealing an ambulance gurney inside. Before he could ask, Louie said, "I called ahead."

Sam carried Longwood to the gurney, and they were off, the lone guard at the airport gate paying them no heed. "Where are we again?" he asked.

"This is Antigua," the driver answered with a heavy Bronx accent. "It's the bigger of two islands that make up the island state of Antigua and Barbuda. It's windy right now because Hurricane Betsy just went through, but Salvatore's villa is in a cove on the western side of the island, the Gulf side, and the hills around it block the Atlantic breeze there."

Louie announced, "Mr. Calder, this is Bruno. He's a good driver, a lousy cook, and a terrible shot."

"Hey, watch it," Bruno responded. "You know I got that dyslexia thing." He glanced over his shoulder at Sam. "I accidentally shot him once, and the big gumbah never lets me f'get about it."

"Hey, you shot me, asshole."

"Okay, okay, but I wasn't aiming at you."

Sam realized the two were comrades-in-arms, so to speak, and on good enough terms for friendly banter. *I remember living in that world with my brother and fellow SEALs a million lifetimes ago.* The thought brought a wave of sadness.

The van cut across the island along a winding road cluttered with palm fronds and other debris left by the recent storm. After a twenty-minute ride, they began to descend a hillside. The now clear sky and full moon gave Sam a hint at the cove's size, and he got an elevated view of the well-lit grounds below.

It looked enormous and appeared to be the only residence in the inlet. He could also make out a wide beach with a lighted dock and boathouse framed against the bay. After the van passed a front gate that opened as they approached, Sam looked out at an expansive, manicured lawn. Widely spaced palms with flowering plants surrounding their bases were scattered across the mowed grass, along with more hurricane debris waiting for cleanup.

A wide, circling drive brought them under a large portico in front of the opened double front doors of a single-story structure resembling a Spanish hacienda. Two heavyset women wearing brightly patterned sarong-style dresses stood there to greet them. To Sam, it seemed as if they were arriving at an island resort.

As Louie and Sam unloaded the gurney, Bruno announced, "The one on the left is Michelle, and the other is Marlene."

Sam nodded at the identical women, each in her mid-twenties and pushing two-hundred pounds.

"They're my daughters, so hands off," Bruno said menacingly, then added with a jovial smile, "Just kidding. Are you married? If not, they come with a dowry, and it's a big one if you take both."

Louie laughed raucously as the twins cajoled their father to stop. They rolled the gurney down the entry hall to a bedroom off a large living room with double-width, sliding glass doors overlooking a stone veranda and the bay below.

As Sam gently moved Longwood onto the room's wide bed, the blanket fell away, revealing the missing forearm. No one commented on the sight. Sam's earlier trepidations began to fade into a more comfortable sense of calm after that. *We should be safe now*, he thought.

The group left Sam alone and closed the door as they departed. After locking it, he uncovered the president's head and examined him, finding a strengthening pulse and better color in his face. The injured arm appeared to be doing fine, too. It showed no signs of bleeding or even the redness of infection.

Sam was concerned about the fact that he'd been

forced to keep Longwood doped up on morphine for more than twenty-four hours. But he thought Longwood should be able to recover now that they were out of harm's way. Sam had just finished re-bandaging the man's head when someone knocked. He opened the door to find Bruno with the bag of medical supplies.

"The other bag was garbage. I threw it out," he explained.

While Sam went about administering fluids and antibiotics to Longwood, Bruno said, "Tony called, so I arranged for a doctor to come by this morning. He's good." He pulled up the bottom of his island shirt, revealing two scars Sam recognized as healing gunshot wounds.

"Hunting accident?"

"Yeah, it was something like that. Anyway, Salvatore let me come down here with my girls so Doc Stephano could patch me up without the cops poking their noses into it."

Louie came through the open door. "The girls made a nice breakfast, Mr. Calder."

"Sounds great, and please call me Sam, fellas."

"Okay, Sam. How's your friend?"

"He's doing fine, but I need to keep a close eye on him. He's been on a morphine downer for a while. He just needs to sleep it off."

As if Sam's words were a challenge, a low moan escaped Longwood's lips just then. Sam leapt to his side, whispering, "Relax. You're safe." That quickly, Longwood was asleep again, but Sam knew the man had to have a concussion, and the fact that he was beginning to wake was a good sign.

With the president resting comfortably, Sam joined the others in the kitchen for a meal of fried Italian sausage, seasoned scrambled eggs with onion and tomato, and some strange but delicious island fruit.

Famished, he devoured everything placed before him.

After checking on the still-sleeping president again, he retreated to the villa's large veranda overlooking the bay. He wanted to better assess his surroundings now that dawn was breaking. Then he returned to the veranda, picking up several loose palm fronds on the way, and sat on a comfortably cushioned lounge chair.

Louie appeared with two filled glasses in hand. "I know it's early, but this is that rare Sambuca from Salvatore's private stock. It goes down real good after a meal."

They sipped and then Sam asked, "How long have you been with the Delucas?"

"I grew up in the neighborhood with Salvatore. I married his sister, but she's gone now—breast cancer."

"I'm sorry. So you're actually Tony's uncle."

"I am. Did you see your family while you were in Montana? I remembered you mentioned them to Salvatore at the club."

The question pained Sam. "Yeah, I saw them," he said, his voice subdued. "I think I'll grab a shower and clean up now."

"There are clothes that should fit you in the closet next to your friend's room. I leave them here for when we come down."

"Thanks," Sam said, setting his empty glass on a table.

He showered and dressed in slacks and an island shirt from Louie's collection, then went to check on the president. Surprisingly, he found the man lying as he had last seen him, except both eyes were partially open, and his bandaged head turned to face him as he entered the room.

"Good morning, sir."

His lips barely moving, Longwood only managed to mumble something unintelligible before his eyes closed and he drifted off again. Sam checked his vitals, finding the pulse steady. At that moment, Bruno entered, accompanied by an older man carrying a medical bag. "This is Doctor Stephano."

With Sam looking on, the doctor examined Longwood, leaving his head bandaged, as instructed. Afterward, he asked Sam, "Did *you* cauterize the amputation site?"

Sam nodded.

"He was lucky you knew what to do. You likely saved his life, and the wound is healing nicely. He does have a concussion, but his pupils are responsive and his vitals are steady. His blood pressure's a bit low, but that's to be expected. I can see the effects of morphine, too."

Sam explained what he had done.

"He needs to rest, but he should recover well. There will be significant discomfort at the amputation site. The morphine can help with that, but you don't want him on it too much longer. I'll leave some painkillers, but those are also addictive and should be used sparingly."

Bruno escorted the doctor out, and Sam returned to the veranda for another glass of the anise-flavored liqueur with Louie.

"If everything is settled with you here, I gotta head back to New York," Louie said before taking a final sip from his drink. "Bruno and the girls will be here to help you with your friend."

CHAPTER 23

W ho did you see?" Frank Crowley asked as his lookout climbed into the back of the large utility van parked in an alley one block from Salvatore Deluca's private club.

"They got here a few minutes ago." He held out his cell phone to display the photo on its screen.

Crowley studied the picture. "That's the old man and his brother. What about the son?"

"I didn't see him. Those other three are younger, but they look like muscle for the old man. They had to unlock the front door, so there's probably no one else in there."

Crowley turned to the rest of his team sitting on bench seats on each side of the van. "Okay, we can't wait around for the kid to get here. Remember, the two old ones have to be taken alive. They probably know what we want to find out." He turned and tapped the driver's shoulder. "Let's go."

Crowley and the other eight men, dressed to resemble a SWAT detail, swarmed out the back of the van as it pulled to a stop in front of the exclusive mobster social club. There were few bystanders to watch the action. Crowley wasn't worried about witnesses, though. He knew they would be in and out quickly, and in another borough within minutes. *Besides*, he thought, *why call nine-one-one when you think it's the cops to begin with, and you know the people there are gangsters?*

The team spread out on both sides of the door as Crowley spotted someone peeking out its curtained window. One man immediately rammed a heavy penetrator into it, causing it to slam open. The assault force rushed inside, and Crowley followed, closing the door behind him.

Salvatore Deluca sat at a table sharing a frothy *cappuccino* with his brother. The other mobsters were scattered around the room but not drinking. The entire group seemed prepared when the door slammed open, and all five raised their hands in surrender, most of them smiling.

"May I offer any of you gentlemen a beverage?" asked Salvatore Deluca.

Crowley smiled evilly and pointed at Salvatore and Luigi. "Not those two."

The other mob men already had red dots on their chests and foreheads. In seconds, all three lay dead. The team swept up the surprised-looking brothers, hooded them, and rushed both out the door.

芝芝芝

"What kind of injuries does the other guy have?" Tony Deluca asked.

"I think I should tell you that in person," Louie said. "I'll be landing in less than an hour."

Tony let it go, acceding to his uncle's wisdom. "Okay, I'm headed over to the club. I'll send the car for you."

"I'll see you there."

As Tony hung up, the front door chimed. He knew that never happened without the building's door attendant calling up first. While guests used the private elevator, maintenance and service people were required to use the door, but never without prior notice.

Peering through its peephole, Tony was surprised to see one of the FBI agents who had been watching his father's club the past several months. The agent was not alone. Tony quickly placed his pistol in a hidden wall opening as someone knocked on the door hard.

"Who is it?"

"It's the FBI. Open the door, Deluca."

As a parolee, Tony knew he had no right to refuse. He released the locks, and the group of three men and one woman entered quickly.

The leader spun him around and shoved him against a wall for a frisking while the others rushed past with drawn pistols.

"Do you mind telling me why you're here?"

"I'm Special Agent Peppers. We have some questions for you."

"He's the only one here, Nick," an agent called out as Tony was escorted back to his sofa.

"I'd be happy to answer your questions, Special Agent Peppers," Tony said as he sat down. "Should I call my lawyer first?"

"Have you committed a crime?"

"Not that I'm aware of, but there are so many new laws these days, who can keep up?"

Peppers did not smile at the mobster's sarcasm. Instead, he held out a photograph. "Know him?"

"Sure, it's Sam Calder. I knew him in prison. I suspect you already knew that, though."

"Have you seen him recently?"

"Yeah, he came by after they let him out. We had dinner, and he left."

"Where'd he go?"

"He said he was going home, but he never said where that was, exactly."

"What *did* he say?"

"Just that he had family out west, in Montana, I think."

Peppers's cell phone rang, interrupting their conversation. He took a step back, answered it, and listened for nearly a minute.

Tony saw an uncertain look on the agent's face when he turned back to him. "Is something wrong?"

"NYPD just responded to a multiple homicide at your father's hangout."

"What?" Tony shouted, jumping to his feet.

Peppers held both hands out to block Tony's movement. "Hold on. Three men were found shot to death, but your father and uncle weren't among them."

Tony knew that meant the killers had taken them. *That makes no sense*, he thought. There were no ongoing grievances with any other faction of the mob or any other criminal organization in New York, for that matter. He knew none would be stupid enough to challenge his father after what he had done to the now-extinct Kingston Yardies. Everyone in their business understood that his father's response to even a minor offense would be far more violent than any reward they might hope to win. He was distraught, though, uncertain what to do, and surrounded by federal agents. "I need to use my cell phone."

"Go ahead."

He called his father's cell and got no answer. He tried his uncle next, with the same result. "Someone took them."

"How do you know? Maybe they weren't there or escaped."

"My father always goes to the club at this time, and with the same men. You know that, Peppers. You've been watching the place for months. Pop's not answering his cell now, and I talked to him an hour ago. If he or Uncle Luigi got away, they would have called me immediately. That means someone took them both. We need to go there."

"Okay, let's go."

✦✦✦

Tony followed Peppers's team into the crowded club through its shattered front door. A dozen NYPD uniforms and suited detectives were moving about the room, examining and photographing the three gruesome corpses splayed across its floor.

Tony angrily stared at a nearby detective he overheard telling another that someone had done them a favor by killing the mobsters.

Peppers apparently heard it, too. He flashed his credentials to the tactless cop and commanded, "Shut up or get out!"

Cowed to silence, the mouthy city homicide investigator slipped away as Tony stepped over the bullet-mutilated corpses of men he had known for years. "Whoever did this took them by surprise. Probably cops, or at least disguised as cops."

"How do you know that?" Peppers asked.

"Their guns are still holstered. Those three would have pulled on anyone smashing in the door, except cops." Tony stopped to stare at the two full cups sitting on his family table and knew he would never see either his father or his uncle alive again.

"I need to put you in protective custody, Deluca."

"Yeah, sure," Tony responded, feigning nausea from the gore, "but I gotta go to the can first. I think I'm gonna be sick." Without waiting for approval, he turned and walked briskly toward a hallway with a restroom sign.

Entering the men's room, he pushed open a hidden panel behind the closed door and disappeared into a dimly lit tunnel. He was in the basement of the building next door in fifteen seconds and exiting the back of the Excelsior Hotel across the street thirty seconds after that. He was already talking to Louie on his cell phone.

"This wasn't local talent or cops," Tony said. "They were hit with heavy caliber stuff, up close."

"Got any ideas?"

"I think it's about Sam Calder. Whoever did this took Pop and Luigi for information. The FBI came to my place looking for him, too."

"You know Luigi can't take the rough stuff, Tony. He'll break."

"I know."

"How do you want to handle it?"

"You stay with the jet. I'll call in some more of the boys and meet you when you land. Tell the pilots to plan to head back to the island right away and let Bruno know we're coming and why. Also, tell him to have Sam ready to leave as soon as we get there."

e∽e∽

Handcuffed to a chair beside his brother, Salvatore Deluca stared icily at the man before him. "Who are you working for?"

Ignoring the question, Frank Crowley backhanded the old man's face. "Where's Calder?"

"Who's Calder?"

Another backhand came quickly, even more stinging than the first. When Salvatore spat blood and a dislodged crown, Luigi struggled against his restraints, yelled something obviously profane in Italian, and spat at Crowley.

One of Crowley's men slammed his fist into the side of Luigi's head, and Crowley asked Salvatore the question again.

Salvatore remained silent.

"I know you assholes think you know how to torture people. But after that little outburst just now, I'm not sure your brother here is gonna enjoy watching what we're going to do to you next." He motioned to a pair of men standing nearby. "Let's try a more enhanced technique."

The two men tipped Salvatore's chair until its back lay flat on the floor. One draped a heavy towel across the mob boss's face, and the other turned on a faucet connected to a hose. He raised the hose over the towel, and cold water flowed over Salvatore's covered face.

Already breathing heavily from Crowley's blows, Salvatore began gagging.

"Now ain't this fun?" Crowley taunted.

Watching his brother tortured, Luigi began yelling again. He strained at his cuffs and tried to kick at the man nearest him, the one who had struck him.

The hose routine was repeated, forcing Luigi to watch his brother suffer. After several seconds of simulated drowning, the hose and towel came away, and Crowley again asked where Calder was hiding.

Salvatore retched but remained otherwise silent.

The towel went back on, and the process began again. It lasted longer this time, but when given the opportunity to end it, surprisingly, the old man held fast.

Luigi did not, though. "Stop, I'll tell you!" he screamed.

"No!" Salvatore gurgled.

Crowley ended Salvatore's protest with a kick to the head that rendered him unconscious. He turned to Luigi and ordered, "Tell me! If you don't, I swear I'll push him to a heart attack."

Luigi hesitated only long enough for Crowley to order Salvatore repositioned for another bout with the towel and hose.

"We sent him to the island," Luigi said.

"What island?"

"Antigua. We got a place down there."

"Was he alone?"

"He brought another, an injured man."

"What sort of injury?"

"I don't know."

"How many men did you send with them?"

"There's only one there now."

CHAPTER 24

Devlin was angry when Preston Maddox, Mandrake's chief of staff, called to summon him to the White House. *I don't have time for any of Mandrake's bullshit right now*, he thought. Still, he responded, "I'll be there within the hour."

He had hoped to send Crowley's team to Antigua, but now felt rushed because of the White House call. Fortunately, what was left of Lloyd Armstrong's group was about to land.

He had been furious to learn that the man Armstrong sent to the hospital had not returned, but Armstrong reassured him that he had gone there himself and discovered that an FBI agent had killed a gunman, who in turn had shot a sheriff's deputy and a nurse. In addition, cops had been seen moving a patient out of the building. Devlin realized he would have to find out where they had taken the rancher and try again to have him silenced before he came out of the coma. *First*, he thought, *I need to deal with his brother, and, hopefully, Longwood.*

Devlin waited in the back of his staff car as Armstrong walked off the transport and summoned him over. In the car, he briefed the mercenary on the situation and handed him a large envelope. "These are satellite shots of the villa. Do you still have that hand-held GPS unit I gave you for Montana?"

"Yes, sir." He pulled it from his bag.

Devlin programmed it with the coordinates for the Antigua villa he'd managed to get from satellite imagery. "I was going to send Crowley to do this one, but I can't wait for him. I have to go to the White House, so you're going down there to finish this. I've arranged for another C-130 the Air Force believes is supporting a DIA exercise. It'll take you to Nevis Island. The pilot says flight time down there will be four hours because you have to go around a hurricane moving up the east coast of Florida. After that, it'll probably be another hour on the boats to reach your target. That'll put you at the villa just after midnight."

"Why not just land on Antigua?"

"A bunch of combat-equipped men at such a small airport would certainly alert Calder's benefactors. Nevis is only forty-five miles away and much more cooperative, for the right price. I've arranged for a pair of fast boats you can take directly to the bay where the villa is located. That GPS unit will guide you there. No one on Nevis will know where you went, and they won't ask questions when you return."

"I understand, sir."

"There's only one mob guy down there with Calder and the other. Do you have enough men left?"

"Yeah, I've got more than enough, especially when they don't know we're coming. We'll be back for breakfast."

Hoping he was right, Devlin dropped the matter. "Okay. If it turns out to be Longwood down there, be sure to weigh him down and sink him someplace deep. I can't have him floating up on some beach."

Armstrong climbed out of the car. "I'll slice him into chum and feed him to the sharks myself."

Devlin shut the door and ordered his driver to take him to the White House. He hoped Armstrong would find that the person with Calder was not Longwood and the whole nightmare would be over, but he couldn't shake the feeling that his plan might be slowly unraveling.

❧❧❧

As Armstrong's flight headed south, Devlin walked into the Oval Office, where Mandrake sat alone behind the desk.

"Hello, Tom, have a seat. I asked you to come by because I have a favor to ask of you."

"Just name it, Mr. President."

"Langford's fighting me about cancelling those talks between the Jews and the A-rabs."

Devlin saw an opening. "Fire her."

Mandrake's silence indicated that he was considering Devlin's suggestion. "You know, I was thinking about doing just that, and I do plan to install my own cabinet. I was only concerned that it was too soon after…well, you know."

"*You're* the president now, sir. You have to do what *you* believe is best for the nation, regardless of what others may think. You know I'll back you."

"Thank you, Tom. You've been a great source of support and counsel."

"You need your own people around you now, Mr. President—people who think about things the way you do, not the way Longwood did. You need a new cabinet, sir, and I'd also recommend a new CIA director."

"What's wrong with Calvin Stone?"

"He was very supportive of Longwood's Middle East policies, especially the peace talks. I'm not sure you can trust him to support your views any more than Langford."

"You may be right. I don't really know Stone. By the way, the Secret Service director resigned this afternoon."

"Did you accept her resignation?"

"I certainly did. Longwood died on her watch. I'm not going to let her get me killed, too."

Devlin's mind screamed, *You're such an idiot*, but he said, "I understand, sir."

"You know, to tell you the truth, there's a lot more pressure to this job than I imagined. It's a real hornet's nest around here, and there are too many godless nonbelievers running amok. I could really use someone like you, a God-fearing man, to help keep my ship of state afloat, so to speak. In fact, that's the favor I wanted to ask of you."

Devlin held his breath and remained silent. He sensed an even bigger opportunity coming.

"You and I think alike, Tom, and I trust you. How would you like to be my vice president?"

Devlin was stunned. He had intended to blackmail his way into the VP job by faking evidence that Mandrake was part of the assassination plot, which would explain why he had avoided going to the lake. *Jesus, he's handing it to me on a platter*, he thought. "I'd be honored to serve, Mr. President."

"That's terrific. I'll bet you sail through confirmation. There can't be any skeletons in your closet, being a three-star general and all. You'll have to retire from the Army first."

"That can be arranged overnight, sir. My deputy, Major General Conway, can take over the agency in my stead."

"Terrific. Let's make it happen."

Devlin left the White House feeling exalted.

I'm about to be elevated to the second most powerful position in the nation and the ideal spot for my next move, he thought. *Plus, I'll still have the DIA under my control.*

Lee Conway had demonstrated no initiative while serving as his second-in-command at the agency, preferring to spend his days on the golf course and nights trolling area bars. Devlin recalled how he had encouraged him to do just that. He had wanted no interference as he manipulated DIA assets. He had even gone so far as to have Conway seduced by a couple of fifteen-year-olds and secretly filmed in the act. After that, the married father of four was *his* man, and even if he somehow uncovered Devlin's mercenary operation, he would never open his mouth for fear of exposure.

Besides, he thought, *I can always set Crowley on him.*

CHAPTER 25

Sam was about to check on Longwood when Bruno rushed up.

"We got a problem. Louie just called. Someone killed Salvatore's crew and took him and Luigi."

"Does he know who did it?"

"I asked, and he said no, but he said the FBI came to Tony's place looking for you."

"Did he tell them where I am?"

"No way Tony would tell the feds anything. He's on his way down here now with some of the boys, and he wants you ready to leave on the jet as soon as they get here. We got maybe four or five hours."

"So Tony thinks someone's coming?"

"Yeah, it looks that way."

Sam was disappointed they would have to leave the comfortable island villa, but he understood that to be the safest move for the president. Then he considered that, if whoever had taken the Deluca brothers was after him and had been able to coerce his location from their captives, they were likely already on the way there, too. He had no time frame with which to estimate who would arrive first, so he decided to play it safe. "Are there any weapons here?"

"Are you kidding? Come on."

Bruno led Sam to a door in the kitchen that opened into a pantry. Behind a false wall was an armory of sorts, with handguns, shotguns, and AR-15 rifles on two of the walls, as well as extra magazines, ammunition, and knives arrayed on a long table next to a stack of Kevlar vests. Bruno opened a wooden box, revealing a dozen hand grenades lying in straw.

"How did you guys get your hands on those?"

Bruno shrugged. "Hey, stuff falls off trucks in Jersey all the time."

"Is there anywhere on the island we can go that's more defensible than this place?"

"I don't know. I've only been down here once before, and I never had any reason to leave the villa except to go to the airport."

"Okay, just in case the bad guys get here first, you need to get your daughters someplace safe until the jet lands. I'm going to come up with a defensive plan."

"Mind me asking why these people want you bad enough to attack someone like the Delucas?"

"I took something they want."

Bruno nodded, stuffed a pistol in his waistband, and walked off.

Sam slipped on a Kevlar vest, shoved a .45-caliber pistol in its built-in holster, slung an AR-15 over a shoulder, grabbed two extra magazines for each weapon, and secured a long-bladed knife to a sheath against his right calf. Geared up for battle, he decided to scrutinize the villa more carefully.

First he walked the unfenced perimeter, pleased that, aside from the widely spaced palms, there was no solid cover within a hundred feet of the house. He next considered an enemy's probable line of approach. He knew the bay would have been his choice, but he wondered if the enemy would think that way. *Probably*, he surmised, *since an armed force landing at the airport and moving on the only road across the island would likely garner someone's attention and possibly provide warning.*

He walked through the house next, locking all the windows and hurricane shutters. He knew that would not stop a determined enemy, but it would slow them down. While he was doing that, he saw Bruno and the twins pull out in the van. With the girls gone, Sam went about setting trip-wired grenades between the palms.

Lastly, he walked down to the boathouse. Inside, he found a luxurious thirty-five-foot cabin cruiser with a tall observation deck. He checked that its fuel tanks were full and the ignition key for its V-12 engine was there. He turned the key, and the engine started smoothly. He turned it off and hid the key behind a seat. *If necessary*, he thought, *I can take Longwood out to sea.* He knew that would be a good idea only if the enemy did not have access to faster boats. If they did, the open ocean would be a killing ground aboard the mostly fiberglass vessel.

Once he was satisfied the estate was as prepared for attack as he could make it, Sam went to check on Longwood. He found him still unconscious and decided that he would have to keep him that way until they were safely off the island, especially if there was another gunfight. Reluctantly, he gave him a third morphine injection and moved him to the gurney for transport.

∽∾∽

Bruno had been gone for several hours, and Sam began to worry he had run off with the twins. To his relief, the van returned, and several men, including Louie, piled out its sliding door as Tony emerged from the front passenger door.

Tony was not smiling as he approached. "Trouble's coming, Sam, and I'm not certain, but I think it's you they want. I got word an hour ago that the cops found my father and uncle, both shot in the head."

"I'm sorry, Tony. It's not me they want, though—it's the man I brought here."

A nod was all Tony gave before stepping past Sam into the house. The rest followed.

"The girls are already on the jet," Bruno told Sam. "They'll help you with your friend. I'm staying here with Tony."

Tony led the group to the large living room overlooking the veranda and bay. The only light in the villa Sam had left on was in that room, and all could see that the sliding glass doors there had been shattered.

"What happened here?"

"I did it," Sam confessed. "I wasn't sure who would get here first. The broken glass crunches on the patio stone. It's dark out there, so it'll act as a sort of early warning system against someone sneaking up from that direction."

"Louie, get the boys spread out."

Before anyone moved, Sam warned, "Hold on a second. I set up some surprises around the property with that box of grenades. There are trip wires between the palms on the north and south sides of the house. I left the front and beach approaches clear. Once the grenades start detonating, the enemy is likely to set off more as they run for cover. Wait until that stops before coming out to fight."

"Bruno, go keep an eye out from the boathouse," Louie ordered, then directed the others where each should go.

"Do we know for certain that someone's coming?" Sam asked.

"No," said Tony, "but my source with the cops said

the assholes did that water-boarding crap on my old man before they killed him. They wouldn't have done that unless they wanted information. I figure it was you they wanted to know about, since we got no beefs with any other syndicate right now, and the feds are looking for you, too." Tony paused a moment. "Look, Sam, my uncle wasn't tortured like my father. If they didn't get what they wanted from my old man, they would have tortured Luigi, too. In any event, we can't take the chance. We need to be ready. Now, can you tell me why that man in the other room is worth so much killing? Louie told me something interesting about his injury."

Sam beckoned for him to follow and went to the bedroom, where he carefully removed the bandaging from the president's head.

A litany of rapid Italian followed, bringing Louie rushing into the room. He, too, stared at the face of the unconscious man before beginning his own declarations of astonishment.

Sam replaced the bandage on Longwood's head and said, "It's a long story, but the one everyone's been told isn't true. My brother and I were there. Those actually responsible attacked my family's ranch, killing several people, including my father and brother."

"I'm sorry to hear that," Tony said. "Do you know who this enemy is?"

"No. I thought they were a military unit because they have some high-end equipment usually reserved for special ops forces, but they lost several men during the attack at the ranch, even though they had better weapons and the element of surprise on their side. I think they have military backgrounds, but they don't have a good skill set. They're probably just soldiers turned mercenary. Still, don't underestimate them."

"Well, they won't have the surprise thing going for them here," Tony said. "We will."

"Even so, I'm not comfortable risking him," Sam said, nodding toward Longwood.

"Take him and go in the van. My jet will get you both off the island. I told them where to take you. It's all set."

"What about you?"

"We're staying. I owe the bastards for what they did to my old man and uncle."

Part of Sam wanted to stay and take his own revenge, but he remembered his promise to his father. Instead, he began pushing the gurney toward the hallway.

Bruno rushed in then. He smashed the lone light and breathlessly announced, "A couple of boats without running lights just came in fast and beached near the boathouse."

Not wanting Longwood caught in the open, Sam realized it was too late to run and reversed direction. "Could you see how many there were?" he asked.

"I didn't count 'em, but there has to be at least a half dozen with two boats."

"Okay," Sam said, taking charge. "They hit our ranch from the front and back, but I expect they'll come at us here from every side. They'll come in quietly to start, probing to ensure they have the element of surprise. Let the booby traps deal with that. When that's over, they'll hit us hard. Remember, these guys don't take prisoners."

"We don't, either," Tony declared as he and the other two rushed off.

Sam knew the mobster's bravado was meaningless, given what Sam expected was about to happen, but his only option now was to fight.

He lifted Longwood from the gurney and laid him on the floor against an inner wall. He covered him with the bed's mattress, pulled a sofa from the living room in front of the bedroom door, and crouched behind it. Several quiet minutes ticked off in the dark house before a thunderous explosion sounded outside.

Another followed almost immediately on the opposite side of the house. The din of falling debris pelting the roof hadn't ended before two more of the trip-wired explosives went off. After a brief pause, gunfire erupted from what seemed every direction.

Sam could discern AR-15 rifles and shotguns firing, and figured those had to be Tony's men, since the enemy was likely still using suppressed weapons. *That*, he thought, *is how I can judge how many of the gangsters stay in the fight.*

He hunkered down and peered around the side of the overturned sofa toward the broken glass doors at the veranda. His vision quickly adjusted to the dark, and he spotted an armed man in silhouette emerging from the bushes on the beach side of the veranda. The intruder began creeping across the patio. Between gunshots, Sam heard crunching glass and saw the man pause briefly and continue forward. *You really aren't very good*, Sam thought as he raised his rifle.

Before he fired, one of Tony's men stepped into the living room from a hallway on the other side and opened up on the intruder with a pistol. He missed, and a suppressed burst from the veranda stitched several bullets across the mobster's chest in payback.

Flash-blinded now, Sam fired two rounds where he had seen the enemy's muzzle flash. He realized he had not hit his target when another suppressed barrage tore into the sofa. He stayed low and waited for the volley to end. Then he heard the *tink* of a magazine hitting the patio stone. With his enemy focused on reloading, Sam rose up, rushed forward, and put a bullet in the man's head at the corner of the patio.

Chaos seemed to reign for the next several seconds. Someone yelled something in Italian, and another grenade went off at the kitchen side of the house where Bruno had gone. When he heard no more gunfire from that direction, Sam suspected the enemy had likely breached the villa there.

Gunfire from the opposite side seemed to crescendo for a moment before going silent there, too. Sam sadly assumed that meant Tony and Louie were now down. Moving back to Longwood, he spotted the tip of a rifle coming into view from the hallway door to the kitchen. The suppressor at the end of its barrel confirmed it was not Bruno. As the silhouette of a head emerged, Sam put a single bullet through the side of it.

Another attacker quickly stepped over the headless corpse and sprayed the hallway and living room with suppressed automatic weapons fire.

Sam had already moved to the wall and raised his rifle to put him down, but before he could pull the trigger, a gunshot sounded, and the attacker fell to the floor atop the other that had fallen there.

A moment later, Bruno appeared in the kitchen doorway.

"I thought you were dead," Sam said.

"They did, too. I only had one round left and there were two of them, so I faked it. Thanks for dropping that first one for me."

Sam handed Bruno his rifle, lifted the mattress, and hefted the president to his left shoulder. "I'm getting him out of here. We're too vulnerable in here."

"Where are you going?"

"I'll take him to the yacht and head out to sea."

Bruno cradled the rifle. "Good luck. I'll cover you."

Sam, holding his pistol in his right hand, moved around the shredded sofa into the living room. The large area was in flickering shadows, and some of the furniture was burning. Sam hugged the wall a moment, preparing to sprint across the veranda into the dark greenery along the beach path. He hoped for gunfire to mask his feet crunching the glass outside, but the earlier clamorous battle sounds had become sporadic now.

Then an AR-15 opened fire at the front of the house, and a pistol sounded from the side. Sam took advantage of the noise and moved rapidly onto the veranda. *If we can get to the cabin cruiser, we might have a chance*, he thought. Then he considered that the enemy might have disabled the boat. *If they did, I'll have to find a way to get to Tony's jet.*

Ten steps across the patio, Sam felt a searing pain burn across the front of his right thigh as he heard the telltale pop of a suppressed gunshot. He spun around just as a loud shot sounded from the living room, and a dark figure at the side of the house crumpled to the stone.

Bruno stepped into the doorway. "Go!"

Sam wheeled and limped off for the boathouse. Creeping along the dark trail as stealthily as he could, he listened to random gunfire continuing behind him. He was surprised that the gangsters had held their own as well as they had against what he assumed was a better-trained and better-equipped force. It crossed his mind that he might have misjudged the thugs' abilities. *After all*, he thought, *they've got a combat history of their own.*

At the dock, he could barely make out the silhouetted fast boats on the beach and debated taking the time to disable them to prevent pursuit. Then he realized the gunfire had ceased. It was quiet now. *No time.*

He entered the boathouse through the side door and stepped aboard the opulent cruiser. He laid Longwood on its teak deck and retrieved the ignition key. The moment he started the big engine, the enemy would know his location, if they didn't already. He would have to be ready to move out quickly. First he had to open the garage-style door at the front of the structure and hope nobody heard him do it.

He jumped back to the dock and ran to the pulley chain that opened the wide door. As he yanked down, it rose smoothly and quietly, but as he turned back, a tall figure stepped through the side door, cutting off his route.

He and the other man both raised their pistols and fired without hesitation, but Sam did so while dropping flat to the dock boards. His attacker's weapon had a suppressor, but Sam's did not, and his rapid shots were deafening and blinding inside the dark aluminum enclosure.

Sam felt another burning sting, this time across his left forearm, but continued to pull the trigger until his handgun emptied. He was flash-blinded again and unable to hear a thing now, but he suspected he had hit his target when the dock shook and he felt a splash of water.

Knowing the others had to have heard his pistol, Sam got to his feet and blindly rushed to untie the ropes attached to the boat's bow and stern. He was about to step aboard when strong hands gripped both of his ankles and yanked him off balance. He fell against the boat's hull and into the water. His attacker's grip shifted, first to his waist, pulling him under, then moving up and seizing his throat.

Under the dark water between the dock and boat, the men struggled. Sam sensed the bigger man's strength and knew his attacker was trying to drown him with brute force. He pretended to resist meekly and stopped struggling altogether, as if he were losing consciousness, and allowed his assailant to hold his neck a moment longer. As his unseen enemy continued squeezing, Sam raised his right ankle very slowly so his attacker would feel no movement. He pulled the knife from the sheath on his calf and rammed it into the man's fully exposed left arm-pit.

Sam heard the man gurgle a scream as the hands came loose from his neck. He pushed the knife in to its hilt so its eight-inch blade reached his assailant's throat, then twisted the handle a full ninety degrees before yanking it out. He quickly grabbed the man's uniform with his left hand and pulled him closer while repeatedly stabbing the torso until the body went limp.

Sam felt warm blood mixed with the cool saltwater. He knew by the stinging sensations that some of it was his. He surfaced, took a deep breath, and pulled himself onto the dock, pausing only a moment to catch his breath. Looking down as he stood up, he spotted the dead man's dark form just below the surface.

Sam struggled aboard the cruiser and hoped there was nothing in front of the boathouse he would not see in the dark. The instant the engine started, he gunned the throttle and ducked low, expecting enemy gunfire that did not come. The big boat's nose rose as it accelerated, and then dropped as it planed-out and reached its maximum speed of fifty-five miles per hour. At the mouth of the bay, knowing there would be nothing but open water ahead, Sam finally glanced back.

He wondered if the enemy was giving chase. He couldn't see any pursuers in the dark. Looking around, he spotted a few distant lights on the ocean and steered away from them as he motored farther from land and the battle, which must have ended. *Our best hope*, he thought, *is distance and darkness*. He was worried, though. He knew the enemy's boats were much faster than the cruiser. *We could be in trouble when daylight gets here.*

CHAPTER 26

Devlin was nearly frantic, having not heard from Armstrong and knowing it was now dawn in the Caribbean. Adding to his angst, the C-130 pilots had just contacted his command center and reported that they had waited as long as they could before diverting to an air base on Puerto Rico. Devlin knew his mercenaries had to have made it to Antigua hours ago, and Armstrong should have called shortly after that if things had gone as planned. *They obviously didn't*, he concluded.

He redialed the satellite phone Armstrong carried, again getting only a not-in-service message. He knew that likely meant the man had failed. He thought back on Armstrong's actions, trying to identify something incriminating that he had missed. The only threat he could think of was Armstrong confessing everything, but that would mean exposing himself to a lethal injection. *Of course, they might offer him some kind of deal*, Devlin considered. He knew the man would sell out his own mother if he thought it would be to his benefit. *If Armstrong isn't dead*, he thought, *I'm going to have to make him that way, quickly.*

The only other people who could cause trouble were Frank Crowley and the *Post* reporter, though all her testimony could prove was that Devlin had not been loyal to Longwood, and Mandrake already knew that. *Still*, he thought, *she has to go. I don't need any loose ends with my confirmation hearings coming.*

Devlin relaxed, knowing Crowley could eliminate the reporter's potential threat. The rest of his mercenary force was not a problem, since they had been misled to believe they were DOD contractors. Only their leaders, Armstrong and Crowley, knew their true employer.

He refocused on the positives. Even if Longwood lived, his own cabinet had constitutionally replaced him, and his injury would probably prevent him from being able to carry out the duties of the presidency, at least for a while. *If Mandrake can get his own cabinet in place quickly enough,* he thought, *they can ensure the job stays in Mandrake's hands—and after my next move, mine.*

He punched Crowley's speed dial and began speaking the instant it was answered. "I want the *Washington Post* reporter, Donna Jones, removed right away. She carries a laptop with her everywhere. Get it and destroy it."

"Yes, sir."

A sneer turned up the corner of Devlin's thin lips as he hung up. He began to put together a mental list of suitable cabinet secretaries he would recommend to Mandrake. People *he* could control. People he knew who would willingly trade their soul for a position of power and influence. *People like that naïve Ben Branson*, he thought. He chuckled as he tried to picture Branson's face when he finally realized there was no sniper hiding in the woods at the lake but mortars instead.

Devlin felt better about the situation as he went to his command center with another idea in mind. He knew he couldn't take the chance that someone there might see Longwood, but he desperately wanted to know what was happening, or had happened, on the island.

"Do we have any assets over the Caribbean at the moment?" Devlin asked the young lieutenant on duty.

"I'll check, sir," she responded as she brought up a program on her computer screen. "We don't, sir, but the CIA has a KH-14 satellite passing over that area in sixty minutes. It's customary to call the other agency for permission to access their hardware. Would you like me to do so?"

Devlin knew if she did, Calvin Stone might find out about it and would undoubtedly look into it. "Is that all that's available?"

"That's all that's available for at least four hours, sir. That's not a routinely viewed area."

Devlin handed her the GPS coordinates of the villa. "I'll contact Director Stone myself," he said, knowing he would not actually do so. "Notify me when you've accessed the bird and give me an overhead of that position when you get it. This is for my eyes only, Lieutenant. I don't want the feed going anywhere except my computer."

ഇന്ദ

Sam moved Longwood to a bed below deck and used the man's head wrapping to bandage his own wounds. Neither bullet had done more than slice a shallow groove through tissue.

Shortly after dawn, he climbed to the boat's observation platform and scanned the ocean as the cruiser bobbed in the swells. He debated moving farther away from the island he could still see on the horizon, knowing that even if the enemy had not heard his gunshots or the cabin cruiser racing away, they would have realized it was gone by now and would undoubtedly be searching for it.

Then another thought came. *Maybe they don't know*

what the cabin cruiser looks like. He scanned the horizon, spotting several vessels in the distance, but all looked to be commercial fishing boats or large freight haulers transiting the area. His was the only pleasure craft in sight and stood out like an oil platform on the nearly calm gulf waters. Still, he'd seen no sign of pursuit and was beginning to relax. A moment later, a dark object appeared on the horizon.

Sam quickly realized it was a fast-moving boat headed directly toward his position. He powered up the engine and sped away, changing course to see if it followed suit. It did, turning on a new intercept.

His pursuers were closing quickly, and Sam could tell the smaller boat was much speedier than the one he had commandeered. He remembered seeing two of them. Realizing they would almost certainly have radio contact with each other, Sam figured the other was likely coming his way now, too.

He stopped running and shut down the engine. With the rising sun behind them, he was able to make out two heads silhouetted over the windscreen of the rapidly approaching vessel. Since the cruiser's fiberglass hull provided little protection against bullets, he decided he would have to surprise them if he and Longwood were to have any hope of surviving the next few minutes.

He climbed down and crawled to the bow, slipped over the side, and hung by his fingertips, listening for the approaching engine to slow from its full-speed run. When he gauged it was nearly upon them, he let go and slipped into the ocean.

He dove down fifteen feet, hoping the enemy would not see him in the clear water, and swam under the cruiser and the enemy boat that was pulling up on the cruiser's port side. With the reloaded pistol in hand, he rose to the surface at the rear left corner of the enemy's boat. He decided that if he succeeded in killing the two men, he would riddle the cabin cruiser below its waterline with their rifles and race to the other side of the island in their boat. He hoped Tony's jet was still waiting.

Sam was surprised they had not already opened fire as he slowly pulled himself up one-handed to peer over the side, figuring they would be looking the other way. Ready to shoot, he froze.

Tony and Louie were standing at the controls, their backs to him.

"Sam, it's us," Tony yelled. "Come on out."

Sam pulled himself to their deck and asked, "What's up, fellas?" as he holstered his pistol.

Both mobsters jumped, startled.

"Damn! You scared the shit outta me!" Louie exclaimed.

Tony smiled. "Didn't I tell you he was off-the-charts good?" He patted the boat's steering wheel. "We taught those assholes what happens when you fuck with *la famiglia*. How do you like my new boat? I got two of 'em."

"I'm glad to see you guys made it."

"Two of the boys are dead, and the other two are shot up," Louie said, "but Dr. Stephano is there now. Bruno took a round in the leg, but he'll be okay. He says he's getting used to it."

"Sorry it took us so long," Tony said. "Bruno told us where you went, but we had to wait for daylight so we could spot you. Are you ready to head back?"

Sam jumped back aboard the cruiser.

❧❧❧

Back at the boathouse, a badly limping Bruno had already lined up the seven attackers' bodies and was readying them for disposal at sea.

Louie jumped to the dock and went to retrieve the gurney while Bruno and Tony began grabbing the corpses by their shoulders and boots and unceremoniously tossing them to the cruiser's rear deck.

Sam examined each as it plopped down, trying to determine who they worked for. They all wore first-rate camouflaged combat uniforms with built-in tourniquets in the sleeves and legs. None had rank or any other type of insignia, though all had high-and-tight haircuts, and several bore tattoos reflecting an affiliation with the Army or Marine Corps.

"These guys aren't active-duty military," Sam finally announced. "They're mercs." He noticed that one of them, a large black man with knife wounds he recognized, had a satellite phone attached at his waist. It was full of water and inoperative, but it worried him because it meant someone might have been monitoring the battle. *More could already be en route*, he thought. "I need to get the president away from here right away."

"What president?" Bruno asked.

Ignoring him, Tony asked, "Why don't you just turn him over to the feds?"

"I can't tell who these guys work for. If they're working for someone in the government—and I think they might be—there are probably a lot more of them. There may be some heavy hitters involved, too, being able to mount ops as rapidly as they have from Montana to New York to here. I don't want to hand the president to them on a serving plate. I need to get him somewhere safe until he can tell me what *he* wants to do."

"What president?" Bruno asked again.

Louie arrived with the gurney, which was stacked with body bags and cinder blocks. While the three mobsters bagged and weighted the enemy corpses, Sam retrieved Longwood from below and placed him on the gurney.

Bruno glanced at the man's uncovered face and calmly said, "Oh, *that* president. I thought he was—"

Tony cut him off. "F'get about it, Bruno. Just go get rid of these bodies and make sure you leave the bags cracked so the crabs can get in."

Sam started pushing the gurney up the path toward the villa. He heard the boat's motor start.

Tony rushed up to help push, saying, "We'll leave as soon as they get back."

"I need to bandage his head again," Sam said. "I don't want anyone else to recognize him."

❧❧❧

Devlin returned to the command center when the lieutenant notified him that she had tied into the CIA satellite about to pass over Antigua. A camera looking down from nearly one hundred miles above the island sent a live picture of the smoldering and heavily damaged villa directly to his monitor.

"How long do we have?" he asked as he zoomed in.

"The satellite will be beyond its field of view in five minutes, sir."

Devlin saw a van in front of the home and scanned west toward the ocean. He spotted two small boats pulled up onto the beach near a boathouse and knew they had to be Armstrong's. Suddenly a cabin cruiser pulled out from the boathouse.

He zoomed closer and counted seven body bags on its rear deck and noted that the two men at the helm wore civilian clothing.

Well, that clears up what happened to Armstrong, he thought with some relief, but then swung the camera back toward the villa and immediately saw something that made his stomach lurch. Two men were pushing a gurney up a path, and a man lying on it was missing the lower half of his left arm. "Shit!"

"Can I help you, sir?" the lieutenant asked from across the room.

Devlin ignored her as he zoomed in on the one-armed man's upturned face and quietly gasped. His mind immediately began trying to figure out how to destroy the man he was staring at without anyone finding out he was the same man supposedly buried under boulders in Pointer Lake.

The challenge seemed impossible at first. Then it dawned on him that he only had to figure out where they would go next. *They certainly won't stay there*, he thought.

The image fluttered and went out as he watched the gurney disappear into the villa. Devlin deleted the feed he had viewed and left the command center without another word.

CHAPTER 27

The Gulfstream was airborne moments after the survivors boarded. Tony spent most of his in-flight time on the phone, giving orders to one person after another as if he were a CEO. In a way, Sam realized, he was. *He runs a multi-million dollar enterprise that employs hundreds of people*, he thought. *He even has competitors, just no shareholders.*

Louie had fallen asleep right after takeoff and remained that way throughout the four-hour flight.

The twins huddled together in seats at the rear, both wearing headphones plugged into iPods and bobbing their heads in unison.

Longwood also slept soundly.

When they got to where they were going, Sam planned to transition him to the painkillers Doctor Stephano had provided. He hoped he had not already created an opiate-addicted president.

"How's he doing?" Tony asked as he sat down across from Sam.

"He's hanging in there. Are you sure it was a good idea leaving Bruno and the others back there? There might still be more bad guys headed there."

"Doc Stephano moved them to a safe place on the other side of the island. The jet will go back down to bring them and our guys' bodies back once things cool down."

"So, what's our game plan?" Sam asked.

"We'll be landing in a few minutes. The pilot had to fly farther west than planned to get around that hurricane moving up the coast."

"Where's it at now?"

"It's off the Carolinas, but it's only a level one."

"So where are we going?"

"We have a place in upstate New Jersey that should be safe."

"What about customs? New Jersey's not some Caribbean island."

"No problem; we're landing at Teterboro. We bring all kinds of things in and out of there all the time. We run nearly every union at the airport and have an arrangement, so to speak, with most of the customs agents. It's all been taken care of."

Sam wasn't surprised to hear that. "Look, Tony, I want to thank you for everything, and I'm sorry for what happened to your father and uncle."

"F'get about it," Tony said quietly, moving away to wake Louie.

The jet landed several minutes later and taxied into the hangar Sam remembered. The twins left in a waiting car.

"They're going to Bruno's place in the Bronx," Louie told Sam.

They moved Longwood to a van that had been left there with keys in the ignition. Louie took the driver's seat while Tony sat in the front passenger seat. Sam rode in the back with Longwood, who lay on a rear seat. Late in the evening, the van arrived at a gated driveway that led to a large, dark house not visible from the entrance.

As Sam carried the president up the steps to the front door, Tony punched a code into a security panel there.

"It'll only be us here," he said. "I didn't want any more men coming because the FBI's been following some of them. They're probably looking for me since I ditched them in New York."

Once Longwood was sleeping soundly in a second-floor bedroom, Sam joined the others in the kitchen. The two mobsters were drinking bottled beer, while Louie ate a thick sandwich.

Tony handed Sam a beer. "You should get some sleep. Louie will keep watch tonight, since he slept through the flight."

Sam felt his exhaustion taking control and only responded by swallowing a mouthful of alcohol. He set the bottle down and walked away, yawning. He was soon asleep in the room next to Longwood.

He woke after what felt like only minutes, but realized it had been much longer when he noticed daylight through a crack in the window curtains. When he glanced over at a clock on a nightstand, he saw that he had slept most of the morning. He jumped from the bed and rushed to check on the president. Longwood was awake and touching the bandage around his head with his one hand.

He glanced at his bandaged stump and turned to Sam at the door. "What happened to my—"

"I'm sorry, sir, but that was how I found you," Sam said as he approached. He pulled the ring from his pocket and placed it in Longwood's hand. "I removed that from what was left of it."

The president held his hand open, stared at his wedding ring, and slowly closed his fist around it.

"Is your wife—"

Longwood interrupted him with a questioning look. "She died just before my election, from a stroke."

"I'm sorry."

Longwood touched his fist to his bandaged face.

"There's nothing wrong with your head or face, other than a concussion and some lacerations. You're bandaged like that because I've been trying to keep people from knowing who you are. The other two men here know now, so I can remove it if you'd like."

"Please."

As Sam unwound the bandages, the president asked, "Why does my identity need to be guarded, and who are you?"

"Do you remember anything about what happened at the lake, sir?"

His head uncovered, Longwood's forehead wrinkled, as if he were trying to recall something. He finally said, "I remember fishing and…" His voice trailed off again.

Sam pulled up a chair and sat. "Okay, sir, my name's Sam Calder." He spent the next thirty minutes explaining everything that had occurred at the lake and afterward.

"There were no other survivors?"

"As far as I could tell, you and the guy I found with your arm were the only ones. He was messed up real bad, though, and we were in a hurry to get you out of there, so I don't know if he made it or not."

"Who's running the country?"

"According to the last news I saw on the island yesterday, they swore in the Speaker of the House as president."

"Mandrake is president?" Longwood sounded either amazed or sickened. Sam couldn't tell which.

"Sir, do you have any idea who might have been behind the attack? Were there any threats beforehand?"

"No to both questions."

"The FBI is saying a group called the Montana State Militia was behind it, and that some of them escaped and are still being hunted. Of course, *we* know that wasn't actually the case. The real killers were either military or military-trained with access to some first-rate equipment. In fact, I'm sure they were using a Predator I caught sight of on the way back to the ranch. That's the only way they could have known where Mark and I took you."

"I can't believe the military would…" His eyes closed.

Sam figured the man was still coming down from the morphine and had had enough for now.

Partially opening his eyes again, Longwood quietly said, "I'm sorry saving me has cost you so dearly, Mr. Calder. Maybe you should—"

Sam cut him off. "My father's last wish was for me to protect you and get the bastards responsible. I intend to do both, Mr. President."

Longwood only nodded.

"And please call me Sam, sir."

At that, Longwood's eyes closed again and did not re-open. Before his breathing became steady, he managed to say, "Okay, Sam."

In the kitchen again, Sam found Tony and Louie eating sandwiches and drinking coffee. He told them about Longwood waking while he enjoyed some food and drink with them. Afterward, he returned to Longwood's room, expecting to find him still asleep. Instead, he found him awake again.

"Sir, would you care for something to eat?"

"No, thank you. My arm hurts."

Sam pulled a small bottle from his pocket. "I have some painkillers if you'd like."

Longwood swallowed the proffered pill and grimaced at some agony Sam assumed originated from the missing limb.

"I still can't believe all of this has happened, and I'm somewhere in New Jersey being hidden from my own government by the mafia. Are you a member of that organization, Sam?"

"No, sir, but I *was* an inmate at Attica State Prison for five years until just a few days ago. That's where I met Tony Deluca."

Sam noticed Longwood's eyes widen, but he only said, "That explains why you didn't know about my wife's death. If I may ask, why were you incarcerated?"

"I was convicted of manslaughter in *my* wife's death and assault against three NYPD detectives." Sam saw the look on Longwood's face change from curiosity to concern, so he added, "It didn't really happen that way." As painful as it was, Sam felt Longwood needed to know the truth if he were to gain the man's trust, so he explained what had really happened, up to seeing Judith lying there.

"How the hell did *you* end up convicted for that?"

"To be honest, sir, everything after that moment is still kinda squirrely. I remember the old woman in the burqa standing there, screaming something in Punjabi, I think. Then police were everywhere—paramedics and ambulances, too. And a big mob formed behind yellow tape someone stretched across the sidewalk. Most of them were holding up cell phone cameras pointed at me. Even a few TV news cameras showed up. I found myself in the back of a police cruiser at some point, handcuffed, but the only other thing I remember clearly is watching some cop cover Judith with a white sheet. And what happened after that has always seemed even more surreal."

"What was that?"

"The Navy turned its back on me. A court-appointed defense attorney told me they gave in to public pressure to allow the civilian courts to deal with me. That made no sense, until I caught part of a TV news story with some reporter claiming I was a drunken sailor who assaulted three of NYPD's finest, simply for trying to prevent me from harming my pregnant wife on a public sidewalk. The secretary of the Navy personally sanctioned my dishonorable discharge. The paperwork my attorney showed me said it was based on my heinous and confirmed criminal conduct."

"So you were in the Navy?"

"SEAL Team Four, sir."

"No shit?"

"No shit, sir. That's another sore spot, actually. I'm sure they were pressured to follow the secretary's lead, but I still get angry about how my teammates ignored my calls for help raising bail. I wasn't even allowed to go to Judith's funeral. Of course, her parents accepted the media reports as gospel and didn't want me there, anyway.

"Then, on the first day of my trial, the detectives' blood-alcohol tests taken the night of the incident came back clean, but inexplicably, mine didn't. It showed a level more than twice the legal limit, even though I clearly remember having had nothing to drink in that grimy restaurant, or beforehand. Adding to that, the old woman testified that she ordered me to leave the restaurant because my loud profanity was offending their other patrons. But the *coup de grâce* came when those two lying cops—the third was killed in a car accident before the trial began—testified they ran into Judith and me exiting the restaurant as they were about to enter for a meal and identified themselves as police officers when Judith begged them for help. One even claimed he heard me threaten to kill her while I was trying to wrench the pistol from the other cop's holster.

"Eleven minutes was all it took the jury to find me guilty and responsible for everything that happened."

"Remarkable," Longwood said. "So how'd you get cleared?"

"Five years into my sentence, someone found a security camera video of the whole thing that one of the cops hid back when it went down. It proved they framed me."

"I wonder why they didn't destroy it."

"The cop that hid it was the one who died before the trial."

"Well, please pardon the pun, but I do feel somewhat better armed knowing I have a SEAL at my side. I'd like to meet the others here, too."

As if telepathically summoned, the two mobsters came through the open door then, and Tony announced boldly, "Mr. President, I'm Tony Deluca, and this is my uncle, Louie Briganti."

Longwood held out his hand and shook theirs, wincing at Louie's exuberant squeeze. "I want to thank all of you for what you've done for me," he said. "I know it has cost you dearly, and I am grateful."

"F'get about it," Tony replied with his thickest Bronx inflection.

After the gangsters left, Longwood asked Sam to turn on a television in the corner. Sam did so and found the Fox News channel Longwood requested. After an update on Hurricane Betsy, which was slowly approaching the nation's capital and forecast to hit Long Island in the next forty-eight hours, the newscaster began speaking over video of a funeral at Arlington National Cemetery.

"Holy shit, they buried me."

"That's gotta be weird to watch."

"I'm only concerned about my daughter, Carolyn. This must be especially painful for her after her mother's loss."

The TV reporter switched to another somber scene showing numerous people standing under umbrellas and hundreds of uniformed men and women standing at attention in the rain. "Shortly before President Longwood's burial today, Admiral Jeffrey Campbell, the president's national security advisor and longtime friend, was also laid to rest…"

Sam glanced at Longwood. His face was pale, and there were tears in his eyes. "I'm sorry, sir."

The anchorman began a new story about someone's confirmation hearing, and Longwood showed more vigor than he had yet. "You've got to be kidding me!"

Sam had no idea who Thomas Devlin was, but he was alarmed by the president's apparent ire.

"I need you to contact someone for me, Sam," Longwood said.

"Do you really think that's safe, sir?"

"There's one person I know who definitely won't be part of anything involving Tom Devlin. He's also in a position to help us."

CHAPTER 28

Vice President Thomas Devlin was ecstatic as he listened to the TV anchorman.

"The congressional confirmation process, often a lengthy and partisan confrontation, was over so fast that most in America still don't know they have a new vice president. From what I hear, Thomas Devlin's meteoric rise to power took most in government, the military, and even the media by surprise. Trying to enlighten audiences about the new number two at the White House has been next to impossible, because all the details on the just-retired general's military career in the intelligence world remains cloaked in secrecy."

As Devlin hoped, in the absence of anything revealing to say about him, most news programs instead focused on Longwood's hurried and rain-soaked funeral. He switched to another channel covering that story.

The anchorwoman was saying, "President Longwood's daughter, Carolyn, led the subdued burial march through a somber crowd of onlookers braving gusts of wind-driven rain earlier today. President Mandrake gave a brief graveside eulogy under a windblown tent at the interment, which the administration says they rushed due to the impending storm. The White House also omitted other rituals that usually accompany a nation's farewell to a beloved leader."

A clip of Mandrake's chief of staff came on screen. "The burial was somewhat rushed," Preston Maddox explained, "because President Mandrake was overwhelmed with emotion and a pressing need to both avenge President Longwood and move on with his own promise to restore America's sense of normality and preeminence in the world. Besides, would you really want to pay homage to a casket lying in state when you knew it held only half an arm? Frankly, that would be a little creepy, don't you think?"

Devlin's head had swiveled constantly during the funeral as he worried that Longwood would suddenly walk in on it. Afterward, Devlin was rushed to Capitol Hill for his confirmation hearing.

Using his influence as president and former Speaker of the House, Mandrake had managed to expedite the process by convincing the Senate and House majority leaders, both of his party, to hold a single joint confirmation hearing. He told them, "Expediting the process is a matter of the utmost importance to the proper governance of this mourning and leadership-challenged nation."

Though both houses of Congress agreed to Mandrake's request, Devlin suspected they really only wanted the matter finished so they could leave the District before the hurricane shut down air travel. The joint questioning itself was also rushed. Only those who sat on congressional intelligence oversight committees had any real knowledge of Devlin's background, and none were able or willing to offer their colleagues anything of substance to ask him about.

With the hearing and voting over within hours, Devlin was given the oath of office and confidently followed Mandrake into a crowded White House conference room.

The entire Longwood cabinet—excluding Elizabeth Langford—stared silently at their new vice president.

In Devlin's mind they should all be envious of him, and he could hardly wait to flaunt his new status before them. *I wish Stone were here now*, he thought.

Unlike the straight-to-business Longwood, Mandrake strode toward his seat with an air of pomp and circumstance, until it became apparent that he was not going to be able to squeeze his humongous frame between the floor-to-ceiling windows and the people standing behind their chairs.

After a few uncomfortable seconds, the secretary of agriculture, whose chair was at the end, offered Mandrake his seat.

When the doors were closed and everyone was seated, Mandrake flatly announced, "We will begin this meeting, and all others, with prayer." Everyone stared as the new president bowed his head and began what turned into a nearly two-minute oration, pleading for God to bestow His favor upon him as he reinvigorated America's Christian-based legacy.

Devlin saw a few heads bowed but noted that most sat staring at their new leader as the man's voice became progressively louder and more beseeching.

Mandrake finally finished, opened his eyes, and raised his head. "As you can see, Elizabeth Langford is no longer a member of this cabinet. Nor will you find Calvin Stone at the table during National Security Council meetings. I would caution each of you not to make the same mistake they did. Specifically, do not fight me on matters critical to this nation's national security and moral fiber. President Longwood's assassination at the hands of our own proves that America has been following a path toward anarchy and hedonism for far too long. That must change. It will change."

After no more than five minutes' discussion of unimportant issues, Mandrake inconsiderately dismissed the cabinet. "We will now move on to national security matters. Only NSC principals need remain."

While most of the cabinet quietly departed and a few new people joined the assembly from the hallway, Mandrake took advantage of the openness and moved to the president's regular seat in the center of the long table with his back to the windows overlooking the rose garden.

The NSC meeting began with Mandrake announcing the termination of the peace talks in Denmark. "I will not make deals with groups that support terrorism, and the Hamas-led Palestinian Authority is such a group."

Devlin noticed that, without Langford, no one voiced any protest, including her deputy, now acting secretary of state. Stone's deputy, appointed acting CIA director, was in attendance but also remained silent. Devlin paid little attention to what the council discussed after that. His thoughts remained focused on finding Longwood again. Moments into that, he had an epiphany.

No one in the room was willing to object to anything the new president announced, and the subdued NSC meeting ended quickly.

Once the cowed participants departed, Devlin walked with Mandrake to the Oval Office.

As the door closed behind the new executive team, Devlin said, "Mr. President, there's a matter I'd like to discuss with you."

"What's that?"

"I believe you should demonstrate your support for finding President Longwood's assassins by appointing someone from *your* administration to oversee the investigation."

Mandrake plopped onto the custom-made oversized

chair he had had brought over from his old office. "I don't have my own cabinet yet."

"Well, to be honest, sir, I'd like to offer *my* services for the job. That way, no one can accuse you of not placing someone of import to the task. And frankly, I'm at a loss for something more important to focus my efforts on with you now leading this nation along God's path." Devlin could almost smell the man's self-absorption as he drew him in deeper with each praising syllable.

"You make an excellent point, Tom. Okay, the job's yours."

CHAPTER 29

Calvin Stone sat at his Langley desk, angrily pondering Mandrake's sudden and unexplained demand for his resignation. *Of course Devlin was behind it*, he thought and wondered who Devlin would push Mandrake to replace him with. He knew the job would not stay in his deputy's hands. *Devlin will want someone he can control*, he thought.

He was disappointed that Devlin had been confirmed and given the oath before Stone could gather the proof he needed to expose him for the narcissist he knew him to be.

When the story about the Middle East peace plan came out, Stone had called the *Washington Post* reporter and flatly asked who her source was. She initially cited the freedom of the press rhetoric he expected and switched to the reporter's taboo against revealing sources but had stopped cold when he interrupted her. "So it *was* Devlin, huh?"

It had really been nothing more than a hunch based on a rumor he'd heard about her having been seen dining with the DIA chief several times just before leaks came out under her byline. Her silence, and the click he heard as she hung up, spoke volumes.

Stone felt that if he could confront her face-to-face, he might convince her to at least volunteer the truth in a closed session before the House and Senate Intelligence Oversight Committees. Even though Devlin was already in the VP's seat, there was still a remote chance that exposure for violating the Official Secrets Act might force him to step down. *It happened to Spiro Agnew*, he thought. *Why not Devlin?*

He called the *Post*, identified himself, and asked to speak with Donna Jones.

"Ms. Jones isn't available. I'll connect you with her editor, Mr. Gleason."

The line changed over with a ring. "This is Melvin Gleason."

"Mr. Gleason, this is Calvin Stone. I'd like to speak with Donna Jones, if I may."

"Donna was killed last night, Mr. Stone."

His inner alarm bells started ringing. "How was she killed?"

"She was mugged going out to her car."

Disappointed, Stone hung up and called a friend at Metro PD. "Hey, John, Calvin Stone. What can you tell me about the Donna Jones case?"

"I can't tell you much," a gruff voice responded, "except that I don't think it was a mugging like they reported."

"Why do you say that?"

"I ain't ever seen a mugger nearly cut someone's head off and leave the victim's wallet and car behind."

"Did he take anything?"

"The only thing missing was her laptop. She had a charger for it in her car, and he left that behind."

"Okay, thanks, pal."

A moment after he hung up, his personal cell phone chimed. The caller ID read *Unknown*.

"This is Calvin Stone. Who's this?"

"My name's Sam Calder. You don't know me, but we have a mutual friend who asked that I pass on a message."

Cautious and curious how this man—*the name sounds familiar*—knew his private number, Stone typed the name into his computer. "Who's this mutual friend, Mr. Calder, and what's the message?"

"His name's Robert Longwood, and—"

"Is this some kind of sick joke?" An FBI bulletin with Calder's name and face popped up on the screen.

"No, it's not a—"

"Wait a minute! Are you telling me President Longwood's alive?"

"He and I would like to keep that a *very* closely held secret, for now."

Stone was standing now, holding his phone so tightly his hand hurt. "Where is he?"

"He's safe at the moment, but there have been two additional attempts on his life since the lake."

"Attempts by whom, the MSM?"

"It was never the MSM. Look, it's a long story, and I'll tell it to you when we have more time. To be honest, I don't know who the enemy is, but based on what I witnessed at the lake and elsewhere, it's someone with access to high-grade military equipment, including a Predator."

Stone's mind reeled. He remembered the task force meeting he had attended at the FBI building, where Devlin claimed credit for using a Predator in unveiling the assault at Pointer Lake, and the man certainly had access to military equipment and personnel. The implications of what Calder had said were extraordinary—and very threatening. So many questions were flooding Stone's mind that he couldn't think clearly.

"Are you still there?"

"Yeah, I'm here," Stone answered. "What's his physical condition?"

"He lost a lot of blood, but he'll survive if we can keep him safe."

"Who else knows about this?"

"There are two others here with us."

"I need to see him, in person."

"You're only about a hundred miles away, less than an hour by chopper, if you can fly in this weather."

"Just tell me where."

"Okay, I'll give you the coordinates where you can land, and we'll pick you up. Remember, he wants to keep this close-hold for now. Tell absolutely no one."

"I hear that."

Stone told his secretary he had a personal matter to attend to and would return for his belongings later. He then had her call to arrange for an agency helicopter.

At Langley's heliport, the senior pilot said, "Winds are still within limits, sir, but we'll need to make it a quick trip, or we risk being stuck out there."

⁊ݣ⁊ݣ

As the newly appointed overseer of the assassination investigation, Devlin ordered Director Pearson of the FBI to come to the White House Situation Room and brief him on their latest findings. He also directed Pearson to bring along Special Agent Peppers as the man most closely involved with the New York mob's tenuous connection.

"The bureau has questioned and polygraphed all known members of the MSM from Noxon and elsewhere," Pearson said. "We found no evidence of deception on anyone's part, and as far as we can determine, none had any knowledge of their dead comrades' intentions at the lake."

"What's the latest on locating the mortar teams?" Devlin asked.

"Every member of the MSM has been accounted for, and there are no missing folks from Noxon or any other MSM chapter."

"So where did they come from, and where did they go?"

"We can't yet prove it, but we're confident the six unidentified bodies recovered at the Calder ranch are those missing suspects. We believe they may have gone there during their escape and stumbled into that sheriff there on a medical call. We're hoping the survivor can help prove that. Unfortunately, there's been no change in his condition."

Devlin was relieved to hear that. "Why do you think he can help you?"

"He was attacked again in the hospital. Someone's trying to keep him quiet. The assassin at the hospital may well have been the person who took the missing weapons from the ranch and set the fire. We can't be sure, because he was killed by one of our agents."

"Tell me you have this comatose man somewhere safe."

"He's in protective custody at the Missoula Regional Hospital. Frankly, we really don't know his—or his brother's—role in all of this yet. We're just going to have to wait until he comes out of the coma or we locate his brother."

"Was there any physical evidence recovered from the MSM suspects that could help in identifying the missing suspects?"

"Yes, sir," Pearson answered. "Four of the eight suspects killed at the lake had cell phones on them. Three were examined and found to have only been used to call each other. The fourth belonged to the group's leader, Howard Jackson, but it was hit by a bullet from one of the Secret Service Uzis. The lab says its data is unrecoverable."

Devlin already knew that from attending the task force briefing, but he pretended displeasure at Pearson's lack of leads while inwardly relishing every word, except that Jackson's phone was damaged. As far as the missing mortar men, he knew exactly where they were. Four, in fact, had died at the ranch. Another died trying to kill the coma patient, and the last met his end on Antigua.

Devlin persisted in misdirecting the FBI's efforts in order to further insulate himself from scrutiny should Longwood reappear before he could find him again. He pulled a photo from the files before him and asked, "Do you have any leads on where this Samuel Calder may be?"

Pearson shook his head. "He seems to have vanished."

Devlin turned to the other agent present. "This probably doesn't seem relevant to the assassination, but I heard about Salvatore Deluca and his brother being murdered, and I remembered you said Calder was seen in their presence. Have you found out anything more about who killed them? Maybe it was Calder—some sort of cover-up of their involvement in the assassination."

"Our informants are emphatic that no rival criminal organization was responsible for the Deluca brothers' deaths, sir, and we can't find a link between the mob and the MSM. We still haven't found Tony Deluca, Salvatore's son, either. He skipped out on me in New York. He's probably lying low so his father's killers don't get him, too. As far as Calder's involvement and whereabouts are concerned, we don't have a clue, sir."

"You have no idea where Deluca could be hiding, either? Maybe Calder's with him."

"Actually, sir, I believe Deluca's in the Caribbean."

"What makes you think that?"

"The mob owns a place on Antigua, and the FAA says their jet flew down there the same night Salvatore and Luigi were killed and Tony ditched us. It had no passengers listed on its manifest, but I think Tony Deluca may have actually been aboard. The jet returned to Teterboro Airport in New Jersey the following day. Customs agents claimed that no one got off, so I sent an agent to speak with the pilots. Both swore they had not seen Deluca and had flown to Antigua for training. I'm not buying their story, though. I think Deluca's down there, hiding from the people who killed his old man and uncle. Unfortunately, the Antiguans are refusing us access to the villa. The mob has a lot of pull down there."

Devlin listened with fascination. He knew Peppers's deduction to be logical, but wrong. *Deluca is definitely not on Antigua any longer. Calder would not leave Longwood at risk like that*, he thought, then asked what he really wanted to know. "Does the mob own any other properties?"

"Yes, sir," Peppers replied, pulling a file from his briefcase. "They're quite extensive. They have commercial holdings that exceed many large corporations—"

Devlin cut him off. "What about residential properties?"

"Let's see," Peppers said, scanning the list before him. "There's a penthouse in Manhattan, a couple of houses in the Bronx, one on Staten Island, another in Atlantic City, and one in upstate New Jersey. They even own a villa in Italy, and of course, the place in Antigua. We're working on search warrants for the stateside properties now."

Devlin pretended to idly flip through Peppers's files.

"Well, it sounds like you've got your hands full tracking Deluca down," he said. "Okay, thank you for coming, especially in this horrible weather. Keep me posted, Director Pearson."

The meeting had been nothing more than a pretext for getting at Peppers's files without raising suspicions. Devlin knew Calder was likely hiding Longwood at one of the mob man's other properties, and he now had a good idea which ones to look at.

Peppers had said the jet landed at Teterboro when it returned from Antigua, and Devlin had managed a peek at the addresses of the mob's Atlantic City and upstate New Jersey properties. It only made sense to Devlin that they would land as close to their destination as possible after the fight on the island. Once the FBI men left, he pulled his secure cell phone.

"This is Crowley, sir."

"I'm emailing you a couple of addresses where they may be hiding Longwood. Both belong to the mob. Check them out."

"Yes, sir."

"The FBI's looking for Tony Deluca and might show up at either location, or they may already have them under surveillance by the time you get there, so make sure you stay off their radar. If you find someone at either place, get your team together and hit it." Devlin paused. "Armstrong's dead, and so are all the men he took with him. Calder is proving to be a very dangerous opponent."

CHAPTER 30

Hurricane Betsy had slowed its march north, and though the winds remained within the helicopter's limits, the ride from Langley was a bumpy one and took more than an hour. The location Calder provided turned out to be a municipal park in the upstate New Jersey woods, empty of people due to the inclement weather.

Stone climbed out of the helicopter as a van pulled up. "I'm not sure how long this will take," he told the pilots. "Wait here, and tell no one your location. If it looks like we're running out of time with the winds, or a problem comes up, text me."

He walked to the van's front passenger door and opened it.

The driver was a large, thuggish-looking man, not the face he had seen on his computer.

"Get in," the driver ordered.

The van drove a short distance before stopping again. Another man stepped out from the trees with a suppressed rifle strapped to his shoulder. He opened the sliding rear door and climbed in the back seat, and the van took off again.

Stone turned in his seat, recognizing the new face, and

offered his hand. "Not taking any chances, huh, Mr. Calder?"

"The president says he trusts you implicitly, but it's been a rough couple of days for the rest of us."

"I can imagine. How long a drive do we have?"

"It'll take about twenty minutes."

"Okay, start at the beginning."

The harrowing tale ended moments before they entered a gated driveway leading to a country manor. The front doors to the house were held open by another man he recognized, Tony Deluca. Stone nodded at the well-known mobster as he followed Calder inside.

He froze when they entered an upstairs bedroom and saw the president propped up against several pillows. He looked pale and banged up, and was missing half an arm, but he was definitely alive. That was all Stone cared about.

"Hello, Cal. Good to see you."

Stone moved to the bedside and gently shook Longwood's hand with both of his. "I can't tell you how good it is to see *you*, sir."

Calder stepped up behind and asked, "Would you prefer privacy, Mr. President?"

"That won't be necessary, Sam." Longwood turned to Stone. "I'm only alive right now because of this young man, and the others."

Calder's story about what had happened at the lake and ranch house seemed incredible enough, but when he added how the Mafia had gotten involved and what they had experienced since, Stone was speechless. Finally he said, "I understand, sir. How do you want to handle this?"

"First off, I can't simply reappear and demand my old job back. I'm not physically capable of performing my duties as president just yet, and the cabinet has already constitutionally replaced me. Even if Mandrake voluntarily stepped aside, Devlin would likely take charge because of my current condition. So, what I propose is that while I recover, we use the time to unravel this clusterfuck."

"I believe I know who at least one of the conspirators may be, and you aren't going to like it."

"Who is it?"

"Mr. Calder said he thought a Predator was used to lead an assault team to his family's ranch."

Longwood shrugged. "Yeah, he mentioned that to me, but I don't know anything about a Predator."

"Well, you wouldn't have needed to know about it, sir, but the DIA had one over you on the day of the lake attack. In fact, it was the Predator that spotted the men who were blamed for it all."

"Do you think the attackers were Devlin's people?" Longwood asked, sounding astounded.

Stone nodded. "Everything seems to point in that direction. He had access to the right equipment and personnel, and he was the only one using a Predator. I also believe he leaked info to the *Post*."

"What makes you think that?"

"I'm pretty sure that reporter had a thing going with Devlin. I called her when she broke the story and tried a little reverse psychology by claiming I knew her source was Devlin. She was stunned silent and hung up on me, but she didn't deny it."

"Do you think she'd testify against him? That was a breach of national security."

"Unfortunately, she was murdered. I heard about it just before Mr. Calder called."

Longwood's eyebrows lifted slightly. "Do you think Devlin was responsible for that as well?"

"Yes, although I have no proof. The news report said her attacker mugged her but only took her laptop. He left her purse and wallet. My bet is that Devlin had her killed while cleaning up loose ends." There was a moment of silence before Stone added, "There's another aspect of this that must be considered, sir. Mandrake may be involved."

"Why do you suspect him?"

"He stayed at the lodge the morning you went to the lake, and he didn't waste any time nominating Devlin to fill the VP slot after he became president. He even appointed him to oversee the investigation into your assassination."

Longwood shook his head in dismay. "That's putting the fox in the henhouse."

"Look, sir, I think your plan to recuperate before making a move is the right way to go, but I think you should have more protection. What about the Secret Service?"

"No. I'm better off with just Sam and the others for now. The fewer people who know I'm alive, the safer I am. Besides, the Secret Service works for Mandrake and Devlin now. I can't take the chance that someone might slip up and Devlin finds out where I am again."

"How about moving to a more secure location? The agency has a safe house up in Maine that's very isolated and reachable only by floatplane or helicopter. I can arrange to have you moved there with nobody except me knowing about it."

"I'll think about it."

"I'd like permission to tell my deputy, Harvey Monson, about this, sir."

"Why?"

"I'm out, and Harvey's the acting director at the moment. We might need his help."

"What d'ya mean, you're out?"

"Mandrake fired me. Elizabeth, too."

Longwood's eyes opened wide. "What?"

"She argued with him about cancelling the peace talks, and since I've never even met Mandrake, I'm certain Devlin talked him into canning me as a revenge move. As I'm sure you're aware, Devlin and I haven't exactly been the best of pals."

"I know." Longwood's lips pressed together, and his hand curled into a fist. "I want you to contact my daughter. I'm sure she's in pain, but make sure she and her husband understand why they need to keep absolutely quiet."

Stone nodded. "I'll take care of it. What about Monson?"

"No. Leave Monson out of it. I'm going to need Trevor Pearson down the road, though."

"That's a good call, sir. Trevor needs to know he's being hoodwinked by Devlin. He's also in a position to search for evidence that can be used against him and possibly Mandrake."

"Get Pearson to secretly arrange some protection for my daughter in case Devlin tries to use her to lure me out."

Stone's cell phone beeped and he glanced down to see a text from his pilots. "I think I'd better leave while I can, sir. I have a lot to do, and that hurricane's closing in."

Stone shook hands with Sam and Tony at the front door and gave Sam a cell phone. "Use this to reach me from now on. It's secure. I'm speed dial number one."

CHAPTER 31

Devlin answered Crowley's call at the first chime. "I found them, sir, but we have a problem," Crowley said.

"What kind of problem?"

"They're at the upstate New Jersey house. I had to climb a wall to get close enough to see the place, and as soon as I got there, a van pulled out of the garage and a guy I recognized from TV came out and left in it."

"Who was it?"

"It was that CIA dude Mandrake fired."

Devlin's heart began thumping like a jackhammer. "Are you certain?"

"Yeah, I took a picture of him. I'm emailing it to you now."

"Did you see anyone else?"

"Yeah, there were two others at the door with him. They were all shaking hands like they were old buddies."

Devlin's mind was spinning as he opened the email and stared at the photo. "That's Deluca holding the door, and the other one is Calder."

"I thought he might be Calder. He's a big one, all right."

He had a fix on Longwood again, but now Devlin had

to worry that Stone also knew the man was alive. "Okay, get the men ready to hit the house."

"What about Stone?"

"Leave Blevins and Stanton behind, and tell them they'll receive their orders by secure email shortly. I need to set up a few things first."

e⁄ɔe⁄ɔ

Longwood's daughter had not yet left Washington, and Stone immediately went to her hotel to explain the truth about her father. He reiterated that she would see him soon but had to maintain silence in order to ensure his continued safety. She seemed so relieved to learn of his survival that her anger at having had to attend his funeral faded quickly.

Stone called the FBI director's office next.

"Director Pearson has gone home for the day, sir," an assistant told him.

"Thank you," Stone replied. "Please call him and let him know I'm driving over there right now. It's urgent."

He wearily made his way to Annandale, Virginia, in his personal car. He would be going home afterward and no longer warranted a driver and agency car. He had been to the FBI director's home on several occasions. The large brick house was set a hundred feet back from the road at the end of a cul-de-sac. As he approached, a black SUV cut him off, forcing him to stop short of the long driveway.

Two large men emerged, both holding automatic weapons. One demanded identification and said, "Oh, excuse me, Director Stone. We didn't recognize the car. He's expecting you."

"Thank you."

The bodyguard FBI agent raised his radio, and the

front porch lit up. The door opened, and Pearson stepped out and waved.

Inside the expansive home library, the two men sat on fine-leather chairs facing a large, unlit fireplace. Pearson first went through the cordiality of offering a beverage. When Stone declined, he said, "Okay, what's up? You seem a bit out of sorts."

"Bob Longwood wasn't killed at the lake." Stone was certain the look on Pearson's face would have been the same had he informed him that little green men from Mars were invading.

"Are you saying you have evidence he was killed somewhere else?"

"No. I'm saying he's alive."

"What the hell are you talking about?" Pearson said, flabbergasted. "They found his arm—"

Stone cut him off. "Look, I think I will have that drink after all. Make it a scotch, neat. This is a wild and complicated story. You'll probably need one, too." He told Pearson all he knew of Longwood's past few days, except for the location of the New Jersey manor.

Stone swallowed the last of his Scotch, sat back and asked, "Any thoughts on how we can nail Devlin?"

Pearson's face couldn't mask his anger. He finished off his drink and threw the expensive crystal into the fireplace. "I'm gonna hang that son of a bitch. Mandrake, too, if he's in on it."

"I know. I feel the same. But that doesn't help us right now. Devlin—maybe Mandrake—holds all the cards. Longwood isn't strong enough to resume his duties, so he wants to hold off on his reappearance until he is. In the meantime, it seems Devlin's aware he's out there and is doing everything he can to finish what he started at the lake, while covering his ass if he doesn't."

"First off, it seems to me that Longwood needs more protection."

"He doesn't want more, not yet. He's concerned that word will get out and make it easier for Devlin to find him again."

"I still think he needs more than a couple of mobsters and a former SEAL fresh out of prison."

Stone sighed. "I don't know. That SEAL seems to have done a pretty good job so far."

"At least get him to let me send in an agent, someone with the legal authority to begin an official investigation."

"Who do you have in mind?"

"Vince O'Malley, the SAIC out in Montana. I can have him here by morning. He's a good gun hand, too."

"Okay, give me a minute, and I'll call and ask."

Stone called the secure phone he'd left with Sam. After a few minutes on hold, Sam told him, "He says okay to the agent joining us. He also changed his mind about that safe house up in Maine. He wants to go there."

"What changed his mind?"

"I convinced him an isolated location would offer better security."

"Okay, I'll set up the move. It'll take a few hours. The pilot will call you with the pickup instructions after I speak with him." Stone paused. "I'll text you his number so you'll recognize the call. His name's Dave." Stone hung up and turned back to Pearson. "Okay, O'Malley's in, but I've got to move them first, and we'll get your man to their new location."

"I'll have him here by morning."

"Don't tell him about Longwood."

"I won't. Do you think Mandrake's in on this, too?"

"He might be, but my bet is Devlin's behind everything that's happened, and Mandrake's just a patsy, probably until Devlin can remove him, too."

"Jesus. That would give the bastard the presidency."

"Exactly. I'll bet that's been his real objective all along."

"What's our next move?"

"I need to set up the move for Longwood, and I'm going home to make sure Alice and Tammy are ready for the storm. She called while I was driving here and said the White House removed our home security detail, claimed I'm not entitled to it any longer."

"Do you want me to send a team over to your place?"

"I don't think that's necessary. I'm sure Devlin's just throwing his weight around, trying to poke me in the eye one last time. Longwood does want you to send some secret protection for his daughter, though. She and her husband are staying at the Watergate. She knows, but don't tell your team or anyone else."

"Okay, I'll take care of it right away."

As Stone left Pearson's home, he texted Sam the pilot's contact number and then called it himself.

"Hello."

"This is Stone, Colonel. I need you to move some people to the lodge ASAP with nobody at the agency knowing about it, and you're going to need Kathy. One of them is injured."

"How many are going?" the pilot asked.

"Four, plus you'll need to get an FBI agent named O'Malley up there separately. He's not here yet, so plan on him going up sometime tomorrow afternoon."

"Okay, where are they?"

"They're a couple of miles from Lake Hopatcong in upstate New Jersey."

"That'll work. And you want me to keep the agency out of it, huh?"

"That's right. You'll understand why when you meet

them. The group's contact person is a guy named Sam. He's got your number."

"Okay, I'll call him with the pickup instructions as soon as I take a look at the weather and that lake on a map."

"Thanks."

Exhausted, Stone drove to his neighborhood almost robotically, his mind overwhelmed by the day's events. His street was quiet and the house dark, which was typical when he returned late. His wife and daughter would have already gone to bed, though Alice was usually watching TV, waiting for him to come home or call. His home's three-man security detail had been removed, but he still had the alarm system the agency installed when he became its director. He turned it off with his remote, keyed the garage door open, and pulled in.

As he stepped out of his car and headed to the door leading into the kitchen, something moved in his peripheral vision. He instinctively turned to it, and a mist sprayed him in the face. The sedation took effect instantly, and he collapsed to the floor.

CHAPTER 32

Longwood had taken more painkillers and slept, not becoming clear-headed until late in the evening. He still had difficulty with solid foods, and Sam noticed he had not touched his dinner. Knowing the man needed protein, Sam brought him a plate of cheesy scrambled eggs.

Longwood smiled. "Thank you."

"How're you feeling, sir—pain wise, I mean?"

"There's some. Actually, quite a lot, but I'd rather not take any more painkillers. I keep nodding off, and I can't focus my thoughts." He paused a moment while he began eating the eggs. "I don't mean to intrude, Sam, but I'm curious about something."

"What's that, sir?"

"When I lost Cynthia, I had the presidency to focus on, to keep me from wallowing in my grief and get past it. How did you manage to cope with your loss in prison, especially being innocent and disgraced like you were?" Sam didn't answer immediately, so Longwood added, "You don't have to answer, Sam. I didn't mean to intrude."

Sam walked to the bedroom window and pulled aside

the curtain. He gazed at his own reflection in the dark glass for a moment before answering. "It's just that it's been a long time since I had a conversation with a regular person," he said, "someone not willing to kill me in my sleep for fun or stab me for a couple of cigarettes. You have to understand that prison's not like living a normal life. There aren't any weekends or holidays. You don't get to start your day deciding when you'll get up, what clothes you'll wear, what you'll have for breakfast, or even what you'll do today. Every day is exactly like the one before it, and you don't get to make any of those decisions for yourself. You just exist, nothing more, and you're surrounded by the most dangerous and revolting people you can possibly imagine. I saw men lose it. Some killed themselves. In time, I came to realize that even though I couldn't change my situation, I *could* affect how I dealt with it."

"How did you do that?"

"I went through each day thinking of it as if I were still going through BUDS out in Coronado. That's where they run the SEAL selection program. Believe me, it's a bitch."

"I've heard that."

"The guys who make it through do so by accepting that no matter what is happening to you at any given moment, you *can* survive it, and it *will* end. Don't get me wrong, though. There were plenty of moments when I thought my life was over. I couldn't see any purpose to my life, even after I was released. The only thing I'd wanted to do for the last five years was get revenge on those cops, and I couldn't even do that now." He paused and breathed deeply. "I'm sorry, sir. I probably sound like a whiner."

Longwood stared at him for several seconds, and then said, "Not at all, Sam. I think you're a remarkable young man. After everything you did in service to your country, you lose your wife, and the nation takes away your honor and throws you in prison. Still, when you finally get reprieved and find your way home, you don't even hesitate when it comes to saving my ass, at great personal cost, again. I know it's no consolation, but I am grateful. When this nightmare ends, and it will end, we're going to have another talk." He paused a moment before asking, "So when do you think we'll be moving to that safe house?"

"Stone said the pilot would call when he's got it set up. I expect we'll go early tomorrow."

Tony stepped into the doorway. "Sorry to interrupt. I forgot I turned the security system off when Stone came by. I just turned it back on, and one of the front sensors tripped the moment I did. I'm gonna go check it out."

"No. Get him ready to move," Sam ordered as he rushed out of the room and down the dark stairs to the front door. They had kept all the main floor lights out and the curtains closed throughout the house. Sam peered through the door's etched-glass window and immediately spotted a dark figure coming through the trees a hundred feet away, then another, and another. He raced back up to Longwood's room. "They found us. Do you have a safe room, Tony?"

"No, but we have a way out. Follow me."

"Sorry about this, sir," Sam said, pulling Longwood to his shoulder. Longwood only grunted at the manhandling.

Louie joined them as they rushed down the stairs and continued farther down, into the basement. Sam heard the tinkle of breaking glass above as Tony pulled on something hidden behind a beam. A panel in the wall opened, revealing a dark tunnel.

"You guys really like tunnels," Sam whispered as he stepped inside.

Once they were all in, Louie closed the panel and

locked it, and Tony turned on dim, widely spaced lights and led the way. Ten seconds later, they were at a staircase and up through a hatch in the unattached garage floor.

Louie jumped into the driver's seat as Tony opened the van's sliding side door and climbed in the front passenger seat. Sam laid the president on the van's floor and glanced through the garage door windows toward the main house as he climbed in. He could see flashlights moving about just inside the now-open front door.

"I don't see anyone in our way outside," Louie said. "Ready?"

Sam pulled the suppressed pistol he'd brought from Antigua from his waist. "Go!"

The van's engine started, and the big mobster floored the gas pedal, ramming the two side-by-side carriage doors open. As the van raced out and down the long driveway, Sam saw several flashes coming from men rushing out the manor's front door. A couple of bullets hit the back of the van but did not stop it.

"Open the gate!" Louie yelled.

Tony hit a remote, and the wrought-iron barrier swung clear just in time.

The van sped out at nearly sixty miles per hour, fish-tailing and nearly tipping over as Louie maneuvered a ninety-degree turn onto the roadway. "Where am I going?" he asked.

"Just drive," Sam answered.

The back window exploded, and the rearview mirror fell from the windshield as its safety glass spider-webbed.

"What the hell?" Louie said.

A second later, something heavy rammed the van's rear, jolting everyone inside.

Louie pressed the gas pedal to the floor as Sam leapt over the back seat and began shooting his pistol out the shattered rear window. His target was a blacked-out Humvee. The bullets didn't even nick the military vehicle's armored glass.

Tony jumped past the president and joined Sam with a shotgun he had grabbed from a rack in the tunnel.

"Save your rounds," Sam yelled. "It's armored. We're faster, though, so keep up your speed, Louie."

The Humvee's overhead hatch opened, and Sam saw a figure lifting a large weapon out. "Shit! They're mounting a heavy gun," he yelled as he tried in vain to shoot the turret gunner hiding behind the upraised steel hatch cover. When Sam saw the man feeding belted ammunition into the weapon, he yelled, "Louie, swerve left and slam on the brakes, now!"

Louie did as ordered, and the van rapidly slowed in the other lane while Sam swung around and opened the side door, shielding Longwood with his body.

The much heavier Humvee was unable to slow down as quickly. As the van passed beside and behind it, Sam opened up on the surprised and now unprotected gunner. The man's head snapped back from the impact of a bullet before his body collapsed back through the hatch.

Behind their pursuers now, Louie spun the van around and headed in the opposite direction.

As they were rounding a wide bend, the Humvee, its lights on now, turned to pursue. "Switch your lights off and pull into those woods on the right," Sam directed. "Keep your foot off the brakes." As Louie did that, Sam added, "As soon as it goes by, get back out there and go the way we were originally. We're faster, so they shouldn't be able to catch up when they figure out what we did. Remember to keep the headlights off and your foot off the brakes."

The Humvee raced past a moment later, and Louie put the van back in gear and pulled out.

Ten minutes later, Tony said, "I think we lost them."

"Yeah, there were probably only two in it," Sam replied, "and I got one. Let's keep moving, though, and I'll call Stone." He tried but got no answer.

"We need to ditch this van," Tony said.

"No problem," Louie announced as he pulled into the driveway of a motel. He parked between two SUVs in its back lot, grabbed Tony's shotgun, and stepped out. He walked to the older of the two cars and broke out its driver's window with the weapon's stock. No alarm went off, and the car's engine started a moment later.

As Sam moved the president to their new ride, Longwood said, "I'll bet I'm the first president to be an accessory to a car theft."

"You're gonna give me one of them presidential pardons, right?" Louie asked.

ে৯ে৯

"I'm sorry, sir. I took a dozen men into the house, but the targets slipped out a tunnel to the garage. I had two guys in a Humvee out on the road keeping an eye out, and they chased after them, but Calder killed one and got away."

"Shit!" Devlin was furious, but another idea quickly formed. "Okay, stay there. I have another solution for finding Longwood that requires your special skills. Blevins and Stanton will bring it to you."

ে৯ে৯

After several unsuccessful attempts to reach Calvin Stone, Sam dialed the number Stone had texted him. It was answered on the first ring.

"Hello."

"My name's Sam."

"I'm Dave. I was going to call you in a few minutes. What's up?"

"Where's Stone? We can't reach him."

"I have no idea. Do you still need a pickup?"

"Yes."

"Okay, Lake Hopatcong is—"

Sam cut him off. "We had to move. Now we're outside Troy, New York."

"Okay, standby." Several quiet moments passed before Dave said, "There's a reservoir three miles north of town. Be in the parking lot of its northern boat launch at oh-five-hundred hours."

"We'll be there."

CHAPTER 33

Calvin Stone came back to consciousness slowly. He could hear someone weeping. His mind told him it was a woman, but he could not process the voice. Nor could he move. His eyes opened slowly, and what he saw when his vision focused horrified him. He was in a basement with his wrists and ankles strapped to a wooden chair. The woman he had heard sobbing was his wife. She stood ten feet in front of him, nude, her arms held by a man at each side. A black bag covered her head.

"Hello, Mr. Stone," a man's voice said as he stepped into view.

Stone did not recognize any of the three men before him. "What do you want?" he asked.

His wife's cries increased. The muffled sound told him they had also gagged her.

"What I want is your cooperation, and as you can see, I'm prepared to force it."

Stone remained silent. Alice's moans were the only sound for a moment.

"We are time constrained, so I'll get right to business. Where's Longwood?"

Stone's silence continued.

The interrogator stepped to his wife and groped her bare breasts, then moved his hand down her body. The two men holding her arms braced as she squirmed, unsuccessfully trying to fend off the assault. With her feet kicking out and Stone repeatedly screaming for him to stop, the man molested her roughly for several seconds before withdrawing. "Where is he?" he growled threateningly.

Stone's heart pounded and his breathing quickened as his mind screamed for a solution that would not come.

"Tell me, or I swear I'll kill her. I don't bluff, Stone."

"Longwood's dead, for chrissakes. He was assassinated in Montana."

The scrawny interrogator pulled a suppressed pistol and nodded to the two men holding her arms. They released their grips on her and stepped aside as he raised the pistol to the black bag and pulled the trigger.

Stunned, Stone watched her body slam to the cement floor with all the grace of a dead fish. He strained against his bindings and screamed until his tormentor slapped the barrel of the hot, smoking pistol against the side of his head. Dazed, but unable to move his tear-filled eyes from his wife's corpse and the dark blood pooling from the bag, Stone sobbed.

"I warned you. I don't bluff, and I'm in a hurry. I gotta get *real* ugly now." With that, the man waved a hand, and another man entered, dragging Stone's eight-year-old daughter by one arm. She wore her nightgown and was bagged and gagged like her mother. Her muted cries told Stone how terrified she was.

As they placed her where her mother had stood, the child's bladder let go. Urine ran down her thin legs, mixing with her mother's blood.

Stone's heart felt as though it would tear itself in half. His only relief was that his daughter could not see her mother lying only feet away. "Please, don't hurt her."

"Then answer my question."

Tammy, recognizing her father's voice, began trying to call to him through the gag.

In that moment, Stone knew he could not witness any harm done to her, no matter the cost. Since the intruders had not concealed their faces, he knew they would kill him, but maybe not her, he prayed. "Please tell me you'll spare her if I give you what you want."

"I'm not a kid killer unless I have to be. Tell me what I want to know, and she walks. You have my word."

Stone bowed his head, giving up all hope but that one, and almost whispered, "He's at a house in New Jersey."

"Bullshit! Where the hell do you think you are? I want to know where he went from here."

Confusion added to his desperation and terror for his daughter. Stone could only stammer, "I don't understand what—"

Stone's words froze in his throat as the man pressed the pistol to his daughter's head. "Remember, I don't bluff."

Stone desperately shook his head, and a possible answer came to him. "He was in New Jersey when I last saw him, but…"

"What?"

"He was going to be moved to a safe house up in Maine."

"Give me its location."

"It's a lodge on Lake Umbagog, near the southeastern border. It's the only thing on the lake."

"Okay, next question: Who else knows about Long-wood?"

"Nobody, I swear."

The man tore the nightgown off with one pull, leaving the small girl in only her mermaid-decorated underwear, struggling ineffectively to escape a horror she could not see.

"Pearson, Trevor Pearson! That's it, I swear to God! Please." The last came out a whimper.

The interrogator smiled cruelly, turned without pause, and fired his pistol into the black hood. As Tammy's fifty-five-pound body flopped atop her mother's, the pistol mercifully swung toward Stone's forehead.

CHAPTER 34

The stolen SUV carrying President Longwood pulled into the reservoir's boat launch parking lot as a breezy, overcast dawn arrived. They were at the fringe of the storm that a radio weatherman said was moving up the East Coast. Still a level one hurricane, it was expected to bring gusty winds and rain across a wide portion of the northeast.

It was not raining there yet, and Sam knew fishing was always good just before a weather front passed. He realized the locals knew that, too, because several fishing boats were scattered across the slightly choppy water and a few anglers stood along the shoreline.

"Are we waiting for a boat?" Longwood asked.

"I don't know, but—" Sam stopped mid-sentence when he heard an airplane motor. He climbed out with Tony and searched the gray cloud cover only a few hundred feet above.

Suddenly a large red and white single-engine propeller floatplane popped out of the cloud deck and passed directly over their heads. It descended low over the water and seemed to be intentionally buzzing the boaters. Once past, its nose came up sharply, and it rose to maybe a hundred feet before banking hard left and turning around for what Sam first thought was another buzzing pass, until it began to descend even lower than the first time.

"What the hell is that guy doing?" Tony asked.

"I believe our ride's here," Sam replied.

Louie muttered, "Aw, shit!"

Boaters along the airplane's path scrambled to get out of its way, and then it was down, splashing across the water directly toward the ramp.

Sam turned to Longwood. "Ready?"

The president only nodded. His head was once again bandaged to protect his identity, and a blanket draped over his shoulders hid his missing arm.

Louie and Tony helped him from the van, and the group began moving down the ramp to the water's edge.

Anglers standing along the bank nearby stared at the odd foursome, and a couple pulled out cell phones when a gust blew away the towel covering Tony's shotgun.

Sam figured that if the New Yorkers recognized Tony, they probably thought they were witnessing a mob kidnapping. *Of course*, he thought, *if Devlin hears about it, he'll know the truth.*

The plane's propeller threw spray as its nose spun around to give the group access to the wide pontoon on the plane's right side. Sam waded into the water to help steady the craft.

A woman who looked to be in her fifties opened the side door and ordered, "Hurry up. We need to haul ass before the cops get here."

Tony and Louie maneuvered Longwood inside and slid him toward a stretcher laid out on the airplane's floor.

"Hello," Longwood said to her.

"Shut the fuck up. We got no time for hugs and kisses."

Everyone climbed in, and the packed airplane began

taxiing back to a position it could use to take off into the wind.

Louie maneuvered to the front passenger seat, while Sam and Tony filled the rear one, with the president lying at their feet.

The woman was on her knees next to Longwood, feeling for his pulse.

Sam watched her a moment and glanced out to see several boaters giving the airplane a one-digit salute as it passed them.

"Are you a doctor?" the president asked his caregiver.

"I'm better than that. I'm a nurse. Now, I told you to shut up. I'm trying to take your pulse in a bouncing airplane."

As they taxied across the reservoir, the pilot said, "We're heavy, so everyone strap in. It could be a might sporty getting this baby airborne on this puddle."

Sam glanced at Louie and noted his white-knuckled grip on the armrest. "Hang in there, Louie."

The mobster glanced at Sam, but did not respond. His wide-eyed look was the same one Sam remembered from their flight in the Cessna in Montana.

Once they were across the small, man-made lake, the pilot turned the plane's nose into the wind again and pushed the throttle all the way forward. The engine roared, and they began bouncing and splashing as they accelerated.

Sam stared ahead at the quickly approaching boat launch he had been standing on moments before. It did not seem far enough away.

Tony leaned forward with a hand on the pilot's shoulder. "You don't have a lot of runway, pilot."

"Don't I know it," the aviator yelled as he pulled back on the yoke with both hands. "Up, up, and awaaaay."

With that, the airplane leapt into the air, and the

bouncing stopped, but the thrills did not. Sam knew they couldn't have cleared the ramp by more than a few inches, and a tree line now stood a hundred feet in front of them.

"You can make it over those trees, right?" Louie pleaded.

"Don't worry about that," the pilot responded. "The top five feet of every tree in the world bends. It's those damn power lines on the other side of 'em that have my attention."

As the airplane's pontoons skimmed the top branches of the leafy maples, Sam looked beyond and saw horizontal lines of heavy-gauge cable directly ahead. It was obvious to him that they wouldn't make it over them.

The nose dropped suddenly, and everyone went weightless.

Sam's stomach lifted as if he were going over that first big drop on a roller coaster. He saw Longwood float off the airplane's floor and reached out for him.

Louie screamed as the windscreen filled with the approaching ground, but just as quickly, the nose came back to level, and the old de Havilland Beaver roared across the terrain now no more than twenty feet below it, passing under the drooping cables.

A blink later, the pilot raised the nose again, and they began to climb. Longwood and the nurse dropped back to the floor unharmed as Louie leaned forward and vomited on his shoes.

"That's gross," the pilot shouted, looking over. "I ain't cleaning that up."

While the men were recovering from what Sam had briefly thought was their impending deaths, nobody noticed the nurse unwrapping Longwood's head. With the bandages in one hand, she looked at her patient and fell back onto her butt. "Oh, fuck."

"What's wrong?" the pilot asked, turning his balding head toward the back. When he saw Longwood's sallow face looking up at him, his eyes went wide. "What the—"

"How do you do, folks?" Longwood said, smiling.

The pilot reached back and shook the president's hand. "How do you do, Mr. President? I'm Dave Stevener, and your potty-mouthed nurse there's my wife, Kathy."

She smiled awkwardly and said, "Sorry about the cursing, Mr. President."

"That's quite all right, Kathy. I've been known to use a bit of profanity myself now and then."

The airplane went into the clouds then and immediately banked to the left. Dave asked, "Hey, doesn't this make my airplane Air Force One now?"

Ignoring the odd question, Sam asked, "Where are we going?"

"We're headed to Maine, but I wanted to go south until I got back into the clouds and far enough away from that reservoir so anyone watching us leave wouldn't know which direction we actually went."

After a few minutes in the soup, they descended to just below the cloud deck again, with Dave announcing, "We'll be staying below radar coverage from here on. We don't want some nosey FAA controller knowing where we're headed, either."

"Did you ever hear from Stone?" Sam asked.

"No. All I know is that he wanted me to take you guys up to the lodge and go back and pick up some FBI guy named O'Malley."

Sam figured that would likely be the same O'Malley he had covertly listened to at the ruins of his family's home. The thought brought on a sigh and a sense of loss that stayed with him as he stared out the misted side window.

No one spoke much for the next hour. Sam noted the

terrain below becoming more and more remote as they flew northeast. Finally a lake appeared ahead, and the airplane began to descend. He had not seen a road for some time and saw only one structure at the north end of the pristine-looking body of water, which was surrounded by dense forest.

The floatplane set down smoothly and taxied under a carport-style cover alongside a dock. As the propeller slowed and the airplane came to rest, Dave said, "Welcome to Lake Umbagog. This entire section of southern Maine is a national wildlife refuge. Flight below two thousand feet above the ground is prohibited, and this lake is off-limits to everyone. It's supposedly a migratory bird sanctuary."

Once the group climbed out onto the dock, Dave wrapped a tie-down rope around a cleat to secure his airplane while telling them, "The CIA built this place back in the Cold War days." He retrieved a bucket with a sponge in it from a compartment in the back of the airplane, dipped the bucket in the water, and handed it to Louie. "Okay, big fella, you get to clean your puke out of my airplane now."

Sam saw Louie give the pilot a look that should have made him change his mind, but Dave merely smiled at the gangster and turned away. The rest followed him down the dock. Sam and Tony carried Longwood's stretcher while Kathy held an IV bag in the air above it.

After climbing twenty steps to reach the massive log structure that sadly reminded Sam of his lost Montana home, they carried the president through a large, rustic great room and down a hallway on the left, into a room containing a hospital bed.

Once Longwood was on the bed, Kathy said, "Let me handle things now. You guys go back out there with my husband."

"Come on, fellas," Dave said. "Let's get you settled while she does her thing. Don't worry. He's in good hands."

The men stepped back into the great room, and Dave informed them, "Guest rooms are upstairs. Ours is next to the medical suite so Kathy can stay close to her patients. There's only one bathroom at the end of the hall up there, but it has a hot-water shower. The kitchen and communications room are on this level, down that hallway on the right."

"I knew the agency had safe houses overseas," Sam said. "I had no idea they had any in the states. Why does it have a hospital room?"

"Well, in the old days they used to do interrogations and debriefings here. Sometimes those folks needed medical attention afterward. Times have changed, though."

Sam let that pass. "It's a nice setup," he said.

"Yeah, we've got a satellite dish and full comms. We even get HBO."

Louie came in the door then, and the two mobsters settled onto a sofa.

"I need to go refuel my airplane and pick up that O'Malley fella now," said Dave. "You knew about him, right?"

"Yeah, Stone told me," Sam answered.

Louie mumbled, "I don't like FBI agents."

As Dave walked out, Kathy appeared and plopped down on a chair. "So, can someone please tell me what the hell's going on?" she said. "That man in there was just buried at Arlington. At least, part of him was."

CHAPTER 35

Devlin was exhausted, but unable to sleep after the failed assault at the New Jersey house. Now Crowley had discovered that Longwood might have gone to a CIA safe house on a lake in southern Maine. Devlin's mind was spinning. He knew they would move him again as soon as they discovered Stone was missing. *Speed's critical now*, he thought. *The longer this goes on, the more likely Longwood will recover enough to go public.*

He also feared that Mandrake might roll over for his more dominant predecessor if Longwood walked through the White House's front doors. Even though he was a legally appointed vice president, Devlin knew that if Longwood managed to get back into office, he would find some justification to remove him from the VP job, possibly even imprison him, or worse.

As his mind worked through scenarios, a rudimentary plan formed. Based on what Crowley had learned, Devlin knew he needed to get rid of Pearson now, too. And yet, having the former CIA director and the FBI director killed right after Longwood was supposedly killed might garner a lot of scrutiny he did not want. *The conspiracy theorists will go nuts*, he thought.

He made a call to his replacement at the DIA and dialed Frank Crowley. "I've just arranged for a DIA Blackhawk to take your team up to that lodge. The pilots will be regular Army, so tell your men not to say anything about Longwood. They've been told they're supporting civilian contractors hired to hunt the missing MSM assassins."

"Okay, we'll get ready to leave immediately, sir."

"No, let Blevins lead it. You and two others need to stay here. Pearson and that comatose guy need to be handled, too."

cↄcↄ

Vince O'Malley was not happy. His investigation was stalled, and the director had forced him to leave his Montana home for Washington, D.C., in the middle of the night, without explanation. *I can't believe he sent a chartered jet to pick me up.*

O'Malley knew FBI headquarters was where most agents yearned to be. *Or at least where the politically motivated sycophants hanker to be*, he thought. He, on the other hand, knew he belonged in the sticks, where his daily attire hardly ever included a tie, and his lunch options were a few diners specializing in chicken fried steak or meatloaf, not sushi. That was why he had requested assignment to the Montana field office twenty years before and voluntarily remained there.

Nonetheless, he accepted that seniority, and being in the wrong place at the wrong time had finally caught up with him. First it had forced him to assume responsibility for the investigation at Pointer Lake, and now this. On Pearson's order, he was secretly meeting some mysterious pilot along a Maryland riverbank. From here, he was to fly to an undisclosed location to meet an unidentified person who supposedly knew something vital to his investigation. *It's all a bit too hush-hush for my liking*, he thought as he stood on the short dock, sipping coffee in a windblown drizzle.

A floatplane suddenly swooped down out of the low clouds, landed on the river, and taxied straight toward the dock.

"Are you O'Malley?" the pilot yelled out a side window, not bothering to shut off the engine.

O'Malley nodded.

"Come on, get in."

The moment he was in the passenger's seat, the pilot motored out into the channel for a bouncy takeoff, and the plane quickly climbed to just below the clouds.

"My name's Dave," the pilot said, sticking out a hand. They shook.

"I'm Vince. Where are we going?"

"I can't tell you, Vince."

"Why?"

"You'll understand when we get there. Just sit back and relax."

Yep, definitely too much cloak-and-dagger going on around here, O'Malley thought. He sat looking out the window at a dreary world. They were heading north, but that was all he could determine.

An hour later, they touched down on a lake in what looked to him to be the middle of nowhere. Once the plane had pulled alongside a dock, O'Malley climbed out first and froze in place as a man tying the airplane to a cleat stood up and faced him.

"Special Agent O'Malley, I'm Sam Calder."

O'Malley just stared, his jaw slack.

Dave passed behind, muttering, "If *he* surprised you, you're gonna pee your britches in a minute."

"Come on, let's go on up to the lodge," Calder said, turning to follow Dave.

O'Malley chased after the pair, baffled. Then he stepped inside and saw the well-known mobster Tony Deluca casually sitting on a sofa next to a beefy man he didn't recognize, and O'Malley gave up any hope of knowing how to handle the situation.

Deluca and the other man stared back at him with distinctly unfriendly glares. He heard the big one mutter something to Deluca in what sounded like Italian.

"Come on," Calder said. "Your surprises aren't over yet."

O'Malley could think of nothing to say as he followed Calder down a hallway and into a room with a hospital bed in its center. He was dumbstruck at the sight before him.

"How do you do, Special Agent O'Malley? I'm Bob Longwood."

His head bobbing slightly, O'Malley barely managed to say, "You're alive."

"I am, thanks to all these fine folks."

"I mean, how did you—where have you—what the hell's going on?"

"That's a long story, and Sam here will explain it to you. I wanted to meet you first so you'd understand why secrecy was so important in getting you here."

"To be honest, sir, I don't understand anything right now." He turned to Sam and added, "But you definitely have my attention, Mr. Calder."

"Make it Sam."

"I'm Vince."

A woman appeared in the doorway. "Okay, fellas, it's time for the president's bandage change. Get the hell outta here, unless you're gonna help."

After wary introductions with the mobsters, O'Malley

listened to Sam's tale without interruption, mostly because he was so astounded at how wrong he and so many others had been. *So much for the FBI being the nation's greatest brain trust of criminal investigative minds,* he thought.

"Well, that's where we stand at the moment," Sam said at the end.

"At least I know who cut the president's wader suspenders now *and* what happened to my damn satellite phone. I'm glad I was right about those bodies we couldn't identify at your ranch. I can happily tell you something *you* got wrong about that part of the story, though."

"What's that?"

"Your brother ain't dead."

Sam leapt to his feet. "What? Mark's alive?"

"He was hit in the shoulder, but the second round only clipped him on the side of the head. I'm sure with all the blood a scalp wound produces, it must have looked fatal, but he was only unconscious. He must have come to and made his way outside before passing out again. First responders found him just off the front porch."

"How is he?" Sam asked, joyful tears welling in his eyes.

"Well, he was in a coma the last I checked, but he's alive and expected to be fine once he comes out of it."

Sam's broad smile told O'Malley he had made the former SEAL's day. It felt good to surprise someone else for a change.

"There was a second attempt on his life, though."

"What happened?"

"A gunman showed up at the hospital and tried to kill him. I stopped him."

"Thank you."

"Yeah, well, we moved him to a hospital down in

Missoula after that, and I put a protection detail on him. At least now I know why the bastards wanted him dead."

Solemnly, Sam said, "I wish my dad had made it, too. At least he got to go out with his boots on like he wanted."

"He did just that, and I believe he took at least one of them out, too, since you made nothing but head shots."

Tony, who had remained silent, cleared his throat. "So, can the FBI do anything to stop Devlin?"

"He may be the vice president, but he's still subject to the same laws as everyone else."

"I hope he doesn't find out about this place," Louie said.

Just then, the picture on the television in the great room blinked out.

Dave came in a moment later and announced, "That storm's coming in. A gust just tore the satellite dish off its mount. There's a sat phone around here somewhere for emergencies." He took off in search of it and returned after a few minutes with the phone. "The battery's dead."

"Got a spare or a charger?" Sam asked.

"Yeah, there's a charger for it somewhere."

"Well, it looks like we're cut off until you find it."

CHAPTER 36

Late in the afternoon, Sam joined Tony on the lodge's wide covered porch. Sitting on one of a half-dozen Adirondack chairs lined up there, he stared out at the water and surrounding woods. The view brought on an unwanted memory of Pointer Lake and the disheartening thought that, if he lived through this, he would likely never go there again.

"Are you okay?" Tony asked.

"Yeah, I was just thinking about something unpleasant."

"There's been a lot of that lately. How's the president doing?"

"He's fine." As Sam said it, a faint but familiar sound teased his ears above the gusting wind. It brought him to full alert, and he jumped to his feet.

"What's wrong?"

"I hear a helicopter." He scanned the southern horizon.

Dave stepped out the door then. "I've looked everywhere. I can't find that damn charger for the life of— what're you fellas looking at?"

Sam continued to stare out over the lake and trees as he said, "I'm pretty sure I heard a helicopter. Tony, go tell Kathy to get the president ready to move."

Tony took off.

"Do you have a safe room here, Dave?" Sam asked.

"No one's supposed to be able to find this place."

"There!" Sam declared, pointing. A small black dot appeared in the distance as the faint sound of its heavy rotors came on the wind again. He turned to Dave. "It's a Blackhawk. We need to fly your airplane outta here."

"We can't. It'll take too long to get airborne, and a Blackhawk's faster than the Beaver anyway. It'll chase us down, and they can just gun us outta the sky. Maybe Stone sent more men up here."

"We were emphatic that only Vince was allowed to join us. Besides, we haven't heard from Stone. I think we would have by now if he was okay."

"He might have tried to contact us. Remember, our comms are down."

The chopper was getting louder. O'Malley and Louie rushed out the door next.

Sam turned to Dave again. "We can't take chances with that man's life on the line. Is there some other way out of here?"

"There are a couple of ATVs in the shed out back, but that's it. There aren't any roads, and it's a good fifty miles to the nearest town." He pointed. "It's that way, west."

The chopper was approaching slowly up the eastern side of the lake. It stopped halfway to the lodge and hovered there. The group watched as six dark objects descended from it.

"Well, that settles who sent them," Sam declared. "We probably only have minutes before they make their way here. I'm taking Longwood out on one of those ATVs. I want Tony and Louie on the other one to provide cover." He turned to O'Malley. "You and the Steveners need to hightail it into the woods. Go north a half mile and turn east. I saw a small lake over that way on a map I looked at earlier. We'll meet up there."

"Yeah, that lake's about three miles east of here," Dave confirmed.

"I should stay with the president," O'Malley said.

"No," Sam replied. "If we don't survive, you're our best hope of getting the truth out."

"Hey, look!" Louie called out, pointing. The chopper was moving west now, across the lake. It stopped on the other side, and six more bodies came out of it. "How the hell did they find us?"

"That doesn't matter now," Sam said. "Let's go. Grab a rifle off that rack in there, Louie, and get the ATVs out of the shed. I'll get the president." Sam grabbed his pistol from a table, pushed past Tony and Kathy, and hefted the confused president over his shoulder. "Sorry about treating you like a slab of meat again, sir, but we gotta go."

Longwood grunted but did not resist. As they went out the back door, Dave called out, "Kathy, over here with us."

Sam and Tony joined Louie as he was pushing the second ATV out of the shed. Sam dropped the president onto its seat and sat in front of him. "Louie, get that rope over there and tie him to me." While Louie did that, Sam started the engine and watched Vince disappear into the woods behind the Steveners. He also saw the .50 caliber *Desert Eagle* in Vince's hand.

With Sam leading the way, the ATVs moved into the trees. The first thing Sam noticed was that, unlike the pine-covered mountains he knew in Montana, the Maine forest was a potpourri of broadleaf growths—mostly maples and birches—often spaced only feet apart. Having to steer around and between them, as well as scattered rock outcroppings left behind by ancient glacial retreats, made it slow going and difficult to navigate a straight line. Sam worried the noise of the ATV engines would give away their position, but he had to accept that he could not run faster, or far, carrying Longwood.

He tried to ensure that they were not going in circles, but couldn't tell the position of the sun because of the tree canopy and cloud cover. After only a few minutes of the turning and twisting ride, he felt almost disoriented. Then the Blackhawk passed directly overhead. Sam had not heard it approaching because of the ATVs' noise.

He stopped and stared up through the leafy canopy, waiting to see if it returned. He hoped the cover above was too thick to see through, but surprisingly quickly, the huge military aircraft was hovering less than a hundred feet above them, its downwash causing a minor wind-storm.

Sam gunned his throttle just as a heavy machine gun began firing above them.

The gun's thunderous roar was louder than the heli-copter and ATVs. It shredded trees all around, showering them with leaves, splintered bark, and hot shell casings. The earth erupted a few feet to Sam's right as bullets slammed into the moss-covered ground, some sparking as they ricocheted off rock.

Sam figured the gunner must have recognized Long-wood strapped to his back, because he was focusing his firepower on their ATV. As Sam maneuvered, frantically trying to avoid trees and bullets, Longwood's one-handed grip tightened, and Sam desperately sought some avenue of escape. He knew it would only be seconds before the gunner adjusted his firing angle and the huge slugs began tearing them to pieces.

Without warning, the gunfire ceased. A moment later, a man's body crashed through the branches above and slammed into the ground only feet away.

Sam stopped and stared at the badly broken and nearly

headless corpse for a moment before the helicopter moved off, allowing him to hear Tony say, "That idiot was so fixed on you, he forgot about us."

Sam turned and saw the mobsters sitting on their ATV. Louie smiled broadly as he slung the AR-15 he had grabbed at the lodge back over his shoulder.

Sam gunned his throttle again and took off. The terrain remained fairly level, though partially buried boulders occasionally jarred them so hard he knew Longwood would have fallen off had he not been tied to him. After several minutes, he stopped again and asked, "How're you doing, sir?"

"I'm okay," Longwood responded.

Sam noted how breathless the president's voice sounded. He glanced around a moment but was unable to determine their position because he could see no land-marks. His gut told him they had likely traveled no more than a half mile. As the other ATV pulled up alongside, Sam pointed the direction he thought east to be. "We'll go that way now, toward the rendezvous point."

After another hour of the constant maneuvering and bouncy riding, Sam came to a stream and stopped to check Longwood's condition again. This time, the presi-dent asked to be untied and allowed to stand and pee.

Sam loosened the knots, and Louie helped Longwood to a tree where he could brace himself.

Sam drove the ATV across the stream and waited for Louie to carry the president across. He and Tony shut down their engines to check fuel levels, and the moment it quieted, they all heard a woman scream. Two gunshots followed instantly.

"That sounds close," Tony said.

Sam nodded. "That was Vince's gun."

"What now?" Louie asked.

Before Sam could respond, Longwood ordered, "Go

see if you can help them, Sam. I'll be okay with Tony and Louie."

Sam jumped back across the stream and headed off, calling back, "Follow that stream and get him to the lake. We'll meet you there." He heard the ATV engines a moment later and hoped no one else could.

🙟🙝

Fifteen minutes into his stealthy search, Sam heard a man's voice and stopped short. He couldn't make out the words, but the tone sounded angry. He dropped to his belly and crawled closer through the trees. It didn't take long before he spotted them.

Two men, armed with suppressed rifles, stood above a prone Vince O'Malley. The body of another enemy lay several feet away, where Dave sat with his back to a tree, Kathy at his side. Both had their arms behind their backs.

As Sam took in the situation, he noticed the enemy wore earpieces and throat microphones. Neither man was maintaining any sort of defensive watch.

One of them kicked O'Malley in the ribs while the other touched his own throat and said too loudly, "Yeah, we heard engines a few minutes ago, but we couldn't tell which direction the sound was coming from in this damn wind." After listening, he added, "Okay, I'll pop a flare, and we'll get rid of these three." He reached for something on his vest as his partner pointed his rifle at O'Malley's head.

Lying prone next to a tree, Sam fired then stood and rushed forward with his finger to his lips as he came in front of the Steveners. He pulled a knife from one of the men he had just killed and cut the plastic ties binding the couple. "Be quiet," he whispered. "They have comm gear and may be able to hear you if you speak loud enough."

Sam turned both of the enemies' microphones off. "Okay, now you can talk."

Kathy had already jumped to Vince's side, while Dave stood and faced Sam. "We walked right into them. There were three, but Vince got that one over there before those two managed to get the drop on me and Kathy."

"How badly is he hurt?" Sam asked.

Before she could answer, Vince rolled over and smiled through bloody teeth. "I had 'em right where I wanted 'em."

Sam chuckled. "I'm sure they were about to surrender, you being FBI and all." He began stripping the dead of their equipment. Stuffing an earpiece into his own ear, he said, "I'm gonna listen in for a moment. Be quiet."

He heard someone ask, "Did anyone see a flare?"

"No," another answered. "Did they say who they caught?"

"Only that they had a woman and two men, but not the target. The idiots weren't sure of their position, though. That's why I asked for a flare. I was hoping you'd see it."

"I heard a couple of gunshots a while back, but I couldn't tell which way they came from in this wind."

"Okay, keep searching. Our target's apparently on one of the ATVs. If anyone spots them or hears them, call out and mark your position with a flare. Be careful. They have a shooter who shot Browning right outta the damn chopper."

"We need to move," Sam announced as he pulled out the earpiece.

CHAPTER 37

Devlin fidgeted in his chair, anxious to hear what the team in Maine had found and what they had done about it. *This could be over soon*, he hoped.

Preston Maddox called. "The president would like you to join him in the Oval Office, sir."

Too fixated on his personal dilemma, Devlin ignored greetings from passersby as he walked the West Wing hallway. Then he heard a female voice he couldn't ignore.

"Can I have a moment, Tom?" Marcy Mandrake asked.

"Sure, what's up? I'm on my way to see him now."

Her tone desperate, she whispered, "He's what I wanted to speak to you about. You're his good friend, and a confidant I know I can trust to do the right thing."

"What's wrong, Marcy?" Devlin asked, trying not to lose his patience.

"He isn't sleeping. In fact, he stays up praying most nights. He doesn't think I know his blood pressure is through the roof, too, and the medications they're giving him for it aren't helping. It's the job, Tom. It's too much for him."

"What is it you want *me* to do?"

She broke down and wept openly. "Help him. He can't keep this up. It's killing him."

Devlin noted people trying not to stare as they passed the heavyset, sobbing first lady. None stopped to offer assistance, though, and he wanted to get away, too. "I'll speak with him about it, Marcy. Maybe I can take some of the burden off his shoulders."

"Would you? Oh, thank you, Tom."

"I have to go," he said, turning away.

He started down the hallway again but stopped as a new thought came to mind. He stood there a moment, ignoring people walking past, as he reconsidered his original plan that he had thought an errant bullet ruined. *Or did it? Is he really that gullible, that dumb?*

A moment later, he nodded several times. *Yes*, he told himself. *He is.*

Outside the Oval Office, he said to Preston Maddox, "Don't interrupt us for anything short of a nuclear attack."

"Yes, sir."

He entered and closed the door behind him, finding Mandrake at his desk eating from a tray of hors d'oeuvres.

"Good afternoon, Tom. Are you hungry? These pigs-in-a-blanket crescent rolls are delicious. Help yourself."

"No thanks, Mr. President. I just ate."

Mandrake shoved one of the miniature weenie rolls in his mouth and attempted to say something more, but failed miserably. He gulped it down half-chewed and tried again. "Excuse me. I was trying to say that I want to discuss your ideas about my cabinet, if you have some free time."

A half-chewed chunk of roll fell from the man's mouth as he spoke. Devlin was disgusted that someone weighing more than three hundred pounds could ignore even common-sense eating habits. *Hors d'oeuvres are fine, but not an entire tray of them.*

"I wanted to speak with you, too, but not about that. Something very important has come up."

"What's that?"

Devlin sighed for effect. "In my capacity as head of the investigation into Longwood's assassination, something has surfaced that I find very troubling—something concerning you."

Mandrake stared at him, even setting down the roll in his hand. "What?"

"The FBI recovered a cell phone from one of the assassins killed at the lake that shows a call received the night before the attack. I examined that phone and recognized the number the call came from. It's your number."

"What?" Mandrake almost screamed. "That's impossible!"

"Where's your cell phone?"

Mandrake pulled it from his pants pocket.

"Let me see it."

Mandrake handed it over, and Devlin scrolled through the recent calls list, finding the one Branson had made. "Oh my God," he said. "It's true."

"What's true?" Mandrake breathlessly asked, reaching for the device. "Let me see that."

"That number's the same one the bureau recovered."

"I didn't make any damn phone call that night! I was asleep."

"The evidence says otherwise, Phil. Not only that, but the bureau is aware that all of the MSM assassins who were killed were constituents of yours. They all came from *your* congressional district."

Mandrake was visibly shaking now, so Devlin pressed onward. "Investigators are also looking into why it was that *you* didn't go to the lake that day."

"I told you, I was sleeping. No one woke me."

Devlin noted that Mandrake was now hyperventilating and sweating profusely. "They're also aware that you personally invited President Longwood to go on that trip and set everything up with Ben Branson."

"It was Ben who came to *me* with the idea," Mandrake almost pleaded.

"Unfortunately, he's dead and can't corroborate that. He certainly didn't walk into a mortar ambush that he set up. It also doesn't explain that cell phone call you made to one of the assassins only hours before the attack."

"I didn't call anyone!" The man's face turned a deep purple, and his eyes blinked rapidly.

"Are you all right?"

Mandrake was gulping for air now, pulling at his tie. "I don't feel well," he gasped. "I'm gonna be sick. I don't know what to do."

"Look, I'm your friend, Phil. I can help you."

"How can you help?"

"Everything they have is conjecture, circumstantial, except that cell phone. I can make it disappear."

Mandrake's face snapped up. "You can?"

"I'm in charge of the investigation. Trust me, I can do it. But to make this work, you'd need to do something to remove the incentive to go after you."

"What?"

"If you were to step down for health reasons, and they no longer had any solid evidence to make a case against you, they'd have no choice but to drop the matter. The attorney general isn't about to indict an ill former president on circumstantial evidence and conjecture alone."

"But I didn't have anything to do with Longwood's death."

"Again, the evidence says otherwise. Think of your family, your legacy. You'll still go down in history as a president if you resign, and nobody's going to fault you for doing so for health reasons. Otherwise, there's a strong probability you'll be indicted, impeached, and charged in the assassination. That will mean disgrace, prison."

"But I'm innocent."

"I'm your friend and a loyal supporter, but the facts speak for themselves. I recommend you consider what I've proposed. I promise I will continue your plan for this country."

Mandrake had tears in his eyes as he stared at Devlin for several moments and sighed. "I don't believe I have any choice. Marcy's been pushing me to quit anyway. Can you really make that cell phone disappear?"

"Consider it done," Devlin answered, knowing Mandrake would never learn of the phone's actual fate.

CHAPTER 38

It was nearly dark when Sam finally led his group into a wide clearing at the lake's edge. He saw no one at first, but there was just enough light to spot Louie stepping out from behind a tree a hundred feet away.

"How's the president?" Sam asked as he neared, noting the gangster's wet pants.

"He's okay, but the ride took it out of him."

"Where'd you put the ATVs?"

"I pushed them into the water. They're almost out of gas."

Louie led the tired group to where Longwood lay, and Kathy immediately went to the president's side.

Before anyone could say more, the faint sound of a helicopter came to Sam's ears again. "Everyone be quiet." He listened a moment. "Shit! It's coming this way." Looking around for somewhere they could hide, he saw only one option. "Everyone get in the water, quickly!"

"Aw, shit," Kathy grumbled.

Sam bent over the president. "Sorry about this, sir, but it can't be helped." He lifted him to his shoulder again.

There were several fallen trees at the lake's edge, their top branches lying in the water. "Get over there into those branches and stay as low as possible," Sam said.

Each walked into the chilly, dark water. Longwood gasped audibly as Sam lowered him under it. Sam tried to ease their discomfort while they waited with only their heads exposed, hidden in the fallen foliage. "It may be cold, but it's better than a bullet," he said. "It's nearly dark now, so we should be difficult to spot. Try not to move around a lot so the water stays calm. Stay low, and slowly dunk your head every thirty seconds or so. The Blackhawk has an infrared imaging capability."

The chopper was over them moments later, its nose-mounted searchlight moving slowly across the water.

It appeared that they were flying a search pattern, and, for a moment, Sam thought they might have made it undetected, but then the chopper swung around and returned to hover not far from where they had been standing on shore. Sam figured they had probably seen the ATVs Louie had apparently not put in deep enough water.

The loud *whomp-whomp-whomp* of the down-drafting rotors caused the small group to huddle closer. It was less than five feet deep where they hid, so all could stand.

The helicopter continued to hover for several minutes, turning its nose in different directions, and descended to the ground thirty feet from the water. With the rotors still turning slowly, Sam watched a man armed with a suppressed assault rifle climb out and begin searching the ground with a flashlight.

"Can you fly that thing?" Sam asked Dave.

"No. I'm a fixed-wing guy only."

The searcher was closing on where the group had been standing, and he stopped to examine the ground more closely. His flashlight beam moved across the water like a lighthouse beacon.

Sam knew more would be coming once word got out they had a lead on their prey, and he could see no avenue of escape. Not one to hesitate in the face of the obvious, he released his grip on Longwood to Tony and turned to the others. "Stay low," he said before slipping under the murky water.

Hardly a ripple marked his reappearance nearly a hundred feet away. Splayed flat in the shallow water and marsh grass, he could see the searcher with the flashlight standing a hundred feet from the chopper. The man was now speaking into a satellite phone, facing away from him. Sam could see the two pilots sitting in their seats through the open door on the left side of the helicopter. He slowly crawled from the water, using the grass and darkness for cover. His eyes darted back and forth between the man on the phone and the pilots as he made his way to the right side of the aircraft. Rising at the rear of the sliding door on that side, Sam saw both aviators still looking toward the third man, oblivious to any threat to themselves.

He quickly slid the door open and jumped in, his pistol pointed. The startled pilots raised their hands, and Sam noted that neither carried a weapon. He intended to force them to fly his group to safety, but a hailstorm of bullets began striking around him, forcing him to dive out the door he had just entered.

Sam rolled once and spun, swinging his pistol up just as a loud gunshot sounded. The searcher with the assault rifle collapsed, and Sam saw Vince standing in the water, his huge pistol still raised.

Sam quickly turned to the pilots, fearing they might lift off. Instead, both were slumped forward in their harnesses. Jumping back inside, he discovered that the bullets intended for him had pierced them instead, tearing into the aircraft's instrument panel and destroying the radio.

He examined the pilots more closely, noting that both wore military flight suits with rank insignia. They were

Army warrant officers. Searching their pockets, he found that each carried an Army ID card and DIA credentials. He pocketed the IDs and reached to a panel to shut down the Blackhawk's engines. He then pulled the pilots' bodies from the cockpit and concealed them at the tree line. Meanwhile, O'Malley brought over the body of the man he had killed. That one had no ID.

As the shivering group climbed inside the helicopter for cover from the rain that had finally joined the wind, Sam retrieved a package from one of several survival kits he knew were standard equipment aboard the military helicopter. He unfolded a small square of shiny silver material resembling tin foil into an eight-foot-long emergency blanket and handed it to Kathy. "Wrap the president in this. There are more in there."

"What's the plan now, Sam?" Tony asked.

"The president's nearly hypothermic," Kathy said. "Hell, we all are."

Sam slid both side doors closed. "You'll be able to warm up in here, and there's food and water in those survival kits, too."

"We should go back to the lodge," Tony suggested. "We need to get in that airplane and go somewhere else."

Sam put the dead searcher's earpiece in his ear. "Everyone be quiet. I need to listen in for a moment."

He listened for several seconds before he heard, "Blevins, this is Crawford. Where the hell are you?"

There was no answer, which told Sam that the dead searcher outside was probably Blevins. Then he heard, "If you can hear this, Blevins, we're headed back to the lodge to wait this storm out."

Another voice announced, "Crawford, this is Johnson. My team will meet you there."

"Yeah, okay. Did you hear that gunshot a few minutes ago?"

"Yeah, but we couldn't tell where it came from. It's getting too dark to see anyway."

"Okay, we'll meet you at the lodge."

Sam disengaged the earpiece. "They're all headed to the lodge."

Everyone sat silently, shivering.

Louie had opened a second survival packet and was chewing on something. He swallowed and immediately said, "Yuck! This is horrible. The package said it was spaghetti and meatballs."

Sam chuckled. "It's an MRE—Meal Ready to Eat. You're supposed to heat it in hot water, though. Otherwise it's like chewing on a bar of soap."

"Stay away from the ones that say burrito, too," Dave added. "They taste like wet dog."

Sam remembered the satellite phone he had seen the searcher using. He opened the side door and jumped out to hunt for it. He found the instrument near where the man was shot, only to discover that Vince's bullet had gone through both man and phone. "Damn."

Considering his next course of action, Sam climbed back inside the chopper. "You and Kathy stay with the president," he said to Dave. He turned to Tony. "You and Louie stay, too."

"What are you up to, Sam?" Longwood asked.

Sam slung Blevins's assault rifle over his shoulder and slipped two extra magazines into a pouch on his vest. "Vince and I are going back to the lodge to take it away from those guys."

"We are?" O'Malley asked.

"We can't walk out of these woods, and Dave can't fly this thing. We need that airplane, and the president needs the meds in the lodge."

The FBI agent climbed out, and Sam climbed out behind him, nodding for Dave to join them. Away from the others, he told him, "If we don't come back by noon to-morrow, the chopper's emergency locator transmitter is in the tail-boom compartment. A passing plane might pick up the signal and notify the FAA of your location. Hide after you activate it, though, in case the bad guys get here first."

With that, Sam and Vince headed off in the dark, rain, and wind.

CHAPTER 39

Mandrake's untelevised and sudden resignation shocked everyone. He summoned the chief justice and attorney general to the Oval Office and handed both a copy of his letter of intent to relinquish the office immediately for health reasons. Thirty minutes later, he and his wife left the White House without fanfare in a blacked-out SUV rather than a presidential limousine.

Devlin made a show of appearing to be in shock when told of Mandrake's actions by a sobbing Preston Maddox, but he entered the East Room of the White House with elation two hours later and walked briskly to the platform at its front.

The remnants of Longwood's cabinet, having been hastily notified of Mandrake's resignation, showed up looking numb. Within the hour, they reluctantly signed their second affidavit in support of the Constitution's twenty-fifth amendment.

With most of America already in bed for the night, only those West Coast denizens alerted by television and radio news flashes were even aware that the nation was once again embroiled in an executive office transition of power.

"Mr. Vice President," the chief justice solemnly asked, "are you prepared to take the oath of office at this time?"

"I am," Devlin responded as he pressed his left hand to the Bible the chief justice held.

The oath completed, Devlin stepped to the microphones, knowing most of America would first hear his words with their morning coffee. "America has once again suffered an unanticipated loss of leadership. However, our nation's strength lies not in its leaders, but in its people, united. It is true that we have many enemies, and as President Longwood's death attests, they do not all come from beyond our borders. Still, we shall prevail against those who would do our nation harm. I promise to root out those enemies and destroy them."

He stepped away from the podium and walked out of the room without saying another word.

Preston Maddox and two Secret Service agents followed him to the Oval Office, but he closed the door, leaving them outside.

He was euphoric. *I have the upper hand now*, he thought, *even if Longwood reappears. I simply need to install my own cabinet as soon as possible.*

He called Crowley. "Have you heard from Blevins?"

"He called a few hours ago and said he had them cornered at some lake, but his sat phone's offline now."

Disgusted by his mercenaries' incompetence but unable to think of other options, Devlin said, "Let me know if you hear from him. I doubt Longwood will stay there much longer."

"He may not have much choice. Blevins said that storm was closing in on them, and the pilots were claiming the winds were almost out of limits. He was planning to wait it out at that lodge after he took care of business."

Another idea dawned on Devlin. "If Blevins was successful and the storm keeps him there a while longer, no problem. But if Calder got the upper hand again and *they* have control of the lodge, there may still be another way to end this once and for all."

"What d'ya got in mind, sir?"

"I'll let you know later." He hung up and summoned the man who had replaced him at the DIA. When Major General Lee Conway arrived, Devlin met him in the Situation Room.

"Congratulations, Mr. President."

Devlin ignored the man's insincere words and motioned for him to sit as he began his prepared lie. "I'm sure you're aware that the FBI has been hunting for the mortar teams responsible for President Longwood's assassination. That's what that chopper of yours is currently involved with."

A familiar oblivious look appeared on the man's face, but Conway nodded. "Yes. I've heard about that, of course."

"Well, the FBI has discovered where they're hiding."

"That's terrific, sir."

"Under my leadership, the DIA revealed the initial attackers approaching the lake in Montana. Now, under yours, the agency is going to end this conspiracy once and for all."

"What do you propose we do, sir?"

"They're hiding at a lodge up in Maine. I want you to drop a big-ass bomb down their throats."

Devlin knew Conway had never been part of, let alone directed, a strike operation while at the DIA. He waited for the man to balk.

"But, sir, an attack like that on American soil? Wouldn't that be against—"

Devlin sharply interrupted him. "It's not against anything, Conway. Those men are seditious traitors, and I'm the President of the United States." He paused a moment.

"Listen, it's a very isolated location—a federally protected nature reserve, in fact. Nobody will even hear the boom. Now, I have the authority to get this done and to have it remain an official secret. If you can't handle this—"

"No, no, no. I can handle it, sir. What's our time line?"

"We need to recon first, verify that they're still there. If they are, we'll need to be prepared to strike immediately."

"That storm might be a problem. I believe it's moving in that direction."

"Use a Predator. It can fly in weather a pilot can't, and its infrared imaging system can see through the clouds. You make this happen, Conway, and there'll be a third star in it for you." Devlin saw the man's face light up at the promotion enticement, so he added, "I want the drone's video feed sent directly to this room, and limit the number of people in your command center. Remind everyone involved that this is a national security operation and have each sign a nondisclosure agreement."

CHAPTER 40

Sam and Vince moved through the dark woods without light to avoid the enemy spotting them. The rain, diminished somewhat by the thick canopy above, continued throughout their nearly three-mile slog. As they neared the lodge, both were soaked, miserably cold, and exhausted. Through the trees, Sam saw light coming from the great room's windows. He knew the lights had not been on when his group rushed out earlier.

Vince knelt next to him. "Well, it looks like they're in there. What now?"

"We need to find out how many there are and where they're located in the building. Then we can come up with an assault plan. Cover me while I do some recon."

"Tell me something first. Why'd you bring me along instead of your mob pals?"

"Those fellas are tough, and they'll protect the president until they're both dead, but they're also city boys. I knew this little jaunt would require someone with a few Montana winters under his belt."

Vince nodded, a barely perceptible movement in the dark, and Sam started forward, now grateful for the rain. It not only enhanced the darkness cloaking him, but kept their enemy foolishly cooped up inside.

Though the upstairs windows were dark, he couldn't take the chance that a lookout was perched in one. It took five uncomfortable minutes for him to crawl to a spot where he could see into the great room. He spotted six men there, and another joined them from the kitchen.

He thought about what he intended to do next as he watched the men. After what he had seen them do, especially to his family, part of him wanted to charge in blasting. Still, something told him they might prove more useful against Devlin as guilty, but living, co-conspirators.

He noted that none had yet to glance out a window, so he rushed toward the covered porch for a closer look. Halfway there, a splashing sound to his left caused him to glance that way, and he spotted a large form bearing down on him.

Before he could wheel to face it, the charging juggernaut slammed into his side like a linebacker. Sam was sprawled onto his stomach in the wet grass and mud with the giant on his back, brutally pummeling his head with both fists.

With his right arm pinned beneath him, Sam could block the powerful blows with only his left, while trying unsuccessfully to raise his torso enough so he could roll over or squirm from beneath the goliath. He had a flashback to those MMA fights on television, where the fighter in his position always ended up unconscious very quickly.

That thought spurred a surge of adrenaline that nearly worked, but the huge man compensated for Sam's thrashing and remained on top, continuing to deliver blow after unrelenting blow.

Suddenly the man's weight was off him. Dazed, Sam pulled his knife and crawled to the motionless figure now lying next to him. He discovered that most of the man's neck was missing, then Vince was beside him.

"You okay?" Vince asked.

"Yeah, thanks."

"I saw a cigarette glowing down by the dock, but I couldn't get off a shot before he went at you."

"He must have been why they aren't even looking out the windows."

"Well, as soon as you feel up to it, how about we deal with the rest of them? I'm getting cold."

"I counted seven inside. The Blackhawk carries fourteen, plus the pilots. We know both pilots and six of the enemy are down. That means there could be one more we haven't spotted in there."

"Okay, what's your plan?"

"We need to get this over with while we still have the element of surprise. They might get suspicious when King Kong there doesn't come back. You go to the back. When I see you coming down the hallway, I'll come in from the porch."

The way the FBI man checked his rifle's magazine gave Sam the impression he didn't intend to take prisoners.

"We need to take them alive if we can," he added.

"Why?"

"They could be useful against Devlin."

Vince looked disappointed but didn't argue. As he rushed off, Sam crawled to the porch door and peered through its window.

The mercenaries displayed no tactical awareness that he noted. The seven men were lounging on the sofas and chairs, their weapons stacked on a nearby coffee table. *They probably think their gargantuan comrade will warn them of any threat out here*, he thought.

He saw Vince enter through the lodge's back door and begin creeping along the inside hallway. As he stepped into the great room, Sam entered from the porch. In seconds, the seven mercenaries were lying face down on the hardwood floor with their fingers interlocked above their heads.

Sam went to the stairs and whispered, "I'll clear the upstairs. You keep an eye on them." He went up the steps, quietly leaping up three at a time. As he hit the landing, he heard two muted pops from below, and Vince let out a yelp.

Sam spun around and looked down. Vince lay on the floor, gripping his right thigh. His rifle had skittered across the room toward their still-unsecured prisoners.

From the landing, Sam fired one round into the top of the shooter's head as the man emerged from the kitchen with his gun still aimed at Vince.

One of the five on the floor made a move toward the rifle. Sam saw it and shot him in the head, too. That stopped all movement by the other captives.

Vince crawled over and retrieved his weapon. "Shit, that hurts!"

Sam ignored the agent's complaint and whirled around to continue clearing the building. When he found the up-stairs rooms empty, he returned to clear the main floor. Once he checked that level, he knelt at Vince's side. "Okay, let's take a look at your leg."

Vince took his hand away from the bloody wound. "Damn, I was hoping to get through this career without being shot."

"It's a flesh wound," Sam said after a quick exam. "You'll need a few stitches, and you won't be doing any squats for a week or two." He went to the hospital room and rummaged through Kathy's supplies, finding a pair of crutches in the medical closet alongside a satellite phone charger. He returned to the great room and held out the charger. "Happen to know your boss's number?"

Sam searched until he found a bundle of plastic quick-ties and secured the ankles and wrists of the six surviving mercenaries before cleaning and bandaging Vince's leg. Helping him to the sofa, he said, "Kathy can stitch you up later."

Sam dragged the two dead men outside and laid them at the end of the covered porch, then moved the big man's corpse from the yard, covering all three with a tarp. Back inside, he cleaned up the puddled blood and goo, and set Vince up with food and water so he wouldn't have to move around. "I'm going back for the others," he announced. "It'll probably take a while to get them back here. Will you be okay?"

"Yeah, I'll be fine. If any of them causes trouble, I'll shoot them all in the feet."

Sam smiled. "Once that phone's charged up enough, call your director and get him to send help."

"Where the hell are we?"

"Dave said we're on Lake Umbagog. It's some kind of wildlife reserve in southern Maine."

⁊ঌ⁊ঌ

"I apologize for the delay, Mr. President," said Conway. "The Air Force had to send a C-17 to Nevada for the Predator. There weren't any available on the East Coast. It's en route and expected to be here in three hours. Then they'll have to fuel it and load the ordnance. It should be over the target by this afternoon."

Furious, Devlin was about to hang up when Conway added, "The meteorology folks say the storm is heading straight for our target. They won't be getting out of there before the Predator arrives."

Frustrated still, Devlin grumpily responded, "Just get it over with, Conway."

CHAPTER 41

The rain and wind had not let up by the time Sam made his way back to the helicopter, exhausted. As the storm worsened, he realized they were probably going to be stuck at the lodge longer than he wanted to be there. From his days living on the East Coast, he knew most hurricanes turned out to sea and fizzled, but occasionally, one type—a nor'easter—would circle back, sometimes stalling for days.

He walked into the small clearing at the lake just after dawn. The side door of the helicopter opened, and five tired faces stared out at him as he approached.

"Where's Vince?" Longwood asked with concern in his voice.

"He's okay, sir. He took one in the leg. He's watching the prisoners."

"You took prisoners?" Tony asked. "What the hell are we gonna do with prisoners?"

"We found that sat phone charger, and Vince was going to call his boss for some help."

"You look like shit," Kathy stated flatly. "You need to get in here, dry out, and get some rest."

"Not yet," Sam replied as he pulled a folded litter from the helicopter's emergency supplies. "This will probably be more comfortable than my shoulder, sir, but I'm afraid it isn't going to be a fun ride in this weather. Ready?"

Longwood slid onto the litter without complaint, and Kathy covered him with two of the emergency blankets.

"Better cover his face," Louie said as he and Tony each grabbed one end of the litter. Dave and Kathy took opposite sides to help steady it.

The group quieted as they moved off into the maelstrom, focusing on staying in line behind Sam and not dropping the president.

ɛ∕ɔɛ∕ɔ

The trek was miserably cold, wet, and slow, but late in the afternoon they finally climbed the porch steps and marched past the tarp with three sets of boots sticking out of one end.

"Dammit," Dave called out. "Someone cut my plane loose."

Sam saw him staring out over the lake. The airplane was floating several hundred feet from the dock. *Probably what that big fella who jumped me was doing down there*, he thought. "I'll swim out and get it in a few minutes."

"I'll need to gas it up," Dave replied.

Inside, the exhausted group only glanced at the six men sitting with their backs against one wall of the great room. Louie and Tony carried Longwood to the hospital bed, where a tired and wet Kathy tended to him.

Sam had held the porch door open and entered last. He stared at the prisoners, who were now gagged and blindfolded.

"They were getting mouthy, but I didn't want to waste my bullets," Vince said from the sofa. His injured leg rested on the coffee table.

"Did you reach Pearson?"

"Yeah, he's sending a team up as soon as the weather breaks, but you ain't gonna like what else he told me."

Sam was in Longwood's room moments later. "We think we know how Devlin found us up here, sir, and it's not good."

"What happened?"

"Vince contacted Director Pearson on the sat phone. FBI agents found Calvin Stone murdered, along with his wife and daughter."

Sam could tell Longwood was upset, though he only bowed his head.

"It gets worse, sir," Sam added.

Longwood looked up.

"Mandrake resigned, supposedly for health reasons."

Longwood looked deflated. "Shit. That means Devlin's the president now."

"Sir, it looks like we're stuck here until this storm lets up. As soon as that happens, though, we need to leave, with or without FBI help. Devlin's people will undoubtedly be coming back for their friends out there, and us."

Longwood lay back on the pillows, looking pale, and closed his eyes.

Kathy stepped in and said quietly, "He needs to rest, Sam."

Sam returned to the great room, where he found Tony and Louie stretched out on the sofa, still drenched. Both were snoring. Sam was exhausted, too, but he wanted a hot shower and dry clothes more than sleep. And his stomach was growling.

Vince stood on the porch, leaning on his crutches. "Hey, check this out, Sam. It looks like the storm's letting up."

Sam joined him and discovered that the rain had stopped. He stepped off the covered porch and looked up in surprise to see a partly clear early-evening sky above. Then he saw blackness in the distance and knew what it really meant. "It'll get bad again," he announced. "It's still a hurricane. We're in its eye right now."

As Dave joined them, Vince asked him, "Any chance we could take off in your airplane while it's calm?"

"The winds may be calm enough in the eye, but we'd never get above it before we hit the other side. I don't know about you, but I don't want to be in an overloaded, sixty-year-old, single-engine airplane in a hurricane."

"There's nothing we can do for now except get some rest, dry clothes, and hot food," Sam said.

As he stepped back inside, Vince called out from behind, "Well, somebody's flying around up there."

Curious, Sam stepped outside again and looked up to where Vince pointed. It was now dark on the ground, but the setting sun glinted off a small aircraft only a couple thousand feet above the lake. In the next half second, Sam's mind was screaming at him. He rushed into the lodge and grabbed a pair of binoculars from a table. Outside again, he stared at the aircraft. "Crap!"

"What's wrong?" Vince asked.

Sam hurried inside again. "Tony, Louie, wake up! Shit's gonna hit the fan again." Without slowing, he continued toward Longwood's room, yelling, "That's a drone. It may be armed. We gotta get outta here!"

ოჳეო

"We have a five-hundred-pounder hanging under the left wing, Mr. President," Conway stated.

Devlin smiled as he stared at the Situation Room's wall-mounted screen, which showed a live feed from the nose camera of the Predator circling above the lodge. *More good fortune brought the eye of the storm directly over the lodge at this crucial moment*, Devlin thought. *Fate is definitely on my side.*

Two men stepped off the covered porch, both illuminated by light coming from the lodge. As they looked up at the sky, Devlin could tell they were not his men. He was wondering if they could see the drone above when a third stepped out and looked up with what appeared to be binoculars.

It was dark on the ground there now. As Devlin watched, the camera operator switched to infrared, and the image changed to various shades of gray and white. The men at the porch, now glowing bright white in contrast to the darker, cooler colors around them, disappeared inside the building.

"Are you ready, General Conway?"

"We're all set, Mr. President. We'll keep the drone's camera zoomed on the building. Even if the clouds obscure the area again, the infrared will allow you to see what's happening."

"I've done this before, remember? Do it."

☙❧☙

As he pulled the exhausted and aching president from his bed without explanation or apology, Sam called out, "Go out the back and run for that ridge to the left."

With Longwood draped over his shoulder, Sam raced for the back door, again.

"What about those guys we left tied up in there?" Dave yelled as the group took off through the trees.

Sam didn't answer, except to think, *Karma's a bitch.*

The group was headed for a shallow drop-off a hundred feet away. *If we can make it over the ridge*, Sam thought, *we might have a chance.* He wasn't certain an attack was coming, but he knew a drone when he saw one, and had learned to expect the worst from Devlin.

He glimpsed the Steveners ahead and off to his left. Tony and Louie were ahead and to the right.

Inexplicably, the two mobsters abruptly stopped and reversed direction. As they passed Sam, he asked, "Where the hell are you going?"

They ignored him. A moment later, Sam glanced back over his unoccupied shoulder and saw them helping the badly limping FBI man.

Three feet from the rim of the sloped hillside, a thunderous explosion rocked the world. Sam felt himself shoved over the edge, and then he was airborne, with the wind knocked from him. Longwood's weight disappeared from his shoulder just before he hit cold water.

୧ର୨ର

The drone's infrared camera remained focused on the lodge, but its operator backed out of zoom mode two seconds before the bomb's impact. The heat from the blast and subsequent fireball made the infrared sensors useless now. Devlin's entire screen went bright white.

"That went right down their throats, Mr. President," Conway stated.

Devlin sat back and smiled.

"Will that be all, sir?"

"You've done America a great service tonight. Remember, though, this never happened. The final thing I need from you is another Blackhawk to go up there when the weather breaks. I'll have some people aboard to clean up the site."

"I'll set it up, sir. By the way, we haven't heard from the crew of that other chopper."

"They're on a highly classified mission," Devlin lied. He hung up then and sat alone, considering his last problem: Pearson and the other Calder. The comatose man would be easy, but killing the FBI director so soon after Stone's murder would almost certainly lead to inquiries he did not need. Then he realized that with what he had just accomplished, Pearson could no longer prove any assertions he might dare to make. *There's no evidence left*, he thought.

He called Crowley. "It's over. They were at the lodge, and the DIA just dropped a five-hundred-pounder on them. They'll have another chopper for you when the weather breaks in the morning. I want that place sanitized."

"Yes, sir. But I only have two men left, unless Blevins's group made it."

"I doubt they'll turn up anytime soon. Calder was at the lodge. Two men should be enough, and Crowley, get rid of them, too."

Crowley did not immediately respond, and Devlin sensed the man's concern, so he added, "Don't worry, your unique skill set is still needed, but I don't need the others any longer. I own Delta Force now."

"Good point, sir. I'll take care of it."

Devlin emerged from the Situation Room. Several Secret Service agents were waiting in the hallway, along with Preston Maddox.

"Mr. President, is everything all right?" Maddox inquired. "I mean, you've apparently been engaged in something serious, but no one else seems to know what's going on."

"That's because you don't have the proverbial need-to-know, Maddox. Now, I want that list of new cabinet nominees I gave you submitted first thing tomorrow. I'm going upstairs to eat and get some sleep."

CHAPTER 42

S am lost consciousness for only a moment. Cold water flowing down the slope, overflow from the lake, quickly revived him. Even though it was now fully dark, he could see quite well. He quickly realized that was because of the fires burning above the ridge behind him.

He sat upright as soon as he determined he was intact, then crawled to dry ground and fell onto his back, exhausted. Looking up again, he saw stars and realized that they were still in the hurricane's eye and that the tree canopy above was missing, shredded in the blast.

Sam rolled to his side and scanned the area in the flickering firelight. Longwood lay motionless ten feet away. Thankfully, the president's head was on dry ground. Sam crawled to him, expecting the worst, but he found a pulse and no indication of broken bones. *The drop-off protected us both*, he thought.

A mist in the windy air made it feel like they were in a cold shower, and Sam knew hypothermia was the last thing Longwood needed on top of everything else he had suffered. He needed warmth, quickly, and Sam did, too. He also knew the storm wall would be returning soon, and with it, more rain and wind. Accepting that he had no alternative, he summoned all his stamina to hoist the president over his shoulder once more and slowly began trudging up the slope.

Partway there, he stopped. Tony lay in a heap at the base of a huge tree with its top half missing. Sam only had to glance at the mobster's twisted form to know he had died on impact. Sam exhaled deeply, and his anger returned, stirring him to push on. It also made him think of the others, fearing they were dead, too. "Please don't be," he said aloud.

As he breathlessly crested the ridge, his thighs and back in agony, Sam saw that the warmth he and Long-wood needed so badly lay just ahead. The area now re-minded him even more of Pointer Lake. Broken and splintered trees lay everywhere, and all seemed to be burning. Where the lodge had stood was a field of scat-tered bonfires lighting the dark sky for hundreds of feet in all directions. Even at a distance, he could feel the heat.

Sam carried Longwood through the debris and laid him on the ground under a large piece of unburned wall propped up against a shattered tree stump. He pulled a thick, burning branch closer, piled more on top of it, and collapsed next to the president, absorbing the fire's warmth and feeling his strength return.

After only a few minutes, Sam forced himself back to his feet and set out to find the others. He knew where he had last seen the Steveners and headed that way.

He found Louie first. The big gangster lay on top of Vince with a three-foot-long tree branch the size of a baseball bat puncturing his torso. Sam gently rolled him to the side and examined the FBI man beneath him.

Vince was unconscious and his leg wound was bleed-ing again, but he didn't appear to have any other visible injuries. Louie had taken the brunt of the blast. Sam car-ried Vince to where Longwood lay, tore off his own shirtsleeve, and wrapped it tightly around the agent's wound before taking off again in search of the others. A few moments into his quest, he caught sight of Dave approaching from the shadows with Kathy in his arms.

"She's alive," Dave said. "How's everyone else?"

"The president and Vince made it. Tony and Louie weren't so lucky."

Sam led the way, and Dave laid his wife next to Vince and knelt at her side.

Sam walked over and began scanning the crater where the lodge had stood.

"What are you looking for?" Dave asked.

"I need to check out the damage."

"It looks pretty total to me."

"I'll explain later. That storm's going to be back on top of us again any minute, and I'd like to look around while I can still see in the firelight." He walked off.

Just as the winds began to pick up and the stars disappeared behind clouds, Sam found what he was hunting for. The prisoners they had left behind were no more, but what was left of the bodies he had placed on the porch had somehow ended up near the edge of the blast area. One was in the condition Sam hoped to find. He ignored the remains that were nearly cremated but had to make several disgusting trips to remove the other men's body parts scattered around the area. He buried those in a shallow hole he dug with a piece of burnt lumber and covered the spot with scorched debris. Afterward, he returned to the others, saying nothing about what he had done.

Longwood was the first to regain consciousness. "What happened?" he asked.

Sam explained, and the three were quiet after that.

Sometime later, Kathy and Vince began to stir.

Kathy hugged her husband as Vince asked, "The others?"

Sam just shook his head.

"Those guys could have escaped, but they came back to help me. Why?"

"You might have been foes under different circumstances, but here and now, you were allies. Their code wouldn't allow them to abandon you."

After that, the five quietly huddled together under their makeshift shelter, trying to stay out of the rain and gusting wind that had returned in force.

As dawn arrived, Sam braved the elements again to scan the lodge's wreckage once more.

The fires were out now, and he was surprised to see the airplane apparently intact, floating twenty feet from the bank near where its dock had sat. The winds must have pushed it there.

When he returned to the group, Dave told him, "I'll help you bring the bodies up."

"As much as I hate doing it," Sam replied, "we need to leave them where they are."

"Why?" Longwood asked.

"I expect Devlin will send in another team to verify that he got everyone and get rid of your remains if they weren't destroyed. If they found Tony and Louie laid out here, they'd know someone survived, and the search would start all over again. We're better off with Devlin believing he got all of us." Sam didn't explain what else he had done to ensure the enemy took the bait. Instead he said, "I know the weather sucks right now, but we need to move away from this place before Devlin's people show up. Any chance your airplane will fly, Dave?"

"I didn't have a chance to refuel it, and the fuel tank was next to the dock. It's gone."

"Okay, let's move to the south end of the lake and wait for Vince's people to get here." Sam looked around and realized the FBI man was missing. "Where's Vince?"

Kathy pointed. "He was over there by Louie for a while, and he limped off toward the ridge."

Sam walked to the edge of the hillside and spotted him. He was kneeling next to Tony, his hand on the dead man's shoulder. Sam knew a farewell when he saw one. He left him alone and returned to the others. "Let's give him a minute."

The somber federal agent limped back into their midst a few minutes later and dropped to the ground without a word.

Sam gave him a chance to catch his breath before speaking. "We need to move now," he said a few moments later. "I want to go before it stops raining so we don't leave prints in the mud."

Vince struggled back to his feet, and the Steveners braced him at each side.

Sam hefted the president to his feet. "Would you be more comfortable riding piggyback style this time or over my shoulder again?"

Longwood moved to Sam's back. "Let's try this for a change. If I have trouble holding on one-handed, we'll switch to the shoulder."

Sam knelt, and Longwood climbed onto his back.

Kathy chuckled. "Now that's a picture that would definitely go viral on YouTube."

It took them two hours to make their way into the trees at the south end of the lake. A short time later, the winds and rain began to lesson in intensity. A few hours after that, they switched direction, and the cloud cover began to break up.

જાજા

Another Blackhawk arrived midday and descended to the ground where the lodge had been.

Sam had left the others an hour earlier and taken up a hiding spot closer to the blast area, hoping the FBI would be first to show up. If that were the case, he planned to have them hide their helicopter and ambush Devlin's thugs when they arrived. Unfortunately, the chopper that landed first did not have FBI markings. It was another Army bird with a fifty-cal mounted at its right side.

When the rotors slowed to a stop and the blowing ash settled, Sam found he could hear quite well from where he was concealed.

The first of three men to climb out of the chopper was obviously the one in charge. He turned to the pilots, still in the cockpit, and yelled, "You two get out and help with the search."

"What are we looking for?" one asked as the pair exited their bird.

"Dead terrorists, and let's make it quick. I want to be out of here as soon as possible."

The group spread out and began walking through the site. A few minutes in, one of the pilots called out from the ridge. "Hey, Crowley, there's a body down here."

The man named Crowley made his way there and stared down at Tony's broken form.

"That's one of 'em," Crowley said. "Get a body bag and load him up."

The DIA pilot headed toward the helicopter for one of the black plastic bags, calling to the other pilot for help.

A moment later, one of Crowley's other men found Louie.

"I have no idea who that big son of a bitch is," Crowley said. "It ain't Calder, though."

"He was probably vaporized," the other man said.

"Bag him," Crowley ordered.

"Hey, Crowley, there's a nasty one over here," his other man called out.

When Crowley walked over, Sam was relieved to hear him say, "That one's pay dirt. Bag it, and we're out of here."

The group had just lifted off when another Blackhawk came swooping in over the lake.

Sam saw the FBI lettering on its tail boom and a dozen armed men in its rear compartment as it slowed to a hover near the rising Army bird. He then watched Crowley leap to the machine gun mounted at the side door and open up on the surprised FBI men.

The heavy, armor-piercing rounds pounded the engine compartment first and slid forward to the pilots, killing both. The helpless men in the back could do nothing as their ride spun wildly out of control, dropping hard to the lake a hundred feet below.

The helicopter slammed into the water on its side, its still-turning rotor blades tearing themselves apart on impact. Seconds later, the craft sank out of sight.

As Crowley's chopper fled south, Sam saw him swing the door's gun to their airplane—again floating in the center of the lake, thanks to the change in wind direction—but he heard no gunfire. For several minutes, he watched the lake for survivors but saw nothing except bubbles surfacing.

When he returned to the others, he found that they, too, had witnessed the carnage.

Vince was livid. "Did you see what those bastards did?"

Sam nodded. "The gunner was a rat-faced runt named Crowley. He tried to shoot the airplane, too, but I think he was out of ammo or the gun jammed."

"What now?" Dave asked. "Do you think Pearson will send another chopper?"

"I don't want to wait around," Sam answered. He was concerned Devlin might check the DNA of the corpses and determine neither was Longwood, and the hunt would be on again.

Without saying more, he walked to the lake's edge and dove into the cold water. He swam out to the floatplane, which was intact, and used the cut tie-down rope to pull the plane to shore.

Once the group was inside the plane, Kathy pulled out its first aid kit and went about cleaning, re-stitching, and bandaging Vince's leg wound.

"Will this thing fly?" Sam asked.

Dave examined his machine for several minutes before saying, "It'll fly, but we've got no gas."

"Does it use the same fuel as that Blackhawk we left at the other lake?"

"No, the Beaver has a piston-driven engine. It uses low-lead aviation gasoline. The Blackhawk's turbine engines use jet fuel. That stuff's like kerosene. It would burn my engine up in less than two hours."

"Yeah, but will it run on it?"

"It'll work in a pinch, I guess."

"Well, this is a pinch. How far can you go in, say, an hour or so?"

"If I had a full center tank, we could probably make it to Everett Lake before the engine seizes. My cell phone will work from there."

"Who're you going to call?" Sam asked.

Kathy answered for her husband. "We live near there, and we left my brother house-sitting when we came up here. He can pick us up, and we can go to our place. Nobody will look for us there. Our summer job's a secret nobody but Calvin Stone knew about."

"Now we just need to find something to carry the fuel in," Sam said, thinking.

"I have some tools in the storage compartment," Dave said. "I should be able to disassemble one of the chopper's tanks, and we can haul it back here and siphon it out."

"Okay, you and I need to hike back there while we still have some light." He turned to Longwood. "Will you be okay, sir?"

Longwood nodded wearily.

"We'll take care of him, Sam," Vince said.

CHAPTER 43

I t's finished," Crowley said over the phone. "We collected a couple of intact bodies outside the rubble. Deluca was one of them, and we found one crispy critter with his left arm missing."

Devlin, alone in the Oval Office, pounded the top of his new desk and gleefully asked, "What did you do with him?"

"We shoved everything through a chipper, poured gasoline over the goo pile, and torched it all."

"Well, that's done, then. No sign of Blevins and the others?"

"No, but since Longwood was at the lodge, we can assume they're all dead in the woods up there somewhere. Animals and the elements will take care of them soon enough."

"What about the helicopter Blevins had? Conway asked about it."

"Lost up there somewhere, I guess. It's a wildlife refuge, though, no trespassing allowed. I doubt anyone will stumble on it anytime soon. Oh, by the way, the FBI showed up at the lake as we were leaving."

"What!"

"Don't worry. I put 'em down. Their chopper went into the water and sank like a rock. Unfortunately, the DIA pilots I had with me didn't seem too happy about that, so I had to drop them, too, as well as our last two men like you wanted. They were all part of that goo pile. I torched the chopper, too."

"Well, since there aren't any witnesses left," Devlin said, "there shouldn't be a problem, unless Conway makes a stink about his missing pilots and machines."

"Just give me the word, and I'll handle him."

"Okay, here's what I want you to do..." Devlin laid out his plan for Conway and concluded, "I'm going up to Camp David tomorrow, and I want you to come along as my guest. You've earned it. We can discuss how to tie up a few loose ends while we're there."

❧❧❧

Sam rigged a drag litter from saplings while Dave dismounted one of the Blackhawk's fuel tanks. Hauling the heavy load back to the de Havilland was exhausting, but they finished transferring the fuel into its center tank by late afternoon.

"I know you're tired, Dave," Sam said, "but we really need to get out of here. Can you fly?"

"Don't worry about me."

He started the engine and spent a few minutes making sure the floatplane was airworthy, and then they took off. Less than an hour later, they touched down on a small lake and taxied to shore near a boat ramp.

Sam was grateful the weather had been so bad that no one else was around, because he had no way to hide Longwood's face. Vince's leg had needed the only bandages available from the airplane's first aid kit.

Kathy made the call to her brother, who showed up in an SUV an hour later.

As Sam joined Longwood and Vince in the car's back seat, Kathy introduced the man behind the wheel. "This is my brother, Mike Downey, sir."

Kathy's demeanor and words seemed to cause Downey to take a closer look at the three men seated behind him. Seeming confused, he muttered, "What the fuck?"

Dave squeezed onto the front seat next to his wife and turned his face to Longwood. "I warned you, Mr. President. That Irish potty mouth runs in the family."

Longwood chuckled. "Thanks for your help, Mike."

"I thought they buried you," Downey weakly responded.

"Not all of me."

Downey's eyes widened as he turned to drive without another word. It was dark by the time they pulled into the Steveners' driveway.

Sam and Dave helped Longwood upstairs to the master bedroom, and the president immediately requested to use the toilet.

As he emerged from the bathroom under his own power, Kathy appeared in the doorway.

"I'd like to try to take a shower on my own," Longwood said.

"Sure thing," Kathy replied. "I have to change Vince's bandage again anyway."

Not long after, Sam found Longwood resting comfortably in the Steveners' bed.

"Have you ever tried drying off and dressing with one hand?" the president asked.

"I think it's time to call Director Pearson again, sir."

Longwood nodded. "Okay, get Vince to join us and put Pearson on speakerphone."

❦❦❦

"This is Trevor Pearson."

"It's me, sir."

"Vince? Holy shit! I thought you were dead."

"We damn near were, Trevor," Longwood added through the speakerphone.

"Oh my God," Pearson responded. "It's good to hear your voice, sir, especially after what I was told."

"What do you mean?"

"Devlin called me to the White House and said you'd all been erased."

"Several good men were," Longwood said. "The bastard used a drone to drop a bomb on us, and his people butchered the men you sent."

Pearson was quiet a moment. "What do you want to do, Mr. President?"

"This is Sam Calder. The first thing we need is more muscle in case we have to fight again."

"I'll send whatever you need."

"One team, no more, and absolute secrecy," Longwood said.

"No helicopters or tactical outfits, either," Sam added. "We don't want to attract any attention from the neighbors. Have them park behind the house."

Dave gave Pearson his address, and Longwood asked, "Are any of my Secret Service detail still around?"

"I can check."

"If anyone from my detail is available, bring them, but don't tell them about me."

తుు

Hours later, four SUVs that Pearson had obtained through a commercial rental agency, pulled into the Steveners' long driveway with their lights out and parked behind the house as instructed.

Twelve large men wearing casual clothes and carrying assault weapons piled out of the vehicles alongside Trevor Pearson and Angel Washington.

Kathy, standing at the back door, waved everyone into the kitchen. In single file, with Pearson at the front and Angel behind him, they moved quickly through the kitchen and into the living room.

Mike Downey, asleep on the sofa, woke at the commotion and immediately scurried into the kitchen, where he joined his sister and brother-in-law. "Are we having a party?"

"Yeah, and it's bring-your-own-machine-gun," Kathy answered.

The group standing in the living room kept quiet, though a few gave each other confused shrugs.

Angel began to ask Pearson, "When are you going to tell me what—?" She stopped mid-sentence and breathlessly muttered, "Oh, my God."

All heads turned to the staircase.

Longwood stepped gingerly down the stairs wearing blue jeans and a polo shirt Dave had loaned him, his injured arm in a sling.

Sam was at his side, his right hand gripping a pistol hidden at his back, just in case. He relaxed his grip when he noted the surprised look on every face staring up at them.

"Good evening," Longwood said.

"Mr. President," Pearson began, "I can't tell you how pleased we are to see you."

As Longwood reached the bottom of the stairs, agents moved to take up positions on each side, muscling Sam back. He did not resist. He faded into the background as Longwood greeted Pearson with a handshake and turned to Angel.

"Mr. President, I tried my best to—"

Longwood stopped her. "I know, Angel, and I'm so thankful you survived."

"She's the only one from your detail not already reassigned, sir," Pearson explained.

"I'm still on a medical hold," she added.

"Okay, let's get down to business," Longwood said as Angel helped him move to the sofa.

Pearson gave a few commands, and his men moved to the front and back doors. Three stepped out into the dark. He then sat in a chair opposite the president and began by saying, "Based on everything I've been told, this nation owes Mr. Calder a great debt of gratitude. That said, sir, I recommend you allow me to move you, along with Agent Washington and my men, to a safer location."

"No, Trevor," said Longwood. "I just came from a safe house that proved not so safe, and I've grown rather confident in Sam's ability to keep me alive under tremendous duress. He's already saved my ass several times these past few days. Now, I asked you to find out where Devlin is. Did you?"

"He's at the White House tonight, sir," Angel answered, "and scheduled to go to Camp David tomorrow afternoon."

"Are you certain?"

"Yes, sir. I'm still assigned to the presidential detail while I'm on medical leave."

Longwood pondered that for a moment and nodded several times. "Okay, I'll confront him when he returns to D.C. We'll need—"

Pearson cut him off. "May I ask how you plan to confront him, sir?"

"Frankly, I'd like to beat the shit out of the man on the steps of the White House, but he'd likely win the fight right now."

"I don't understand what you plan to do, sir. We can

certainly prove that you're still alive. Unfortunately, we have no evidence that connects anything that happened to Devlin, and like it or not, he is currently the constitutionally appointed president and cannot be removed from office without cause."

Longwood angrily answered, "He's a treasonous psychopath who used murder and sedition to cut in the constitutional line of succession. This nation cannot endure him as its president."

"I understand how you feel, sir. I assure you I feel the same. Nonetheless, we are a nation of laws, and the nation will demand to see what evidence we have to back up our allegations."

"They used an attack drone and a bomb at that lodge," O'Malley said. "The military has to have some record of who authorized that."

Pearson nodded. "I looked into that after you told me about it on the phone. The Air Force authorized the use of the drone and the weapon based on the DIA director's word that it was in support of my agency's manhunt for missing assassins. No one else at the DIA seems to know anything about who authorized the attack. They got their orders from their director. The only other person who *would* know the truth is Devlin himself."

Sam, listening from the back of the room, pulled the two helicopter pilots' IDs from his pocket as Longwood said, "Well, squeeze the DIA director to testify that Devlin put him up to it."

"Unfortunately, we can't, sir. He was a general named Conway. This afternoon, someone posted a video on the Internet showing him having sex with a couple of very young girls, and he apparently blew his brains out rather than face a court-martial and his family."

"I bet he had some help holding the gun," Vince mumbled.

Sam handed the IDs to Pearson. "I took these off the two chopper pilots who flew those guys to the lake. They were killed by one of Devlin's men named Blevins. What about those guys who were shot down over that lake?"

"Again, we can recover them and prove that the incident occurred, just like we can recover those chopper pilots and their bird. Unfortunately, there's no link to Devlin. That's our problem. None of it connects to him personally." Pearson turned to Longwood. "You should also know, sir, he's already vetting a list of new cabinet nominees."

Sam knew Pearson was right. Devlin was now in the perfect position to ensure that accusations of wrongdoing fell on others' heads. As Longwood and Pearson debated, he angled away and went into the kitchen, finding the Steveners and Mike at the table. He joined them, though his mind was not on the conversation. Instead, it stayed focused on the past days' events. After a few minutes, he excused himself and stepped out the back door onto a large deck.

He stood at the railing and spotted an FBI agent lurking in the shadows near the line of hidden SUVs. The summer air was warm, and the mosquitoes the Steveners had complained about seemed to be taking a break from their nighttime feasting. Staring up at the star-filled sky, he let his mind wander to his father and brother and the others this horrible misadventure had killed or injured. He briefly wondered if Mark had returned to consciousness yet and hoped he was beyond Devlin's reach.

After a few minutes, he went back inside and returned to the living room. Longwood and Pearson had finished their conversation, deciding that the FBI would redouble its efforts to come up with something tangible they could use to convince people of Devlin's culpability. Until then, Longwood would remain in hiding and recuperate. Sam could tell the president was unhappy with that, but he apparently accepted that there was no other option under the circumstances.

"At some point I'm going to come out of hiding and go public," Longwood declared.

"Let's hope we can uncover evidence we can use against Devlin before then," Pearson responded, "or we'll undoubtedly end up with a constitutional nightmare in the courts, and possibly even in the streets."

Pearson left in one of the SUVs a short time later so he could get back to his Washington headquarters before anyone noticed his absence. Mike Downey left for his own home, and everyone else began to settle in for the night.

Longwood asked Sam to help him back to the master bedroom, which the Steveners insisted he use.

"Is there anything you need, sir?" Sam asked as Longwood relaxed back on the raised pillows.

Longwood surprised him. "What made you become a SEAL, Sam?"

Sam stared into the president's eyes for a moment before answering. "I couldn't stand by and allow people to get away with the kinda shit Devlin's getting away with."

"Do you have any regrets about what you did as a SEAL?"

"No, sir," Sam answered without hesitation.

"And I'm sure you would have sacrificed your life for your country, if necessary."

"Any SEAL would, sir, and many have."

Longwood was quiet again but continued gazing at him. After a long moment, he closed his eyes. "I'm tired, Sam."

"Good night, sir." Sam turned and closed the door. Two agents stood in the hallway there. With everyone else apparently down for the night, Sam returned to the rear deck to think. He was beyond exhaustion, but as before, the faces of those he had lost kept painfully flashing through his mind. *Longwood's right*, he thought. *The nation deserves better. It's inconceivable that a maniac is running this country.*

At that thought, Sam came to a terrifying realization. There was only one implausible option left to him if he was to avenge his father and all the others—one mind-boggling alternative that could make things right for the nation, and possibly the world.

The back door opened, and Angel Washington stepped out. "I'm too hyped to sleep. You, too?"

Stone-faced, Sam asked, "Is there any way to penetrate Camp David?"

"Why in the world would you even want to try?"

"Vince O'Malley told me what happened to you and the other folks in that forest."

Her face instantly hardened, telling Sam his words had had the effect he'd hoped.

"I'm sure those agents were good people, Ms. Washington, just like my father and all the others who have died or been injured since."

Her eyes wet now, Angel turned her back to him and gazed out at the darkness.

Sam hoped she was thinking about those agents who had run with her, as well as the others viciously killed by the mortars and snipers. *Most had to have been friends*, he thought. "What Devlin did, using his position to commit murder and sedition, is a capital offense punishable by death. But it won't matter, because, with no evidence to back up our allegations, his new cabinet will make sure he stays in office. All those folks will have died in vain."

She slowly turned to face him. "Mr. Calder, I agree with everything you've said. I really do. Nevertheless, if you're thinking what I think you're thinking, you're out of your mind. Camp David may look like a summer camp retreat on television, but it's not. It's actually a highly secure military encampment. I'm talking about a specially-trained Marine combat unit two hundred strong and nearly a hundred staff and support personnel, including the Secret Service, when the president is there."

"I didn't think it would be easy," Sam replied and remained quiet, waiting for her commitment or repudiation.

Finally she nodded and exhaled deeply. "I think you're crazy. You'll never be able to pull it off, but if you even get close, you have to promise me one thing for my help: you won't harm any agents or Marines, no matter the cost."

"You have my word. If it comes to that, I'll surrender."

CHAPTER 44

After checking that the president was sleeping and secure, Sam and Angel walked out to one of the SUVs without revealing their intentions to anyone.

"You'll have to drive," he told her. "I don't have a license."

"What?"

"It's a long story."

"Get comfortable, Mr. Calder," she said as they pulled out of the driveway. "We have a long drive ahead of us and a lot to talk about."

"Let's make it Sam and Angel then, huh?"

"Okay. First off, Sam, I can't figure out how you could possibly pull this off. Moreover, you should know that every assassin since 1968 survived only because he or she committed the act in front of the press. There won't be any media at Camp David, just really pissed-off Secret Service agents and Marines. Prison won't be an option."

Sam sighed. "Thank God."

"What?"

"Never mind. Let's start at the basics. How secure is Camp David, really?"

"I wasn't kidding. The place is a fortress. Aside from Secret Service protection, that Marine unit uses special tactics and equipment. I'm talking about roving patrols and snipers deployed throughout the area twenty-four-seven when POTUS is there. There are sensors of all kinds—heat, motion, sound, magnetic anomaly, you name it. They can turn everything on and off at will. One moment a spot can be safe to walk through, and an instant later, with the flip of a switch, it becomes a killing ground."

"My experience has been that the more confident people are in their security measures, the less likely they are to see weaknesses, and believe me, there is always a weakness somewhere. How easy is it for *you* to access the place?"

"I'm still assigned to the White House, on paper at least, but I can't get you inside without having you vetted first. I doubt Devlin will approve you as a guest."

"Okay. When we get to the gate, will they search the car?"

"It doesn't matter who you are. Unless you come in on Marine One with the president, you get searched."

"So sneaking in under a blanket in the back seat probably won't work, huh?"

Angel glared at him.

"Sorry. So where does the president stay while he's there?"

"The main residence is called Aspen Lodge. The other cabins are for guests and staff."

"Okay, how many entry points are there for this Aspen Lodge?"

"Three doors out front and a sliding glass door off the sunroom in the back, but all are guarded by an agent standing outside when the president's inside. The rest of the detail on duty can respond anywhere inside the residence within seconds."

"Are those doors the only ways in or out of the building? What about the roof?"

"The roof is actually steel to prevent a tree from falling through it. There are no skylights, and the three chimneys have grills with sensors halfway up them. The only ways into the building are the guarded exterior doors, except for…"

"What?"

"Well, there are a couple of elevators in Aspen Lodge."

"Where do they go?"

"They drop two-hundred feet to a bunker built back in the fifties—some sort of Cold War thing. It's still functional, though, and officially designated Orange One."

"Where are the elevators?"

"One's just inside the building's main entrance off the kitchen, and the other's in the president's bedroom."

"It opens directly into his bedroom?"

"Yeah, but it stays at ground level for him to use in a hurry at night."

Sam chuckled and sarcastically asked, "Okay, so let me get this straight. You're telling me the Secret Service would send the president to a bunker two-hundred feet underground with those two elevators as his only way out?"

When his real point clicked in her mind, Angel slapped the steering wheel. "I'll be damned, you're right. The more confident people are, the less likely they are to see a weakness—and that's exactly what you just found, Sam."

"Did I now?"

"In the event the elevators become inoperative or Camp David comes under ground attack, there's a tunnel connecting Orange One with what people call the Underground Pentagon. Officially, it's designated Site R. It's a massive complex below Raven Rock Mountain, just over the Pennsylvania border, six miles from Camp David."

"Okay, so how difficult is it to access Site R?"

"The place is minimally manned unless there's a national security crisis."

"What about tunnel security?"

"Generally, only tunnel maintenance personnel and the folks who maintain its special transport vehicles are allowed inside. The rest of Site R is set up for the survival of the government during a crisis. It's where Dick Cheney was taken after Nine/Eleven."

"So how difficult is it to access the tunnel?"

"There's a biometric security system that requires a retinal scan to even be allowed to enter the codes required for access through the nuclear blast doors at each end."

"Well, that could present a challenge."

"Not really. As a member of the presidential detail, my retinal scan is in the system, and I know the codes."

Sam stared out the windshield, smiling.

They continued to develop their plan through most of the long drive. At dawn, they entered Waynesboro, Pennsylvania, less than ten miles from Camp David. They stopped at a crowded diner, where they sat in a corner booth and continued quietly strategizing over breakfast.

"Whenever any sort of maintenance is done in the tunnel," she told him, "a Secret Service agent must be present. That means I'll have to go with you, at least to the base of the elevator in Orange One."

"Is any security maintained in Orange One?"

"It's unnecessary unless the president goes down there, and several agents go with him when he does."

"What about cameras?"

"There are two in the bunker, but they're only activated when Orange One's systems are brought online."

"Will the elevator cause them to be activated?"

"No."

"Any chance we could run into someone down there, or in the tunnel?"

"There's always a chance, but going in the middle of the night should minimize that risk."

After eating, they drove to a mall, where Sam purchased a dark suit and dress shoes. He got a haircut and shave before having several small black-and-white photos taken of his face in a drugstore photo booth.

Angel's cell phone beeped while he was in the booth. She looked at the screen. "It's the Steveners' home phone. I put the number in before we left."

Sam stuck his head out of the booth. "Don't answer it. In fact, turn it off so we can't be tracked."

Angel did so and removed the sim card.

At noon, they pulled the SUV to the back of the mall parking lot. Sam was exhausted and moved to the rear seat to sleep while Angel stayed on guard.

൦ൟൟ

Marine One descended to the helipad at Camp David and bounced gently. Frank Crowley unhooked his seatbelt and followed Devlin and the six Secret Service agents surrounding him. Several more agents stood at the ready outside, their heads scanning different directions.

Devlin, having never been there before, asked the detail leader to guide him to his new weekend retreat.

"This way, sir," the agent said, pointing. "It's the big building in the center of the compound."

Feeling exhilarated as he entered Aspen Lodge, Devlin faced an agent and ordered, "Have the chef prepare a couple of medium-rare rib eyes for dinner." Without waiting for a response, he turned back to his lead agent. "Okay, give me the nickel tour."

Accompanied by Crowley, Devlin followed the agent through the residence and finally into a large living room.

Crowley closed the room's doors, leaving the agents posted at them out of earshot. Then he went to the fully stocked bar against one wall and filled a glass with expensive cognac. "Thanks for bringing me along, sir."

"Calder's brother is still in a coma in Montana. I want you to go out there tomorrow and end him before he comes out of it."

"It'll be a pleasure, sir," Crowley responded as he re-filled his already empty glass. "What about Pearson?"

"He won't be a problem now. He has no evidence to base any accusations upon."

⋇⋇

Angel woke Sam just before evening, and they drove to a large building at the edge of town where the company holding the contract for tunnel vehicle maintenance was located. They had to wait until normal business hours ended and the small night shift crew arrived. Having toured the facility during her training for the presidential detail, Angel was familiar with the building's layout and knew where Sam could locate the company's distinctive utility coveralls and the tool kit he would need for his disguise.

The pair slipped through a side door to the locker room, where Sam found coveralls that fit, while Angel located a company ID badge left in a day-shift worker's locker. The two burglars went out the same side door five minutes after they entered.

Sam attached one of his new pictures to the badge and re-laminated it.

While he was busy with that, Angel mentioned, "If we make it through this, we'll need to return this stuff before the day shift comes on. And don't forget to remove your picture." She put her cell phone back together next and called the Secret Service operations center in Washington, D.C.

Angel gave the agent assigned there on the night shift a special code word to indicate she wasn't under duress, and the console operator entered Angel's Secret Service ID number. "Yes, ma'am. What can I do for you, Agent Washington?"

"The tunnel sweep made for the president's visit to Camp David revealed a few minor maintenance issues with one of the transports. Please send notice to Site R that I'll be supervising maintenance there this evening and will be accessing the tunnel." She looked at the badge Sam had finished and gave the agent the name and information for the maintenance worker.

When she hung up, Sam said, "She seemed awfully eager to help."

"Once they see that you're on the White House detail, they'll do whatever you ask without question."

☙☙☙

Crowley was passed out on the sofa with the empty cognac bottle lying nearby. When he began to snore, Devlin decided to call it a night and told the agents at the door, "I'm going to my room. Let him sleep it off where he is, and tell someone to bring me a club sandwich and a cold beer."

Devlin went to his suite, showered, and put on a set of royal-blue pajamas with the presidential seal embroidered on a breast pocket. Feeling like a king, he slipped on a matching bathrobe and slippers and sat at a small table to eat the sandwich the Secret Service had left while he showered. Afterward, he moved to a sofa and watched the late news while he finished off the beer. Slightly inebriated, he retired for the night at ten forty-five.

CHAPTER 45

Sam and Angel pulled into the Site R parking lot on Raven Rock Mountain at ten forty-five p.m., just before the underground survival compound's graveyard shift went on duty. They sat in the SUV and watched as dozens of men and women arrived, walked to the entry gate in groups, flashed their ID badges, and disappeared into the wide tunnel mouth yawning on the mountain's face. Some wore military uniforms, but most were civilians.

"I thought you said this place was minimally manned. I've counted seventy-eight people going in since we got here."

"Believe me, this is minimally manned for the federal government. Look, Raven Rock is like a small underground city. The place can house more than three thousand people for months in an emergency, but it's primarily just a communications center during peacetime. The majority of those civilian folks going in there work for dozens of different federal agencies and private companies doing contract work for the government. That's actually to our advantage. With so many vendors, they have a huge turnover rate, and the guards see new faces continuously."

With the maintenance bag slung over one shoulder, Sam walked beside Angel, blending with a crowd of a dozen other last-minute arrivals. Some seemed to know each other and talked, so Sam and Angel did so, too, in order to prevent someone else from starting up a conversation that might give Sam away.

The guards had apparently succumbed to the tedium of their unchanging nightly duties. One verified that their names were on the computerized list of scheduled visitors, while the other merely glanced at the badges hanging around their necks rather than checking them for authenticity, although Angel's would have passed scrutiny.

As they entered the mountain opening, Angel quietly commented, "If, by some miracle, I'm still an agent tomorrow, I'm going to have to see that security is tightened up around here. That was way too easy."

"Complacency is a universal weakness when a job is monotonous and there's no specific threat," Sam whispered as they stepped to the back of an elevator that quickly filled before descending into the depths of the granite mountain.

When its occupants stepped out more than a hundred feet down, all moved in various directions with apparent purpose.

Sam followed Angel's experienced lead down a long hallway cut out of solid stone. It ended at a round, shiny, nuclear-blast door. There, she leaned her face into a retinal scanner at the side and keyed in a brief code on a panel that popped up. The panel lit green, and the three-foot-thick door began to swing open.

An amber light flashed atop the door, and an irritating beep sounded during the nearly thirty seconds it took for the fifty-ton tempered steel entrance cover to open fully. Though several people passing by glanced their way, none questioned their presence or actions, or even seemed surprised to see the door opening.

Once inside, Angel keyed the tunnel's lights on, and the door closed. She pointed to a line of small vehicles. "Those are the tunnel transport vehicles. They're electric."

They looked to Sam like the miniature shuttle buses used in airport parking lots. Each was capable of carrying a half dozen people. The tunnel itself was wide and well constructed, with two paved lanes marked for driving in opposite directions and a railed sidewalk on one side.

They climbed aboard one of the keyless carts already aimed the way they wanted to go and took off. Sam spotted firefighting equipment, first aid kits, and telephone boxes along the wall every few hundred feet, but that was all there was to see. The six-mile trip took forty-five minutes, but with the quietness of the ride, they were able to talk through their plan once more. At the other end, they glided to a stop at another blast door identical to the first.

Before opening it with a different code she knew, Angel turned to Sam. "If anyone's in there, Sam, we're done. Understand?"

He nodded without comment but held his breath as she opened the door. He let it out once he saw that only emergency lighting was on. Angel closed the blast door, and they moved directly to the elevator.

She pointed at a smaller door on an adjacent wall and said, "That's the one that comes down from the president's bedroom."

Sam removed his coveralls, revealing the business suit he had purchased. He pulled his new shoes from the utility bag and placed his coveralls and work boots in it.

Angel then handed him the pistol she had carried in case the Site R guards searched or scanned them for weapons.

Sam removed the suppressor hidden at the bottom of his utility bag amongst a socket set and affixed it to the handgun's barrel. As he stuck the weapon in the back of his waistband, he heard Angel exhale deeply and glanced her way. "What's bothering you now?" he asked.

"There are more than a dozen agents up there, Sam, and there will definitely be one directly outside Devlin's suite. Remember what you promised. You can't hurt any of them."

"I give you my word, I won't."

She stared into his eyes a moment and nodded. "Okay. Now remember, when you come out of the elevator, turn right into the kitchen. Then you'll have to go past the living room to the hallway where the bedrooms are located. There'll be three doors to your left along the hallway, but the president's suite is on the right around the corner at the far end." She handed him her large, red-bordered badge. "This is a close-in badge, but if someone sees my face on its front, you'll probably be shot immediately. If you do, by some miracle, make it to Devlin's door, just swipe it against the security pad and the door will open."

"No code?"

"We may have to move inside quickly, and they don't want to take the chance an agent might forget or mess up a code in a crisis." She looked at her watch. "It's twelve-fifteen now, so they've just made a sweep of the interior and exterior of the building. They'll do another in forty-five minutes. Until then, except for the exterior door guards and the one assigned to the hallway outside the president's suite, all the other agents on duty will be in the command post. Other than the hourly security sweeps, they don't roam around inside after midnight, to avoid waking guests." She paused and asked, "So, how *do* you expect to get past the agent at Devlin's door?"

Sam hung her badge around his neck. "Please don't

take this the wrong way, but when people, even Secret Service agents, get comfortable with the routine, they get lax and inattentive, just like those gate guards back at Site R. They aren't paranoid, so they aren't alert. I only need a half-second distraction."

"Are you really that good?"

Sam smiled, winked, and pushed the button summoning the elevator.

"I can't leave without that badge, so I'll be here until you or someone else shows up.

The door opened and Sam stepped then turned to face her. "If things go bad up there and you manage to get out, please make sure my brother is safe and knows the truth."

Angel only nodded.

He smiled at her and pushed the UP button. The door closed, and the elevator started moving. When it stopped and the door slid quietly open to an empty entrance hallway, he exhaled the breath he had been holding again. He had feared there would be one or more agents standing there and his mission, and probably his life, would end right then.

Hearing only quiet, he stepped out and quickly moved to his right, through the dark kitchen. He stayed low and continued into the living room. As he crossed it and headed toward the bedroom hallway, he heard a snort and snapped his head to the left. Devlin's rat-faced killer, Crowley, lay asleep on a sofa. He wanted to kill the ugly little man but feared making a disturbance, so he ignored his urge and continued into the hallway.

Halfway along it, he came to a door on his right and spotted an agent standing just outside. He ducked as he passed the door's window and continued toward the corner.

Sam knew his plan was foolishly simple: cover his face and Angel's picture with his left hand while faking a cough long enough to get close to the agent at Devlin's door. He hoped he could do what he had to do quickly and quietly. If he could not, he intended to surrender just as he had promised.

As he crept along the quiet, dimly lit hallway, his mind wandered to other times he had done similar things as a SEAL. *Each of those missions ended with the kidnapping or death of a terrorist*, he remembered.

Thirty feet from the corner leading to Devlin's door, a shuffling sound from behind him forced his thoughts back to the moment.

His heart pounding, he turned and saw Crowley staggering along the dim hallway. The skinny man leaned against the wall, apparently drunk.

Sam turned back and bent his face down as Crowley quickly closed on him. The intoxicated man did not even seem to notice his approach. He stepped behind and wrapped his arms tightly around Crowley's scrawny neck, squeezing. The small man struggled only briefly before falling limp in his arms.

Sam decided to break his neck, but as he repositioned his arms to do so, he had another thought. Instead, he pulled him through an unlocked door on the left, thankfully into an empty bedroom. He laid him on the floor and slammed his elbow into the scrawny man's jaw, sending him into oblivion.

He then took off his suit coat, removed Crowley's red shirt, and slipped it on himself. It was far too small, but he only intended to wear it for a few moments. He also took the yellow-bordered temporary ID badge from Crowley's neck, hiding Angel's red-bordered one underneath the red shirt.

In the hallway again, he bent at the knees to appear shorter, held his face down, and moved quickly toward the corner again. Once there, he moaned and made a mumbling sound, as though he were drunk.

As he hoped, the agent at Devlin's door peered around the corner, then quietly said, "Mr. Crowley, your room's back—"

The agent's polite intervention was interrupted mid-sentence by Sam's palm swinging up and planting a stunning blow to the young man's jaw. The agent's head snapped backward, and Sam caught him before he hit the floor. Holding him upright, he swiped the unconscious man's badge against the security pad and quickly moved inside Devlin's suite. He laid the agent in the dark entry-way and listened for a moment. Hearing nothing, he returned to the other bedroom.

After putting Crowley's shirt and badge back on the man, who was still out cold, Sam donned his own coat again and laid Crowley next to the agent in Devlin's suite. Then he pulled his pistol and rushed across the carpeted floor to the bedroom.

Inside the dark room, Sam stepped close to the bed he could barely see. Standing at the foot of it, he could not make out Devlin's form and waited for his eyes to adjust. Suddenly a toilet flushed and a door opened, flooding the room with light. The man Sam had seen on television in New Jersey—Devlin—stood there.

Devlin seemed startled but recovered quickly. "What the fuck are *you* doing here?" he demanded.

"Making things right," Sam stated calmly.

Visibly shaken, Devlin glanced at the phone on a nightstand five feet away and back to the long pistol in Sam's hand. "I'm the President of the United States now, Calder. You'll never get out of here alive."

With resignation in his voice, Sam replied, "I know. That doesn't mean *you* should live, Devlin. You're a murdering traitor."

Sam's mind told him to get it over with, but something

held him back— something that surprised him, and he could not get past it. He was suddenly, shockingly aware that he could not go through with it, even though every fiber of his being was screaming for him to pull the trigger. "Shit," he muttered. He accepted that while he could take a life when forced to, he was not a cold-blooded murderer. He slowly lowered the gun.

"Longwood's dead and cremated, Calder, and there's no evidence left that can prove I had anything to do with it."

"You're wrong, asshole. He isn't dead, and he's well protected from the likes of you and your henchmen now."

Devlin seemed stunned by this news.

"Drop the weapon!"

Sam turned to the new voice coming from the doorway to his left. The Secret Service agent he had knocked out stood there, his pistol aimed at Sam. *He looks dazed*, Sam thought, and he instinctively considered his options before remembering his promise. He dropped the pistol at his feet. *What the hell*, he thought, *I couldn't do it anyway*.

"Kill him!" Devlin ordered.

The agent didn't shoot. Instead, he asked Sam, "Is President Longwood really alive?"

"I ordered you to kill him!" Devlin screamed. "Do it!"

The agent stared at Sam, ignoring Devlin.

"He is, no thanks to this asshole. Devlin was the brains behind the assassination attempt."

Devlin dove to the floor, reaching for Sam's pistol.

Sam kicked it away, toward the agent, and his foot swung back, connecting with the side of Devlin's head.

Devlin fell against the side of the bed, stunned but conscious. Then the agent crashed to the floor atop Sam's pistol, his own falling close to where Devlin sat rubbing his jaw.

Crowley now stood in the doorway, holding a piece of firewood like a club. "What the fuck is going on?" he asked, slurring each word.

Devlin and Sam both leapt at the agent's pistol.

Fighting for a grip on the handgun but sensing Crowley's approach, Sam turned his head for a split second and saw the log coming down. He ducked away, and the poorly aimed blow bounced painfully off his shoulder. Still, it prevented him from winning the battle for the pistol.

Devlin sat back against the bed with the agent's gun now pointed at Sam's chest. He breathlessly demanded, "Where's Longwood?"

Seated on the floor next to the fallen agent, his back to the wall, Sam answered, "Somewhere you'll never find him." As he was speaking, he rubbed his head with his right hand as a distraction while slowly sliding his left hand under the agent, feeling for his pistol. He touched what he thought was the tip of the suppressor. Then, to his surprise, he felt it being slowly pushed into his hand. It took him a moment to realize the agent was feigning unconsciousness now and trying to help him.

"How'd you convince Mandrake to step down?" Sam asked, stalling.

"I played that fat patsy from the beginning, even set him up to share the blame for Longwood. He was the easiest part of the whole scheme."

Sam nearly had the pistol in his grip. "So how're you going to explain all this?"

A half inch of the suppressed pistol crept out from beneath the agent.

"It's quite simple, really. I'm going to kill you with the agent's gun, and I'm going to kill him with your gun. It'll look as though you shot each other. It worked at the lake with those MSM clowns and the Secret Service. Afterward, I'll find Longwood again, and Crowley can finish what—"

Sam's bullet entered Devlin's right eye and exited the back of his head. *Shut him off like a light switch.*

The pistol's report sounded loud inside the room, but Sam knew that only someone directly outside the door could have heard it. He also noted that even though Devlin's finger was still on the trigger, the gory splatter on the headboard and wall behind meant Sam did not need to fire again.

As Devlin's gruesome corpse slumped slowly to the side, Sam turned to the doorway just as Crowley stumbled through it.

Sam leapt to his feet, jumped across the slowly rising agent, and chased after Crowley. He managed to catch the staggering drunk before he could flee the suite.

Crowley ineffectively swung his piece of firewood, but Sam blocked it and slung his arms around the man's bony neck, quickly putting him to sleep again. Back in the bedroom, he dropped the unconscious man to the floor.

Sam helped the young agent to a sitting position against the wall and examined his scalp. "You'll be okay, but you could probably use a few stitches."

"I wasn't sure you were going to shoot. I saw you hesitate earlier."

"Yeah, well, turns out I'm not a cold-blooded murderer, but I have no problem killing in self-defense. He was about to do us both in."

The agent stared at Devlin's corpse. "Yeah, I heard everything he said. That bastard was responsible for the deaths of a lot of good people on that mountain—friends of mine." He turned to Sam. "Look, I don't know who you are, but you need to get the hell out of here."

"One more thing to do first," Sam said, and he placed

his pistol in Crowley's unconscious grip. "This guy was one of Devlin's killers. I saw him butcher several good men, FBI agents." He put his own hand over Crowley's and squeezed the trigger, sending the silenced bullet into the mattress.

"You missed."

"No, I didn't. We can't have a post-mortem wound. That one will look like he fired twice." Standing, Sam retrieved the pistol from Devlin's hand and returned it to the agent. "Sorry you got your head busted, pal."

The young agent holstered it as he replied, "Don't worry about it."

Crowley moaned then, and the agent leaned over and choked him into unconsciousness again. "Go on," the agent said. "Get the hell outta here."

Smiling, Sam started to leave, but the agent called out, "Wait! How'd you get in here?"

"I came up in the elevator from Orange One."

"No shit? You'd have to know—"

"F'get about it," Sam said and started moving away again.

"No, wait."

As Sam halted and turned back again, the agent pointed toward what looked to be a closet. "There's another elevator in there. Use that one and send it back up. When it gets back here, I'll know when to let this asshole wake up."

Sam opened the pocket door to find that it was indeed a small elevator. He stepped in and pressed the only button available. The agent called out, "Good luck," as the door closed.

When it opened seconds later, Angel spun toward him, her face ashen. "Oh my God, you did it?"

His heart still pounding, Sam nodded and stepped out, then reached back in and hit the button again. As the small door closed, he grabbed the tool bag from her and turned toward the tunnel entrance. "Let's get the hell out of here. I'll change on the way."

As they rode back to Site R, Sam confessed, "It didn't go down quite as we planned."

"What do you mean?" she asked with concern. "What'd you do?"

Sam explained what had occurred. When he got to the part about Crowley hitting the agent with the firewood, she slammed on the brakes. "You assured me no agent would be harmed."

"I know, and I'm sorry. I surrendered to him just as I promised. I had no idea Crowley was going to come around that quickly. The agent's fine, though."

"Are you sure?"

"Yeah, I'm sure."

Angel started driving again. "We do have a problem, though. When that Crowley fella tells them you were there, they'll discover my retinal scan was used to open the blast doors, and they'll be after us. With this long of a ride, we may not even make it out of Site R."

"I don't think we have anything to worry about. Crowley's drunk, has gunpowder residue on his hand, and *his* prints are on the pistol that killed Devlin. Besides, that agent heard Devlin confess that he was going to kill the agent and me, then find Longwood and complete the assassination. I don't think he's going to say anything about me being there. In fact, he told me to leave in that other elevator and wished me luck."

"You're kidding," Angel muttered. "This just gets weirder and weirder."

ᘒᘔ

Crowley moaned and rolled to his side as he slowly returned to consciousness. Someone was nudging him. Still under the influence of the cognac, his head aching now, he climbed to his feet, dazed and unable to comprehend his surroundings. The room was whirling. Then he spotted Devlin's ghastly corpse and looked down at the heavy, suppressed pistol in his right hand. "What the hell happ—"

"You killed him, Crowley. I saw you do it."

Crowley spun around to the injured agent he vaguely remembered bashing with a piece of wood. Crowley leaned over and clubbed him again, this time with the pistol, and staggered from the bedroom with his still-intoxicated mind giving him one piece of advice: *Run*. He raced from the suite and out the exterior door in the hallway—past the unseen agent posted there—and into the dark woods.

☙❧

When the agent at the door saw the pistol in Crowley's hand as he staggered by, he sent a dozen others racing to the president's suite. Seeing their man missing at its door, the agents charged inside, guns drawn. In the bedroom, they found the suite's door agent holding onto the wall, attempting to stand. Then they saw Devlin.

"It was Crowley," the head-sore agent croaked as blood ran down his face.

Another alarm went out. Seconds later, the forest around Crowley lit up as if the sun had suddenly risen. The brightness did not slow the tottering drunk's escape attempt, but the Marine sniper tracking him through the woods did. He saw the pistol in the running man's hand and pulled his trigger the instant the alarm sounded. The bullet smashed through Crowley's spine and out his chest before making a large hole in an oak.

CHAPTER 46

Sam and Angel returned the borrowed items to the maintenance company's locker room before the day shift arrived, first making sure to remove his picture from the ID card. They then took off on the long drive back to New Hampshire.

Just after dawn, Sam used Angel's reassembled cell phone to call the Steveners' home phone.

"Hello?"

"It's Sam. How's the president?"

"He's fine. Where have you been?"

"Why? What's wrong?"

"He's leaving. Hang on a second. He wants to talk to you."

Longwood sounded concerned. "Where are you, Sam? Is Angel with you?"

"Yes, sir, she's here. We're on our way back now. What's going on?"

"Tell me where you are, and I'll pick you up. I have a helicopter now."

ꞔꞔꞔ

The Marine One helicopter landed in the middle of an

empty parking lot outside an abandoned outlet mall, and Sam and Angel climbed aboard, leaving the SUV for the rental agency to recover.

Vince sat behind the FBI bodyguards with his injured leg propped up on a seat. Behind him, Pearson and another man Sam did not recognize sat next to Longwood.

The FBI director looked up at Sam and Angel quizzically, but before he could ask anything, Vince said, "That bastard from the lake, Crowley, killed Devlin last night."

Angel and Sam exchanged a look, but Sam only responded, "Really?"

Vince smiled. "Yeah, apparently he was Devlin's guest at Camp David. Can you believe that? The fella giving the news flash said the dumb son of a bitch was drunk, cold-cocked a Secret Service agent, shot Devlin, and got killed by a Marine sniper during his escape attempt."

"Nobody seems to even know who the guy really was," said Pearson. "He doesn't have any fingerprint, dental, or DNA files on record."

Sam and Angel took seats next to each other as the big chopper lifted off.

The president seemed to be studying Sam from across the aisle before he leaned over and quietly asked, "Are you okay?"

Stone-faced, Sam only nodded.

Longwood stared at him for several more seconds, pursed his lips, and nodded, too.

"How'd you come to get picked up by this, sir?" Sam asked.

Pearson answered, "As soon as I heard what happened at Camp David, I contacted the acting director of the Secret Service and told him the truth about President Longwood. He sent this helicopter."

"Sam, this is the new Secret Service director, Paul Dooley." Angel said.

The man shook Sam's hand. "I'm very pleased to meet you, Mr. Calder."

Sam glanced around. "I take it Dave and Kathy decided they'd had enough."

Longwood smiled and shrugged. "I invited them to come along, but Kathy declined."

"Actually, she said, 'No fucking way,'" Vince interjected and stormed off."

ⅇﾉﾆⅇﾉﾆ

Forty-five minutes later, Sam looked out a window as they descended to the south lawn of the White House. He could see hundreds of people and news cameras behind ropes and wondered if the nation—the world—was ready for what they were about to witness. He looked over at Longwood. The man, though undoubtedly still in pain, seemed eager. Sam felt a bit like that now, too.

Promise kept, Dad, he thought.

As the helicopter touched down, Longwood glanced at him and smiled. "You know, I've changed my mind. I think I'd rather keep you out of the limelight, Sam." He turned to Pearson. "Put Sam and Vince on a plane for Montana, Trevor. Send them home."

Pearson smiled. "Yes, sir."

Longwood stood and shook O'Malley's hand. "Thanks, Vince." Then he took Sam's hand. "We'll talk again, soon. Go home and take care of your brother. I'll be fine now." With that, Longwood turned and walked off the helicopter with Angel Washington and Paul Dooley at his side and the six FBI men in trail.

Sam watched out a window as the crowd of reporters and camera operators were stunned into silence, and he heard a roar of cheering erupt as the helicopter's engines restarted.

ℰᔆℰᔆ

En route to Montana, Sam watched the FBI charter jet's satellite television coverage of events at the White House. Fox showed footage of a tearful Carolyn Longwood rushing into her father's one-armed embrace before switching to a live shot of a spokesman stepping up to a podium, facing a seemingly elated press corps.

"Ladies and gentlemen, while certain aspects of what has transpired must remain classified for national security reasons, I will brief you on the overall chain of events."

Sam listened as the Secret Service received credit for the president's survival, supposedly kept undisclosed until the last conspirators could be located and dealt with. No mention was made of Sam and Mark or the Mafia. Nor did the Speaker say anything to indicate that Devlin had been responsible for all that had happened. Devlin's death was attributed to a shadowy figure believed to be suffering from an alcohol-fueled psychosis.

"The last of the assassins died following what appears to have been a suicide bomb set off when they were discovered at their hideout in the Maine woods. Unfortunately, several FBI agents, as well as four Army helicopter pilots providing transport, were also killed during that incident. The MSM has been officially disbanded.

"Auspiciously for our nation, the doctors have declared President Longwood physically and mentally fit to resume his duties on a limited schedule for now, and the fully restored cabinet has constitutionally reinstated his presidency. He will address the nation this evening."

Sam switched the screen off and turned to see Vince staring at him from across the aisle.

The agent snorted. "You didn't really expect the truth, the whole truth, and nothing but the truth, did you? Seditious traitors in the government, the mafia and FBI improbably teaming up with a framed ex-convict to save the president. There's no way they're gonna try to sell something like that to a nation addicted to conspiracy theories."

"I guess it does sound pretty farfetched," Sam said as he lay back and closed his eyes. "Wake me when you see mountains."

EPILOGUE

S am sat on the porch of the guesthouse his father and brother had built, examining a *New York Times* article Vince O'Malley had sent him. He smiled ruefully as he read the reporter's words below a photograph: *Following the unexplained disappearance of the Deluca clan, a new boss has reportedly stepped up to take the reins of the New York Mafia.* The photo showed Bruno Cavetti on crutches, his twin daughters alongside, heading into the Bronx eatery Sam remembered visiting.

Mark came out the front door and sat next to him. "Who's that?" he asked, glancing over at the paper's front page.

"That's Bruno. He's a good driver, a lousy cook, and a terrible shot."

"What?"

Sam chuckled, and with a badly faked Bronx accent, said, "F'get about it."

Mark had awakened from his coma the day after Sam returned and had gone home with him two days later. The pair had been nearly inseparable since. At least, they were when Becky Miller and her boy were not around. She and Mark planned to marry as soon as they managed to get the big house rebuilt.

To help with that, Sam was planning to give them a wedding gift—the money he was expecting from New York. Of course, that decision led to a long discussion with Mark about where he had actually spent the last five years and why.

Sam planned to remain in the guesthouse, but for how long he was uncertain. Given the loss of his father, plus Mark's upcoming nuptials, he felt more like a visitor than a truly needed part of the ranch. Mark, he knew, had invested his entire life in the place. Sam had not, and though he loved being there and would always consider it home, he was not sure whether he would stay or not. What he had wanted so badly—his father's embrace—he had enjoyed. His heart told him that joy would remain with him always, no matter where he was.

"Feel up to some saddle work?" Mark asked. "That broodmare in the north paddock is ready to foal, and the weatherman's calling for thunderstorms this afternoon. I'd like to move her into the barn before it gets nasty out."

Before Sam could respond, the sound of air brakes caught their attention, and both looked out to see a line of flatbeds turning onto their gravel drive. In front of them were several dark SUVs.

Both brothers stood. "What the hell's all this?" Mark asked.

Sam stepped off the porch. "You got me. Did you order something?"

The big trucks stopped in a line along the side of the driveway as the SUVs continued past the former main house's bare foundation to the guesthouse and fanned out. Several men in suits and sunglasses exited each vehicle and immediately took up positions facing all directions. One that Sam recognized looked over at him, nodded, and turned away. Sam saw no evidence of damage atop the young man's once-battered head. An SUV in the middle of the line stopped directly in front of the brothers, and the front passenger door opened. Angel Washington climbed out, smiling broadly at Sam. She opened the rear door, and President Longwood emerged.

"Hello, Sam," Longwood said, extending his hand as he approached.

"It's good to see you again, sir," Sam replied as he shook the president's hand.

Longwood turned to Mark. "I'm glad to finally meet you, Mark, and to be able to thank you for everything you did for me."

Mark shook the president's hand. "Thank you, sir. You certainly look a helluva lot better than the last time I saw you."

Longwood held out his new prosthetic left forearm. "It makes drying off after a shower a lot easier."

Sam chuckled and nodded at the heavily loaded trucks. "What's all that about?"

"They tell me those folks are the finest log home builders around. They're going to rebuild your family's home. Please consider it a gift from a grateful nation and a more-than-thankful president, though it will have to remain our secret."

"I understand, sir. Thank you."

"Well, ain't that neighborly," Mark said. "And to think, I didn't even vote for ya."

Smiling, Longwood turned back to Sam and handed him an envelope.

"What's this?" Sam wondered as his mind flashed to the last time someone had handed him an envelope.

"Open it."

He did and found his honorable discharge from the Navy inside. "Thank you, sir."

Longwood then turned to a huge oak about a hundred

feet away. Below it was a fenced-in family burial plot with a half-dozen headstones. "If you'll excuse me a moment," he said, "I'd like to pay my respects to a man I never had the honor of meeting."

The president walked over by himself and stood at Jeremiah's marker for a few moments, then turned back to the porch where the brothers waited.

"Why don't we go inside, fellas? I don't know about you two, but I could use a cold beer."

"Did you bring some?" Mark asked, and quickly added, "Just kidding. Come on in."

Longwood smiled and patted the big rancher's shoulder, then put his hand on Sam's with an affectionate squeeze as they started up the porch steps.

Inside, while Sam retrieved three beers from the refrigerator, Mark asked, "Are we gonna be slammed with reporters now?"

As Longwood took a seat on the sofa, he answered, "No one knows I'm here. That's why all the SUVs instead of my usual car." He took a beer from Sam and asked, "So, what are your plans, Sam? If you don't have any, I've got an idea you might find interesting."

END

About the Author

Dave Bullock got hooked on flying as a youth, leading to a long career as a USAF pilot after college. After retiring, he became an AFJROTC instructor for another fifteen years until finally realizing he had been in uniform far too long. It was time to do what he had been dreaming about for years—grow a beard and write novels.

He has had three novels published by Damnation Books: *False Jihad*, 2010, *Masked Jihad*, 2011, and *Vengeful Pursuit*, 2012. He is especially proud of his fourth novel, *Forced Succession*. It was a Top Three Finalist for the coveted 2014 Tom Clancy Collectors Society Adventure Writers Award.